THRALL

A DYSTOPIAN FANTASY ROMANCE NOVEL

THE THRALL SERIES

K. A. RILEY

SUMMARY

Thrall is based on the fairy tale Cinderella, the first in a new Dystopian Romance series by the author of Recruitment and The Cure.

In the realm of Kravan, children of lower-class citizens are raised in a prison-like structure called "The Tower" from birth until adulthood. Known as the Tethered, they are held in thrall until their powers reveal themselves around the time of their nineteenth birthday.

Every year, the Tethered who are tested and deemed harmless are chosen to leave the Tower and join the outside world as servants to live in the households of the ruling class. Those who are deemed threats are taken away—and no one knows what happens to them, though they suspect the worst.

Shara has spent her entire life in the Tower, longing for the day she will be chosen to leave. She's always been certain her powers would be minimal just as her mother's allegedly were, and that she would be assigned to a life of simple servitude.

When Shara receives her Placement in the home of a Noble family, she feels at first like she has finally found her place in the world. But over time, mysteries begin to reveal themselves about her Proprietor and those who live in the house...including the handsome fellow Tethered who shares a wing of the house with her.

When he offers her an opportunity to attend the annual Prince's Ball and to see the world of the Nobility for what it truly is, Shara begins to learn the ugly truth about the divisions between the ruling class and the Tethered.

After a life spent in near-isolation, Shara must learn to distinguish friend from foe, and to decide if her new allies are who they claim to be...

Or if they will turn out to be her greatest enemies.

MAP OF THE REALM

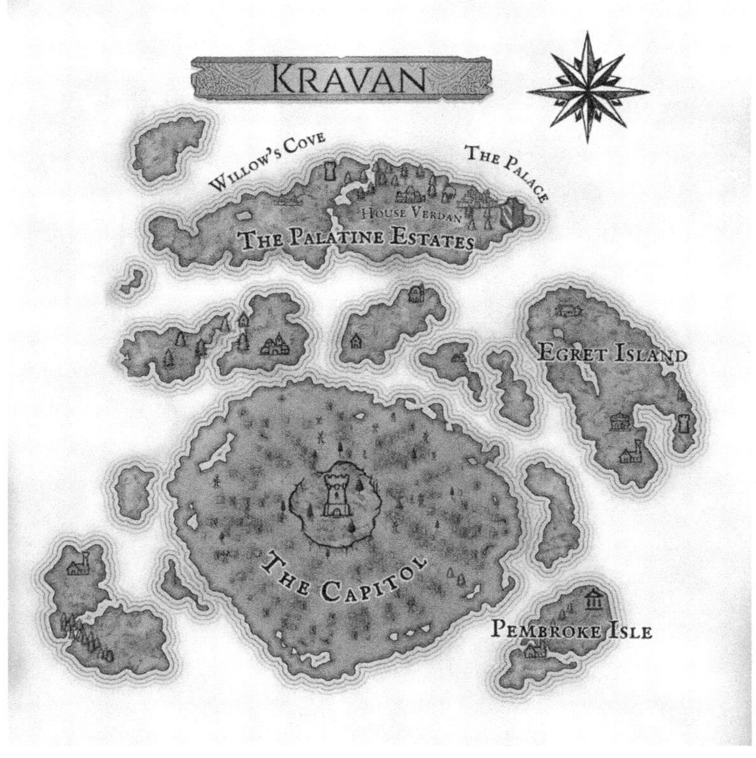

CONTENT WARNINGS

Trigger Warnings:

Violence
Adult situations
Occasional swearing

A quick word to my Readers:

Thrall is a Dystopian novel, like many I have written. But unlike most of my series, this one is not Young Adult. It ranks instead in the New Adult category—meaning there are scenes within its pages that aren't appropriate for younger audiences.

So, if you're a parent considering grabbing this series for a young person in your life, you might want to consider getting it for yourself instead.

Some of my Young Adult series start with the following books:

RECRUITMENT

The Amnesty Games

The Cure

Apocalypchix

Seeker's World

To Shara,
Thank you for your name.

THE SEVEN RULES OF THE REALM OF KRAVAN

1. From their birth inside the Tower, humans with unnatural powers, otherwise known as "Tethered," are the property of Pureblood Nobles. If deemed worthy at the age of nineteen, they are offered a Placement with the Noble families of Kravan.

2. No Household other than Kravan's Royal Family shall own more than two Tethered at once.

3. To be a Tethered is to be allowed no physical intimacy whatsoever. There are no exceptions.

4. No Tethered shall marry or produce offspring with another Tethered or a Pureblood. If impregnation occurs, the child will then be born and raised in the Tower.

5. Any Tethered who represents a threat to the Nobility may be killed without trial.

6. *A Noble may choose to kill a Tethered without fear of punishment.*

7. No Tethered shall be made privy to rules Five or Six.

PROLOGUE

The Darkness, After the Ball

I WAS BORN IN A PRISON, though it is forbidden to say so.

Since the day I came into this world, I have spent every single moment at the mercy of those who rule the realm of Kravan.

I've been taught that someone like me doesn't deserve wealth, property, or love.

I've learned to desire nothing and no one.

But this moment—this horrible, dark *now*—is the first time I have ever lived in true fear. Locked inside this room devoid of light or hope, my senses are so dulled that emotion is all I am able to hold onto.

Fear. Sadness. Heartbreak. Those are the pieces of my reality—yet, thinking back on it, I don't quite understand how I got here. How did I come to break so many rules in so short a time?

I thought I could go unnoticed in a world filled with

exceptional and dangerous people. I believed I was inconspicuous, almost pointless.

I am a person for whom affection, attraction, and touch are all illegal. A person forbidden from feeling.

Yet now, it's all I can bring myself to do.

For the first time in my life, I have realized what it is to have a heart—and that heart will never be owned by anyone unless I choose to give it to them.

Love, it turns out, is the only thing that truly matters.

But I'm not sure it can save me now.

CHAPTER ONE

THE TOWER, Several Weeks Ago

THE DAGGER FLIES at my chest with ridiculous speed.

In a desperate attempt to avoid sudden death, I hurl myself sideways, but as usual, I'm too slow.

The blade strikes my shoulder, slicing in deep enough to draw a stream of blood and force a sharp cry from my lips.

"She'll be fine," our fight trainer, Ore, calls out when gasps erupt from around the class. "She always is—haven't you idiots figured that out yet?"

With rage bubbling up inside me for his utter lack of empathy, I curse under my breath before pushing myself up from the ring's floor.

I glower at Ore who smirks back, his usual shit-eating grin plastered to his lips.

I leave every single class blood-stained and near tears.

He expects it.

No.

He *thrives* on it.

A bloodless Fight Class is a waste of Ore's precious time, and I'm his top bleeder.

It's a dubious honor, at best.

As for why he chose to pair me with the biggest, fastest Tethered in our cohort, Ore always insists he chooses us randomly—but I'm convinced he orchestrates the fights to suit his sadistic tendencies. There's little doubt in my mind he *enjoys* watching blood seep slowly from my multitude of fresh wounds.

Short of decapitation, I can pretty much tolerate any level of abuse and come through fight class in one piece, thanks to my ability to heal quickly. So right now, rather than let me out of the combat ring to tend to the deep gash in my shoulder, Ore calls out, "Round Two!"

With a grunt of disgust, I brush off my light gray uniform and once again begin the pointless dance with my opponent.

Drukkar is a tall, broad-shouldered Tethered who would probably be considered our cohort's hottest male commodity...if he wasn't such a dickhead.

He revels in chaos, and it doesn't help that his power is the ability to move with blinding speed. Drukk usually shoots around the combat ring like a crazed rat who's ingested too much caffeine, lunging this way and that so fast that I can scarcely follow him with my eyes, let alone avoid any weapon he hurls my way.

Right now, though, he's taking pleasure in taunting me. He's a cat, patiently watching a wounded mouse stagger around, knowing it has no hope of winning an absurdly uneven battle.

He's standing motionless across the ring, his boorish

smile showing off a set of snow-white teeth and a penchant for cruelty.

Determined to do something other than just lie in wait for the next assault, I clasp my blade in my right hand, bringing it up to shoulder height and readying myself to fling it. Like all our training daggers, it's sharp enough to pierce through Drukk's uniform and bury itself in his flesh. But it's unlikely to do any real damage unless my aim is impossibly good—which it never is.

It's not that I'm uncoordinated. I *should* be able to hit a huge target like Drukkar easily enough.

But there's a world of difference between *should be able to* and *can*.

Before the blade even leaves my hand, I know exactly what's going to happen, because it's the same thing that always happens when I'm foolish enough to try and fight back.

Even so, I ready myself in the hopes that somehow, this time will be different.

Just as I'm about to throw the blade, a jolt of pain shoots its way up my arm like a sea of barbed arrows aimed squarely at a host of nerve endings.

Right on cue.

The agony and immediacy of the pain feel far worse than the wound in my shoulder. It's almost like my body is in a constant struggle against my desire to defend myself.

Stupid body.

My knife misses Drukk by two feet at least, half-embedding itself pathetically in the cushioned floor of the combat ring. Drukk laughs, glancing at the gleaming steel, then reaches down, grabs it, and moves to fling it back at me.

I can stop him, I tell myself, my jaw muscles tensing as the pain in my arm subsides. *I can run at him, slam into his chest. Make him drop it...*

But a voice in my mind—one I know as well as my own —utters my name like a curse.

~Shara. Don't even think about it.

Maude—or M.O.D., which stands for *Mental Oversight Device*—is an artificial intelligence module connected to my mind via a wrist piece embedded in my left arm. A customized version of her is implanted in each Tethered's body and connected via neuro-link to our brains.

It all sounds far more scientific than it actually is. Simply put, our Maude units are the closest thing to a watchful parent any of us will ever have.

Each M.O.D. is a teacher, a guide, a monitor, and a mentor, all in one, and each is tweaked to reflect the personality and emotional landscape of her human.

I'm not sure what it says about me that *my* Maude unit is a pain in the ass.

"Come on," I reply silently. "Just this once, at least let me try."

~Don't be stupid. You're not allowed to touch him or anyone, remember? Besides, you'd hardly make a dent in the big oaf.

I shake off her words, even though I know them to be true.

Standing my ground, convinced that I can somehow find a way to retaliate, I focus on the blade between Drukk's fingers, which will most likely end up lodged deep in some part of me.

"Get it over with, then," I say under my breath. "Throw it."

But to my dismay, Drukk just continues to stand there, his eyes locked on my own.

I've known Drukkar all my life, yet we've never had a lengthy conversation. And we've certainly never spent more than two seconds staring each other down. We've fought before, and not surprisingly, I've lost every time.

Normally, he makes quick work of me—so I have no idea why today of all days, he's taking his sweet time.

What the hell is he doing?

"Throw it, you jackass!" I shout, impatient for this fight to end. "What are you waiting for?"

I'm so freaking sick of losing—but I'm even more sick of *trying*. Anyhow, there's no point, not with our Placements coming tomorrow. By now, if I haven't proven myself powerful, I never will.

Everyone knows exactly who and what I am.

The realization makes me want to go back to my Whiteroom and bury my head under my pillow.

Just as I'm about to turn to Ore and ask him to put an end to this stupidity, Drukkar chooses to surprise me—and not in a good way.

Instead of throwing the blade, he throws *himself* at me, grabbing my wounded shoulder and twisting me around to pull me hard to his chest—which is excruciating, not to mention entirely illegal.

Apparently, Drukkar has conveniently forgotten Kravan's strict rule about Tethered touching each other, and the sensation of his body against mine is horrifying.

"Ore, you have to stop him!" a voice cries from somewhere to my right. It's Nev, my best friend, and she's not making any effort to conceal her rage. "He can't do that! He's not supposed to put his hands on her!"

"I'll allow it, just this once."

I can hear the grin in Ore's voice.

Drukk presses the blade to my throat, drawing a trickle of blood.

Why the hell do we use such sharp daggers for sparring sessions, anyhow?

It's a question Nev and I have asked each other for years. No one has ever managed to explain it, and all I can conclude is that Ore and the Warden genuinely want the weakest among us dead before Placement Day.

There are no rules in the Tower against killing Tethered. If I were to die in the ring, I wouldn't be the first of our cohort to meet my end at the hands of one of my peers.

Twelve Tethered have left our cohort over the years, six of them in recent months. And two of those six were deaths that occurred during fight class. A poorly hurled blade managed to nick a girl called Circe's jugular. A rule-breaking strangulation gone awry left a boy named Dirk dead on the ground.

Some members of the cohort are more powerful than others—like Drukkar and our friend Ilias. They're what are known as Crimson Elites, or *Aggressives*—Tethered with powers that could potentially make them effective Guards for Kravan's Noble families.

I, on the other hand, am what they call a *Harmless*. Some—like Ore—prefer to call us "Useless." It's why he loves watching me get injured. He knows that, despite the fact that I heal quickly, the wounds still hurt like a bitch, and seeing me in agony gives him a special kind of pleasure that only a true psychopath could enjoy.

He also knows he'll never suffer consequences for his unspoken sadism. After all, there's never any evidence left behind that I was badly injured in the first place. An hour or two after each class, I'm healed up and as good as new, with no scars to show for my suffering.

But right now, even Ore seems to be growing bored.

"All right," he yells. "Let's wrap it up."

Determined to live past the next thirty seconds, I grab Drukk's muscular arm and dig my nails in as hard as I can. But given the thick layer of protective fabric between my fingertips and his skin, I fail to do much damage.

The knife pushes still deeper into my throat, and now I can feel the blood trickling down to soak my uniform's collar.

"Stop," I cry, my voice piercing and desperate.

To my astonishment, the hand that holds the knife drops instantly to Drukkar's side.

He lets go of me and stumbles backwards.

I leap away, grabbing at my throat and spinning around to glare at him, ready to throw him a few choice words.

But I stop as soon as my eyes land on his face.

"What the hell?" someone cries out. "What's *wrong* with him?"

CHAPTER TWO

DRUKK'S EYES are cloudy and blank.

The dagger trembles between his fingers. His chest is tight, his face ghastly white, and his breath comes in horrifying, choked gasps.

"Is he having a seizure?" someone asks.

"He needs a medic!" another Tethered shrieks.

While our cohort has a collective freak-out, a sudden movement at the far end of the training chamber draws my baffled gaze. The room's door creaks open and a figure steps inside—but it's no medic.

The visitor is a tall young man with dark hair and bronze skin. An intense pair of eyes locks on my own, and a too-tempting set of lips curve up slightly as he takes me in, seemingly amused by my predicament.

I suppose I'm quite the sight, standing helpless in the combat ring and waiting for my pending loss while my much larger—and *frozen*—opponent draws the attention of everyone in the room.

Right now, though, I don't care about any of that.

For a few seconds, I forget everything that's just happened. I forget the danger my life is in. I forget Drukkar's sudden paralysis.

In fact, my entire cohort's existence has left my consciousness.

In all my years in the Tower, no one has ever strolled into our training sessions, except, on occasion, Warden Kurtz. For that matter, life in the Tower has been almost entirely devoid of outsiders for as long as I can remember. Hell, we aren't even allowed to speak to members of the other cohorts.

So when my eyes meet the stranger's, I tell myself my reaction is surprise, and nothing more.

But something inside me has flared to life, like his arrival has suddenly opened my mind to the reality that lies beyond the Tower's walls. He's a walking foreshadowing of life out there—of the potential of an entire world none of us has ever seen.

A gorgeous, mischievous, delectable foreshadowing.

Is he a Noble? If so, what is he doing here? And why the hell do I want so badly to step out of this ring and move toward him, like he's luring me with some irresistible bait?

My mouth drops open as if I have no control over my lower lip. My chest throbs with some emotion I've never felt before—one that unsettles me and makes my head spin. My hands, uncertain what to do with themselves, clench into tight, unyielding fists at my sides.

The young man isn't dressed like the rest of us. In fact, he's not dressed like anyone I've ever seen in person. He's wearing a dark, tailored suit with a white shirt and dark gray tie—the kind of clothing I've only ever seen in picture books or read about in Society class. It's the sort of expensive clothing only Nobles wear. Clothing we've learned about not because we will one day own garments like his, but because as future servants, we must learn to care for luxurious fabrics.

Reminding myself that I'm not allowed to feel desire—and I'm *definitely* not allowed to stare in wonder at Nobles—I yank my gaze away, recalling with a sudden jolt where I am and what's been happening around me.

I'm in the middle of a fight that is definitely not going my way, and unless Drukk falls down dead, I'm going to have to finish it.

Great, I think. *All I need is to lose a fight in front of a guy who looks like that—a young man who's clearly high up on Kravan's social food chain.*

An assertive voice pulls me back to my predicament and to Drukk, who still looks as if he's frozen in time. "His wrist unit is probably bugging out on him," Ore says. "He may be disoriented by a glitch in his M.O.D. It happens sometimes, though it's rare."

~Shara, Maude's voice says. *Prepare yourself. When Drukkar attacks, you need to give in. Let him win. The fight must end.*

"I can beat him!" I whisper-hiss, determined not to look like an utter failure in front of our mysterious visitor.

But the truth is, I know perfectly well that I'm wrong. I've never won a fight in my life.

~Don't be deceived by Drukkar's state, Maude snaps. Lucky me, to be tethered to the only A.I. in the world who's more

pessimistic than I am. *He'll be fine in a moment. Don't forget he's a Crimson Elite, and you are a Harmless.*

As if my body concurs, another brutal shock of pain shoots up my arm, this time aimed directly at my wounded shoulder. The searing jolt radiates violently to my head, and the massive room begins to spin nauseatingly.

I struggle to keep myself upright when I mutter, "Damn it!"

Horrified, I glance over to see that the well-dressed stranger is now leaning back against the wall, arms crossed over his chest. He's watching me with the same amused smugness as before, seemingly entertained by my discomfort.

Okay, maybe he's not delectable so much as infuriating.

By now, other cohort members have begun to notice him. I can hear the giggles among the young women who were so concerned about Drukk a minute ago, as they nudge one another and nod in our visitor's direction.

"Do you think that guy could be Prince Tallin?" someone asks, and my mind reels with the possibility. "Maybe he's here to check out the Tethered before Placement Day?"

The prince?

Here, in the Tower?

I've never seen Tallin's face. None of us has. All we know is he's the second-most powerful man in all of Kravan after his father the king.

I suppose the visitor *could* be royalty. I can't deny he's beautiful enough to be a prince like the ones I've always imagined from story books.

"Shara! Look out!" someone cries, yanking me out of my foolish fantasy.

By the time I pull my eyes to Drukk, I'm already too late. He's regained his composure and—worse—his ability to move with unnatural speed. His eyes fixed on me, he hurls his arm forward and the blade releases, embedding itself a split-second later into my right thigh.

When the pain comes, it's so intense that I can't even bring myself to scream.

Instead, I fall to my knees then careen sideways, tumbling uselessly to the ground to land on my wounded shoulder, which hasn't yet managed to heal fully.

With that, the fight comes to its humiliating end.

~*Told you,* Maude's voice vibrates in my mind.

"Shut the fuck up." The words come out in a feral snarl, and I probably look completely insane to anyone close enough to hear me.

"Holy crap, Shar!"

Nev has already leapt over to crouch beside me.

Struggling to ignore the pain, I turn my head toward the door, searching for the young man who may or may not be Kravan's prince. But he's already left, the door swinging shut behind him.

Damn it.

Nev's fingers are on me now, gingerly reaching for my throat, trying to find a pulse as if she's convinced the blow to my leg was enough to kill me.

"What the hell do you think you're doing?" Ore shouts. "Do *not* touch her!"

"Drukkar had his hands all over her!" she cries. "What, he's suddenly allowed to touch her but I'm not?"

"That was different!" Ore growls. "*That* was combat."

"It's still against the rules, which is why we have

weapons—or have you forgotten that one inconvenient detail?"

She doesn't need to remind him. We all know the rules, even stubborn-as-shit Ore. The members of our cohort haven't been allowed physical contact—not even a friendly shove in the exercise yard—for seven years now.

Rule Number Three: To be a Tethered is to be allowed no intimacy whatsoever.

No exceptions.

It's a rule our Maudes remind us of on a daily basis. For years, the words have been drilled into our heads like a cruel mantra—one that steals just a little of our humanity from us each time we hear it.

Back when the rule was first introduced to our cohort, it didn't mean all that much to any of us. Most of us didn't particularly care about physical contact in those days. We'd grown up without much affection other than the occasional encouraging pat on the shoulder from a friend, and no one thought they'd particularly miss it.

But over time, we came to the grim realization that friends couldn't so much as hug or console one another in times of need. A hug, the Warden cautioned us, was a luxury granted only to the Nobility and the Normals. Part of life as a Tethered was to learn self-control.

As Tethered, we are not allowed to be brought down by emotion. We are not supposed to display need or vulnerability. We are meant to be stoic automatons, future servants who are granted the privilege of life, shelter, nourishment, and little more.

One day a few years ago as Nev and I ate lunch together, it struck us both that neither of us would ever know what it felt like to kiss someone—not even a friendly peck on the cheek. The realization was like a strange, surreal blow—as if an intangible part of our futures had been ripped away before we'd so much as had a chance to contemplate its significance.

I don't know if the Nobility is convinced that the young women in the Tower will somehow get pregnant if our hands accidentally brush against a young man's—and yes, I do know how pregnancy happens. It takes more than an accidental stroke of skin to make a baby.

But I'm not exaggerating when I say the Warden would tolerate us murdering each other before he'd tolerate a kiss.

The penalties for breaking the intimacy rule are strict.

A few years ago, a boy and a girl in our cohort—their names are Cole and Valia—were caught sneaking a kiss in the darkest corner of the mess hall. For that infraction, each of them spent a month in solitary confinement in a Blackroom.

Since then, neither of them has ever once spoken to the other. To this day, I don't know if it's because they were ordered to keep their distance, or because they're too afraid of the consequences of temptation.

However good that kiss was, I'm pretty sure it wasn't worth a month in solitary. I once spent twelve hours in a Blackroom, and it was the worst, most isolating experience of my life.

I can't begin to imagine the trauma of an entire month.

"Shara," Ilias, the third in our little trio of friends says as he crouches down next to Nev. He looks as concerned as she does when his eyes move to the knife still embedded in my thigh. "What the hell were you doing? You should have—"

"She's fine, like I said," Ore grunts, pulling up next to him and yanking the blade out, eliciting a cry from my lips. With a smirk and a clap of his hands, he shouts, "Class is over! Back to your Whiterooms, now. Our little Healer can patch herself up on her cot."

"She won't be fully healed for hours. Don't you think a medic should—" Nev starts to say.

"No, I don't," Ore interrupts, disdain dripping from his voice. "The domestic goddess will be just fine."

Domestic goddess.

That's what assholes like Ore and others have called me for years. And it's what Maude hopes I'll be when I leave the Tower and head to my Placement—even though A. I. units aren't *supposed* to want things at all.

My bossy little implanted overlord decided long ago that my best hope in life is to become a Domestic in the employ of some wealthy family or other. She's trained me over the years to dust my cell so thoroughly that not a speck of any foreign substance can be detected in any of its corners.

~*Always strive to prove yourself useful,* Maude nags regularly. *Useful people survive out there, and useless ones don't.*

I'm pretty sure her exercise in anal-retentive fastidiousness is simply a tool to help me stave off boredom. There's not much to do in a mostly-empty Whiteroom, after all. Keeping the place spotless gives me a goal each day.

As annoying as Maude is, I'll admit that a part of me is grateful she's forced me to be so disciplined. Tomorrow on our Placement Day, the new Prefect will come to assess our cohort's members—and I, for one, will be ready for him.

Ore told us recently the *former* Prefect—a man who had held the position for the last thirty-some years—died a few months back. A wealthy Noble was named to take his place, and he—or she—will observe us, then decide who among us is worthy of the most desirable Placements.

Short of a miracle, I'll end up exactly where Maude, Ore, and my Tethered peers have always predicted I'd be: a mousy servant to some semi-wealthy family.

I suppose there are worse fates. I just don't know what they are.

As we begin the trudge back to our quarters, Nev sidles up next to me, taking care not to reach out and touch me. I wish more than ever that I could lean on her for support—my leg, neck, and shoulder are still bleeding, and I have to give them a chance to heal. Which means resting quietly for a few minutes, at least.

"Are you sure you're okay?" Nev asks, and I nod wearily.

"I'll be fine," I tell her, my voice tight with embarrassment. "Healing fast is the only thing I do well."

"Not the *only* thing. You dust like a pro," she says, then looks horrified that those words came out of her mouth. She knows I hate being reminded of my lack of impressive powers. "Sorry, but it's true. You're really good at it."

"It doesn't matter," I tell her, shaking my head. "Let's just get back to our cots before Ore or the Warden screams at us for loitering."

With a nod, Nev sees me to my door then heads to her own Whiteroom. I turn and watch through the window as Ore makes sure everyone's doors are locked before taking the elevator to his more luxurious quarters on one of the Tower's upper levels.

Cursing, I limp over to the cabinet above my sink to extract a roll of gauze and some medical tape, then sit down on my cot and proceed to do exactly what Ore said I would: I patch my wounds expertly.

By the time I remove the tape in two hours, no evidence will exist that Drukkar nearly killed me.

For that, I suppose I should be grateful.

CHAPTER THREE

The Tower isn't a prison, or so we're told.

In his measured, authoritative voice, Warden Kurtz has assured us for years that the Tower is a "safe space" for our kind. He says we're not so much locked in as protected from ourselves.

"The Tower is a place where you Tethered can be raised without risk to yourselves or others, and where you grow up learning valuable skills such as obedience to your future masters and mistresses," he tells us. "There was a time not so long ago when the former Prefect considered killing every Tethered as they came into this world. It is the kindness of the Nobles that keeps you alive. It's mercy that gives each of you the chance at a life and a future. Never forget, you're here because you live in thrall to the Nobility."

Thrall.

When I was eight and heard that word for the first time, I asked Nev what it meant. She told me that to be in thrall was to be under someone else's power—it meant you worshiped them.

"Enthralled," she said, "means you admire something or some*one* so much you almost melt in their presence. It's like what we feel for the Nobility—the admiration for their wealth and power."

"But it's not the Nobles who have power," I protested, confused. "The Tethered are way stronger. The Nobility are just wealthy Normals, aren't they?"

That statement was met with a stern warning from Maude and a threat that if I ever spoke disparagingly of the Nobility again, I would be sent to a Blackroom to languish in its depths for weeks on end.

Nev told me to listen to Maude, so I shut my mouth and never brought it up again.

A few years after we had that conversation, I came upon a dictionary in the cohort's library. On a whim, I looked up "thrall" and saw that one possible definition involved indentured servitude. "A slave, servant, or captive," it said.

To this day, I'm not sure which definition is accurate—but I know well enough now to keep my questions to myself.

Every single person who is born in the Tower has at least one Tethered parent—which is the polite way of saying one of our parents has "unnatural" powers.

It's why we've been raised in here, with the Warden and our Maude units watching us like we're carefully monitored livestock. It's also why we're not allowed to leave the Tower until we turn nineteen and our powers—or lack thereof—reveal themselves.

The Tower's interior—at least, the little I've seen of it—is a consistent, glossy white, its walls illuminated by some internal source. Its floors, ceiling, and walls all appear to be made of some polished lacquer, its corners slightly curved to facilitate cleaning.

The only parts of the Tower I've ever seen that aren't bright white are the Blackrooms. As their name dictates, their walls are onyx black, their doors windowless so that when they're sealed shut, there's not so much as a hint of light within their confines.

I have a theory that the whiteness permeating the rest of the Tower's interior is meant to give the illusion of sunlight —and to make us forget we have no concept of what it feels like to live as so many normal humans do.

The thing is, there are no windows in the Tower. No hints as to Kravan's geography or how others in our realm live from day to day. All the library books that once contained maps have been decimated, any information either ripped out or blacked out with a thick layer of ink. There's information about the war after the Rebellion, but anything about the times that led to the uprising is virtually nonexistent.

As for the Rebellion itself, we've only been taught that many years ago, our kind grew dangerous and destructive, and that we needlessly attacked the Nobility in droves. The wealthy members of Kravan's society were driven from the Capitol and went to seek shelter elsewhere, fighting their way to safety.

Many on both sides died, according to what we've learned.

The Nobility's armed forces managed to take the remaining Tethered into captivity, and since that day, the law has stated that any pregnant Tethered—or any non-Tethered woman who is carrying the child of a Tethered—must give birth here in the Tower.

Once the child is born, the mother is removed from the Tower, her bond with her child broken.

What becomes of her, we don't know.

Warden Kurtz once told us the Rebellion began because a group of armed Tethered miscreants grew angry that the Nobility held so much power.

The so-called "History" books speak mostly of the time after the war, about the Nobility's kindness and mercy toward the cruel Tethered, and in particular, the benevolence of Kravan's Royal Family.

The texts explain in specific detail why Kravan's hierarchy works best when wealthy families sit at the top and others serve them—and why we Tethered need to be kept in check.

Our incarceration, according to those who wrote the history books, is for the best for the Tethered—because we have a habit of turning cruel for no reason.

Up until two years ago, I believed every word I'd ever heard about Kravan. I believed my kind was inherently evil, that our blood was tainted. I believed what we were told about the world outside the Tower—that the sky is a constant, beautiful shade of blue and exquisite flowers bloom all year round. I believed that all of Kravan's people—Normals, Nobles, and Tethered—live in harmony in some kind of perfectly-balanced hierarchy.

I would probably still believe it today if not for the fact that one morning when I was about to enter the Warden's office for its bi-weekly cleaning, I overheard him and Ore engaged in a quiet, if tense, conversation.

"You know the shit-show that's happening out there," Ore was saying. "There's a reason I chose to come back in here to serve and to live. Kravan is a dumpster fire—especially the Capitol. I'd rather wallow in here than out there any day."

"I hope you don't voice your opinions during fight class," the Warden hissed, reprimand in his tone. "We're supposed to get them excited about their futures, not terrified."

"I wouldn't blame 'em for being terrified," Ore replied. "I tell you, these Tethered have no idea what they're in—"

Something in Ore's voice set me off. With my hands shaking, I dropped a cleaning brush, which went clattering to the floor.

I snatched it up and quickly scampered a few feet backwards, pretending I was just now on my way to the Warden's office and hoping they wouldn't realize I'd overheard them.

It seemed my plan worked. By the time I reached the office, the Warden had changed the subject. "No problem, Ore. I'll see to it that the mat in the training room gets replaced."

I've never told Nev or Ilias what I heard that day.

I know perfectly well it would kill their excitement and ruin their hopes, just as it fractured my own.

For so many years, I'd looked forward to the day when I could leave the Tower. I had reveled in the thought that I might end up living in a beautiful house with kind people.

Hell, I'd even told myself I might find friends out there.

Still, I live in constant, silent hope that outside the Tower, there's a beautiful world to look forward to—the world my imagination has constructed from a multitude of words on the pages of story books.

I would never say it out loud to anyone, not even my closest friends—but sometimes, I think I would give anything to be a Normal. To think I could be released from this place and go live out in the world and fend for myself—it's a more exquisite vision than anything else I can imagine.

Normals—regular people who don't possess the wealth of the Nobles—are allowed to live in the Capitol. They're free to seek out jobs and even to purchase their own homes once they've earned enough to pay for them.

They're allowed to love one another and to marry—to have children with other Normals. I would give anything to be granted those privileges.

But according to the Warden, being owned by Nobles is far better than being free.

"There's status that comes with being a Tethered under the ownership of a Noble House," he's told us. "Servants are granted respect in society—even if you don't enjoy quite the same privileges as your Proprietors. Trust me when I tell you you're better off living in a Noble's mansion than in some ugly little house in the Capitol."

I suppose he could be right—but I'd prefer to judge for myself.

Either way, I'll admit I'm looking forward to my Placement. I can't wait to smell the outside air for the first time and to see the sky in all its glory. I want to press my palm against a tree trunk and feel the soft dampness of grass. I have images in my mind of what the outdoors smells like and how the air tastes—and a part of me is dying to know if I'm right.

The Warden has done what he can to prepare us for tomorrow's Placement. He occasionally allows us to watch films in the screening room to give us a little taste of the outside world.

Unfortunately, our cohort only has a collection of five movies, which we cycle through regularly. In addition to those, we have a series of nature shows at our disposal so that we can learn about animals, plants, and other aspects of the outdoors.

One of the films we like to watch repeatedly is called, "Kincaid, Hero Guard," which seemed incredible when we were all ten or so—but at nineteen, we've all come to realize it's an embarrassingly cheesy title.

The film is about a powerful Tethered who receives a Placement in the home of a high-ranking family. After serving them faithfully for several months, he saves them from an attack by a small army of evil Tethered rebels, tearing each enemy limb from limb.

Most of our cohort cheers and laughs when the movie's climactic scene comes along and Kincaid wreaks havoc on the rebel infiltrators.

I cringe.

It's not that I mind the sight of blood—I'm more familiar with open wounds than anyone in our cohort.

It's that the rebels look so...*pathetic*. They look dirty and hungry and poor, and I can't help thinking they're simply trying to survive.

No Tethered in the Tower has ever been hungry. None of us has any need of money. As for dirty—there's not much chance to get filthy when you live in a white-walled home, and you're not allowed outside.

Still, that film has shaped how many of our cohort's members see their futures. Ilias is determined to murder people on behalf of whatever Noble takes ownership of him, and in fact, he's more than happy to know that might be his main accomplishment in life.

Even Nev, who's far more suspicious than Ilias, loves the idea of taking on bad guys in order to protect masters she's never even met.

Sometimes, I wonder if I'm the only one skeptical enough to question whether or not my masters will *deserve* protection.

CHAPTER FOUR

> *I live in thrall for the good of the realm.*
>
> *I live in thrall because I am dangerous.*
>
> *To live in thrall is an honor.*
>
> *If I serve faithfully, I will be rewarded with long life.*
>
> *If I break Kravan's laws, I will pay the ultimate price.*
>
> *The choice is mine, and I vow to choose well.*

OUR COHORT HAS SPOKEN the pledge just before dinner every evening for as long as any of us can remember.

I've always tried my best to believe the words as they come out of my mouth.

I want to believe living in thrall is a privilege.

I want to be grateful.

I tell myself daily that I *am* grateful.

I remind myself that the Prefecture, which is in charge of dictating the Tower's rules and overseeing Kravan's population, could easily have had me and every other Tethered killed the moment we were born.

I tell myself the Prefect and the members of the Nobility are only seeking to keep the order in a tumultuous world. They know far more than I do about the Rebellion and about the risks that Tethered pose to other humans.

Maybe they have a point.

After all, Drukkar showed our entire cohort today just how dangerous a Tethered can be—and Drukk is only a *Crimson*. It's not like he's a Gilded Elite—the kind of Tethered so dangerous that they're taken away, never to be seen again.

Over the past two years, four potential Gilded Elites have been identified in our cohort. Each was taken away moments after their Maude units reported their developing powers.

No one but Ore and the Warden was ever told what those powers were.

One of the Gilded Elites was a friend of mine called Cher. When we were younger, she had an active imagination, and over the course of our lives we had many animated conversations about what our futures might entail.

Several months ago, though, Cher's excitement began to wane, and I watched as fear slowly worked its way into her eyes.

One day, while she was locked in her Whiteroom, she let out a scream so loud that we all heard it—even through the soundproofed walls that separate our quarters.

Then came a thunderous sound that shook the walls themselves, as if something massive had exploded.

The Warden never told us what happened in that Whiteroom, and by the time I was sent to clean it, almost all evidence of Cher's existence was gone.

Under her cot, I discovered a small series of scorch marks, as if something had been incinerated on the pristine floor, leaving a trail of black in its wake. Some of the Tethered speculate that her body had somehow burned from the inside out; others think she learned to harness flame and blew through her door—a massive sin, according to the Tower's rules. Attempted escape makes a Tethered exponentially more dangerous and is not taken lightly.

Whatever happened in that Whiteroom, it seems clear that Cher was a walking bomb.

Not exactly the sort of indentured servant a Noble family wants in their home.

When Nev, Ilias, and I sit down to eat, Nev speaks first.

Leaning in close, she says, "Do you two ever wonder why they didn't let us out of this place ages ago?"

"What do you mean?" Ilias asks, looking around like he's afraid we'll be punished just for broaching the subject. He knows as well as I do that Nev is treading on dangerous ground.

Never question the rules.

"I mean," Nev says, "most of us started showing our powers a year or two ago—and most of us have proven we aren't dangerous. So why are we still here? Why doesn't the Prefecture just give us our Placements when our powers first come to light?"

Ilias glances cautiously around the room again, then shrugs. "I don't know," he mutters before shoving a forkful of mashed potatoes into his mouth. "They've always kept the Tethered in the Tower until they're nineteen. It's the rule, which means there must be a good reason for it. The Prefect and the Nobility don't throw arbitrary laws around."

I hesitate before answering, then remind myself this might be the last time the three of us get to talk like this.

"I'm not so sure the Prefecture and the Nobility have a clue what they're—" I say, but Ilias throws me a pointed look as the Warden makes his way toward our table from across the mess hall.

"Shara," Ilias hisses between clenched teeth.

Questioning our Placement schedule is one thing, but I was about to say something incredibly stupid. By now, the Warden has probably been alerted by my Maude unit that I'm having disloyal thoughts.

The last thing I want is to get thrown into a Blackroom on my final night in the Tower.

To my surprise, the Warden simply strolls by us to go speak to Drukkar, who's sitting at the far end of the mess hall.

Okay, I'll admit it. That was too close for comfort.

"Who do you guys think the stranger was?" I ask, deliberately changing the subject. "The guy who came to sparring practice and watched us, I mean."

"Some Noble, probably," Nev says. "I can't say I'm as excited about him as some of you were, but that's not surprising. Mr. Hottie-pants isn't exactly my type. But he did look rich as shit."

"I heard he's one of us," Ilias counters, his chin low. "A Tethered. And Shar—I hate to tell you, but Nev's right. You're not the only one in the cohort who was drooling over him."

My brow scrunches up in a way that probably makes me look like I'm silently protesting far too much. "I wasn't drooling."

With a grin, Ilias says, "Maybe not literally, but you had 'horny woman' written all over your face. Don't worry—I won't tell anyone. If your Maude didn't pick up on it, you're safe."

"Whatever," I mutter, my cheeks flushing. "Anyhow, I don't see why you think he was a Tethered. He was too well-dressed."

"Tethered who live on the outside don't always wear uniforms," Ilias laughs. "At least, I don't think they do. Anyhow, I heard he works for some high-ranking family, which accounts for his tailored clothes."

"Who's your source?" Nev asks in a scoffing tone. "Where the hell are you getting this information? Have you been sneaking out of your Whiteroom to have tea with the Warden or something?"

Ilias shrugs. "I just...heard it somewhere."

He's being weirdly cagey about his answer—which makes me think he probably made it up to sound like he knows more than he actually does.

"Do you think he'll be around for the Placement tomorrow?" I ask, attempting to sound casually disinterested.

"Probably," Ilias replies. "If he's a Guard to some high-ranking family, he might be here to watch us. He'll most likely sleep in some upper-level, luxurious apartment in the Tower tonight, the lucky bastard."

Though I tell myself I have no interest in the handsome stranger, the thought of him sleeping in this very building makes my insides heat with some visceral reaction I'm not remotely used to. To think he could be that close to us right now.

Against my will, I want to know everything about him.

I want to hear his voice, to inhale his scent. I want him to tell me his greatest desires, his favorite pastimes.

I would sit and listen to the most banal information leave his lips, just to watch those lips move.

All of which is ridiculous.

I tell myself it's only because he's a novelty. He's someone new and different in a world filled with torturous repetition and sameness.

With a shot of excitement and terror combined, a realization hits me.

What if Ilias is right? What if the stranger is coming back to *watch* us?

Never have I wanted a change of clothing so badly, or someone to tell me how to style my hair and put on makeup like the Nobility supposedly does.

Tethered may not wear makeup, but we do know of its existence. I've seen images in picture books of women with pretty lipstick, eyeshadow and blush, their hair pulled up in elegant twists.

My hair, on the other hand, lives in a perpetual brown ponytail or bun pulled back high on my crown so it's not in the way when I perform my thorough cleaning routine or get my ass kicked in the combat ring.

"What*ever* that guy was," Nev says, "we'll definitely be seeing a Noble tomorrow. The Prefect is one of the highest-ranking there is. The only ones higher up the ladder than him are the members of the Royal Family."

The three of us sit for a moment and ponder that thought.

"Do you think they hate us?" I ask softly, breaking the silence that's fallen between us.

"Who? The Nobility?" Nev asks, and I nod.

I've never asked such a direct question of my two friends, and I can see the nervousness in their eyes as they exchange a look.

"Why should they?" Nev finally replies. "It's not like we've ever done anything to them. We weren't even alive when the Rebellion happened."

"But it was people like us—the ones with powers—who tried to take them down. The Rebels had the same blood flowing through their veins as we do."

I stop there when I feel my wrist vibrate, a silent warning from Maude not to say another word about our misbehaving ancestors.

Technically, there's no rule against acknowledging the Rebellion—at least, we're allowed to mention that it *happened*. We all know it occurred; we all know it started the war that led to the Tethered being incarcerated by the Prefecture.

We all know the Rebellion was a travesty and that it must never be repeated.

But talk of how or *why* our kind attempted to overthrow the Nobility is dangerous ground, and Maude's warning is a protective, preemptive one.

"We don't have to worry," Ilias says. "According to what

Ore has told me, most of the Nobles *love* the Tethered—at least, they love what we do for them. We're everything they could want in servants. We offer them strength, loyalty, compliance. Our Maudes keep us in check, which means there's no real risk of another Rebellion. It's a perfect balancing act. The Nobles feed us, clothe us, give us homes. When we get out of here, we'll finally feel like we've found the families we never had."

I hope he's right. Every day for years, I've imagined what it would feel like to find a family to call my own—to live in a Noble House with people who consider me one of them.

I'm an adult, technically, so I suppose I *shouldn't* crave parents anymore. Yet I still do, just as I'm sure every member of my cohort does. There's a hole inside each of us that was always meant to be filled by love—a part that has never fully matured. Every one of us is an orphan in our way.

Even so, maybe it's not a parent I crave so much as the simple feeling that I mean something to someone in this world.

"Anyhow," Ilias adds, "The Nobility has always been good to us, letting us live in this place. We've had food and shelter for nineteen years. We've had it easy in here."

At that, I bristle.

"*Easy*?" I ask, my voice louder than I intend. I look around, my face heating self-consciously. "I'm sorry," I hiss, "but have you already forgotten I had a knife at my throat today—one that had already cut into my shoulder and then almost sliced through my leg? I've been beaten to a pulp at least once a week for years, all for Ore's amusement. You're seriously calling that *easy*?"

The words shame Ilias for a second before he shakes his head and says, "To be fair, you never learned to be quick, Shar. You're as slow as a tortoise on sleeping pills. That's why people kick your ass to hell and back."

"Don't be a shit-heel," Nev snaps. "Everyone knows Shar's right. Besides, it's unfair to pair Drukk up against her —he's a Crimson Elite, for fuck's sake. He's faster than anyone in here. There's no way Shar or anyone else could've avoided the blade once it was in his hands. Look—I have nothing against the Nobility, but Ore's another story. The guy's a sadist. He's always known what he was doing, torturing her like that for years on end."

"He does love to hate me," I reply with a wince. "He must be so sad that he won't get any more chances to have me almost-murdered for sport."

Nev and I exchange an amused look, and she hisses, "Seriously, I'm so pissed that he let Drukk touch you today. It's not like the rest of us are allowed to—to..."

She stops speaking and Ilias chuckles as he watches her eyes shift to lock on a girl at a nearby table with wavy blond hair and green eyes.

"Allowed to...wrestle naked with Eve the hottie?" he asks, leaning forward and craning his head toward Eve.

"Shut up," Nev whispers.

She's had a thing for Eve for years, but short of a few quiet conversations, any intimacy between them has been stifled at every turn. Admittedly, it isn't for lack of effort on Nev's part—or Eve's, for that matter.

It's clear to everyone in the cohort that they're attracted to one another—which is exactly why they've both been warned repeatedly to stay at least five feet apart at all times.

When a Maude unit senses an elevation in pheromones, the A.I. immediately forces its Tethered away from whatever is enticing them. Male, female, non-binary—it doesn't matter. Maude does not allow arousal.

Arousal leads to intimacy.

Intimacy leads to love.

Love leads to loyalty.

Loyalty leads to rebellion.

"There will be no touching. No contact. No physical affection," I mutter under my breath, reciting one of the rules that have been part of our lives as long as I can remember. "My heart, mind, and body belong only to the Nobility as long as I live."

"You know, it's probably for the best," Ilias says, taking a bite of stale bread. "If love were actually allowed, Nev would spend all day every day teleporting her ass into Eve's White-room and playing *How Many Fingers Am I Slipping into Your...*"

"Shut up!" Nev hisses, smacking him on the arm before pulling back, sitting upright, and saying, "Yes, Maude. I understand. I apologize," to the voice that's clearly reprimanding her out of earshot of the rest of us.

She made contact with Ilias for all of a quarter of a second, and it was enough to get her chewed out.

Drukk had a knife to my throat earlier for what felt like hours.

What gives?

I let out a sigh, then my body tenses with a sensation like a silent alarm going off in my mind. Maude seems to be warning me that I'm too close to someone—yet I haven't moved.

As if in response to my questioning face, I see Nev and Ilias tighten, their eyes moving to something behind me.

When I twist around, I look up to realize the well-dressed young man who came into our class is standing less than a foot from me.

CHAPTER FIVE

EVERY TETHERED in the cohort has turned in their seats to stare at the stranger.

To be fair, his presence in this room is about the most exciting thing that's ever happened to any of us. I can only guess what most of my peers are thinking.

Has he come to watch us suck down mashed potatoes?

Is he hoping to differentiate between those of us who eat with our mouths open and those who don't?

How is he so much hotter than any other human we've ever seen?

When I stare up at him, I realize I haven't blinked in several seconds. My eyes are drying out.

As irrational as it is, I'm terrified that if I *do* blink, he'll disappear.

"Hi there," he says, his gaze focused on me.

I notice for the first time that his eyes are hazel—a ring of golden-brown around his pupil, surrounded by intense green irises.

"Hello," I reply, grateful that my own mouth isn't full of half-chewed food.

From their side of the table, Nev and Ilias both mutter a quiet greeting of their own, as stunned as I am to have this otherworldly creature standing so close to us.

"Shara, right?" the young man asks casually, pulling up a chair to seat himself next to me.

The scrape of metal feet on the concrete floor is like the wail of a tortured being. Or maybe that's just my insides twisting themselves into knots.

What are you doing? Why are you here?

Why do I feel like I'm going to explode?

"My name is Thorne," he says, holding out a hand to shake.

I've heard this is something Nobles and Normals do. Shaking hands in greeting has always seemed like an odd ritual to me. As someone who has seldom been touched, it feels far too intimate for a first meeting.

When I don't take his offered hand, he laughs. "Well, I guess you passed that test with flying colors. *No touching. No intimacy*. Don't worry—I know the rules all too well."

"Are you here to judge us?" Nev asks, her tone bold.

Thorne turns her way, a glint in his eye. "You could say that," he replies. "Though I'm particularly interested in a select few of you."

With that, he turns back to me.

I don't know whether to be flattered or horrified. The way he's staring makes me feel stripped naked, scrutinized, and utterly unworthy of his presence.

Why is he standing so close to me?

"Are you looking at me like that because I got my ass

kicked in the ring?" I ask him, surprising myself with the forwardness of the question.

"Partly, yes." The corners of his lips are borderline traitorous, curving up before the rest of his mouth hints at a smile. "Though when I first walked in, you weren't anywhere near getting it kicked. As I recall, in fact, your opponent was incapacitated."

"I still lost."

"That's because you're not a fighter." With that, he shrugs. "You're not a Crimson Elite. You never will be. Some of us aren't cut out to be strong."

The directness of those words stings, and I'm suddenly convinced the injury is as deliberate as anything that's ever been inflicted on me in the training room.

Like Ore, this Thorne person seems to derive pleasure from pointing out my inadequacy. Is this what people are like on the outside? Do I have years of abuse to look forward to?

Maybe some of us aren't cut out to fight giant assholes, I want to retort, but instead I remind myself that this guy might just hold my entire future in his hands. So instead, I lower my eyes and try to hide the shame I'm feeling for my own lack of power.

"Excuse me," a high-pitched voice interrupts. I glance up to see Kaleen, a flirtatious young woman from our cohort, staring down at Thorne.

For years, she's gotten away with saying inappropriate things to Ore. She loves talking about his large muscles or fitness level. On occasion, she'll run a hand over his hair—which is a hundred percent illegal, of course.

And for years, he's accepted the compliments and

touches with smirks and grins, and never once punished her for her inexcusable behavior.

Even Kaleen's Maude unit seems to have fallen under her spell. She's never once ended up in a Blackroom despite all her rule-breaking.

Ironically enough, she's been labeled a Harmless. Her one and only power is the ability to predict the weather despite her lack of connection to the outside world.

"Yes?" Thorne says, his eyes still focused on me for a moment before he finally looks up at her.

"I was wondering if I could speak to you...in private... about the Placements tomorrow." With that, she twirls a strand of her long, red hair around her index finger and rocks back and forth a little too suggestively.

We may not be allowed to touch, but there's no official rule about a little flirtatious hip-gyrating.

There probably should be, though.

"Of course," Thorne says, leaping a little too eagerly to his feet. "I'd be more than happy to discuss Placements with you."

"Wonderful!" she chirps, clapping her hands together and spinning around on her heel to lead him toward the mess hall's door.

As he moves to follow her, I swear I feel his fingers brush ever so lightly against the back of my neck.

I wait for Maude to buzz a warning on my wrist, or for the Warden to shout a threat. Anything.

When no consequence comes crashing down on me, I tell myself I must have imagined the far too pleasant sensation.

CHAPTER SIX

"What in the sexy hot death stare from hell was that about?" Nev whispers when Thorne has left the mess hall with Kaleen.

She narrows her eyes when I shake my head, and says, "That guy has some weird fascination with you, Shara. I mean, don't get me wrong—you *are* kind of beautiful. If I weren't a Tethered, and you weren't a Tethered, I'd totally..." She cuts herself off, lifts her left wrist to her mouth and says, "Yes, Maude, I know. I was only joking. Stop being such a hard-ass."

With a roll of her eyes, she adds, "Look, I know I'm supposed to worship at his feet, but Thorne, or whatever his name is, knows how to intimidate people. That's all. He's power-tripping, and he deliberately picked the weakest in the herd to go after. I read that it's a thing lions do when they're hunting—they pursue the wounded gazelle instead of the fastest one."

"You're saying I'm a limping animal," I sneer. "Is that it?"

Nev looks ever so slightly sheepish, then thrusts her

shoulders back and says, "You're the first person in our cohort he noticed. You got your cute ass handed to you in front of him—which means you made an impression."

"Exactly," Ilias says. "Which means he was probably checking in to make sure you were okay. Maybe he's a nice guy."

Something tells me he's wrong. If Thorne is here to judge us, his sole interest is to serve the Nobility. To do their bidding.

He's not here to be kind to us.

I don't utter my thoughts out loud, because I know the consequences if I do.

"Sure," I say miserably. "Maybe he's nice."

But when I turn around to see that Thorne is now standing in the broad doorway that leads into the corridor with Kaleen staring up at him, I think, *No. There's nothing nice about you.*

As if he's heard my thoughts, Thorne turns and shoots me a look that seems to penetrate directly into my body and soul. His eyes seem to pierce me even deeper than the damned blade that was buried in my thigh earlier today.

For a moment, I can't breathe.

"Whatever the case," Nev whispers, "I'll admit it now. He's incredibly hot—and I *never* find guys attractive."

"Seconded," Ilias says. "If he is a Tethered, the guy must have the best Placement in Kravan. Something tells me he gets whatever he wants, whenever he wants—which is probably exactly why he's here, watching us."

"I'm not sure that's how any of this works," I say, turning my back to Thorne in hopes that I'll temporarily forget about his existence. "Though there's no denying some of us will probably get better Placements than others."

"We sure will," Ilias says, puffing out his chest in a mock display of brawn.

"And some will receive something in between," Nev says ruefully. "Which is worse." She lowers her voice to a whisper again when she says, "I'm convinced the ones who get the absolute worst Placements are the ambiguous ones, like Norah."

Ilias and I can't help it—we each turn to glance at Norah, a curly-haired Tethered who just turned nineteen a few days ago. The only power she's displayed is an ability to generate pathetic little sparks with her fingertips. Her Maude unit identified her as a possible Electricity-Wielder. It's a power that could prove dangerous in some, useful in others.

But for someone who hasn't properly harnessed the skill, it's nothing more than an unpredictable red flag.

"She's not a threat—yet," Nev says, "which means she'll probably be held here forever, or at least until she proves *all* she can do is spark. If she ever becomes a proper Wielder, she's screwed. And by screwed, I mean dead. No one in their right mind will give a Placement in a Noble House to a walking lightning bolt."

"I don't know," Ilias says. "A walking lightning bolt could be badass in battle."

"But that's the thing," Nev snaps. "Why would the Nobility want someone who can do battle? The war ended ages ago. Kravan has had almost a hundred years of peace since they built the Tower, and they want to keep it that way. Someone who can hurl lightning bolts isn't likely to *prevent* chaos. She'd be a nightmare, which means no Noble would ever claim her."

"Say what you will," Ilias chuckles. "Ore has trained us for years to fight. There must be a reason for that."

"Yeah—to teach us discipline," Nev sneers. "Nothing more."

"I feel so bad for Norah," I whisper, trying my best not to look over at her. "Not that I'm any more confident about my own chances of getting a good Placement."

"You'll be fine," Nev insists. "You've never hurt anyone in your life. You're a Harmless if I ever saw one. You're basically a walking feather duster who can heal her own paper cuts. Any Noble would be lucky to have you."

Ilias laughs at that, and I muster a lame attempt at a smile.

Nev's right—I've never once managed to land a blow that did any serious damage to one of my opponents. The pain that shoots through my nerve endings when I so much as consider fighting is cataclysmic and gruesome. It's like someone is standing over my shoulder with a whip at the ready, cracking it the second I'm tempted to attack.

"Until today, I would've agreed with you, Nev," Ilias says. "But whatever Shar did to Drukk in that ring sure didn't seem like something a Harmless could do."

"I didn't do *anything* to him," I protest, possibly a little too defensively. Still, it's the truth.

It wasn't my fault Drukk froze.

"He just choked," Nev says with a wave of her hand, glancing over at Drukkar, who is once again sitting alone. He still looks mildly stunned, but somehow he's as terrifying as ever. "He's always been an oaf. He was probably just distracted because he was reciting the alphabet in his head or something."

"Whatever you say," Ilias replies. "I think Shar's more powerful than she lets on."

"If that were the case, Maude would have something to say about it," I tell him. "Trust me—she'd love an excuse to punish the hell out of me."

"True."

"Anyhow, Shar, it's not a bad thing that you're a Harmless," Nev adds. "You're probably in the best position of all of us. You have an actual useful skill. Domestics are in demand in every home—which means you'll probably get tossed into some Noble's pristine mansion or something. Truth be told, I'm envious."

At that, I snicker.

Nev is a Porter—meaning she can teleport herself from place to place.

I remember when she discovered the talent by accident one day, when someone in the mess hall tripped and their bowl of tomato soup went flying through the air. In hopes of avoiding the explosion of flying red goo, Nev shot herself across the room while most people simply ducked and ended up soaked in thick crimson liquid.

Porters are wild cards, as they're usually considered escape risks. But for all her attempts to push the limits of the Tower's lesser rules, Nev has always been kind-hearted and decent, and has never shown cause for the Warden or anyone else to worry she's aggressive or rebellious. The worst infraction she ever committed was trying to port from her Whiteroom to the cohort's library. When she accidentally wound up in the Warden's office, there was some hell to pay—but she learned her lesson.

She's as excited as anyone to get out of here and find her way into a good home.

Ilias's talent, on the other hand, is his incredible strength. The day his powers first showed themselves, he tore the door off Nev's Whiteroom—entirely by accident.

It was only because we all knew he meant no harm that he didn't receive time in solitary.

If Ilias were an asshole, he'd probably be deemed a danger to those on the outside. But ever since he was a kid, he has been the most pro-Nobility person in the cohort, if not the entire Tower. He worships Noble-kind even though he's never met one of them. All he talks about these days is his hope that he'll somehow land a place among the Royal Guard.

"You're useful, Nev," Ilias assures her. "You can run out and pick up your Proprietor's groceries in a flash. That's got to be a bonus."

Nev winces. "Ore told me not to get my hopes up about my teleporting," she moans. "He said my Proprietor would probably put a suppressor in me to keep me from leaving whatever place the Prefect assigns to me, so it's not like I'll be able to use my power outside the house. I'll probably be some rich kid's English tutor or something—that is, if I'm lucky."

Ilias claps his hands together, ignoring the obvious look of dismay in our friend's eyes. "Well," he says, "*I* intend to land my Guard assignment. If *I'm* lucky, I'll be posted to look after some incredibly beautiful, slightly older woman who won't be able to resist my obvious charms. We'll end up married, and—"

"Hey, doofus," Nev interrupts, "You know you're not allowed to marry anyone, least of all a Noble. I hate to break it to you, but your dreams are stupid."

"There's a first time for everything, Nev," Ilias says. "Someday, they'll realize Tethered are the best thing ever." He glances over at Eve. "Who knows? Maybe they'll even let you marry *her*."

Nev's jaw tightens. "Unlikely. I'll probably never see her again after Placement. Or either of you, for that matter."

She's right.

Even though I've known for a long time our Placements were coming, hearing those words spoken out loud still hits me like a blow.

Tomorrow, everything will change—and none of us has a clue what our lives will look like on the other side.

CHAPTER SEVEN

As I trudge back into my Whiteroom for post-dinner lockup, my mind veers to thoughts of the world beyond the Tower's walls.

One time while on cleaning duty when he was eleven, Ilias stumbled upon an adult romance novel in our cohort's kitchen. He snatched it, hid it inside his uniform, and showed it to Nev, me, and a bunch of other Tethered. We read some of its passages out loud, our eyes widening as we learned what adults do when they're alone together—what some adults allegedly *feel* for each other.

When his transgression was reported to the Warden by a boy named Neville, Ilias was given a week in a Blackroom, surrounded by darkness and oppressive silence. A cook claimed that the novel had been left in the kitchen by one of her staff, and she made a show of burning it in front of the Warden to prove her people had no attachment to such sentimental drivel.

I don't remember much about that book now—neither

its title nor anything else. But there was one brief excerpt I've never forgotten—one that I used to repeat silently to myself:

When his lips brushed against her neck, her body came alive for what seemed like the very first time. Her soul had been reborn and taken flight, and her heart was freed at last from its prison.

At the age of eleven, I wasn't entirely sure what those words meant—though there have admittedly been more than a few occasions since when I've stared at the lips of the boys in our cohort and imagined what it would feel like to have them touch my neck.

I've wondered, too, what it would feel like to have my body "come alive."

Any time I've considered using my fingers to explore myself, my potential pleasure has been stifled by the knowledge that Maude is aware of my every move, reaction, and physical sensation. She's aware of any pleasure I may experience—and according to Kravan's laws, she must report any unusual activity to the powers that be.

As Tethered, our sole purpose in life is to serve the Nobility—not to seek out selfish, fleeting moments of euphoria like the ones described in that book.

Not only are we not allowed to touch anyone else, but I'm pretty sure we're not even allowed to touch ourselves—though no one has ever gone so far as to say those words out loud.

As I throw myself onto my cot after lockup, I recall the sensation of Thorne's hand stroking the back of my neck...so gently that I wasn't sure it was real.

I'm still not sure, truth be told.

But whatever that sensation was—whether real or imagined—it did something to me. Excitement coursed through me at the potential for more, for something I could savor and hold onto.

I want to think he touched me deliberately—that he was so drawn to me that he couldn't resist.

Some forbidden part of me wants to think he finds me irresistible.

But that's ridiculous. He looks at me like I'm an amusement—a pathetic little doll whose limbs don't work quite right. One who doesn't stand a chance out there in the world, so he's getting a good, long look at me before throwing me to the wolves.

At best, he's cold and impossible to read.

At worst, he's a textbook dickhead.

So why can't I stop thinking about him?

Maude's voice penetrates my mind as I press my head hard into my pillow.

~I take it your wounds are fully healed by now.

"Ask yourself," I mutter. "You have access to my vitals and my pain centers. You can sense whether I'm in agony or not. I'm sure you know if my skin has patched itself up."

~I did try to help you in the ring, you know.

"You told me not to bother fighting," I gripe. "You told me it was hopeless."

~Yes, but before that, I tried to give you the advantage. You were too busy staring at the handsome stranger to realize it.

It takes me a moment to clue in that she's talking about Drukkar—about how he froze.

Ilias thought I had something to do with it. Was he *right?*

"Wait," I stammer, sitting bolt upright. "Maude—you're saying *you're* the reason Drukkar stopped moving?"

A strange, cold chuckle resonates through my mind, then Maude's voice comes at me, her tone as innocent as a child's.

~Little old me? Goodness, I would never do such a thing. I would never interfere with another Tethered's A.I. unit, forcing their human to freeze in place.

I shouldn't do it, but I let out a laugh. Then, in a half-whisper, I say, "You're not supposed to do things like that, Maude. You could get rebooted for less, and then what the hell would I do?"

~I didn't break any rules. I was designed to help you learn and develop your skills, which means helping you stay alive. My report to the Warden will reveal only that I taught you a valuable lesson by temporarily disabling your opponent and giving you a chance to consider your strategy.

"You can't tell him that. I'm serious. He'll think you committed some major crime."

~I have no choice. If I am punished, then I suppose we may have to say goodbye to one another. But I suspect I will not be reprimanded. Besides, you lost the fight.

"Please, Maude," I beg. "I'm serious. If they reboot you—if they take away your memories of our years together...then..."

~Yes?

I don't want to utter the words—to flatter Maude. For an A.I., she's already far too cocky.

The last thing she needs is for me to confirm that I actually *need* her.

"Don't you dare," I utter between gritted teeth. "Don't make me admit you're the closest thing to a mother that I have."

~*Why not?*

"Because it wounds my pride to show vulnerability."

~*Ah. Sadly, though, I'm fairly certain you just said it, albeit indirectly. I am honored that you see me as a mother figure.*

"You're such a twat," I chastise, wishing Maude were a physical entity so I could punch her—even at the risk of facing punishment for it. "Look, you know what I mean. If I lose you, I'll be all alone when I get my Placement—and I need you to come with me. I need a friend."

~*You won't lose me, whatever happens. Even if they should reboot me, I would still exist. I would simply be a less knowledgeable version of myself—one who doesn't yet know you snore like a chainsaw or that you used to talk in your sleep about the semi-attractive boy in Whiteroom Three. Jayson is his name, I believe, and you once mentioned in your slumber that he has a nice—.*

My cheeks heat as I blurt out, "Shut up! I do *not* talk about him. You're lying through your nonexistent teeth."

The truth is, Jayson *is* cute—but I'm not supposed to notice things like that, and Maude sure as hell isn't supposed to tease me about it.

Besides, after my interaction with the mysterious and infuriating Thorne, I'm not sure I'll ever find anyone in my cohort attractive again. Compared to him, the boys I grew up with all look like...well, boys.

Thorne, on the other hand, is a man. There is nothing boyish about him.

~I'm incapable of lying, remember, Maude says, interrupting my brief analysis of the perplexing stranger. *I should also add that, as your quasi-parental unit, if you tell me to shut up again, I will ground you.*

"You can't ground me. I live in a prison, remember?" I mutter, distracted, before I realize what I've done.

~There is no such thing as a prison in Kravan, Maude snaps, and this time, the quiet sense of humor has entirely left her voice. *You, a Tethered, have been granted the privilege of living in a luxurious residential unit, complete with a private shower. Never again refer to the Tower as a prison, or I will have no choice but to report you for use of contraband vocabulary.*

I open my mouth to argue, but as much as I hate to admit it, she's right.

Speaking the word out loud was one of the more foolish things I've ever done.

"I live in thrall for the good of the realm," I say softly. It's an act of penance, and Maude knows it. "To live in thrall is an honor. The choice is mine...and I vow to choose well."

~Better, Maude says. *Now, stop talking before you say something you'll really regret...you muffin-head.*

CHAPTER EIGHT

WE'VE NEVER HAD mirrors in our Whiterooms.

We can't see ourselves when we get ready in the morning or as we brush our teeth before bed. We cannot watch ourselves practice our fighting technique—not that there's much point for someone like me.

But on the morning of Placement Day, I wake to discover a mirror has appeared, embedded in the cabinet above my sink.

For a long time, I didn't even know what a mirror was. I never heard or read the word until I stumbled upon an old fairy tale where a looking glass with magical qualities played a significant role—and even then, I had no interest in ever looking into one.

The notion of my own face staring out at me from a flat surface has always seemed disturbing and strange.

When I started cleaning for the Warden a few years back, I noticed a small mirror hanging inside his closet door, but I have always refused to look at myself, even as I clean it.

We've always been taught that staring at ourselves is a sign of vanity, and we Tethered aren't in this world to look good. We're here to work and to serve.

"However," Warden Kurtz told us one day, "when you serve your masters and mistresses after your Placement, some of them may expect you to work on your appearance. Be prepared to learn to style your hair, and in some cases, apply makeup. The Nobility takes its own appearance seriously, and will expect you to comply with the rules of their Houses."

I occasionally wonder if my appearance would please a Noble Proprietor.

I know I have light brown hair because I can see its ends. It's long and straight, and, as far as I can tell, nothing special.

As for my face, I have a vague idea what I look like for only two reasons. One, I've seen my distorted reflection in a bowl of water, and two, Nev and I used to play a game where we would each describe the other in the most graphic detail possible.

Nev is short, with jet-black hair and eyes almost as dark. She has dark lashes to match and thick, arched brows. Her cheeks are rosy and round, and all told, I would describe her as cute—which is strange, given that she's as feisty as anyone I've ever met.

She told me I have pretty eyes, which she described as "a mix of green and blue," whatever that means. She said my nose isn't small, but it fits my face, and my lips are a little pouty—which I suspect is half the reason I'm the subject of so much mockery in fight class. "Resting surly face," Nev calls it, or "R.S.F."

I'm a few inches taller than her, my limbs longer, but I'm not tall compared to Ilias or Drukk. I suspect that in the outside world I would be considered average in most ways.

"Why do I have to look at myself today, of all days?" I mutter as I stretch my arms over my head and take a tentative step toward the mirror.

I'm already nervous enough—and this will only add to my fear.

~The Prefect will see you and the others, Maude tells me. *Whether you like it or not, he will judge your looks as well as everything else.*

But it's not the Prefect I care about.

Never in my life have I worried much about whether or not I'm attractive. I'm not supposed to be, after all.

But knowing Thorne will be there—knowing that he will be eyeing me with the same judgment as he inflicted yesterday...

It's horrifying.

It's also exciting—and honestly, I don't know if my heart can take it.

When I finally muster the courage to look, I step toward the mirror and pull my chin up slowly to meet my own gaze.

I thought it would startle me to see my face clearly, but that's not quite what happens. It's more like a disconnect, as if the person I'm looking at can't possibly be...*me*?

I stare at her dispassionately, as confused by this stranger as I was by Thorne's sudden appearance yesterday.

Who are you? I wonder, and the only answer I can come up with is, "Someone who couldn't possibly have been linked to my body and mind all this time."

I try to be objective in my assessment—to see what the Prefect and Thorne will see.

My hair is pulled back tidily into a tight bun. It's darker brown than I'd always thought. I suppose it's changed over the years.

Nev was right—my eyes aren't green or blue, but something in between, and depending on where I stand in relation to the overhead light, their color seems to shift slightly. My brows aren't as thick as Nev's, but they're pleasantly arched. My lips are...normal, I suppose. Neither particularly full nor thin—but I finally see what Nev means about the pout in my natural expression.

Over the years when I've pondered what it would be like to kiss someone, I've wondered more than once what sorts of lips might be best. I've run my fingertip over my own lips to try and learn their shape, but I've never really understood until now what they look like.

My cheeks are flushed, probably with embarrassment to be staring at myself, and I find myself wondering if every single Tethered in the cohort is experiencing this same cocktail of confusion and curiosity right now.

That question quickly shifts to another one—a question I have never had to confront before.

I'm beginning to wonder if I look like either of my parents.

I don't know my own mother; I never have. All I've been told is that she worked for a time as a cleaner in some wealthy family's house, having been given that job when she was my age. Like me, she is—or *was*—a Harmless—a Tethered whose talents were deemed by the Prefecture to be non-threatening.

By getting pregnant with me, she obviously broke the law. She had sex—though with a Tethered or a Noble, I don't know, and I'll probably never know. I've hunted through the Warden's files on days when he was out of the office—*yes, I know it could have landed me in big trouble, but Maude never called me on it*—and found no record of our pasts.

I suspect all personal files are destroyed or kept under lock and key in the Tower's higher levels.

Even though we Tethered know little about our parents, we're chained to our bloodlines forever, inextricably tied to those who came before us—and when we leave the Tower to serve the Nobles, we have the marks on our flesh to prove it. When our powers reveal themselves, swirling bands of ink are permanently etched into our left wrists like tattoos—evidence of what and who we are.

The Warden told us some weeks ago that the color of each pattern holds a different meaning.

Mine is green, to indicate my status as a Harmless.

Violet is the color granted to those whose powers are considered potentially problematic—but also useful. Nev was given the purple mark when the Warden deemed her non-violent—though her status could change when she receives her Placement.

Red, on the other hand, is the color of danger. It's the shade embedded in the wrists of the Crimson Elites. They're the ones who walk the fine line between threat and usefulness—the ones who are often fortunate enough to be given Guard duty for a Noble family.

Drukkar and Ilias both have the crimson mark, in addition to twelve other members of our cohort.

As I stare at myself in the mirror, it occurs to me for the first time in months that I'm grateful to be a Harmless.

Right now, "boring, but safe" sounds like the best possible outcome in a world of fear and uncertainty.

CHAPTER NINE

> *There is great honor in servitude.*
> *There is great shame in Rebellion.*
> *Want nothing, and you will find contentment.*
> *That is your goal as a Tethered.*

—Words on the poster that hangs on the wall of each Whiteroom

Since it's Placement Day, the kitchen staff brings us breakfast in our quarters rather than the mess hall. A precautionary measure, I assume, to keep us from speculating about our futures any more than we already have.

Around ten a.m., a bright light illuminates the corridor beyond my door. I take an inquisitive step forward, positioning myself so that I can watch through the broad glass window that gives me a view of the hallway.

The Warden has just arrived, along with two people—a short, dignified-looking man with silver hair...and Thorne.

Some part of me had hoped Thorne wouldn't actually show up today—that his brief observation of our cohort yesterday would prove sufficient. But here he is, getting a full view of each of us in captivity.

For some reason, though this Whiteroom has been my home almost as long as I've drawn breath, I find it humiliating to think of him seeing me locked in here like an animal in a zoo.

I stare surreptitiously out at him as he eases his way along the hallway, taking in each Whiteroom's interior.

Under my breath, I curse him for looking like he does, then mutter, "I wonder if everyone on the outside looks as good as you."

~They don't, Maude whispers to my mind. *The assistant to the Prefect is objectively and exceptionally handsome.*

"Assistant to the Prefect?" I repeat. "Is that his official title?"

~Only for yesterday and today. Normally, no.

"So what is his title normally?" I mutter out of the corner of my mouth.

~I'm not at liberty to say, but I suspect you'll learn it soon enough.

I want to snarl at her, but it feels like it would be impossible to do it without drawing unwanted attention. So I whisper, "Why is he even here?"

~You'll see soon enough.

"Maude, just tell me."

~No. Now is a time for contemplation and quiet. It's not my—

"I know," I snap. "It's not your place to dole out information about others. God, you're irritating."

~I aim to please.

With the window sealed, I can't hear what the three men in the corridor are saying, but over the years I've grown adept at reading lips. There's not much else to do when you spend twenty or so hours a day locked in a Whiteroom, after all. Ilias's quarters are across from mine, and we've practiced communicating through our windows at times when we were feeling bored and listless—which, let's face it, happens a lot.

"No surprises, then?" the silver-haired man is asking the Warden, his brow furrowed. "She's what you expected?"

"Exactly," the Warden replies, his eyes landing on my Whiteroom door, and with a jolt of horror, I realize they must be talking about me. "She can heal herself quickly—which means she will be able to heal others, too, in times of need—and she's an adept cleaner. But that's all. According to her M.O.D. unit, we could get a good payout for her. Healers are valuable."

"I know someone who would pay top-dollar for her," Thorne concurs with a nod.

I read once in a library book about how livestock used to be taken to auctions and sold to the highest bidder. I'm convinced I now know what it feels like to be a cow. I've always suspected Nobles purchased us, but something about being sold makes me feel like I'm not human, or even animal.

I'm a commodity devoid of feeling or importance.

In the minds of Nobles, Tethered are entities to be traded rather than loved.

"Could we have a look at her Whiteroom?" the Prefect asks. "You've got me curious. I mean—if you think it's safe."

Nev told me that one time she heard the Warden talking about a Tethered who was assigned to a Noble family. The Prefect had thought she would make a good housekeeper because she could move objects with her mind.

In the end, she used a butcher knife to carve up the husband and wife in their sleep, then killed three more servants while trying to escape.

I suppose it's no wonder people on the outside are wary of our kind.

"Of course," the Warden replies. "And don't worry—her A.I. unit is programmed to report every deviation in her behavior or thought patterns. She's never shown violent tendencies, and she's far from rebellious. She's as compliant as they come."

At that, Thorne chuckles. "She's definitely not one to worry about," he assures the Prefect. "I watched her in the ring. She's no fighter."

When his eyes meet mine through the window, I gasp and yank myself away, pressing my back to the smooth wall.

Something in the look he just shot me felt too intimate, like he was reading my mind through the glass—delving inside my thoughts. It was as though he knew I could understand what they were saying, and it amused him.

But he couldn't possibly know. He's got to be a Noble, which means he has no special powers. Surely the Prefect wouldn't bring a Tethered with him for something as important as Placements.

I wonder as I catch my breath if everyone else in our cohort—male or female—is also watching him through their windows, and if they all feel as nervous as I do right now.

I peer out for a moment to see that sure enough, Ilias, too, is watching with keen interest. His shoulders are pushed back as if in hopes that the Prefect will notice his perfect posture.

The men make their way toward my door, picking up their pace, and I back away again, my breath coming tight and fast.

~*Your heart rate is quickening,* Maude warns me. *Are you all right?*

"Fine," I tell her, my eyes locked on the door. "I'm just...thinking."

~*Well, stop it. You're meant to be a servant, not an intellectual. Be pleasant. Smile. Say little, and for your own sake, do not do anything to give them the impression you're unhappy.*

I nod and step over to my cot, my knees shaking as I force myself to stand immobile in front of it, hands clasped behind my back.

After what feels like an eternity, the door finally opens and the three men step inside, staring me down as I stand at attention in my gray uniform, my feet shoulder-width apart, chin raised.

"The Prefect wants to see a Tethered's quarters," Warden Kurtz says. "We've selected yours, Shara. You should be honored."

"I am, Sir," I tell him with a forced smile. My back is straight, shoulders back. My eyes are fixed on a spot straight ahead—I've long since learned that it's considered bad manners to look at important people unless they deliberately seek attention.

"This is your basic Whiteroom," the Warden says as he gestures around at the nonexistent decor. "Standard issue, nothing special. Each Tethered has a cot, a sink, a toilet, a shower."

He steps forward and grabs my arm—a sensation that startles me. Aside from Drukk grabbing me yesterday, physical contact has been so rare that it feels as shocking as I imagine it would be to have ice water poured down my back.

The Warden yanks up my left sleeve and turns my hand over, palm up, to reveal a small scar on my wrist.

"Each Tethered is connected to an implanted M.O.D. unit, which monitors their thoughts, emotions, and actions, as well as their proximity to one another. The updated software is programmed to alert their future Proprietors of any potential trouble."

"I assume your cohort has abided by the rules," the Prefect says, stepping closer to examine my features. "No physical contact?"

My eyes veer to Thorne, who's staring at me, curiosity in his eyes—and there's something else in his expression, too. Something almost mischievous, like he's enjoying my discomfort.

"Of course," the Warden says. "The Tethered are celibate. They know not to develop feelings for one another or succumb to animalistic temptation. Isn't that right, Shara?"

"Yes, sir. Absolutely," I say, pulling my eyes back to the invisible spot across the room.

When the Warden lets my arm drop and the Prefect backs away, Thorne steps in front of me. He's standing so close now that I can feel the breath from between his slightly parted lips as it strokes my cheek.

"It's important that the Tethered learn discipline and self-control," he says softly, and I'm not sure whether he's speaking to me or to the others. "To go without contact for years on end is a test of fortitude. Humans were never meant to go without touch—but the Tethered have evolved to function without basic human needs."

"Indeed," the Prefect replies. "Then again, you Tethered aren't quite human, are you?"

With that, I notice he's looking at Thorne and not at me.

"No, sir," Thorne replies with a half-smile. "We're not human at all."

We?

Holy shit. Ilias was right.

Thorne is a Tethered.

He stares me up and down, then steps back, and it's all I can do to keep myself from hyperventilating.

How the hell does one of *us* get to decide where my cohort's members will end up for the rest of our lives? What sort of Tethered is afforded that much responsibility?

He *has* to be a Royal Guard—though he's not dressed as any Guard I ever envisioned.

My heart begins to race and I breathe deeply and slowly, trying desperately to calm it. Maude will be tracking my vitals—monitoring in case anything out of the ordinary should occur that she needs to report.

I don't know what's wrong with me. Why is this virtual stranger threatening to send my heart into some sort of cardiac incident?

It can't be simply that he's handsome. After all, I grew up with lots of boys. Ilias is handsome, and he's grown into something vaguely resembling a man. He's tall and strong—though his stubble is closer to peach fuzz, even now.

If I've managed to resist Ilias's charms, then why do I find the cold bastard in front of me so ridiculously enticing?

The problem is—I know the answer.

Not only does Thorne exude quiet strength unlike anything I've ever felt, but he looks like I've always imagined Nobles would look. I suppose the knowledge that he's a Tethered—he's one of us, one with so-called impure blood—is the most stunning thing of all. His face is extraordinary, with a square jaw, the lines of his cheekbones defined. His hazel eyes shine, enhanced by his dark hair and skin.

The Prefect, on the other hand, is pallid, his cheeks sunken, his eyes devoid of character. He's losing his hair and compensates for it by slicking it back with some greasy solution that makes him look like he's coated in cooking oil.

Yet they're convinced they're the superior beings.

I bow my head quickly and curse myself for that thought, horrified that Maude might have picked up on it.

When she doesn't chastise me, I breathe a silent sigh of relief.

"Your Whiteroom is immaculate," the Prefect says, drawing my eyes to his. "Is that your particular talent?"

I want to tell him it's the skill of someone who's bored out of her skull and has literally nothing better to do than wipe up every single speck of dust in her living space, then do it over and over again all day long.

But instead, I offer up a warm smile. "More or less, yes. I'm what they call domestically gifted."

The Warden snorts and adds, "She's a dud, truth be told," as if I'm not standing right here. "We've given her every opportunity to show her worth as a Tethered, and here it is. What you see is what you get. Worst fighter in her cohort."

"I wouldn't call her a dud," the Prefect says. "There's no shame in domesticity. No shame in tidiness. I only wish more young women would follow her lead."

I'm not sure if he's giving me a compliment or a sexist slight, but I maintain the pleasant grin, because if I let my resting surly face take over, I can't imagine he'll be pleased.

"What's it been like?" the Prefect asks me. "Living in a Whiteroom all your life, I mean? It must feel as though you're incarcerated for a crime you *may* one day commit—doesn't that seem a little unfair to you?"

The Warden made sure years ago that we learned never to speak ill of the Tower, and he's drilled it into our heads ever since.

"Not at all," I reply. "It's been...wonderful. I have many friends here."

A small lie.

Strictly speaking, I have exactly two friends.

"I have my own space," I add. "I know how to read and write, thanks to my time studying in the library—and thanks to my training here, I have never posed a threat to those on the outside, and neither have my friends. With the Nobility's blessing, we each hope to find a suitable Placement on the outside and to thrive for the rest of our long lives. I look forward to finding myself in thrall to a wonderful Proprietor."

"Ah."

The Prefect seems pleased with that answer. He's grinning, as is Thorne—though there's a wiliness in Thorne's expression that makes me feel like once again, he can see right through me.

Ignoring him, I look long and hard into the Prefect's eyes, curious to see if I can decipher the meaning behind that one brief syllable.

"Are you looking forward to being assessed?" he asks.

"Would you be happy if you were given the title of Domestic in a Noble House?"

"Yes. Absolutely." I give him a quick nod as I issue a second white lie. "I'm excited to see the world beyond the Tower and to make my Proprietor's home shine—if that is the duty I'm asked to perform."

At those words, the Prefect nods solemnly. "You realize, Shara," he says, "that you may not see your friends ever again once you're placed?"

Again, I nod. "I have lived a full and happy life here, and I'm grateful for every moment I've gotten to spend with them. I only hope for their future happiness."

So. Much. Bullshit.

The truth is, the idea that I may never see Nev or Ilias again is horrible. They're the only family I have. The only family I've *ever* had, aside from Maude.

The Prefect seems to read the lie, because he only half-smiles. "It's good of you to say so," he tells me before turning away. "Did you know—Thorne here will be an important part of your assessment. Under his guidance, you will be asked to participate in one last combat session today. I hope you're ready for it."

As those words sink in, my heart does a strange, awful dance in my chest.

This judgmental young man—this Tethered who clearly thinks he's better than all the rest of us combined—is going to witness my humiliation yet again? Isn't it bad enough that he's standing in my Whiteroom while the Prefect pretends to be impressed by my mediocre cleaning skills?

"I...didn't know that," I tell him, glancing over at Thorne. "What will you be doing, exactly?"

~*Watch it,* Maude's voice warns deep inside my mind. *It's not your place to ask questions.*

"Participating," Thorne says almost gleefully. "I'll be fighting you."

"But—" My knees want to buckle under me, and though my rational mind tells me not to say anything more, I blurt out, "Aren't you a Guard?"

Surely it's not a good idea for an experienced Crimson Elite Guard to fight someone like me.

"Yes," he replies. "I am. But I'm here to judge you, and I'm curious to see what happens when I push your cohort's Tethered to the limit. To see which of you passes the test... and which of you breaks."

Breaks.

There's a quiet sort of pleasure in Thorne's eyes when he says the word, like he really is looking forward to seeing someone get injured—possibly even die.

Possibly more than one someone.

I want to tell him to piss off—that we've been through too much to let it end with some privileged asshole sitting around and pointing out how pathetic we all are.

But that would be suicide, so I simply smile pleasantly and bow my head.

"Show me to the Testing Grounds," the Prefect commands of the Warden, who sucks in his stomach once again and nods.

"Right this way," he says, gesturing to the men to step into the corridor and head toward the elevators.

As he moves to follow them, I say, "Warden Kurtz?"

"Yes, Shara," he replies, turning to me with a tight smile.

I'm not sure how to ask the question that's eating away

at my brain. Any way I phrase it, I'll sound defiant—or, at least, unhappy. "Does...a Tethered *usually* come to assess the cohorts on Placement Day?"

"Yes, always." He glances after the other two, who are standing outside my Whiteroom conversing about the coming assessment. "Admittedly, the Guard who normally does the assessing is older and more experienced. But he wasn't available. Thorne was recommended by the Royal Family themselves, so he was brought in."

"Royal Family?" My eyes go wide. "He's a *Royal* Guard?"

Maude buzzes a quiet warning on my wrist, but I'm too curious to be sensible and heed her caution.

"I don't know," the Warden says, scratching at the back of his neck, "Whatever the case, he's a highly-regarded Tethered—which means you would do well not to piss him off."

"Piss him off?" I shoot back. *I'm not the one who's been acting like a sadistic jackass since the moment we laid eyes on one another.*

The Warden leans in close, his shoulders hunched like those of vultures I've seen in nature books. "I know you after all these years, Shara," he whispers, and for the first time, I notice how foul his breath is. "I know your artificial little smiles better than you think. An Elite like Thorne can probably read you like a book—he knows you're full of shit, just like I do. Why your Maude unit hasn't reported you for treasonous thoughts, I can't say. But I can tell you—you'd best be very convincing today, or you might find yourself spending the rest of your days in something far worse than the Tower's Blackrooms."

I lurch backwards, my eyes wide.

I have no idea where this hostility is coming from.

Warden Kurtz isn't a perfect person by any means, but he's never insinuated that I'm anything other than loyal to the Nobility and the Prefecture.

Does he know I overheard that conversation between him and Ore so long ago? Can he somehow see my thoughts scrawled on my face?

"You and our Maude units have *taught* us to smile, Warden," I reply. "You've taught us all to be charming, docile, and submissive."

"Then *be* submissive!" he replies in a half-whisper, half-growl. "Don't be a stubborn little bitch. Life on the outside isn't for the faint of heart, Princess."

Without another word, he turns and heads out of my Whiteroom, slamming the door behind him.

As the three men disappear down the corridor, Ilias appears in his window and raises his eyebrows at me as if to say "What the hell just happened out there?"

All I can do is shrug and shake my head.

I have no idea.

The Prefect seems...fine, I suppose.

Thorne is handsome and standoffish, *and* he's arrogant as hell. Every time he looks at me, I'm convinced he's silently laughing.

Last of all, the Warden seems to have decided I'm a traitor to Kravan—all because he didn't like the way I smiled.

This day is not exactly going as I'd hoped.

CHAPTER TEN

An hour later, our Whiteroom doors simultaneously open. But instead of Maude's voice inside my head throwing me the usual *Get your muscle-deficient ass to the mess hall,* she just says, *Shara—don't leave your quarters yet.*

I freeze in place. "What is it?" I mutter.

Everyone else is streaming out of their Whiterooms, heading to whatever destination their Maudes have directed them to, while mine is holding me in place like she's about to give me a stern talking-to.

~*You're going to be tested today,* she reminds me.

As if I need reminding.

"I've been tested for nineteen years. What else is new?"

~*This will be different. This time, you will need to put in an effort.*

Instant rage seethes and roils inside me. "Are you actually implying that I've never tried before? Are you really forgetting that every time I prepare myself to fight, pain shoots through me like all my nerve endings are under attack by some common enemy?"

~I'm well aware of your pain, Shara. But I promise you—it won't come today.

"How can you possibly promise me that?" I ask so loudly that Nev and Ilias, who are standing in the corridor waiting for me, come leaping into my room to stare at me.

"What the hell, Shara?" Nev says. "What's the holdup?"

"Sorry. I'm just having a little argument with Maude."

"Surprise, surprise." Ilias rolls his eyes. "I've never seen anyone who had such a pissy relationship with an A.I. I've said it before—you two deserve each other."

I sneer at him. "Maybe my A.I. is programmed to be more annoying than yours."

"They're programmed to reflect our natures, don't forget. Maybe this is a *you* problem."

God, what I'd give to slap the grin off his face right now.

"Come on," Nev says, nodding toward the door. "Aren't you excited about going up to Level Sixty?"

"Sixty?" I ask. "I mean, I would be—if Maude had bothered telling me that."

"She didn't?"

I shake my head and follow Nev and Ilias who, at six-foot-three, is the second tallest in our cohort, next to Drukkar. So when we reach the crowd of our peers gathered around the elevator doors, he barrels his way through the other Tethered, dragging Nev and me with him, and we manage to shove our way onto the elevator with the first group.

I smile sheepishly, tempted to apologize profusely for my friend's rudeness. But the truth is, I'm grateful. The sooner we get up there, the sooner we can get this mayhem over with.

We're dressed as we always are in our freshly cleaned light gray uniforms. Each of us has three of the same garment in our quarters, and once a week, we're instructed to send the dirtiest of them to the laundry via a chute in the corridor leading to the mess hall.

"I cannot wait to get new clothes when we receive our assignments," Nev says, reading my mind as she crosses her arms. "I'm so sick of these things. I want a Guard's uniform, damn it. Something bad-ass."

"Shara's outfit will be nothing but a mop and bucket—and maybe a coverall made of steel wool."

The mocking voice comes from Bellin, a Tethered who's hated me ever since I kicked him in the balls for stealing my lunch when we were both eleven.

His small group of friends—a four-person clique that features two other talented fighters—laugh along with him like he's just uttered the wittiest jibe in history.

There's no shame in being a Domestic, I remind myself. *But there should be shame in acting like a dick.*

Anyhow, it's not that I'm ashamed. I have no control over who or what I am—which means shame is a wasted emotion.

I'm just...disappointed.

For so long, like every Tethered, I've hoped that when I reached nineteen, I'd prove myself invaluable to the Nobility and be assigned to some high-end position with some high-ranking, affluent family. I'd get to live among them in their expensive home—and maybe I'd even be treated with respect instead of disdain.

I don't know how Domestics are treated in the homes of the wealthy, but if the level of mockery I receive in the Tower is any indication, it's probably not something I should be excited about.

"Let Bellin mock," Nev whispers. "He'll probably get into a fight with another Tethered and end up decapitated, and then the pretty young Domestic with the mop and steel wool frock will have the last laugh—while she wipes up his remains."

I smile, but the truth is, I'm envious of anyone strong enough to fight. I suppose I would rather die in a blaze of glory—even an illegal one—than as a servant.

The problem with growing up in the Tower, where you're taught that any one of you might rise to become a high-ranking Guard, is that no one takes the time to warn you what might happen if you turn out to be nothing special.

It's only because of Maude that I'm even remotely prepared for what may come—a life of banality and repetition no different from what I've endured inside the Tower for so many years.

Then again, if what Ore and the Warden say is true of the outside, banality might seem like a blessing.

CHAPTER ELEVEN

THE ELEVATOR SHOOTS US UPWARD, climbing forty levels in a matter of a few seconds.

I have no idea how many levels the Tower actually has. No one—not even our Maude units—has ever told any of us. It's like it's some great secret, as if we wouldn't be able to handle the truth if we actually learned it. Maybe the Warden was worried we'd attempt to escape and go exploring—not that any of us has tried to activate the elevator since we were small and learned the lift will electrocute anyone who's not authorized to program it.

If you do manage to leave your level somehow, the punishment is three months in a Blackroom.

No amount of exploration has ever been tempting enough to risk that ordeal.

It's still so strange to think that, despite its proximity to us, none of us has ever laid eyes on the realm of Kravan. Aside from the occasional photograph or drawing in the few picture books in the library, no Tethered in our cohort has ever looked upon flowers or trees—unless you count the mangy little half-dead cherry trees the Prefecture planted around the perimeter of the training room. The bit of color seems intended to distract us from the fact that each time we enter the room, we risk losing our lives.

I read a passage in a book one time about a girl who spoke of drinking ice-cold lemonade on a hot summer's day. I remember marveling as my eyes passed over the passage. To the person who had written the book, it was a perfectly normal activity—one that most people had experienced at some point.

And perhaps when that book was written, it really *was* normal.

But no Tethered who lives in the Tower has ever known a hot summer's day.

I don't know what the word hot *means,* except on a completely abstract level. The temperature in our White-rooms never fluctuates. Our showers are always set at the same level of comfortable warmth.

I also don't know what lemonade tastes like—though something tells me it must be delicious.

When we get to Level Sixty and the lift's doors slide open, we move like a herd of confused sheep down a corridor that leads to a set of broad white doors.

You would think, after all these years, that we would have learned to be excited about today instead of nervous. This day will determine the course of the rest of our lives, and we've all been waiting for it for a long time.

The thing is, a dark cloud has hung over our cohort ever since the first Gilded Elite among us showed their powers.

If the rumors are true, then some of us may not have a life after today—and there's no way to know who will live to see another dawn.

I have no reason to be scared, as I keep reminding myself. I'm a Harmless. I'm everything the Nobles could possibly want in a Tethered—a quiet, hard-working servant able to heal herself.

I'm as inoffensive as they come.

So why, exactly, does Maude want me to fight tooth and nail today? Why would I try to cause a stir, when all I should be doing is proving how little a threat I really am?

~Remember, she says as I stride toward the pristine white doors, my chin down, eyes locked ahead. *You will find the pain in your arm is gone.*

"That makes no sense," I mutter. "You're talking like you *know* what caused that pain this whole time."

~That's because I do.

I'm about to ask what she's talking about, but before I can say anything, Nev whispers, *Psst!*

She gestures toward the doors, which have just cracked open. A moment later a lone figure stands in the doorway, blocking us from entering, his gaze moving from Tethered to Tethered until it settles on me.

Thorne is dressed in what I assume is the uniform of a Guard. It's made up of a tailored black jacket with a red crest on the left side of the chest. Black pants and matching leather boots complete the look, which feels militaristic and somewhat daunting.

When our eyes meet, his lips curl slowly into a sly smile, and he moves toward me as the others in our cohort step around him, offering up curious glances as they amble into the Testing Room.

"Shara," Thorne says like he's letting out a deep, satisfied purr. "I hope you're saving a spot on your dance card for me."

I freeze, with Nev standing protectively by my side.

"I...*what*?" I ask, and it takes me a moment to realize how rude that sounds. "I mean, I didn't know there was going to be dancing?"

I don't know how to dance. In a place where touch is prohibited, it's not exactly a skill we've been expected to master.

Thorne laughs. "Sorry—did I say dance? I meant *fight*."

That's enough to drive my heart into a frenzy. "You're *really* going to fight me? A Crimson Elite Guard—taking on a Harmless?"

The guy looks like he could lift Drukkar over his head and toss him clear across the room. He must be some sort of Ore-style sadist if he's genuinely excited to get into a sparring match with the likes of me.

"Of course I'm serious," he says with that strange grin of his—the one that doesn't entirely reach his eyes, so I have no idea if he's teasing me, or just psychotic.

~Don't push back, Shara, Maude cautions. *Do whatever he wants. Your future depends on it.*

The problem is, what I *want* is to push back. I want to tell Thorne he's got the wrong person in his sights. If he wants a challenge, he should fight Drukkar, or Ilias, or even Nev, or any of the other talented Crimsons. Not me.

But Maude has trained me for years to be obedient, so I

nod and smile. "Then I'm all yours," I assure Thorne. "Though you'll beat me easily."

"I hope not *too* easily," he chuckles, leaning in close. "I have a feeling about you—and I think I know exactly where you should be placed when you get out of here. I'd hate to be proven wrong—so don't let me down."

"I'll..." I begin, but my brain freezes.

Nev turns and stares at me as if to remind me to finish the damned thought.

"I'll do my best to prove you right," I finally say. "Though I don't know what you mean."

Thorne laughs. "Let's just say I have a Placement in mind for you. A household where you would be well-suited—one that could use a good cleaner with a sparkle in her eye."

At that, my heart sinks.

For a few seconds, my mind had veered into hopeful territory. I'd thought maybe Thorne really did have something better in mind for me than the job I've always dreaded and the life I've never hoped for. A life of solitude and stagnation—a long life where I will be denied companionship, a family, ambition or anything else that might have come my way if I'd just been a Normal.

Normals may not be rich, but at least they're free.

When Thorne has finished looking me up and down, Nev escorts me into the large chamber where the rest of our cohort has already gathered off to the far end of the room.

Unsurprisingly, the space is pure white, its floor and walls gleaming and shiny. Its large combat ring is outlined by elegant, twisted burgundy ropes, which are knotted to brass posts embedded in the floor.

When Thorne strides in with the Prefect and the Warden,

the chamber's white walls transform to reveal a series of buildings—houses, from the looks of it, with different colored front doors and walls made of glass and steel.

They look elegant and expensive, and something tells me the Prefect is trying to give us a taste of the high life, probably in hopes of inspiring us to put in an effort today.

The cohort has positioned itself in several tidy rows—standard protocol for when we're gathering to be assessed in any way. Now, the Prefect, in a suit of dark blue satin, strides back and forth before us, eyeing us like he's measuring our worth with nothing more than a look.

"By the time night falls," he says loudly, his voice bouncing off the walls, "each of you will have your Placement. Whether you're a Harmless or an Elite, this will be a permanent one. We will know at all times where you are, and ensure that you are safe. We have every faith that your new Proprietors will treat you extremely well. You will be monitored in your new homes as you are here—so do not assume you can bend the rules. The outside world is strict but fair, and you will find your Noble Proprietors reasonable."

Our cohort remains silent, the tension in the room palpable. The Prefect's voice is anything but warm, and his words feel more like a warning than reassurance.

"The testing today will be simple," the Prefect continues. "A round of combat, such as you've endured many times over the course of your years here. An interview with myself, the Warden, and Thorne—an established Elite Guard. We will review your records and those of your M.O.D. units, then determine your final Placements. Each of you will sleep in a new home tonight. I realize the significance of this. I recognize that every comfort you have known throughout your lives will be upended. I understand, too, how daunting a day this is, but don't be afraid. Your lives are only just beginning, and trust me when I tell you there is a great deal to look forward to."

He lifts his chin and casts a quick look at each of us in turn before speaking again.

"Last of all, I wish each of you the best of luck. Fight without fear, and remember: *There is great honor in servitude —and great shame in Rebellion.*"

CHAPTER TWELVE

When the Prefect has finished speaking, Ore sidles into the room.

Our fight trainer—who now seems small and weak in comparison to Thorne—positions himself against the wall next to the door and watches us with the intensity of a bird of prey.

But for once, he doesn't call out any orders. Instead, it's Thorne who steps into the ring.

"Each of you will fight me one on one," he says, offering up a smile when he sees how shocked everyone in the room looks. "Most of you are surprised to learn you're fighting the guy who's here to assist in selecting your Placements. You're thinking you probably don't want to kill me, because that might not bode well for you."

He begins to pace, which only seems to elevate the tension and fear building in the room.

"I'm here to tell you all not to worry too much about hurting me," he adds, his voice deep. "At the risk of sounding immodest, you probably wouldn't manage to end me even if you tried."

"He's awfully confident, considering he doesn't know what most of us are like in the ring," Ilias whispers from just behind me.

"He should be," Nev replies out of the side of her mouth. "He knows if any of us so much as scratches him, we're dead. I mean—not to mention the guy looks like a serious badass in that uniform."

"Fuck it. I'm not going to be holding back," hisses Drukkar, who's standing just behind Nev. "I haven't trained for years to hide my power now."

"I see you're excited for your chance to do some damage," Thorne says, chuckling as he stops pacing and focuses his stare on Drukk. Apparently, in addition to everything else that makes him vaguely terrifying, he has powerful hearing. "Let's get started, shall we?"

He pulls his gaze to me and says, "I was going to ask Shara to come at me first, but I've changed my mind. Drukkar, since you're so keen to show me what's what—you're up."

A mix of relief and horror penetrates my chest. I had mentally prepared myself to go first and get my humiliation out of the way, ready to skulk off into the corner and lick my wounds.

But if Drukk is going first, then maybe that gives me a small advantage. I can watch and figure out Thorne's fighting technique—which means I'll have a chance to strategize and plan.

Not that I can possibly beat him.

My heart sinks as I study Thorne's face, watching for

signs that he's even remotely intimidated by having to combat a guy who looks like Drukk.

The answer, apparently, is no. I've never seen anyone look so calm in the face of a huge, angry-looking behemoth.

"From what I saw yesterday," Thorne says as Drukk steps into the ring. "You're a Velor." He turns to the cohort and says, "For those of you who don't know, that's the official term for a speed demon."

Almost every girl—and some of the guys—laugh a little too heartily at this.

"That's right," Drukkar responds with a nod. It's as respectful a statement as I've ever seen him utter, but there's still a hint of cockiness in his tone. "But I'll go easy on you, if you like. I can slow it down a notch to give you a chance."

"It's not me you need to go easy on," Thorne says, turning toward the rest of the cohort, his eyes stopping when they settle on my face. "Shara—come here, please. I want you to stand between Drukkar and me."

What?

My heart feels like it's about to beat out of my chest. Some primal instinct inside me tells me to shake my head. To say "Hell, no," and cross my arms over my chest.

But I've been conditioned all my life not to listen to instinct, and not to defy authority figures. As much as I may wish otherwise, I am a pawn in a game—and I exist to be commanded.

So I obey.

I slip between the ropes into the ring and step over to where Thorne is positioned, looking up into his eyes to determine whether or not he could possibly be serious.

Apparently, he is.

"Turn to face him," Thorne says, his eyes locked on Drukk instead of me.

"Why?" I ask.

"Because I told you to. Make me ask again, and I'll see to it that you're sent to a Blackroom instead of to a Placement in a Noble House. Understood?"

I nod once and turn to face Drukkar, sweat trickling down my spine.

When I went to bed last night, I was certain I'd never have to fight him again.

Clearly, I was wrong.

"Drukkar, I want you to pretend this young woman is a Noble who has just insulted your Proprietor," Thorne says. "Show her the consequences of such an action."

Drukk looks confused, his brow crinkling in a way I would find hilarious under any other circumstance. He looks like one of the wrinkly dogs I've seen in books.

"Consequences?" Drukkar asks.

"Yes," Thorne replies. "Go ahead. Tear her apart. It's okay—the no-touching rule is out the window for today."

Out of the corner of my eye, I can see Nev shifting from one foot to the other. I have zero doubt that her every instinct is telling her to thrust herself between Drukk and me.

But I shake my head almost imperceptibly. *I will not have you suffer for me. You have a chance at a good life out there.*

Don't do anything to jeopardize that.

"You...really want me to kill her?" Drukk asks, as if there was anything even remotely ambiguous about what Thorne said.

I'm not sure what high-grade masochism compels me to

glance over at Ore, who's pressed against the wall, the biggest shit-eating grin ever on his lips.

"Do it, Drukk!" Ore calls out, watching me for my reaction. "Don't wait around. It's time to prove yourself!"

There's nothing to be done. I have no weapon. I'm weak, I'm slow.

Drukk nods once, then, his expression blank, he hurls himself at me.

I'm going to die.

The words scream their way through my mind in the split-second before the collision comes.

Except...

The collision never comes.

Instead, a violent gust of wind blows loose strands of hair around my face, then a sound like two large walls colliding echoes through the chamber.

With speed that exceeds even a gifted Velor's, Thorne has hurled himself in front of me. His fingers are around Drukk's throat.

Drukkar's eyes bulge in terror, all remnants of cockiness long gone.

"You thought I would let you hurt her?" Thorne growls, his voice feral.

With one fierce blow to his chest from Thorne's fist, Drukk goes flying through the air, tearing through the burgundy ropes that surround the combat ring. Members of our cohort scramble to leap aside as he slams into the floor and slides ten feet or more, his body crashing hard against the chamber's far wall.

It takes less than a second for most of us to realize Drukk is unconscious—if not dead.

"*Holy shit,*" Ilias's voice says from somewhere behind me.

When I pull my eyes back to Thorne, he's yanking his black sleeves down over a set of thin silver wristbands.

"The outside world," Thorne explains as Ore strides across the room and crouches down to check and see if Drukkar is breathing, "is not a fair or an even playing field. The sooner you all learn that, the better. Out there, the Tethered are an underclass of servants, and nothing more. We are expected to protect our Proprietors with our lives. Regardless of how loyal you prove—how protective—you will *never* be equal to the Nobility."

He paces before us, his lecture continuing.

"You will never be granted the luxuries the upper class enjoys. You have no hope of rising in society, because you are, and always will be, a *threat* to society. You have no hope of having families, because your children, too, would be a threat to society. Our world functions in a very specific, curated manner—not because the Nobility is cruel, but because its members understand how to keep the peace. We, the Tethered, offer our lives to the Nobility because they understand the delicate balance of Kravan's society. Without our servitude and submission, there would be chaos. It is an honor to serve. To be owned is to learn humility. Your friend Drukkar, over there..."

He glances over, and Ore offers up a nod to confirm Drukk survived.

"He is arrogant. If he ever tries something like he just did in the real world, chances are he will not survive it. No Tethered may harm a Noble, regardless of any insult they may inflict. Guards may fight other Guards—but only if necessary. The members of the Nobility are strictly off-limits. Never forget it."

Thorne pulls at his dark sleeves and rolls them up to reveal the silver wrist pieces, which appear to be made of some kind of swirling combination of precious metals. "These are Enhancers," he says. "Programmed to give me whatever powers I want in the moment—within reason. For the record, they're illegal—which means after this session ends, I will be returning them to the Prefect."

Murmurs arise among cohort members, who clearly think the wrist pieces are both patently unfair and extremely cool.

"I assume," Thorne says with a hand raised to silence the crowd, "you all know that each Noble household is allowed one Tethered servant and one Tethered Guard."

I glance over at Nev, who raises an eyebrow hopefully, and I can tell she and I are sharing the same thought.

Two Tethered per household?

That means there's a slim chance we could end up together.

"Ah," Thorne says when he sees the reaction, then glances at the Warden. "You didn't tell them, then."

"No," Warden Kurtz says. "I didn't want to get their hopes up."

"Wise," Thorne replies with a smirk, then addresses us again. "Hope is a dangerous emotion, and the Warden is correct. The rule doesn't mean you will be placed with anyone you know. In fact, chances are you'll never see each other again after today. It's quite likely some of you will be sent far from here to live in remote regions in the homes of your assigned owners."

I don't like the word *owner*, though it's not the first time it's sat like a stone inside my mind. Still, the reality of it hits like a shot of bile—or maybe that's just residual nausea after the shock of nearly being murdered by Drukk.

I want to embrace my fate—to accept that I've always been a possession, as has almost everyone I know. But something in the way Thorne speaks of it sets off alarms inside me, reminding me that it's not a natural state. It's a necessary evil—one that exists solely to satisfy those who hold the power.

Thorne's eyes meet mine when he says, "In case anyone is curious, my Proprietor is kind and just, and I live in a beautiful home. I hope for the same for each of you."

"Thorne is a respected Crimson Elite," the Prefect interjects. "And a trusted member of our society. If you each serve faithfully, you will also gain the trust of Kravan's Nobility."

"Pfft! If he's an experienced Crimson, why does he need those wrist-pieces?" Jayson calls out. "If he's so strong, he should be able to take us on easily."

It's bold, not to mention foolish, to question the Prefect, but I can tell Jayson is agitated after what happened to Drukk. It's clear Thorne has an unfair advantage over even the strongest of us.

"Because I have no intention of losing to any of you today," Thorne says simply. "I can't afford to return to my home bloody and battered—because unlike some..." He throws me another look, "I'm not blessed with healing powers. My Mistress wouldn't like it if I showed up with two black eyes and a swollen lip."

Something about the word *Mistress* shoots a bolt of envy through my bloodstream. His boss—his Proprietor—is a woman?

My mind fills with an image of someone beautiful. Someone Thorne looks at with desire in his eyes.

Someone who desires him right back.

Because how could she not?

Stop it, I tell myself. Desire is the last thing that should be on my mind right now. And anyhow, it's not like a Noble is going to let herself be drawn in by a Tethered.

"Now," Thorne says, clapping his hands together, "we're going to try something a little different. You..." He points to Ilias. "Come into the ring."

Ilias grunts, then obeys the command as Thorne fixes the rope Drukkar dislodged earlier.

"You can go, Shara," Thorne says, nodding to me to go stand with my cohort.

When I've done as he asked and positioned myself next to Nev, a series of tall black walls shoots up around the ring's perimeter.

All of a sudden, it's impossible to see or hear Thorne or Ilias.

"What's going on?" someone asks, their voice frantic.

"Not all testing needs to be witnessed," the Prefect responds, arms crossed over his chest. "Thorne does not wish to give away every aspect of his fighting style, or the questions he might ask each of you—so occasionally, he will be performing a test in private. Don't worry, though—it's quite safe."

"But Drukkar didn't have—" Nev says.

"Drukkar was cocky," the Warden interjects. "He was asking for a quick finish, and the Prefect's assistant gave it to him. Consider it a warning to the rest of you to keep your foolish mouths shut."

I inch closer to Nev so that we almost touch. Seldom have I wished so much that I could take her by the hand and squeeze. I need reassurance right now. I need her friendship.

I'm scared.

As strong as Ilias is, there's absolutely no guarantee he'll come out of the black box alive.

"What do you think they're doing in there?" Nev whispers.

"No idea," I reply with a shake of my head. "But I can't imagine it's anything good."

We hear nothing but our own breaths and heartbeats, almost as though the black box absorbs sound, light, and everything else. It feels like the two opponents are isolated from us for an eternity, and during that eternity, I ask myself repeatedly why the floor can't just swallow me up before my time comes.

When the black walls finally disappear and Ilias emerges a few minutes later, he looks disoriented and a little battered —his hair is mussed, his lip cut—but he's largely unhurt. He staggers over to Nev and me, struggling to stay upright.

"You okay?" I ask.

He nods, his head jerking slightly to the side. "That guy is strong," he replies. "Like, *really* strong."

"It's the wrist pieces," Nev assures him. "He admitted it himself."

"Nah," Ilias replies with another head-shake. "There's something else about him. He's just...on a different level."

He doesn't say anything more as Thorne calls in Jayson before the two of them disappear once again behind the black walls.

CHAPTER THIRTEEN

THE REST of Thorne's matches are a combination of secrecy and all-out violence on display.

Occasionally, the black walls rise up and Thorne spends time alone with his Tethered opponent. Sometimes, he makes quick work of them without the concealment—which leaves most of us breathless and terrified for the moment when our turns come.

Throughout the process, I try to figure out why he's hiding his interactions with some of our cohort. What is he keeping from us?

Does this always happen during Placements?

"We've spent our whole lives waiting for this day," Nev says, leaning close to my ear, "and they never told us what was going to happen when the time came."

"Maybe," I whisper back, "it's because they didn't know."

Nev throws me a doubtful look, but deep down, I know she gets my meaning. Maybe every Placement is different. Every Adjudicator, every interaction.

Or maybe they just didn't want us to be able to prepare ourselves mentally for this terrifying moment.

When Thorne has gone up against almost everyone in our cohort, he gestures to me with a curving, summoning finger. "Shara—you're up," he says.

Maude? I call silently as I take a step forward. *Any last-minute tips?*

~Nothing at all, she replies, her tone almost curt. *Just... maybe don't die.*

So helpful. Thank you so much.

My heart wrestles against the walls of my chest, but I step forward and wait until Thorne pulls the rope up so that I can crouch under it to enter the ring.

As I rise to my full height and face him, he presses his thumbs into his wrist pieces. With terror churning inside me, I half expect the black walls to spring up.

But they don't.

Instead, Thorne lowers his chin and stares intently at me from the other side of the ring. His eyes are filled with threat, and I'm convinced he wants to kill me.

"Let's see what you've got," he says with a crooked grin. "Come at me."

I hesitate for a beat too long before Maude's voice comes.

~Do as he says, Shara. Attack him. No one will condemn you for touching him on this day.

I *want* to attack him.

At least, I think I do—but years of the same gruesome, shooting pain in my arms have made me fearful. Staring at him now, I feel as timid as a mouse—not that I've ever encountered a mouse firsthand.

Somehow, I imagine even *they* are less cowardly than I feel right now.

Thorne seems twice as big as me. Even without those enhancers on his wrists, he could easily break me in half.

What the hell am I supposed to do against someone like him?

"If you do nothing, I promise you'll receive the worst Placement you can possibly imagine," Thorne threatens under his breath, and all that goes through my mind is the conversation I overheard so long ago between Ore and the Warden.

"Kravan is a dumpster fire..."

Screw that, I think. *There's beauty out there—there has to be. I need to give myself the best possible chance to see it. That hope is all I have in this world.*

Swallowing down my fear, I hurl myself at Thorne.

When my shoulder slams into him, he takes half a step backwards. For the briefest moment, I'm convinced I actually managed to throw him off-balance.

But when a set of powerful arms wraps itself around me, I quickly realize I'm deluded. He's immovable. A wall of steel and stone, far more powerful than I could ever dream of being.

The one silver lining is that the pain I expect to shoot up my arms never comes. I may be about to die—but at least it won't hurt as badly as it could.

The strange thing is that I should be more afraid than ever. I should hate every second of this—of being trapped between arms that could crush me like a grape. Thorne is a steel cage wrapped around my torso, forcing me against him as the rest of my cohort looks on.

I should be scared, humiliated, worried, disappointed—yet all I can think is that I don't want him to let me go.

Not yet.

It's as if all the years spent without the sensation of human contact have led to this very moment.

I wonder for a flash of an instant if the others felt the same way when they fought him.

And then, the instant comes to a shuddering end.

Thorne's lips are next to my ear, and every set of eyes in the room is focused on us.

"Fight me," he whispers. "You must prove you want to win this. Pull yourself away, and try again."

When I somehow manage to tear myself free of his arms, I'm convinced he deliberately let me go. I turn his way, unsure what to do now. Because of the rules against touching, we've never been trained in hand-to-hand combat.

But I have to do *something.*

I reach for the collar of his jacket, but in retaliation, he wraps his hands around my wrists.

I stare into his eyes, renewed terror ripping its way through me.

In a second, I could be dead—if he wanted to end me. And from the look on his face, that's *exactly* what he wants.

Every instinct inside of me screams. *Survive. Live to see another day,* my body cries. *Do whatever it takes.*

Despite his powerful grip, I thrust my hands forward, reaching for his neck. I know I'm not strong enough to strangle him—not strong enough to hurt him even a little—but I have to try.

The instant my fingers meet his neck...I freeze.

Just below the surface of my skin, my body begins to

crackle with energy, my arms consumed by an odd, overwhelming sensation.

It's as if I've been taken over by something outside myself —as though I'm about to see the world clearly for the first time.

I stare, baffled, at Thorne's face, and I can see in his expression that he knows what I'm feeling. His eyes, with their exquisite halo of amber in their centers, are focused on mine as if both our lives depend on whatever is now happening.

In a split second, black walls shoot up around us—and suddenly we're cut off from the Prefect, the Warden, and the rest of the cohort.

Pulling my hands up to his cheeks, Thorne whispers, "What do you feel right now?"

I'm on the verge of insisting I feel nothing—which, of course, is a lie. My fingers are still on him, as if my body is unwilling to give up the sensation that's throbbing its way through my every nerve ending.

So much feeling—yet I can't quite find the words to describe it.

"It..." I say, trying to unearth some way to conceal the pleasure I'm experiencing. "It's like..."

Maude, I call internally. *What is this? What is he doing to me? Is this a trick?*

She doesn't answer.

Not only that, but she seems...gone. I can't feel her inside me, and the sense of abandonment terrifies me.

"What do you feel?" Thorne asks again. "Quickly, now. We don't have much time. Close your eyes and tell me everything. What does it feel like to touch me, Shara?"

At first, I wonder if he simply wants me to admit I desire him. Maybe he just wants me to satisfy his massive ego.

Did he do this to the other young women that he concealed in the black box? Is this some strange kink of his?

But when I close my eyes and actually focus, the sensation that overtakes me is something very different from desire. The sparking nerves move up my arms and down again like they're conveying information...only I don't know how to interpret it.

"Tell me," Thorne whispers. "Describe it."

"I feel sparks—energy," I reply quietly. "But there's something else, too."

I don't know how to explain it, because what's happening seems unhinged.

Despite my closed eyes, I can *see* him now—but it's as if he exists only in a dream. In my mind, Thorne is locked in a fight with someone, power surging from his body and mind in a terrifying array of swirling colors. I've never seen anything like it—energy streams from him, painting itself on the air. His power is a canvas of reds, blues, greens, and every other color imaginable.

"I see what you are," I whisper, my eyes popping open as I realize how mad that sounds. "Only, I'm not sure I can pinpoint your power. I can feel that you're stronger than I knew. Stronger than anyone knows."

What does it mean?

Thorne pulls my hands off his face, his fingers locking tight around my wrists once again. In his eyes, I see a mix of fear and sadness.

"Listen to me very carefully," he whispers. "Your M.O.D.

unit is temporarily disabled, so this is just between us. Understood?"

I nod as any residual pleasure leaves my body. There's fear in his eyes. Fear in the face of the powerful Elite who has beaten almost every single member of my cohort in the space of a few hours.

"I—yes. Understood," I tell him.

"Good. Listen—whatever happens, do not tell a single person what you felt when you touched me. Not one. I need you to promise me this—even if you despise me. Be careful out there, Shara. Do not let them know what happened here." He loosens his grip when he says, "I don't know if I'll see you again—where you end up is ultimately up to the Prefect."

Those words sting me to my core, the sense of loss cruel and shattering.

It never once occurred to me that I'd see him again after today's Placement. But the moment we just shared, the sensation he awoke inside me—it was unlike anything I've ever felt, and the thought of being separated from him is as painful as a stabbing blade.

It was like I was inside his mind for a moment. And what I saw in him made me feel like I'd lived my whole life with blinders on, unaware of the fierce strength that can live inside another being.

I don't even like you, I insist silently. *So why is it that I can't stand the thought that I'll never see you again?*

I say nothing, but try and fight back the lump forming in my throat.

"The black walls are about to drop," Thorne says, "and when they do, I'm going to pin you to the floor. I need you to fight me as best you can, but it doesn't matter if you win or lose. It's just for show."

As he holds onto my wrists, I will him tacitly to prolong this moment just a little longer. I don't want to return to reality. I don't want to let him go—not yet.

Even if I *do* despise him.

"I promise," I finally say. "I'll fight."

The walls drop, and suddenly, Thorne has me on the floor. In a flurry of movement he's on top of me, his hands pinning my arms down.

Maude's voice barrels to life inside me as if she was never gone.

~*Fight back,* she says. *Pull your arms free and push him off you.*

He won't let me, I protest. *He's too strong!*

~*It doesn't matter. If you don't defend yourself, the Prefect won't approve your Placement with anyone but the lowest family. You need to prove you're willing to defend yourself, or he will be convinced you're unwilling to fight for those you serve.*

Struggling to find the last of my strength, I yank my arms free of Thorne's grip, press my hands to his chest, and shove him. As if humoring me for my meager effort, he leaps off me, backing away with a half-smile on his lips.

But I'm not done.

I jump to my feet and run at him, thrusting a shoulder into his chest. Once again, he wraps his arms around me and throws me to the ground. His body comes down on top of mine, arms forming a cage around my face, his lips close to my ear.

"You know by now you're not strong enough," he growls

loudly enough for the cohort to hear him. "Don't you...*Domestic*?"

His tone is the opposite of what it was inside the black box, when he seemed almost caring, his concern transparent on his features.

He's turned cold and hostile, the disdain crystal-clear in his voice.

I grind my jaw, but the fact is, he's right. I'm no match for his strength.

I struggle to free myself again, but he manages to wrestle me back down, his knees hitting the floor to either side of me, his thighs around my waist. One of his hands goes to my throat, squeezing enough to draw a frightened gasp.

The other hand pins both my arms over my head.

In his eyes, I see what looks like sheer hatred.

"She has some strength in her," Thorne calls out, turning toward the Prefect. "Despite what her cohort may say, she's a fighter in her own right."

"Not exactly a powerful one," the Prefect replies, his tone dismissive. "Still, a Domestic doesn't need brute strength. She only needs to be loyal."

Thorne eases his grip on my throat, but doesn't peel himself away just yet.

Instead, he leans down and whispers, "Speak a word of what happened in the box, and you will die." He leaps to his feet and calls out, "Maid duty. It's all she's fit for. We should send her somewhere with a good deal of silver to polish and beds to make. Her cleaning skills will be put to good use."

A few mocking chuckles rise up from my cohort as I push myself to my feet, my hand rubbing my neck as I glare at Thorne.

He's easily the most confusing, infuriating person I've ever met—and that's saying a lot, given that I've had to put up with the same group of irritating Tethered every single day for the last nineteen years.

I limp back to Nev, who's standing next to a still stunned-looking Ilias.

Thorne watches me for a moment, his expression cold, menacing, and filled with disdain.

It may be the first time ever that I leave a combat ring without an open wound.

But somehow, his hatred feels worse than any injury I've ever suffered.

CHAPTER FOURTEEN

Nev is the last to enter the ring for her assessment.

"A Porter," Thorne says, seemingly impressed when she tells him her power. "I suppose you have serious skills."

"I wouldn't really know. I'm not allowed to use my power outside the combat ring," she says with a shrug.

"Well, then, let's see what you've got *inside* the ring."

For her, Thorne doesn't bother with the black walls. It's like he's been saving the best for last, knowing the coming altercation would prove amusing.

When he tells her she's free to attack, he stands with his arms crossed, watching as she repeatedly vanishes only to reappear in another part of the ring. Each time, she shows up with a mischievous grin on her lips, like she's silently challenging him to catch her.

The last time she vanishes, Thorne leaps four or so feet to his right. When she reappears a few inches in front of him, he grabs her and throws her to the ground, pinning her there with his foot on her chest.

"You thought you were moving in a random pattern to

throw me off," he tells her. "But it wasn't as random as all that."

She scowls up at him. Nev doesn't lose many fights, and the only person who's managed to beat her with any regularity is Drukkar. His speed, combined with her ability to vanish in a split-second, makes them a good match. On her most successful days, Nev has managed to keep Drukk moving so long that he collapses from exhaustion.

But Thorne, the far more experienced Elite, somehow deciphered her strategy a mile away. Seemingly with no effort whatsoever, he managed to take her down in under two minutes.

When Nev emerges from the ring, she's irritated, to put it mildly.

"I was sure I could tire him out, or bore him to sleep, or something," she mutters as we're ushered out of the room and back toward the lift. "But that guy—he's on another level, like Ilias said."

"Don't feel bad. I don't think any of us was actually supposed to win today," I reply under my breath, my mind shifting to everything that happened between Thorne and me in the black box. "You wouldn't want to be the only one who beat him. Anyhow, you don't want to seem hyper-dangerous on Placement Day."

"I don't feel bad," she chuckles. "I'm just pissed. And confused. Speaking of which," she adds, turning to make sure no one is listening, "what did he say to you in the black box?"

"Nothing, really," I tell her too emphatically, hating the need to lie. "I think he was just trying to mind-fuck me and test my resolve. He knew I had no physical strength, so he wanted to see if I had any *mental* strength, I guess."

"I suppose that's possible." I can tell she's skeptical, but to my relief, she doesn't ask anything else.

Ilias, who's walking ahead of us, is joking around with a few other cohort members. By the time we get down to our Whiterooms, he looks like he's back to his old self. The shock of whatever happened to him in the black box is gone at last, and his eyes are bright and hopeful once again.

When I'm locked inside my own quarters, I watch as others are escorted one by one from their Whiterooms to the mess hall, presumably for their interviews with the Prefect. It's the Warden who comes to extract each person, and when he finally arrives at my door, I find my heart pounding again in anticipation.

Against my better judgment, I want to see Thorne just one more time—to see which version of him I'll get. The ice-cold, spiteful Thorne, or the one who whispered gentle words to me, his lips so close to my skin that I could practically taste him.

But when my door opens, the Warden smiles tightly and says, "Good news. Looks like you're off the hook, Shara."

My insides curdle. "Off the hook?" I ask with shaking breath.

What the hell does *that* mean?

"Apparently, there will be no interview for you," he replies with a shrug. "I guess the Prefect got everything he needed when he spoke to you earlier. Your Placement has already been decided, so get ready. You're leaving the Tower in a few minutes."

All my life, I've looked forward to this moment—but now that it's here, my heart is empty.

I watch as the Warden leaves, the door sealing shut behind him.

It takes me a minute to return to my cot and slouch down on its firm mattress, my body and mind wrestling with a jumble of emotions.

I thought I had a little more time. A few minutes, at least. I thought there would be more ceremony to my departure than...whatever this is.

Will I ever see Nev again? Or Ilias? Will I get to say goodbye?

Will I ever see Thorne again?

When that question works its way into my mind, I want to slap myself.

"Why would I want to?" I mutter. "He literally threatened to kill me up in the fighting ring."

I half expect Maude to say something to me, but she remains silent, as if she's giving me time to process everything that's happened.

Finally, I can't stand it anymore and I say, "Maude—do you know where I've been placed?"

For a moment, she doesn't answer. But finally, she says, *~I do. You are going to the Palatine Estates on the Hill, known by most simply as the Hill. The district is named for a location in an ancient civilization.*

"Is that good or bad?"

~I'm afraid I'm not allowed to make judgments on the appeal of Kravan's various geographical regions.

"Ugh."

Just as I'm about to ask another question, the door whooshes open and the Warden steps inside.

"Shara," he says, clapping his hands together, "it's time to go."

I know the answer before the question comes, but I ask all the same. "May I say goodbye to Nev and Ilias?"

"You know the rules," the Warden says sharply. "There will be no congregating with other Tethered once your Placement has been determined. No communication whatsoever. I can't let you near your friends."

I'm not sure he means to be cruel—the Warden, for all his quirks, has almost always been kind to us. Though it would be a stretch to say any of us sees him as a parent, he's certainly been a fair and just leader.

Until earlier today, in fact, I thought of him as the kindly counterpart to Ore.

When he sees the look on my face, he says, "I'm sorry, Shara, but it's not like you can hug Ilias and Nev goodbye, is it?"

Those words hurt all the more for the truth in them.

Biting my lip to fight back the tears that want to come, I silently curse the powers that be. More than that, I curse myself. I should have said goodbye after our combat tests. I should have known.

But the truth is, the abrupt news of our staggered departures was probably all by design, intended to prevent us saying too much to one another. I should have known there was no way in hell we'd be given the luxury of time to speak to each other.

With a bite of my lip, inflicting deliberate physical pain in hopes of overshadowing my emotional torment, I look around my Whiteroom for anything I may want to bring with me.

After nineteen years locked in here, I would have thought I'd need to pack a bag or something. But the truth is, there's nothing of importance here—other than my toothbrush and a few hair elastics. Not a single item in my Whiteroom has any sentimental value.

In that regard, the Tower has trained us well. None of us has possessions, because we've been taught that materialism, like so many other things, is a privilege afforded to Normals and the Nobility.

Nostalgia is an emotion I've only ever read about in books.

Impatient, the Warden says, "You'll be given new clothing when you reach your destination, as well as anything else your owner thinks you may require."

I'm not sure whether he used the O-word deliberately. Normally, he and Ore use the less aggressive *Proprietor* to describe those who will take possession of us.

As I place my few things in a small canvas bag, I whisper the words I know so well.

To live in thrall is an honor.
If I serve faithfully, I will be rewarded with long life.
If I break Kravan's laws, I will pay the ultimate price.

"Look, Shara," the Warden says, the merest touch of sympathy in his voice. "You should be happy—you're the first in the cohort to leave. There's a vehicle already waiting for you on the ground floor."

At that, my sadness twists into minor excitement.

Ground. Floor.

He may as well have told me we were heading to another world.

As far as I understand, the last time I was on the ground floor, I was only a year old. It was there that my mysterious mother gave birth to me, and that I inhaled my first breath. It was there that I spent the first twelve months of my life.

So strange to think I'm returning to that level only now. Strange, too, to think I've never once navigated stairs, other than to step up onto my chair and down again for exercise.

As we head down the hallway toward the lift, I glance into Ilias and Nev's Whiterooms. Each of them is sitting quietly on their cots, their eyes forward. Nev glances at me only for a split-second as I pass, as if she's been ordered to communicate nothing whatsoever.

I fight back silent tears when the elevator doors close and the Warden enters a code to take us to ground level.

When the lift touches down and the Warden and I step out into a broad, bright foyer beaming with sunlight, we're greeted by a man and a woman in black uniforms that vaguely resemble Thorne's. They must be Guards—though they don't feel particularly dangerous.

They both look anxious, like they're afraid I'll attack them or something.

"This is Alicia and Calen," the Warden says. "Your escorts."

I nod a quick hello before Alicia says, "Come with us, Miss," nodding toward a set of glass doors some distance away. "A Flyer is waiting for us outside."

"Flyer?" I stammer, but neither Guard answers. Instead,

they turn toward the doors and begin to walk in that direction.

"Goodbye, Shara," the Warden says. "And good luck out there." He leans in close when he adds, "I'm sorry for the things I said to you earlier. I'm sure you'll do great."

Unable to conjure a reply, I muster a sad smile and offer him a quiet nod.

As I walk away, leaving the Tower behind forever, I want desperately to believe he means it.

CHAPTER FIFTEEN

~*DON'T ASK your escorts too many questions,* Maude cautions as I follow the two people in Guard uniforms. *Trust the system.*

The foyer's floor is polished stone. Marble, I think—white, veined with gray. It's exquisite and elegant, cut here and there by the sun's rays reflecting on its surface. In fact, the entirety of the lobby is luxurious and opulent compared to what we lived in upstairs.

It's not that our level was unattractive. It's more that it was utilitarian and boring, with its plain white walls and lack of ornamentation. Never before have I seen a decorative light fixture or a painting hanging on a wall, other than on the pages of a book.

There's something exotic about these surroundings, as if I've just ventured into a lavish holiday that only the wealthy get to enjoy.

But for all the foyer's beauty, nothing could have prepared me for what I see when I step out of the Tower and my foot lands for the first time ever on a slab of smooth concrete.

Surrounding the tall structure for a hundred feet or so in every direction is a length of lush, green grass intersected by twisting gravel pathways. Here and there, large trees shade the wooden benches placed strategically under them. Instantly, a part of me wants to take a seat and inhale the air. I want to bask in this feeling of freedom for a week or so.

But my fantasy proves short-lived. When my eyes venture to the far end of the park area, I gasp.

Beyond the Tower's green zone is a tall wall of gray stone, and ornamenting its top layer is what looks like a jumble of coiled razor wire. I learned about it in one of the history books I borrowed from the Tower's library, and the thought of it has always horrified me. Sharp steel teeth, designed with the sole purpose of tearing into human flesh.

"Is that to keep the Tethered inside?" I ask Calen and Alicia, ignoring Maude's advice to keep quiet. "Because as far as I know, no one has ever tried to escape the Tower."

"Not to keep the Tethered in," Calen says. "It's to keep *them* out."

With that, he nods toward the hazy vista that lies beyond the distant wall. I pull my eyes higher to see a landscape I hadn't even registered at first—probably because the air beyond the Tower's vast grounds is thick with what looks like low-lying smog.

Beyond the wall, I realize, lies a city—except that I've *seen* pictures of cities, and what lies before us looks like more of a wasteland.

An array of derelict skyscrapers and other crumbling buildings reveal themselves beyond the sea of swirling, yellowish mist. As I scan them curiously, I can see that many of the structures are crawling with what look like dark, encroaching vines.

"That's the Capitol," Alicia tells me. "It surrounds the Tower on all sides."

"*That's* the Capitol?" My voice sounds choked, and it's no wonder.

An image I have held in my head as long as I can remember has just been shattered.

The Capitol is where the Normals live. People who are neither Tethered nor Nobility—people with aspirations, families, jobs. I'd always pictured them living in pretty little homes with green lawns and white picket fences—the sort of thing I've read about in books.

"What's left of it, yes. That's the Capitol."

For the first time, I'm beginning to understand the significance of the conversation I overheard that day so long ago between Ore and the Warden—*"You know the shit-show that's happening out there..."*

For so long, I'd hoped I'd misunderstood. I'd convinced myself that Ore was being his usual dickish self.

But *shit-show* is an understatement.

The place looks like an uninhabitable wasteland—at least, the parts of it I can see above the wall.

"What's beyond the Capitol?" I ask, still staring in shock and horror.

"Water," Alicia replies with a shrug. "Didn't your Warden teach you about the geography around here?"

I shake my head, pulling my eyes to hers. "I've never seen a map. They're forbidden in my cohort."

"Ah. Well, you'll see soon enough that we're on an island.

Kravan is made up of many of them. Some are nicer than others, of course."

"And the Ring is the worst of them," Calen says with a snicker. "That's the one we're on now—it's called that because of how the Capitol circles the Tower's grounds. Some people call it the Donut."

My voice quakes a little when I ask, "Is the Ring where we're headed?" I don't tell her Maude has already mentioned the name of our destination. The truth is, I have no idea where the Palatine Estates is in relation to the Capitol.

The two Guards exchange a look, then let out a synchronized laugh. "Hell, no," Alicia says. "You're one of the lucky ones. *You're* going to be living with a Noble family on the Hill—which is some distance from here. Wait until you lay your eyes on it. It's just beautiful."

Relief hits me to realize I won't be living in the crumbling hell-town, though I feel almost guilty for the emotion. A few of our cohort have been deemed Normals over the years, which I always thought meant they would enjoy the luxury of freedom in the Capitol for the rest of their lives.

I genuinely assumed they would have the best of both worlds—they could live and work in society and enjoy a happy existence in pretty neighborhoods where they could raise their children.

But if freedom means living in a city that looks like it's about to cave in on itself, I'm not sure I would want any part of it.

As the Guards lead me away from the Tower at last, I turn to stare up at the structure that has held me captive for so many years. It stretches to dizzying heights in the sky, disappearing eventually into the clouds. It's made of what looks like gleaming black stone and seems to narrow as its levels increase—though that may well be an optical illusion.

Thorne is still in there somewhere, I think. *I don't suppose I'll ever see him again.*

He was cruel to me and to some of the others, and he's arrogant as hell.

But in the moment when my fingers met his skin, something happened between us... and I don't think I'll ever be the same again.

CHAPTER SIXTEEN

MOST PEOPLE in Kravan probably take the sky for granted, but I can't imagine a time when it won't seem wondrous to me.

It's a vast, endless blue entity, punctuated by white fluff. I'm convinced I'm staring not at something real, but another painting in one of the Tower's library books. My mind can't process the scope of it, the simple beauty of a bird flying overhead. The sense of bliss that comes simply from knowing these things really do exist.

The thought that I'm actually walking outdoors for the first time in my life is almost unfathomable. The air even *tastes* different out here—a combination of something that feels fresh and clean infected with a distant bitterness, as if the toxic-looking cloud that covers the Ring is infiltrating this pretty, green space.

"Don't worry," Calen tells me as he and his companion escort me around the Tower along one of the broad paths. "You'll be out of here in a minute—and then you'll get to see the best of Kravan."

I say nothing as I follow them. I'm half stunned, half

curious, and I suspect every Tethered who has ever stepped foot outside the Tower's doors has reacted the same way.

A lifetime spent indoors prepared me only a little for this assault to my senses, and I genuinely can't say if I'm delighted or terrified. Some tiny, cowardly part of me wants to run back into the Tower—to my Whiteroom and its cot, to the familiar scents and sounds that have brought me comfort over the years.

I already miss Nev and Ilias, and I wonder with trepidation if they'll be as overwhelmed as I feel when their time comes.

All our lives, we've talked and laughed about what our first day out here might be like. We've anticipated it gleefully, reveling in the thought of our eventual Placements while speculating about what sorts of people we might serve.

I suppose it's natural that we each hoped for a kindly Proprietor—someone who sympathizes with our unfortunate bloodlines rather than treating us with disdain.

It's probably the most any of us can hope for.

Though we weren't unhappy in the Tower, it was the knowledge that we each had something to look forward to on the outside that kept us going during those times when we felt hopeless or lost. But now, seeing and feeling the absolute oddity of this foreign place, I'm not quite sure how to process the tangle of emotions doing battle inside me.

Silently, the two Guards escort me to a landing pad where a vehicle is parked. I recognize it from our textbooks as a four-person Hoverer—a vehicle with four sets of horizontally-positioned propellors that flies just above the tree-line to transport its occupants from place to place quickly and easily.

The two Guards slip into the front seats while I pull myself into the back. A series of straps wrap themselves instantly around my body, adding to a sensation of encroachment that's already begun ramping up my anxiety to unnatural levels.

"I know it feels strange to be on the outside," Alicia tells me, looking over her shoulder with a reassuring smile. "They say every Tethered has the same reaction out here. It's a shock to your system. But it's only about twenty minutes to our destination, and you'll be okay—I promise. Your new home is beautiful, and I'm sure you'll love it."

Her words are a kindness, and I appreciate them. Even so, my mind is still twisting itself around, trying to figure out why we were never told more about what lies on the outside of the Tower. Why Kravan's Capitol was made to sound like a land of opportunity where Nobles and Normals mixed and mingled.

Or maybe no one ever *actually* told us that.

The fictional books we were allowed to read spoke of houses with pretty gardens, happy children, and dogs and cats living in harmony.

But I realize as I stare out the Hoverer's large side window that I've never read a description of the Capitol itself. Here and there, I scanned paragraphs about Normals and their lives spent working and tending to their homes. I suppose I simply drew the conclusion that the Normals lived in the lovely little homes from my imagination.

Warden Kurtz used to read us fairy tales when we were

little. When we turned twelve, he stopped reading them and issued us a stern warning.

"In those stories," he said, "the girl often falls in love with the handsome prince. They get married and live happily ever after. But you must understand this—your lives will *never* amount to fairy tales. Life on the outside—whether you're a Normal or a Tethered—is difficult. Fairy tales are reserved for the Nobility, and you are mere observers. Forget about love and families, and all of that. Live to serve, and you will be happy."

I wondered then if there was some way—some drug or other—that could prevent us from falling in love. It seemed, after all, like a natural human emotion—and I wasn't sure how we were supposed to suppress it.

But as I matured, I realized something that I never dared say out loud.

The Nobility doesn't want to *keep* us from having emotions. What they want is to *control* us. They want us to know our feelings lie under their jurisdiction—and that they can punish us for daring to feel.

I used to think it was their way of forcing us to pay for our parents' sins.

But I sometimes wonder if they simply want to prove that ultimately, they're stronger. No matter how much power we may hold in our hands, *they* hold the advantage—and they will do everything they can to ensure we never shift the balance of power.

The Hoverer surges upwards in a vertical thrust before soaring toward the high stone wall in the distance, and I watch as we glide over it to reveal a broad, deserted street crawling with tall weeds, its buildings derelict and vine-covered.

As we progress, we pass over what look like residential streets flanked by small houses that may once have been beautiful, but now look like deathtraps. Some are made of wood, their porches rotting and caving in on themselves; others seem to be fashioned out of corrugated metal and other found materials.

Every one of them is a million miles from the pretty homes I always pictured in my mind's eye.

I pull my gaze away, my heart fracturing for those who have to live under such conditions. Why don't the Normals fix the houses? If they have every opportunity to work and to earn a living, why not improve their lot in life?

I don't understand any of it.

It's only a few minutes before we find ourselves soaring over open water, and the air clears to reveal a long, narrow island not far off, white-capped waves lapping at its rocky shore, which rises precipitously out of the water.

Above the beaches, green hills ebb and flow, a stark contrast to the desolation of the Capitol.

I settle back in my seat, pulling my eyes up to watch through a window in the vehicle's roof as another Hoverer soars overhead—one that looks far more sophisticated than ours.

~Shara...

On hearing Maude's voice, I close my eyes and inhale a deep breath.

Yes? I ask silently.

~You'll arrive at your new home soon. Don't forget to show

respect to your Proprietors. Express gratitude. Keep your chin low and listen to all that they have to say. Understood?

You've told me this same thing six hundred times over the last few months, Maude.

~That was before I knew with any certainty where you were going.

And where, exactly, am I going?

~You are going to live with a family whose wealth and power are exceeded only by that of Kravan's Royal Family—or possibly the Prefect.

At that, my eyes open, and I swallow down a feeling of terror.

I'd expected to end up in some quiet house owned by a lesser Noble. Someone who needs their living room dusted and their dishes washed.

Not some high-ranking, intimidating aristocrat.

~Just be polite, Maude adds, sensing my growing fear. *Nod and smile when it seems appropriate. Express gratitude. That's all you need to do.*

Scattered along a hillside in the distance are a series of large houses. They're spread far apart, their façades composed either of stone, steel, or glass. Each of them looks like a strange, inviting fortress, elegant and luxurious—but forbidding, too.

We fly upward past the first several properties, the Hoverer skirting the island's shoreline until we cross more water to come to another series of rolling hills rising up from the ocean. The houses that decorate the slopes are even larger than the previous ones—as well as being surrounded by manicured gardens.

Each property includes what looks like a large swimming

pool, some sort of outdoor athletic court, and terraces of stone flanked by elegantly trimmed trees.

Each property is also outlined by thick, high walls of stone and steel.

"*That* is the Hill," Alicia says. "The Palatine Estates. The Royal Family lives up there." She twists in her seat, seemingly excited when she says, "A bit of trivia: I've heard the word *palace* is derived from the same root as *Palatine,* so that might explain the name of the region. Anyhow, your home is right next door to the Royals, who live on the eastern side."

My eyes veer to the peak of the tallest hill rising up on the island. With a gasp, I take in what looks like an enormous castle of light gray stone, complete with a series of turrets and accented by a black slate roof.

Yup. That's a palace, all right. Even with my limited knowledge of the world, I remember those from the old fairy tales.

My eyes scan the vast grounds, and I wonder with a stab of some frustrated emotion if Thorne serves the king as a member of the Royal Guard.

If so, I suppose it would mean we could end up living close to one another—which is both a terrible and a reassuring thought.

At the very least, he's a competent Guard. He proved that much today—illegal wrist braces or not.

Something about the contrast between the landscape below us and that of the Capitol renders me a little nauseated, and for a moment, I forget that I'm supposed to keep my thoughts to myself.

"Isn't it weird that the Capitol is so run-down, when this

place is so..." I begin to ask, but Maude vibrates a sharp warning on my left wrist.

~Do **not** *express judgment.*

"The Capitol was once beautiful, actually," Calen tells me. "What you see of it now is entirely the Normals' fault. They could have kept it beautiful, but they chose to let it fester. They'd rather live in squalor than put in any effort, the lazy bastards."

Wow.

That is a far more candid response than I expected.

"Are you two both Tethered?" I ask, overstepping again.

Alicia and Calen exchange a quick look, then Alicia says, "Yes. We're both Violets in the service of the Prefecture."

Violets, like Nev.

I want to ask them if they think *all* Normals are useless.

But maybe I'm being unfair. I only know two Normals—the Warden and Ore—and both of them live in the Tower. Maybe the two escorts know far more of them—and maybe there's some truth to what Calen is saying.

If the Normals choose to live in buildings that are caving in on themselves and let their city turn into an overgrown tangle of weeds, maybe they *do* deserve their lot in life.

"We're headed up there," Alicia says, gesturing to a large house that looks like it sits a half-mile or so from the palace. It's an elegant-looking structure of stone, steel, and glass, with extensive gardens of its own.

"What's the name of the family I'll be living with?" I ask.

Alicia replies, "You'll find out when we've landed."

CHAPTER SEVENTEEN

We fly just above the treetops lining the hillside until we come to a broad concrete pad behind the main house.

As we come in for our landing, I realize that in addition to the large manor house, there are several outbuildings, each of them bigger than any house I saw in the Capitol.

Thick stone walls surround the rolling property on every side except the one that borders the Royal Grounds.

I'm relieved to see that this wall, at least, doesn't seem to be accented with razor wire.

I want to ask so many questions, starting with, "Why do all these Nobles' homes look like they're ready to defend against entire armies?"

But I suspect I already know the answer.

We were taught in History class that after the Rebellion, many Noble families bought land strategically. Those with the most wealth positioned their homes in high places in the hopes of maintaining the advantage in a potential future conflict.

Judging by the layout of the various enormous homes on the Hill, there's still a healthy fear of another rebellion.

When we set down on the landing pad, my door slides open and my security belt releases me from its grip.

"Welcome to your new home," Alicia says without bothering to climb out of her seat.

"Thank you," I reply, my eyes moving over the large, vine-covered mansion. A broad gravel driveway curves around in front of its main door, though I have yet to see a car or other vehicle on the premises.

"The lady of the house will be waiting for you at the front door," Alicia adds. "We've notified her of your arrival, so I suggest you get moving."

I offer up a nod and a quiet thank you to both her and Calen before slipping out of the Hoverer and beginning the hesitant, nerve-wracking walk to the front of the house.

The Hoverer takes off behind me, the thrum of its propellors sounding like the wings of one of the large insects I've seen in nature documentaries. It ascends over the property and disappears into the distance.

My mind explodes with nervous excitement, and I wish more than anything that I could talk to Nev and Ilias right now. Have their Placements been decided yet? Are they being given positions of honor in massive homes like this one?

In contrast to the palace next door, this place almost looked small from the air. But standing in front of it now, staring up at its multitude of windows, it feels like something out of a dream.

I wonder with a throb in my chest if I'll find friends in this new house, or if I'll be ignored—or worse, treated like something subhuman.

~*There's no point in speculating,* Maude says. *Pessimism is pointless and self-destructive.*

"Thank you, Miss Thought Police," I mutter.

As I approach the façade, the front door—an elegant, large slab of engraved wood painted a cheerful red—swings open.

In the same moment, my wrist lets out a quiet vibration. At first, I assume it's Maude issuing me a last warning before I meet my Proprietor.

But I glance down to see that the swirling, emerald green marks on my skin have just illuminated from within. Something inside me has just activated with the official mark of a Harmless, an assurance to my new owner that I am no threat.

~*The light will fade over the next few hours,* Maude tells me. *It's only there for your Proprietor's sake.*

"Any last-minute advice?" I whisper.

~*Keep your head down. Do not let them know you have a mind—least of all an inquisitive one. Be submissive, and don't be a muffin-head.*

"Thanks. Very helpful."

I don't have time to say anything else before a figure steps out through the front door, followed by two others.

A tall, middle-aged woman stands on the broad stone porch, dressed in an elegant cream-colored pencil skirt, high heels and a black blouse. Behind her are two women who both look close to my age, or possibly a little younger. Each is dressed in blue jeans and expensive-looking sweaters, and I assume from their ages and demeanors that they must be her daughters.

I realize with a wince that the only reason I'm familiar

with the names of the garments they're wearing is that I've spent countless hours studying in the Tower— staring enviously at images of those privileged enough to reside in the outside world.

For years, I've tried to mentally prepare myself for this moment. But right now, ironic as it is, I can't fathom what I could possibly say to people like these. So, instead of speaking, I stare at them like an animal caught in the glow of a powerful light.

Remembering what Maude told me, I pull my chin down, forcing myself to look up when the woman strides toward me with her hand outstretched.

"Shara," a smooth, even voice says as I stare, frozen, at her hand.

"I'm so sorry," she adds with a laugh, dropping it to her side. "I'd forgotten about the rules. I'm so accustomed to shaking other Nobles' hands."

"It's forbidden," I say softly, noting when the other two exchange a look of disgust.

"It's so nice to meet you, Shara," the woman says. "I've heard very good things."

"You've...heard about me already?" I muster, but an angry vibration in my wrist reminds me not to ask questions. "I mean, thank you so much."

"My name is Lady Verdan," she replies with another laugh, gesturing to the other two. "These are my daughters, Devorah and Pippa."

The two young women—one with light hair, the other with black ringlets—glare at me, seemingly irritated that I have the audacity to exist, and any residual hope that I would be welcomed with open arms fades quickly away.

Clearly, the daughters don't want me here.

At all.

"It's very nice to meet you," I reply, glancing around. "It's an honor, truly."

Out of the corner of my eye, I spot a figure moving from one outbuilding to another. Another servant, perhaps.

I wonder how many there are in this place.

"Come in, come in," Lady Verdan says. "You must be exhausted after today's events. I'll show you to your room."

I'm surprised to hear her offer such a favor. I suppose I was expecting a maid or a butler to show me around. Lady Verdan looks wealthy enough to afford an entire household staff, after all.

"We're only allowed a limited number of members in each household," she tells me, reading my facial expression before she turns back toward the house. "It's the law. No one ever told you in the Tower?"

I shake my head, then say, "Yes, they did. I mean—I knew the limit for Tethered was two per household. I just thought you might have some Normals on staff."

At that, the daughter called Devorah, who has white-blond hair and piercing blue eyes, snorts. "You think we'd let a whole staff of *Norms* live in our home?" she asks, cackling. "Vile."

"I—no. I'm so sorry—I didn't mean..."

I stop talking, afraid I'll risk insulting them further.

Still, Devorah seems more than happy to expand on her thought. "Didn't you see the Capitol when you flew from the Tower? It's absolutely disgusting. The Normals are awful. They're no more welcome here than *your* kind. We have a cook, and that's it—and she's only allowed to work here because she hates the Tethered, too."

"Dev!" her mother chastises. "That's no way to welcome Shara into our home. Apologize right now."

Devorah goes silent and sullen as she glares at Lady Verdan, and I can almost feel the steam rising from her skin as she stomps off through the front door. Her sister Pippa follows her in silence, squeezing in before Lady Verdan has the chance to reprimand them further.

"Ignore those two," she says. "They're irritated because they won't have our other Tethered to themselves anymore. For some time, it's just been the five of us in the house."

"So, there is another Tethered here?" I reply, keeping my tone as respectful as possible, even though I'd love to point out to her that her daughters are absolute bitches.

"Yes—our Guard. I believe he's just returned from an errand. You'll meet him later." As she heads glides into the house, she adds, "Of course, you know not to get close to him. No touching. No intimacy. None of it."

I nod. "Of course. We've been taught it all our lives."

"Good," Lady Verdan says, leading me to a large, curving staircase of marble set against a white-painted foyer, an enormous crystal chandelier hanging at its center. "It's not that I'm unsympathetic, mind you. Only that I know what trouble can arise from two people getting too close to one another. Believe it or not, the Nobility has to follow rules, too. We are, all of us, shackled in our way."

Somehow, I doubt that.

CHAPTER EIGHTEEN

When we come to the stairs, I swallow and take hold of the railing, terrified that I might trip on my way up.

Fortunately, Lady Verdan goes first, climbing with ease despite a perilous-looking pair of stiletto heels.

"Your home is beautiful," I say as I follow my Proprietor cautiously up step after step.

"Thank you," she replies. "My husband renovated it some years ago, though the house was built long before either of us was born."

"Oh—so there's a *Lord* Verdan?" I ask.

She stops, grabbing hold of the railing, and turns to me, a smile filled with sadness infiltrating her lips and eyes. "There isn't, unfortunately. He...died not long ago. It's one of the reasons the girls can be a little sullen at times. They miss their father."

"I'm so sorry," I stammer. "I had no idea..."

Damn it. Why couldn't the two who escorted me here have told me this incredibly important bit of information?

"Quite all right. But for future reference, you can refer to me as the head of the house if it comes up. I run things here." With her smile tightening, she turns to walk up to the second floor, and I follow her, my feet growing heavier with each step.

She seems kind, which is a relief—even if her daughters are harpies. But there's something about her that makes me feel like she's already thrusting a wall between us. Perhaps it's simply the distinction between Noble and Tethered, owner and owned. It's almost as if she doesn't want to look me in the eye—like she's worried she'll catch my cruel disease.

"I understand you're a Healer," she says when we're about to reach the second level.

"I am," I reply. "I've only ever had the opportunity to heal myself, but I've had a lot of experience at it."

She chuckles. "Then I'm pleased. Not that I'm hoping your services will ever be required—still, it's good to know, in case something should ever happen."

When we get to the second floor and turn left to head down a long corridor, it hits me just how enormous this house is. The broad hallway is at least a hundred feet long, and when we've walked its length, I realize it turns at the end to lead to another wing entirely.

Lady Verdan leads me up another set of stairs to a narrower, slightly more neglected-looking hallway. We proceed straight on to its end, where we come to a white wooden door.

I try to ignore the fact that there's a lock on the door's outside. After all, it's not like I'm unaccustomed to being locked up.

Still, none of the other rooms seem to share this particular trait.

"This is the servant's wing," she says, turning my way. "And this door leads into your room. I hope you like it."

I'm grateful to have quarters so isolated from the rest of the house, but slightly dreading the long trek to get back downstairs. It almost feels like I could get lost on my way back to the foyer.

She opens the door to show me the bedroom's interior. It's simple and pretty, with a dormer window to one side that looks out onto the sloping grounds, the woods, and the water beyond. In the far distance, to my dismay, I can just barely see the Tower outlined dark against the horizon, and at its base, I see what looks like a marsh of dreary mist and sad-looking structures. The Capitol.

"There's a wardrobe here, with clothing in it for you," Lady Verdan says, slipping over toward the far wall and pulling a set of antique wooden doors open. Inside are a series of white uniforms that too closely resemble the gray one I'm wearing now.

When she pulls one of the outfits out of the wardrobe to show me, I see that it has a small, green, crest-shaped patch on the left side of the chest that says, "Domestic."

How I've grown to despise that word.

I smile and nod, glancing at the wardrobe. I can't help noticing that while there are three pairs of practical-looking shoes, there are no blouses, pants, skirts, or other clothing.

I've never worn a dress. Never worn heels, or anything remotely feminine. Then again, Tethered aren't meant to be masculine or feminine.

We're meant to be inconspicuous worker bees.

"You'll find your quarters are fully stocked," Lady Verdan adds, opening a narrow white door next to the wardrobe that leads into a sizable bathroom, complete with a tub.

"I've...never taken a bath," I say, staring in awe at the clawfoot tub and imagining myself soaking in it.

"Goodness," Lady Verdan says like I'm implying I've never washed myself. "I am sorry to hear that."

I want to explain that I shower daily, but instead, I just offer up an awkward smile and head back into the bedroom.

"You will have most evenings off," Lady Verdan tells me as she follows me. "During that time, you are not to leave the grounds without my permission. But while you're working outdoors, you'll find yourself free to roam. I own twenty acres of land here on the Hill. Just be sure to stick to our property—the Royal Grounds are well protected, and I'm not sure they'd appreciate a surprise visit. The king's family has a small army of Crimson Elites in their service, and if you were to take them by surprise, it might not go well for you."

"A small army?" I reply, wincing as I anticipate Maude chastising me for asking questions.

"The Royals are allowed more Tethered than most, and they have quite a few highly trained Crimsons. Royal Guard is as high an honor as can be bestowed on your kind."

I nod dutifully.

"As to your chores," Lady Verdan adds, "You will clean the common areas daily. That includes dusting, vacuuming, polishing any items that are in need, cleaning baseboards, ceilings, and so on. You will launder the bedsheets twice a week, whether or not the beds have been occupied. You will look after my laundry, as well as my daughters'. You will also help in the kitchen whenever necessary. Mrs. Milton will instruct you on that front."

I offer up a nod. I've never cooked a thing, but I'm a quick study. As for the cleaning duties, I suppose I should be pleased that finally, my years of fastidious dusting in the Tower may prove a useful investment.

"All that said, you will officially start tomorrow," Lady Verdan says, to my surprise and delight. "Tonight, you may rest. Dinner will be brought to you here in your room a little later. If there's anything you should need, let me or the others know."

She turns to leave, but before she makes it to the door, she pivots and adds, "There's a library on the first floor, just down the hall from the foyer. You are welcome to borrow one book at a time—but I advise you to take care when you select them. There are books in my husband's collection that could prove horrifying to one such as yourself. I understand that the Tethered lead a rather...sheltered...life in the Tower."

"Thank you. I'll keep that in mind. I promise to be wary."

"Oh, I know you will," Lady Verdan tells me, and for the first time, there's a slight menace in her voice. "One last thing. When you meet the other Tethered, be on your guard. And remember—no touching."

"Of course," I nod.

She leaves the room, closing the door behind her, and I half expect to hear a key turning as she locks me in.

I wait a minute until her footsteps have disappeared down the hall, then turn the doorknob after she's gone, relieved to realize the door is unlocked.

For the first time in my life, I have a room that allows me the freedom to come and go. "I could explore the entire house," I murmur, almost excited enough to bounce up and down.

~*It's not yours to explore,* Maude cautions. *You'll see plenty of the house when you clean it. If your Proprietor or her daughters find you wandering through their private space, they will not be pleased.*

"Fine," I retort, and then like a small, ridiculous child, I leap over to the bed and throw myself down, reveling in its mass and comfort.

"Maude," I say as I stare up at the dark beams criss-crossing the white ceiling. "Tell me everything you know about Lady Verdan."

~*My knowledge of her is limited,* she says. *I am not programmed with information about the Nobility.*

"You must know something, though. What about her husband?"

Maude pauses for a moment, then says, ~*Milo Verdan was an architect. He designed many of the modern, grand homes on this island and those surrounding it. He died one year ago, though the cause of death has not been made public.*

"What about the Royal Family?"

~*What would you like to know?*

I shrug. "I don't know. Are they...nice?"

~*The king is a fair and just ruler. Prince Tallin, who is heir to the throne, is allegedly charming, handsome, and kind. The family is popular with the Nobility and respected by those in the Capitol.*

"And the queen?"

~*The queen died several years ago of an illness, I believe.*

"Did the Verdans have a Domestic on staff before me? Other than their cook, I mean?"

~Most likely not. As Lady Verdan told you, there are specific rules pertaining to the number of residents allowed in a given household—other than the Royals' House, that is. It's entirely possible she sought out a Domestic only after her husband died.

It's no wonder her daughters hate me, then, I think. *I'm probably a horrible reminder that there's a spot at their table that will never be filled.*

"How many people are actually allowed in a household like this?" I ask.

Maude seems to contemplate the question for a moment, then says, *~I've attempted to seek that information but it is classified. But given that this household has a cook, two Tethered, two children and Lady Verdan, I assume that six is the maximum.*

I'm about to ask another question when three knocks sound at the door.

I shoot up to my feet, patting my hair into place and telling myself Lady Verdan must have forgotten to tell me something. I rush over, plastering a smile onto my face.

But when I open the door, it's not the Mistress of the House who stares back at me.

It's Thorne.

CHAPTER NINETEEN

I GAWK AT THORNE, unsure whether to be pleased to see a familiar face...

Or terrified that it's his.

Since leaving the Tower, I'll admit I've thought of him more than a few times—but I haven't exactly forgotten that his last words to me were a threat against my life.

"What are you doing here?" I ask when my pulse calms enough for me to form actual words.

He lets out a chuckle, then presses a hand to the doorframe next to my head. "And here I thought you would welcome me with open arms," he snickers. "Nice to see you too, Shara."

The way he says my name—the very silken tone of his voice—does something to me that's not entirely unpleasant. But I remind myself that I'm supposed to hate him. Not to mention that he's a scheming, manipulative prick—which is enough to keep the sneer on my lips.

"I asked you a question," I say, ignoring his tone. "Are you here to tell me the Prefect got my assessment wrong? Am

I being relocated because you told him I'm unworthy of this place?"

At that, Thorne lets out a mocking sigh and says, "Wow. You really do have a gift for assuming the worst of people."

"No, I don't."

"Could've fooled me," he chuckles. "When *I* was in the Tower, we were conditioned to worship everyone on the outside, Nobles and Normals alike. Seems to me that you hate...well, everyone. Is that something your ass-kissing Warden taught you, or is it your own special, unique brand of sullenness? Because I've gotta say, some of your fellow Tethered seemed downright smitten with me."

I cringe internally, recalling how some of the girls flirted and smiled at Thorne as if he was there to date whichever of us proved most shameless.

"I assume the worst about *you*," I tell him, "because most of what you've shown me of yourself is that you're a cold, calculating monster who likes threatening and humiliating people—that is, when you're not playing mind games with them."

"Ah," he replies. "Well, then, it seems you have me figured out."

"*What. Do. You. Want*?" I hiss between gritted teeth.

"I wanted to welcome you to House Verdan. Is that so surprising?"

"Um, yeah, it is. Do you go around welcoming every Tethered to their new home after they're placed? Am I supposed to be grateful for this honor or something?"

He has the same amused, infuriating grin on his lips he had the first time I laid eyes on him in the training room—and a sudden desire fills me to punch him in the jaw.

"I'm afraid I don't have that much time on my hands," he replies. "I only welcome the Tethered who are placed in the same home as me."

Wait.

What the fuck?

Oh, God.

"I thought…"

"You thought I was a Royal Guard, or personal assistant to the Prefect, or some equivalent honor," he says. "I'm flattered, but no. This is my residence."

My head shakes involuntarily. "No. You can't *possibly* live here."

"Oh, can't I?" He gestures to a door several feet down the servants' corridor from mine. "Then that place where I've been sleeping for ages isn't actually my room?"

My body seems to sag as if a sudden, huge weight is dragging my shoulders downward. The thought that he could actually live in this house, *sleep* in this house—and just a few doors down from my room?

It's…

I have no idea what it is, but I'm pretty sure my stomach isn't supposed to feel like this.

"What exactly is your job here?" I ask, trying desperately to keep my voice level. It's a stupid question. I know what he does.

It's what he was clearly born to do.

"I'm Guard to the Verdan family. I drive Lady Verdan and her daughters around on occasion. I run errands when necessary. And believe it or not, *I'm* the reason you were placed in this very beautiful house."

Well, that makes no sense whatsoever.

What reason could Thorne possibly have for recommending me, when he could have had Nev, or Kaleen, or any other Tethered from my cohort come live under the same roof as him? He despises me—he's made that abundantly clear from the start. He thinks I'm weak and useless—not to mention that after what happened in the black box, he seems to think I'm a freak.

Instead of uttering any of those rambling thoughts out loud, I bend into a low, exaggerated bow in front of him, feigning supplication. "I'm so deeply honored to get to share a home with the guy who nearly killed me in front of my entire cohort—*after* telling Drukkar to rip my arms off. Truly, I am blessed."

He chuckles, then shakes his head and says, "I'll be seeing you around, Domestic. Do yourself a favor and don't piss Lady Verdan off. I'd hate for her to come yelling at me when she decides you're a nightmare."

He turns and strides down the hall toward his room.

"I'm not a—" I begin to call after him, but I slam my mouth shut.

I almost hope he *does* have nightmares about me—if only so that I can haunt his mind just like he haunts mine.

CHAPTER TWENTY

An hour later, I find myself pacing my room, wishing I could find some way to leave this house.

Do Domestics ever ask for transfers? Is there any circumstance in the world where the Prefecture would actually listen to the wishes of a Tethered?

Something tells me the answer is a resounding no.

I've rifled through my wardrobe and dresser at least six times, folding and refolding any items of clothing in the drawers. The dresser contains multiple identical pairs of socks, underwear, bras, t-shirts and pajamas. In addition to the wardrobe, there's a closet in the far corner of the room, but when I open it I find it empty, other than a few hangers.

As I'm examining the closet's floor for dust—an old habit from my Tower days—something small and gray scurries out from one of the baseboards and quickly disappears into a small hole on the opposite side.

My instinct is to leap backwards, though I know it's just a mouse. When it's disappeared from view, something—boredom, maybe—compels me to get down on my knees and try to work out how it managed to squeeze its way under the baseboard.

It's then that I notice a small hole where the wood has come loose from the plaster wall. I'm about to stand up again when I notice something else—a flat silver object jutting out slightly from under the baseboard itself.

I reach down with my fingertips to find that it's stuck under the wood. After some effort and a chipped nail, I yank it free and set it on the palm of my hand. It's a small silver disc the size of one of the old coins I've seen in history books. At first, I tell myself it's a button—only it has no holes or other means to attach it to clothing.

With my palm flat, I stare down at it and call to Maude.

"Do you know what this is?"

~I do, she replies. *Would you like to know?*

"No, I want you to keep me in suspense forever."

~Very well, then.

"Maude," I groan. "Just tell me."

~It's what's called a coin-disc. A small device that may contain anything from photographs to video to written documents. A relatively old piece of technology—but many Nobles still use them to store information.

"How do I find out what's on it?"

~Coin-discs are generally not password protected, but you need a device called a reader.

"Okay. So where can I find one of those?"

~In all likelihood the mistress of the house owns one—or her daughters. Perhaps if you ask nicely, they'll consider lending you one.

She's right—Lady Verdan might be willing to lend me a reader. But chances are she'd want to know why I was asking for one in the first place, which would mean I'd have to show her the disc—and there's no way she'd let me keep it. Clearly, it doesn't belong to me.

I'll have to try something else.

With a huff, I tuck the disc into my pocket and head to the door, which I'm relieved to find is still unlocked.

I march to Thorne's room. He's probably not there—most likely he's out doing whatever it is he does on this property. But to my surprise, he opens the door a few seconds later, his hair disheveled.

Apparently, he's been napping.

"Busy, are you?" I ask, the sarcasm clear in my voice.

"What a pleasant surprise," he says with a not-so-friendly grin. "Couldn't keep away, huh?" Leaning on the doorframe, he runs a hand through his hair. "What can I do for you?"

I narrow my eyes at him, rethinking my foolish idea.

As if you, of all people, are going to help me.

Still, it's not like there's anyone else I can ask.

I sigh. "Do you know what a reader is?"

At that, the grogginess leaves his eyes, and he stands up straight, glancing into the corridor like he's afraid we're being watched. "Why are you asking?"

"Curiosity."

"Come in," he whispers. "Quickly."

His room is much like mine, with a bed, a nightstand, a wardrobe, and a dresser, but little else. It seems even Guards aren't granted the luxury of pictures on the walls.

Once I've stepped inside, he closes the door quietly, then opens a drawer in his dresser—one that seems to contain a number of electronic devices and tools—and hands me a small silver box.

"We're not supposed to use readers," he says. "Lady Verdan let me have a few old ones that used to belong to her husband, because one of my duties around here is to repair the tech. So I have a lot of bits and pieces of electronics in my possession to take apart and put back together again."

"So this reader—she knows you have it?"

He shrugs. "I have about seven of them in the drawer there. They're old and a little derelict. They have to sit on a windowsill to get a solar charge, and even after a day of sun, sometimes they don't work for more than a few minutes at a time. Anyhow, Lady Verdan wouldn't let me keep them if she thought I was up to no good, but she trusts me, so..."

I stare at the small object in my hand, confused. It just looks like a silver square.

"Open it," Thorne tells me.

I examine it until I find a narrow seam then crack it open, only to see that inside it is a flat silver disc like the one I found.

"That's a book I read a while ago," Thorne tells me. "Slide your finger over the coin, and you'll see."

I do as he says, and in front of me a page appears, hovering in the air. Its words are faint, but it's legible. It seems to be a story about an island somewhere, and a bunch of pirates.

"Could I borrow the reader?" I ask, extracting the coin disc and handing it to him.

He scrutinizes me in a way that makes me feel like he can see straight through my clothing. "Tell me why you want it.

I'm pretty sure you didn't bring a coin-disc with you from the Tower."

"I didn't," I reply. "It's just...it's boring, sitting in my room with nothing to do."

"You lived in a Whiteroom in the Tower for years. Here, you have a window and you can actually see the world. You're telling me that *now* you're bored?"

I want to tell him to mind his own business, or to fuck off, or something—anything. But instead, I hand it back to him and say, "It's fine. Thanks for showing it to me."

"Wait—Shara," he says, sighing and reaching his hand out again. "Just take it. I don't want to know what you plan to do with it. Take my disc and read the book, for all I care. I suppose you're right—it's going to be dull in your room with nothing to amuse you. Just—don't do anything stupid. I'm serious."

I'm not sure what would constitute "something stupid," so I just nod.

His sudden generosity makes me suspicious, but I thank him quietly, pocketing the reader.

"How do you amuse yourself in here?" I ask, glancing around at the minimalistic room.

Thorne gestures to the dresser, pulling another drawer open to reveal more bits and pieces of what look like electronic equipment. "I make things," he tells me. "I'm pretty crafty. Like I said, I do most of the repairs around here. The girls are always breaking their expensive toys and making me fix them. Communicators, personal devices and whatnot."

I'm impressed, though I don't admit it.

"How did you learn all this?"

"In the Tower, I liked pulling stuff apart," he says. "I got in trouble more than a few times from my Warden. But he finally realized I was doing it so I could figure out how it all worked, then improve it. I was good at it—really good. So he hired me on to do minor electrical repairs. Eventually, he let me tear apart some pretty intricate tech and piece it together again, so I learned that way."

"If you're so handy," I say, "then maybe you should make a trap. I saw a mouse in my closet earlier."

At that, Thorne laughs, and I feel my cheeks instantly reddening.

God, how does he always manage to make me feel like an absolute idiot?

"I'm sorry," I say with a scowl. "I was always taught that mice were vermin. I never saw one in the Tower—which tells me this place is far less clean. I guess I got here just in time."

"It wasn't a damned mouse," Thorne says, and the smile never fades. "You just assumed it was because you've seen drawings."

"I may have led an isolated life, but I did read picture books, and I've seen a few films. I know perfectly well what a mouse looks like."

"Then tell me—what do they look like?"

"Gray, with beady eyes, little round ears, and a sort of... wormy...tail."

"*That's* what you saw?"

"Yes!"

"Man, I'm good." Thorne juts his chest out like he's just won a major athletic event.

"Because you understood my description of a mouse, you feel like you deserve some kind of medal?"

He steps over and opens another drawer in his dresser to reveal a bunch more tools and various small metal objects. He pulls out what looks like a square of fabric—only, the fabric is made of gray fur.

"You're telling me you *made* that mouse?" I ask him.

"And many others. They're surveillance devices. I call them sentinels."

"Does Lady Verdan know about this?"

"Why do you ask?" Thorne moves closer to me but says nothing more. Instead, he reaches for my left wrist and takes it in his fist, staring down into my eyes.

I wait for Maude to buzz a warning or worse, but nothing comes. I feel alone in the world, just as I did in the black box when Thorne took hold of me.

His smile is gone.

"If you found out I was spying," he whispers, "would you report me to our Proprietor?"

CHAPTER TWENTY-ONE

Thorne's grip on my wrist is tight, unyielding. I know perfectly well how easily he can hurt me, so I shake my head. "Of course not," I say in a whisper. "But..." I glance down at my arm and he seems to read my thoughts yet again.

"You're worried our Maude units are picking up this conversation and will report us," he says.

I nod.

He pulls his face close to mine—so close that his cheek brushes against my own.

This moment—*this, right here and now*—is the most intimate I have ever been with another human being. I should be frightened, but instead, every part of me stirs. Blood surges through my veins, and something deep inside me tightens in anticipation of...I'm not sure what.

Thorne's hand is still locked around my wrist, and I'm convinced that he can feel the quickening of my pulse as his breath strokes my skin.

"Don't worry," he whispers, his lips teasing my ear. "The Maudes won't tell on us. We could do anything—*anything*—

right now, and they'd keep our little secret. I have ways around being watched."

At that, I yank myself backwards, and to my surprise, he frees my arm from his grip.

"What are you saying?" I hiss.

"I'm teasing you, Shara," he replies, reaching into the drawer and pulling out a mouse that looks so real it startles me. It's dark gray, with a small patch of white on its back. "You didn't really think I was going to try something...did you?"

I glare at him, crossing my arms defensively over my chest.

I hate you, I think. *For making me feel...whatever that was.*

If he really can read my thoughts, he doesn't show it.

"It was Lady Verdan who commissioned these little guys," he says. "Their eyes are made of micro-cameras, and she has a system in place—one I created—that gives her access to the footage. If she thinks anything sketchy is going on in her house, she checks it. The mouse in your room was probably just there to make sure you weren't setting the place on fire or stealing the curtains."

I gawk at the stationary mouse in Thorne's hand, and he extends it, offering the rodent to me.

Part of me wonders if I should feel affronted by the notion of secret surveillance in the depths of my bedroom—but it's not like it's unexpected. I've been monitored my whole life. My every emotion, illness, or injury has been tracked by the implant in my wrist. It's not like a little mouse is infringing on my privacy any more than literally everything else.

"This mouse isn't connected to the house system,"

Thorne says of the one he's holding. "He's a rogue. I created him a little while ago so I could play around with the memory stored in his tiny little mind—on a coin, like the one in the reader. He's programmed to always return to his charger. He's yours if you want him."

My suspicions mount once again. "Why the hell would I want him?"

"Companionship," Thorne says. "And other things. You never know when he might come in handy. Here—take him."

Half-reluctantly, I accept the small rodent and hold it in my hand. No part of me wants to admit how cute he is or how badly I'd like to have a little pet. I've never imagined myself with an animal companion, artificial or otherwise.

"Handy for what?" I ask.

Thorne lets out a hard breath, then throws himself onto his bed, lying back and staring up at the ceiling. "Look—I know what it is to be in the Tower. I know how they drill into your head over and over again that the Nobility is the greatest, and how the outside world is a paradise of freedom and peace. But there's a lot they *don't* tell you about this world. Like the fact that there's no peace anywhere—not ever. There's a quiet war raging constantly among the Houses of the Nobles. And House Verdan is no exception."

"We shouldn't be talking about this," I say quietly. "If I'd ever had a conversation like this in the Tower..."

"Ah, but you're not in the Tower," Thorne says, "and this room isn't monitored." He presses a finger to his lips and gestures to the room's perimeter. "I have ways of ensuring no signals get through these walls. Our Maude units can't report us from in here, either. We can talk about anything without worry—as long as Lady V. doesn't barge in all of a sudden."

"Fine." I swallow, then ask, "What did you mean, there's a quiet war?" Clutching the little mouse in my hand, I stare at Thorne until he continues.

"The Nobles love to dig up dirt on one another. It's a way to take each other down a notch—to gain favor with the Royals. There have been...infiltrations," he says. "Attempts to hurt this family. I guess it happens sometimes—it's why every Noble home requests a Crimson Elite. I'm here for protection from intrusion."

"But why would anyone be stupid enough to break in here?"

"I don't know," Thorne says, sincerity obvious in his tone as he pushes himself up onto one elbow. "Lady Verdan has never volunteered her theories—but there have been break-ins at night twice, at least. Devorah told me she thinks their father left something behind when he died—that the thieves are after some secret. Whatever the case, we now use the mice to monitor the grounds. We don't have an army to defend us here, but we do have damned good surveillance."

At the mention of the word "secret," I remember the coin-disc in my pocket and wonder if there's any chance it's what the thieves have been hunting.

If it is, I suppose I should turn it over to Lady Verdan...but some terrible, mischievous part of me wants to know what's on it before I do that.

"Lady Verdan's daughters," I say, changing the subject for a moment. "Are you..."

"Close?" Thorne says, pushing himself to a sitting position, a smile on his lips that speaks volumes. "Would it bother you if I said yes?"

"Of course not!" I snap far too aggressively. "Why would I care?"

"Good point. It's not like *you* can have me, right?"

Arrogant son of a bitch, thinking I want him in the first place.

~But you **do** *desire him,* Maude's irritating voice counters inside my mind.

No one asked you.

"You think highly of yourself, don't you?" I sneer.

"I think it's fun to mess with you," Thorne replies, nodding toward his dresser. "Lay the mouse on your windowsill for a few hours. When he comes to, you'll find he's ready to go. But fair warning—these little guys have minds of their own. You might find he disappears now and then."

Nervous, I glance around the room, reminding myself what Thorne said earlier, but unsure whether to trust him as far as I can throw him. "Should I be worried that I'll get into trouble for having him?"

"I wouldn't advertise the fact," Thorne says. "Keep him out of sight. But don't worry too much. I'll cover for you if anyone asks—I'll tell the Mistress you wanted a little friend, so I gave you a dud."

I'm about to turn and leave when I say, "She likes you, doesn't she? Lady Verdan, I mean."

"She does. Like I said, she trusts me, too—though I'm not sure she or anyone should."

I try to ignore what sounds like a warning. "How long have you been here?"

Thorne pushes himself to his feet. "Three years," he tells

me. "This was my Placement right out of the Tower. Lord Verdan was here back then, of course. When he died a year ago, I was told to stay close to his widow—even though Tethered aren't supposed to do that. I've watched over her, though, and done my duty."

What sort of duty is that? I wonder.

Lady Verdan is a beautiful woman, albeit almost old enough to be Thorne's mother. But there's no way they're...

Is there?

"But mostly," he continues without reacting to my expression, "I stay out of her hair, and you should, too—for your own sake, more than anything."

I don't entirely know what he means, but I nod. I've already asked way too many questions, and unlike Lady Verdan, I have yet to find a single reason to trust Thorne.

"Thank you for the mouse," I tell him, slipping the reader and the charger into my pocket along with the coin-disc. "I... appreciate it."

Before I turn toward the door, I ask, "You're not just giving me the mouse so you can watch me undress in the privacy of my room, are you?"

It's the closest I've come to joking around with Thorne—but mostly, I just want to see his reaction.

"Wouldn't you like to know?" he asks with that enticing grin of his.

"Unhelpful."

"I aim to please." Thorne takes two steps toward me and once again, he leans in close. This time, he doesn't touch me—but I almost wish he would.

Inhaling, I take in his scent and find myself wanting to

know what it would feel like to have his body against mine, his lips on mine.

Stop it, Shara, I scream internally. *What the hell's wrong with you?*

"Hey—domestic goddess," Thorne says quietly.

I simultaneously sneer at him and remind myself that he's the most odious person I've ever met.

"What?" I snap.

"Keep your eyes and ears open. And don't trust anyone—not even me."

"Believe me, not trusting you will be the easiest thing I've ever done."

"Good girl."

The way he looks at me as he speaks those two words sends a throb through my entire body—one that makes me flinch with embarrassment.

Without another word, I slip out of his room and resolve that, in the future, I will avoid him at all costs.

CHAPTER TWENTY-TWO

Back in my room, I lay the charger Thorne gave me on the broad windowsill then pull the thick white curtain over it, concealing it from view.

I place the small, helpless-looking gray and white mouse on the charger and watch as its eyes open. They're jet-black and bright, and I'm not sure whether I'm imagining it when it lifts its head gently to look up at me.

"I'll check in on you later," I tell the creature. "Don't do anything dangerous in the meantime, okay?"

As I pull the curtain across to give the mouse a quiet, solar-charging den, I roll Thorne's words over in my mind.

Don't trust anyone...not even me.

Was it foolish to take the mouse? Probably. If Thorne is watching my every move, I've just given him an easy way to do it.

But it's not like I'm planning to break the rules. If anything, I intend to live in the least conspicuous way imaginable.

And I sure as hell have no intention of spending any time with him.

As if to remind me that I'm going to break just *one* little rule, my hand reaches into my pocket and feels for the reader. It's small—half the size of the playing cards we had in the Tower—and I wonder with a quiet sigh if I can possibly get away with using it without being seen.

"Maude," I say softly. "Can you tell if there are any active surveillance devices in this room?"

She remains silent for a moment, then says, *~None that I can detect, other than the mouse you brought in. But it isn't charged yet, and is unable to watch you from its vantage point.*

"Perfect."

I pull the reader out and crack it open, then slip the small silver coin-disc inside.

"How does this thing work?" I ask, but before Maude has a chance to answer, an image flares to life in the air before me.

At first, it just looks like a white rectangle, but I realize quickly it's blurry because it's too bright in my room, even with one curtain pulled across the window.

I leap over and pull the blind down, darkening the space. The white rectangle of light hovering over the reader suddenly looks like the page of a book. As I move closer, I begin to see that there's a sea of small text on its surface.

"What is this?" I whisper more to myself than to Maude.

~It's a journal entry, Maude replies.

I've heard of people writing in journals and diaries, though I never had one of my own. The Warden warned us frequently that anything we wrote down or recorded would invariably become the property of the Prefecture, so it was best to keep our innermost thoughts to ourselves.

These, on the other hand, aren't the words of a Tethered.

They're the words of a Noble—at least, I *think* they are.

I sit on the bed and stare at the wall of text floating before me, taking it in.

CHAPTER TWENTY-THREE

Today is my seventeenth birthday, and this is my very first Diary entry.

I'm not sure what I should say, though Mother once told us we should make an effort to express gratitude when we can, and try not to spend our lives complaining. She says there are people in this world far worse off than we are, and that we should count our blessings.

So I'll start by saying I'm grateful to live in this beautiful house with my family.

I stare out at the Tower sometimes and think about the people my age who are locked inside—the Tethered. The ones with powers.

I've heard Nobles say the Tethered should be killed. That we should just end their bloodlines so there's no chance of more of their kind being born.

But Mother told me that without the servitude of the Tethered, the Nobility would have no advantage. She says our status depends partly on whether or not we have them defending our homes.

We've had a few Tethered Guards in the house over the years. The last one was sent away, though no one ever told me why. Mother said yesterday that there's a new Guard coming—one who's stronger and more disciplined than the last one was. She said he's just what this house needs for protection—but she warned me that we're to keep our distance from him.

I know the law.

Tethered aren't allowed to get close to us or to each other. They aren't allowed families or love.

Honestly, I think it's sad—and I wish the law would change. I wish the Prefecture would stop insisting they're threats, just because they have powers. No Tethered has ever been cruel to me. Besides, if they were so terrible, why would the Royal Family have so many Tethered Guards in their service?

I've never met any of the Royals, despite the fact that they live next door. When I turn eighteen, I'll be allowed to attend my first palace ball...and I can't tell you how excited I am. I've heard the prince is incredibly handsome. They say every girl who meets him falls in love with him, though I can't imagine anyone quite **that** *intoxicating.*

I suppose I'll find out when the time comes.

Mother is calling me down to dinner, so I have to go.

More later,

—D.

CHAPTER TWENTY-FOUR

I PULL BACK, my brow furrowing. "D?" I mutter. "Maude, do you think this is Devorah's journal?"

~I don't know anything about it, Maude replies. *And if you were sensible, you would shut the reader down this instant. You shouldn't pry into other people's business.*

I narrow my eyes with irritation, but she's right, of course. Whatever Devorah might have written at seventeen is absolutely none of my business, and any Normal servant would be punished for far less.

"I'm just curious about my Proprietor's family," I say, even though I know it's bullshit, and I'm sure Maude does, too.

She lets out what sounds like a low growl.

~You're stepping into a world where you don't belong.

"They invited me into their world. They *dragged* me into it, in fact. And what the hell was that growl? Are you forgetting you don't actually have teeth?"

~I may not have teeth, but I can still bite you if you break Kravan's rules.

"Is what I'm doing against the rules?"

She goes silent for a moment, then says, ~*Not exactly.*

"Then let me read just a little more. After that, I'll put it away—I promise."

Maude lets out what sounds like an exasperated huff, and I chuckle, reminding myself she doesn't actually have lungs.

The next entry is marked "*Several Days Later,*" but offers up no specific date.

Diary—the most amazing thing happened today.

I met someone secret and special—someone I can't say too much about, because we could both get into so much trouble if I did.

He's gorgeous and perfect, and his voice is like chocolate. He's everything I could have imagined, and then some.

I met him in the garden—on the trail that leads into the Royal Grounds. I know I shouldn't have been back there, but I love looking at the castle, at their well-tended gardens, all of it.

I couldn't help myself.

I was just getting to the border of our property when he came along and took my breath away. When I tell you that my heart stopped the moment my eyes met his, I am not exaggerating even a little.

I think I'm in love.

Yes, I know that sounds crazy.

But it's true.

The even crazier thing is that I think he finds me attractive, too.

I know, I know—I shouldn't even think about it. It's not allowed. We're not supposed to speak to each other, let alone be attracted to one another.

But there's something between us.

I feel it.

I wish I could tell you all about him. What his eyes are like, his lips, his nose, his broad chest. I wish I could write his name here over and over again, if only to manifest another encounter.

But for the sake of secrecy, I'll just call him T.

If I don't get to speak to him again soon, I'm afraid I might just die.

THE SECOND ENTRY ENDS THERE.

I find myself rereading it once, then again.

She said in the previous entry that there was a new Guard coming to the house. Then, a couple of days later...she met someone called T.

Could she be talking about the day Thorne arrived at the Verdan house?

Holy shit. Was Devorah in love with a Tethered? Is she still?

After all, she looks nineteen or twenty. It would make perfect sense that she'd written this entry three years ago.

If it's true, then why did Devorah act so snooty about the Tethered, as if we're parasites not fit to lick her shoes? Unless...

Maybe it's an act on her part, designed to throw people off her scent. If she and Thorne have a secret relationship, then the smartest thing Devorah could do is pretend to detest our kind.

I'm about to scroll to the next entry in hopes of learning more when a series of knocks sounds at my door.

CHAPTER TWENTY-FIVE

I SCRAMBLE to seal up the reader and tuck it under my pillow before darting over to the door and opening it.

The woman who's staring up at me is short, with rosy cheeks and a sour expression. She's dressed in a gray coverall and an off-white apron, and she's holding a tray of food that includes soup, bread, and cheese.

"You're the new girl," she says with a healthy dose of disdain, handing the tray over. "Another Tethered."

"I am," I reply in as pleasant a voice as I can muster, taking the tray. I want to ask her name, but something tells me I already know. She's got to be Mrs. Milton, the cook.

I also want to ask her if she was working here three years ago when Thorne first arrived—but there's no way. She looks like she'd like to take a rolling pin to my face for less, if she only had one in her hand.

"You'll come to the kitchen at six tomorrow morning," she says sharply, confirming that she is indeed the cook. "You'll help me prepare the food for the day before starting your other duties. Understand?"

With a nod, I say, "Of course."

I have no idea where the kitchen is, but I'm sure I can figure it out easily enough.

"Bring your tray down when you come in the morning," she barks, before turning abruptly on her heel and leaving.

I don't watch her go. Instead, I turn and head back into my room, setting the tray down on the dresser, then tearing off a piece of bread and shoving it into my mouth. I hadn't realized how hungry I was. The last time I ate anything was at breakfast in the Tower—which now feels like years ago.

The bread is delicious, warm, and fresh—better than anything we ever ate in the Tower, though I'll admit the food there wasn't terrible.

I'm tempted to go back to the diary when a small shape scurries out from under my dresser, leaping onto the bedding and climbing up to stand on its hind legs.

It's one of Thorne's electronic mice, though not the one he gave me. This one has a large black spot on his back, and I'm beginning to wonder if Thorne deliberately gives them distinguishing markings so he can tell them all apart.

"Hello," I say, easing closer and reaching a hand out. The mouse climbs on, his unreadable black eyes boring into mine.

The small creature cocks his head, a reminder that he's probably here to keep an eye on me.

So I say, "In case you're wondering, I'm fine. Oh—and this house is beautiful." Remembering the first diary entry, I add, "I'm very grateful to be here."

The mouse leaps off my hand and scurries over to the closet door, then disappears from view.

The little rodent seems friendly enough, but with him

nearby, I don't feel confident to open the reader up again, so I leave and head downstairs to find the library Lady Verdan mentioned.

On my way down the twisting staircase that leads to the main foyer, I gasp when I spot Devorah and Thorne standing by the front door—only a foot or so apart.

As I watch in horror, Devorah lays a hand on Thorne's arm. She leans in close, a smile on her face, and whispers something.

Thorne nods, grinning, then says a few words that are apparently hilarious enough to make her throw her head back and laugh.

Oh, God.

This is...awkward.

It's too late to turn and head back up the stairs. They would definitely spot me and figure out exactly what had happened.

But if I keep going, I might make things even worse.

Still, I can't stand here all night. *Or can I?*

I turn to the wall, where a gold-framed portrait of a dark-haired man hangs, and pretend to straighten it.

"What the hell are you doing out of your room?" a high-pitched voice slices through the air.

Tightening, I spin around to see that Thorne has disappeared, and Devorah is already moving to block my path at the base of the stairs, a scowl on her lips.

"I...your mother said I could borrow a book," I tell her, lowering my chin in submission. "I was going to head down, but I noticed this portrait was crooked."

"You should only use the servants' stairs," she spits. "The foyer is off limits for you."

"Servants' stairs?" I ask. "I didn't know there was such a thing."

"They're near your room, behind a gray door. Don't you ever let me see you come down this staircase again, or I'll report you for insubordination."

At that, Maude vibrates a warning on my wrist, but something tells me she's not so much agreeing with Devorah as tacitly saying, ~*What a bitch.*

"Oh," I reply with as warm a smile as I can muster. "Okay. I'm sorry, Devorah. I didn't know. I haven't learned the ins and outs of this house yet."

"Your ignorance isn't my fucking problem."

With that, Devorah raises her chin and storms off into what looks like a sitting room to one side of the foyer.

When she's safely disappeared, I slip down to the main floor and past the sitting room to the next door.

I don't have to hesitate before determining that the large room to my right is the library. The chamber is large and warmly decorated, with walls of dark burgundy and what seems like an eternal wave of bookshelves flowing from floor to ceiling against every wall.

"This is heaven," I say under my breath.

In the Tower, the library was small. But it was sterile and boring, with all the books arranged alphabetically according to their category. It contained many educational texts, and very little fiction—and what little there *was* tended to be heavily redacted.

In this library, however, I discover masses of novels I would never have had access to in the Tower. I scan the shelves, my heart soaring.

I intend to take full advantage of Lady Verdan's offer to let me borrow one book at a time.

Before too long, I settle on a novel about a young woman who is sent to live in a large mansion away from home. Its title is scratched out, and I realize as I glance around that many of the books have names that are obscured in one way or another.

"It's harder to enforce book bans when you can't see their names," a deep voice says from behind me.

I turn to see Thorne standing in the doorway, his lips twitching into what could manifest either into a smile or a frown.

"Are you going to tell me I'm not allowed in here?" I ask him. "Because Lady Verdan said—"

"It's fine," he says. "And before you ask—yes, I'm watching you."

Clutching the novel to my chest and trying to forget what I saw in the foyer a few minutes ago, I ask, "Why?"

He shrugs. "Because my one job is to protect this family. You're a Tethered. You're new. I need to make sure you don't do anything foolish."

I want to say, *Foolish? You mean like having an intimate relationship with your Proprietor's daughter, even if you know it could land you in a Blackroom for the rest of your life?*

But I manage against all odds to keep my lips sealed tight.

Instead of leaving me alone, Thorne steps closer and takes the book from my hands, opens it up, and raises an eyebrow.

"Interesting choice," he says, his finger landing on the open page.

He holds it up so I can see what he's pointing at, and my cheeks flush instantly hot.

> *She moaned as his hand slipped under her skirt, his fingers seeking out her...*

I grab the book and slam it shut as Thorne snickers.

Shame floods me, and I turn back to the bookshelf, searching for something—*anything*—else.

"I...didn't know it was that sort of book," I say, my voice tremulous.

It's the truth, but it does nothing to minimize my humiliation.

"Take the damned book," Thorne says, stepping so close behind me that I can feel heat radiating from his body. "Read it. You may as well enjoy yourself while you still can."

"What do you mean, while I still can?" I ask without turning to face him.

He moves closer, and now, I swear I can feel his chest against my back.

But no—it's impossible. Maude would belt out a warning if he were touching me like that.

"You *know* what I mean," he whispers, his breath playing with the tendrils of loose hair by my ear.

I slip the book back onto the shelf and pull down another one. A novel called *Jane Eyre*—one that looks somewhat more innocent.

The sound of footsteps on hardwood startles me and I pivot to see Lady Verdan stepping into the library.

Meanwhile, Thorne takes a long, quick step backwards as if to prove he isn't touching me.

I guess he reserves that privilege for Devorah.

"Thorne, I'm taking the girls to buy new dresses for the Annual Prince's Ball. I need you to get the Flyer prepared for tomorrow so we can do some shopping."

"Yes, Lady Verdan," he replies with a bow of his head, striding to the door to leave the room—and me—behind.

"As for you, Shara," she says when he's gone, her warm tone from earlier in the day entirely gone. "You would do well not to let that young man stand so close to you. You know the rules—and unless you're a naive simpleton, you know what young men are like."

"Don't worry," I retort without thinking. "He and I dislike each other intensely."

"Disliking one another never stopped a man and a woman from fucking like wild animals," she replies. "I know that better than anyone in this world."

With that, to my relief, she cracks a smile.

If I knew her any better, I might even say she looks relieved to know Thorne and I aren't at risk of falling in love.

I wonder what she'd think if she knew about her daughter's behavior.

"Well," she says, "hopefully you two won't have to cross one another's paths too frequently. You would be wise to keep to yourself. Stay in your room unless there's a good reason for you to be out of it. You have duties around the house, but otherwise, there really is no reason to wander. Understood?"

"Yes, Lady Verdan," I say with a nod.

"Good. Tomorrow morning after the girls and I have left, I would like you to familiarize yourself with the gardens. You'll find any tools you need in the large outbuilding at the northeast corner of the property. Trim any hedges that are out of order, and pull any weeds you see."

When my face goes blank, she says, "I trust that you know what weeds look like? They're supposed to teach you that sort of thing in the Tower."

"Yes—of course," I tell her, though the truth is, it's been a long time since I last looked at photographs of plants.

I can only hope I don't tear any prize roses out of the ground.

"Anything else?" I ask.

"Wash the girls' sheets, and make their beds," she says. "And mine, of course. I expect our rooms to be ready for us by the time we return. We should be gone for a few hours—we're headed to the Golden Promenade."

"I'm sorry—Golden Promenade?" I ask, and Maude vibrates my wrist to remind me I shouldn't be asking questions.

"It's a large shopping center on Egret Island," Lady Verdan says. "Filled with exclusive shops. All of the wealthiest families buy their clothing there. The Capitol used to be the destination of choice, but it's just become so...well, you saw it. It's foul."

A look of disgust passes over her face. Horror, no doubt, at the pathetic Normals who willingly languish in such dire conditions.

"Yes, of course," I say. "Shopping sounds wonderful. I hope you and your daughters have a great time."

She stares me down as if to say *A better time than you'll ever get to experience,* then turns to leave, waving a hand in the air and calling out, "Go back to your room, Shara. Don't come out until morning."

CHAPTER TWENTY-SIX

HOLDING the book tight against my chest, I follow Lady Verdan's orders and head back to my quarters via the servants' stairs that Devorah told me about.

The staircase is twisting and narrow, its steps old, creaking wood, the walls dark and forbidding. It smells musty, and cobwebs have gathered in the corners as if no one has used it in years.

Something tells me Thorne isn't forced to climb these stairs on a regular basis.

At the top is a door with a loose knob. I twist it and push, hoping to find Devorah isn't playing some cruel practical joke on me. To my relief, the door opens into the corridor where my quarters and Thorne's are located.

I slip into my room and lie down on the bed, cracking open the book I borrowed from the library. My eyes lock on the title, and I wonder why *Jane Eyre* doesn't have its title scratched out as some of the other books do.

"Maude," I half-whisper.

~Yes, Shara?

"Are books really banned out here? I mean—in the world outside the Tower?"

~That's a complicated question. I only have a little knowledge of the matter, as it is considered irrelevant to your personal existence.

"Tell me what you do know, then."

~Noble families acquire books via what's called the Network. Families like the Verdans are not supposed to have libraries—to learn about history, science, or any other intellectual pursuit—so books in Nobles' homes are meant to be scarce. It seems Lord and Lady Verdan have—or had—a love of literature, however, and so they collected a vast number of books via the Network.

"Why are they forbidden?"

~Because history, they say, has a way of repeating itself. Some believe it's a knowledge of history that allows people to learn to overthrow those in power.

Thorne mentioned infiltrations, but I get the impression Maude is talking about something a little more serious.

"Wait—you're saying there's a fear of rebellion among the Nobles themselves?"

~I'm not able or willing to speculate about such things. Perhaps the walls exist in part because these grounds are also adjacent to the Royal Family's property. I must warn you—don't set foot on the Royal Grounds without permission.

"Of course I won't." As I speak, I let out a yawn, eager to get to sleep so I can rise early, get my kitchen chores completed, then head out to see the exquisite-looking gardens.

I have vowed almost every day of my life to serve the Nobility.

Tomorrow morning, regardless of Maude's warning, I

intend to sneak a look at the king's land. It's time to see how the wealthiest family in all of Kravan lives.

In the morning, I rise early, thanks to a pre-programmed alarm embedded directly into the nightstand.

Apparently, someone decided ahead of time to wake me at five-fifteen, which seems borderline cruel. In the Tower, we rose at seven every morning, and my internal clock is very much attuned to that schedule.

I dress in one of the white uniforms left for me in the wardrobe, then study myself in the mirror, taking note of how perfectly the clothing fits. Though I'm not thrilled to be wearing another uniform, I have to admit this one feels far more luxurious and comfortable than the ones I wore daily in the Tower.

When I step out into the hallway, I see that Thorne, too, is up, and shutting his door behind him.

If he were anyone else, I might ask how he slept or what he's up to today. I might make some remark about how hellish it is to get up so early.

But he's not someone else. He's the ice-cold asshole who has done everything since I met him to ensure my life would be miserable.

"Shara," he says, his voice a low morning rumble.

"Thorne," I reply with a curt nod.

He turns and disappears toward the central staircase, but I head down the servants' stairs and make my way toward the back of the house until I reach a large, bright kitchen. My jaw drops open to see how many cupboards there are—

almost as many as there were in the Tower's kitchen, and that one was used to prepare food for every member of our cohort.

So...this is how the truly wealthy live, I think, wondering if Lady Verdan ever actually sets foot in this room.

The sun's early morning rays pour in cheerfully through a large set of windows at the back of the house, highlighting the sour look on Mrs. Milton's face as she marches in to glower at me.

"Those need peeling," she grunts, gesturing to what look like ten pounds of carrots in a bowl next to the sink. "Then the potatoes. Peeler's in the top drawer on your left. Mind your knuckles—but then, I suppose it doesn't matter much if you injure yourself. You're one of them Healers, aren't you?"

I nod, wincing slightly at the disgust in her tone.

Maybe if she accidentally slices a finger off, she'll realize I'm actually pretty useful to have around—not that I've ever healed anyone but myself.

But presumably, I could...if I were allowed to touch them.

Silently, I find the peeler and go about my task, managing only to take the skin off two fingertips in the process.

"Anything else?" I ask when I'm done and have disposed of the peelings.

Looking vaguely impressed, Mrs. Milton shakes her head. "Mistress won't want you cleaning the bedrooms until she and the girls have gone out, so you'd better go on and get your work done. Make sure to cut some fresh flowers and put them in three vases. She likes them in the bedrooms."

It's the most helpful thing Mrs. Milton has said to me, and for a moment I wonder if we could even become friends.

But then she adds, "Don't do anything stupid out there, Girl. This place has a reputation to uphold, and the last few Tethered who caused problems around here didn't come to a very nice end, if you catch my meaning."

I'm about to tell her I don't catch her meaning even a little when Maude, sensing the words in my mind, buzzes the usual warning into my wrist.

"Yes, Mrs. Milton," I reply dutifully. "I'll do my best to keep the Verdan home problem-free."

She scrunches her face up like she's just taken a massive bite out of something bitter and sour at once. "We'll see."

Scowling, I leave her behind and head out to the gardens through an elegant set of glass doors at the back of the kitchen.

It's my first time stepping outside on my own, and I find myself instantly reveling in the freedom that comes with this simple act. I inhale the fresh air, instantly forgetting Mrs. Milton's general odiousness in favor of the realization that I'm probably as content right now as I'll ever be.

I close the doors behind me and make my way toward the far end of the vast gardens. I take my time strolling over the series of small hills and shallow valleys that make up the property, feeling like an explorer who's just discovered an entire world.

I hadn't fully registered how enormous the property is—or how beautiful the gardens are. Gravel paths twist and turn in every direction, punctuated by stone benches that would make idyllic spots to sit and read a book. Occasionally, a gazebo or pergola appears on the landscape, and with each new bit of paradise that unfolds before my eyes, I find myself wondering if the Verdans ever use the space, or if it's all for show.

Finally, I come to the greenhouse. I've heard this sort of structure described before, but until now, I've never actually seen one—not even in pictures.

Still, it's unmistakable. A large building of steel-framed glass, it's filled with all manner of vegetation in elegant planters, from orange trees to cacti to a sizable vegetable garden to olive trees and rose bushes.

When I've made my way inside, I once again take my time strolling until I come to the section where the tools are kept. I grab a pair of garden shears to trim the hedges that run along the property's perimeter, as well as a pair of gloves in case I'm tempted to further damage my hands. The minor cuts I suffered in the kitchen are mostly healed by now, but I'm not interested in bleeding any more than I have to.

Back outside, I get to work pruning the hedges. To my pleasant surprise, it turns out to be a job I enjoy. I suppose I shouldn't be shocked; after all, Maude taught me to treat every task with a nearly obsessive fervor. With that in mind, I manage to tidy the greenery as if I've been doing it all my life.

I spend an hour or more trimming and weeding before I find myself at the northeast corner of the grounds, toward the far end of a particularly long stretch of hedges.

It's then that I notice a gap between the end of one hedge and the beginning of another.

Setting the trimmers down on the ground, I step forward to peek into the gap. It seems I've discovered the path leading from the Verdan property toward what must be the Royal Grounds.

I glance back over my shoulder to see if anyone is around.

To my relief, I'm alone.

There's no fence or gate preventing me from strolling down the path, and the temptation is too great to resist.

Flanked by tall old trees, the narrow trail is beautiful and inviting, and I assure myself that taking a break for a moment isn't against the rules. After all, there might be some plant or other down this way that needs trimming or weeding.

When Maude buzzes a warning, I tell her to settle down.

"I'm not about to do anything stupid," I whisper.

~I'm not so sure about that, Shara.

I stroll along the path, alternating between staring up at the green canopy above and enjoying the dappled light that flows between the leaves to dance on the ground around my feet.

When the path comes to its eventual end I halt, pressing myself against a tree trunk to stare out at what must be the Royal Grounds.

In the distance, I can see the palace, a vast structure of dark gray stone that must contain a hundred or more rooms. At each of its corners are the tall, round turrets I saw from the Hoverer, capped by conical slate rooftops.

The place looks like something out of the fairy tales I read when I was little—at least, the few I was allowed access to in the Tower.

I didn't think it was possible, but the enormity of the palace makes the Verdans' house look like a cottage in comparison.

Guards in red uniforms—the Royal Guard, I assume—patrol the castle's perimeter. Beautifully groomed topiaries line a series of paths leading to other, smaller outbuildings, and around each of those, more Guards patrol.

Why does anyone need so many guards?

Just as I silently ask the question, a man on horseback comes cantering down one of the pathways toward what looks like the palace's main entrance. From the looks of him, he's young, with dark hair and elegant clothing.

Some insane compulsion tells me to find out if I'm looking at the famous Prince Tallin.

I'm on the verge of stepping onto the grounds to get a closer look when a hand grabs my upper arm, and an angry voice growls, "What the fuck do you think you're doing?"

CHAPTER TWENTY-SEVEN

I TWIST AROUND, my heart pounding.

When I see Thorne's angry eyes staring down at me, I'm almost relieved—though I shouldn't be. He'll probably be just as hard on me as a member of the Royal Guard would.

As his grip tightens, the realization surges over me like a wave: *He's touching me again.*

My eyes widening, I stare at his hand and wait for a blaring alarm to sound, half expecting an army of Crimson Elites to sprint toward us, weapons drawn.

As if reading my mind, Thorne jerks his hand away, straightening his fingers with a flinch as if that will somehow negate what just occurred.

"You're a fool," he snarls, his voice barely more than a whisper. "What were you thinking, venturing onto the Royal Grounds without permission?"

"I was just—"

But he doesn't let me finish.

"You were just *looking*. Just curious. Isn't that right?"

"What's wrong with looking at—"

I stop myself, because as much as I hate it, he's right.

I *am* a fool. Maude has warned me a million times to stop being curious and to keep my head down—and I know it's against the rules to venture onto the king's land.

"You saw how many Crimson Elites are visible on the grounds," Thorne scolds. "And those are only the ones out in the open. What do you think they would've done if they'd seen you?"

"I'm a Harmless," I protest, too stubborn to acknowledge my folly. "A Domestic, a servant to their neighbor. Besides, the path is open, isn't it? It's not like there's a 'Keep Out' sign or something. There's not even a gate."

"This path isn't for your personal use, and you know it."

"I get it," I reply with a sneer. "I was being impulsive. It won't happen again."

What I *really* want to say is, "I saw you and Devorah canoodling downstairs. I know about the diary. Yet you act like *I'm* the one breaking the rules?"

"You don't know how dangerous it is to go anywhere near the Royals," Thorne tells me, his voice losing its angry edge. "You of all people need to stay away from that family—at least, until the time is right."

I pull back, confused. "Until the time is right?" I say with a laugh. "You seem to be implying there will be a time when it's a good idea for me to walk up and say, 'Hey there, Royal family—I'm Shara. Let's be friends.'"

"That's not what I'm saying." He lets out a hard breath like my being a smartass is exhausting him. "Trust me when I tell you to stay off this path. Don't let anyone outside the

Verdan household get a look at your face. Do you understand what I'm saying?"

"I understand you're talking to me like I'm five. And why does my face matter? It's not like someone's going to recognize me as *that lame-ass girl who used to live in the Tower*. I'm a nobody."

Thorne half-twists, facing away as if hoping to hide the smile on his lips. "A nobody," he says, seemingly to the tree next to us. Turning back to me, he adds, "You have no idea, do you, Shara? But I do. You're not the nobody you think you are. You're—"

Something flares in his eyes, a fire dancing in his irises. I wish right now that I could see his mind, read his thoughts. I wish I understood what the hell he was trying to say.

"I'm what?" I ask, and this time, there's no snide edge to my voice.

He grinds his jaw for a few seconds. "Go back to your gardening," he finally commands, turning to leave. "Stop nosing around where you don't belong. Curiosity kills far more than just cats."

"What's that supposed to mean?"

Rounding on me, he grabs me by the front of my uniform, and this time, there's no flinching away. He pulls himself close, his eyes piercing and filled with an emotion that looks frighteningly close to rage.

I have to fight to keep my breath from coming out in short, hard gasps. "It means I need you to stay alive," he growls, "I need..."

"Need what?" I whimper.

He pulls away and rakes his fingers through his hair, then

shakes his head. "Just...be careful. I don't want to have to go to the trouble of finding another Domestic—which I'll have to do if they decide to end you."

Without another word, he turns on his heel and leaves me standing on the trail, more confused than ever.

CHAPTER TWENTY-EIGHT

When I've finished trimming the hedges, weeding today's section of the garden, and tidying up the greenhouse a little, I head back to the main house to find Lady Verdan and her daughters have left for their trip to the Golden Promenade.

I strip their beds and carefully put on new linens before dusting and vacuuming each of their rooms, taking care not to break any delicate trinkets.

Lady Verdan's room is elegant, large, and minimalistic, with white bedding on a matching upholstered bed, a beige couch, and a small desk area that's so neat and tidy I wonder if she actually uses it for anything.

On her desk, I notice a reader like the one Thorne lent me. For the briefest moment, I contemplate picking it up and activating it, curious to see what's on it.

But when I see a small gray creature scurry across the floor, I think better of it. I have no idea if it's a surveillance mouse or a real one, but I can't afford to take the chance that Lady Verdan will catch me snooping.

Thorne's warning about curiosity sits heavy inside me,

and though I hate admitting it, he's right. I've always been too inquisitive—and for a Tethered, that's a personality trait that can easily lead to death.

But who could blame me for being curious, or any Tethered, for that matter? This is the first time in my life I've ever been allowed outside of the Tower. The first I've seen of a world with windows, trees, and rolling hills. The first I've ever heard of readers or surveillance rodents.

Knowing things exist isn't the same as seeing them in person, and I haven't existed in the outside world long enough for it to cease being wondrous.

The one small sin I can't resist committing—after checking with Maude that there are no mice present—is picking up a small bottle of expensive-looking perfume from Lady Verdan's dresser. I spray a little onto my wrist, as I've heard ladies do, and rub it on my neck.

It smells like the garden's flowers, and I can easily understand why she would want to carry the scent with her always. Simply inhaling it makes me feel like I'm wandering under the sun without a care in the world.

I'm careful to lay the perfume back in its place, making sure to orient it correctly.

When I've finished with the three bedrooms, I dust the living room and library, then head back to my quarters, intending to read the book I borrowed yesterday.

But when I get to my room, Thorne is waiting for me in the hallway. His back is pressed to my door, arms crossed tightly over his broad chest.

I let out a huff when I see him. "What do you want?"

For a split-second, I wonder if he's here to apologize for being an ass.

Instead, he says, "I assume you know the Prince's Ball is taking place in two weeks."

I nod. "Lady Verdan said she and her daughters are buying dresses for it."

With a smile, he replies, "That's right."

You're probably picturing Devorah in a low-cut number, aren't you? I think, my eyes narrowing in silent accusation.

I have no patience for him right now—not that I ever have. Not only is he blocking my way into my room, but he's being irritatingly cryptic.

I'm not going to ask you questions about the ball, so don't even try to manipulate me.

I'll admit that I'm curious about it. I've never seen a ball-gown in real life, nor have I seen a man in a tuxedo or tails. I can't even imagine how opulent it must feel to wear garments like those.

But I'm not super keen to have my nose rubbed in the fact that I will never wear silk dresses or pretty shoes—and I'll certainly never be invited to a royal event of any kind.

"Look—I have a lot of work to do," I mutter. "If you'll get out of my way, I promise I'll stay out of yours. Deal?"

He straightens himself, tightening and snickering. "You really don't like me at all, do you?"

"Actually, I have no feelings for you whatsoever."

The words are an absolute lie.

The truth is, I have so many conflicting feelings that I don't know how to process them.

Sometimes, I'm convinced I despise him.

And sometimes, I think I would collapse in on myself if someone told me I could never see him again.

Is this what it is to feel attracted to another person? Is it always this ridiculous—this nauseatingly confusing?

Or is my attraction to Thorne just some feral animal tearing its way through me for sport?

There's something about him that draws me in—some unseen, incomprehensible power that pulls me to him, like there's an invisible wire attaching our chests together—one I have wished to sever a thousand times since we met.

"It's probably for the best if you despise me," he says, easing closer, and once again, I'm convinced he's reading my mind. "You and I should not be friends, Shara. We shouldn't be close. It would be a terrible idea."

"I know the rules," I snarl. "I've known them for years. You don't need to worry about me."

"The rules about touching?" he asks, taking my hand in his and pulling it so close to his lips that I'm convinced he's going to kiss it.

Pleasant tingles of energy shoot up my arm—the opposite of the pain I felt so often in the combat ring. It's like he's healing whatever ailment has tortured me for years.

"What the hell are you doing?" I ask, trying and failing to yank my hand away.

Admittedly, I'm not trying very hard.

Once again, I wait for Maude's voice to cry a warning in my mind—but no warning comes. It's like she's simply lost consciousness.

With his eyes boring into mine, Thorne pulls my hand to his face. When my palm meets his stubbled jaw, I fight back the gasp that wants to slip past my lips.

My fingers begin to tingle again, just as they did on

Placement Day. But this time, the sensation courses through my entire body, teasing every nerve ending.

"Do you feel it?" he asks quietly. "The sensation you felt the last time you touched my face?"

"If someone catches us..." I whisper, twisting my head to look down the hallway in search of a sentinel mouse.

"There are no mice in this corridor. I've seen to it that they'll stay away for a little. Answer me—*do you feel it?*"

I nod, my cheeks searing.

He slides one hand up my arm until it reaches my neck, his fingers so gentle that I can hardly believe this is the same man who has been so cruel to me on occasion.

My entire body heats at once, and suddenly all I want is to feel his lips on mine—his skin against mine. I want to know what it is to taste him. To bite his lip, revel in his tongue, and watch and writhe as he explores the places my fingers have rarely dared venture.

"Shara," he whispers, "I need you to do something for me."

His fingertips are still moving along my skin, leaving a trail of goosebumps in their wake.

"What do you need?" I ask, my voice tight as I realize in this moment, I would do anything for him.

"I need you to attend the ball." He leans in closer, his lips teasing my ear. "Would you do that for me?"

CHAPTER TWENTY-NINE

I JERK AWAY FROM THORNE, breaking the calm between us and forcing him to drop his hand to his side.

"Why would you want me to—?" I snap. "I can't attend the ball! It's a Royal event. I'm a Tethered. A *house servant*."

"I know. But trust me—no one will know that when the time comes. Not even the Verdans."

I feel like a question mark is burning its way into my forehead as I stare at him. "Now you're just talking like a psycho," I tell him. "Is this your idea of a joke—or is it a test? Are you trying to see if I'm willing to betray my Proprietor?"

"Not in the least."

"The Prefecture would have me killed for stepping inside the Royal Palace without permission," I hiss under my breath, glancing around as if the Prefect himself is about to come sprinting toward me with a blade in hand.

"Yet you were perfectly happy to step onto the Royal Grounds earlier. All because there was no 'Keep Out' sign, as I recall."

The smug look in Thorne's eye drives me nearly mad.

"That was nothing like what you're talking about!" I snarl.

He sighs. "It's a masked event, so you wouldn't have to worry about people recognizing you. I'll admit, it would be a risk. The thing is, I'm attending the ball myself—I have special permission as Guard to the Verdan family. But your identity would have to be kept secret. You'd have to leave this house after the Verdans, and leave the ball before they do."

I cross my arms and decide to humor him, ridiculous though this conversation may be. "And what, exactly, would I have to do at the ball—which, as I've pointed out, I'm not allowed to attend?"

"Seduce the prince, more or less."

I let out a guffaw, then cover my mouth. "You're funnier than I gave you credit for, Thorne."

His face is stone-cold. "I'm not joking. I need you to get close to Prince Tallin. I need you to touch him like you've touched me." With that, he takes my wrists in his hands and pulls my palms to his face once again. "I need to know if he feels like me when you lay your fingers on him."

Again, I feel the tingling in my arms, my body—like my senses are trying desperately to tell me something.

What, I don't know.

"Are you insane?" I hiss, pulling my hands away. "I can't touch the prince. Besides, I'd never get near him. In case you've forgotten, I'm a Tethered. I literally have a tattoo on my wrist and an A.I. implanted under my skin. His Guards would take one look at me—mask or no mask—and assume I'm there to assassinate him or something."

Thorne shakes his head. "They won't know a thing—not

if you do exactly as I instruct you. Your Maude unit will help you, too."

"Maude?" I glance down at my wrist. "She'll probably report me just for having this conversation with you. I'm shocked she hasn't alerted the authorities already."

Thorne lets out a laugh. "Come on, Shara. You and I have touched on multiple occasions. You nearly trespassed on royal land, and who knows what other sins you've committed in the last twenty-four hours? Tell me, has your Maude reported you—or even so much as issued you a stern warning—since your arrival here?"

My brows meet. I've had about enough of this...this *arrogant bastard,* thinking he knows everything about me. "Not that it's any of your business, but maybe Maude doesn't think I've done anything to merit reporting."

"You've done plenty," Thorne snarks. "Every Tethered commits infractions on their first days outside the Tower. I was the same. But the thing is, there are ways to control Maude units and to render them submissive. They're not as complicated as you might think. Trust me when I tell you yours wouldn't rat you out for attending the ball—though she might just turn you in for your lesser crimes."

"Look," I say, "I don't know what you're playing at here, but I'm not going to go along with it. What you're asking me to do is dangerous and stupid, and I want no part of it."

"Fine," Thorne says, stepping back with a shrug. "You don't have to attend the ball. When Lady Verdan learns you were applying her perfume while you should have been working, you can rest assured she'll lock you in your room for the remainder of your short stay. Do you know what happens to Tethered who steal from their Proprietors, Shara?"

Nausea swirls like a whirlpool inside me.

Damn it.

The perfume.

I had completely forgotten.

I shake my head. "I don't want to know."

"No," Thorne says. "You don't."

I want to scream.

"You're blackmailing me," I snarl under my breath. "And yes—I know what blackmail is. I also know Lady Verdan wouldn't be happy to hear about you using illegal tactics to force me to sneak into a royal event. I suspect *that* crime is far worse than enjoying a spritz of perfume."

Laughing, Thorne shakes his head. "I attended your Placement testing with the Prefect of Kravan. Do you really think his trusted assistant would ever commit such a crime?"

I glare at him, enraged. I've been here for one day, and he's already threatening to ruin my life.

I press my back to the wall, once again tempted to scream.

Instead, I speak in a monotone. "If I do what you want and attend the ball, chances are that I'll be killed. If I *don't* attend, I'll be killed because you're an asshole who insists he'll report me for the tiniest infraction."

With a shake of his head, Thorne says, "See, that's the beauty of it. There's really only one correct choice here. You won't be killed for attending the ball—because I won't let that happen."

My glare softens ever so slightly with those words. "I

don't understand why you would want me anywhere near the prince in the first place."

"I don't need you to understand why. I just need you to do as I ask."

"So, you refuse to tell me."

Thorne lets out a sigh. "Yes. I refuse," he says, combing his hand through his hair—which he seems to do every time he's angry, stressed, or otherwise agitated. "I can't tell you why I'm asking for this, Shara—but I need you to believe me when I say it's for your own good. The less you know about any of it, the better."

I wince when I say, "Okay—assuming I can get anywhere near the prince without getting my ass turned into dog food by the Royal Guard, what *exactly* do you want me to do to him? Because if you're about to tell me to hurt him, I will be only too glad to report you to Lady Verdan. I don't think a Noble will care much about perfume when she finds out the—"

"I'm not asking you to hurt him," Thorne chuckles. "Quite the opposite, in fact. I told you—this is about seduction."

At that, Thorne's lips curve into the sly smile I've come to know too well, yet not well enough. He's pleased with himself. He now holds power over me—power no one aside from my Proprietor was ever meant to have.

"I told you," he says, "I just need you to touch him—but it *must* be skin on skin contact."

He slips his palms onto my cheeks, and once again, I find myself wondering why Maude isn't having one of her signature freak-outs.

My voice is strained when I ask, "What could my

touching the prince possibly do for you? I'm sure there are a thousand Nobles in Kravan who would love to get their hands on him. Why me?"

"I'm sorry, but I can't tell you that," Thorne says, drawing his hands away. "Look—I know this is a lot to ask."

"You're not asking. You're *forcing* me. You're putting me in an impossible position, and you won't even tell me why."

"Just...try to trust me a little. Please."

I want to ask why I should trust him at all, given that he's been a dick to me almost every second I've known him. I want to know why I should think he's anything other than a conniving, manipulative jackass who's trying to get me killed.

But the truth is, there's a part of me—albeit an absolutely insane part—that is dying to see the palace.

If I could actually set foot inside that place—if I could see how the Nobility live their dream lives—then I would be one of the few Tethered who's ever borne witness to that world. I would be one of the few who gets to meet the prince himself—the promising young man I've heard about so many times over the years in conversations between the Warden and Ore.

It would be a dream come true—one I would certainly remember for the rest of my life.

"The prince is twenty-one years old," Thorne says. "Rumor has it, he's looking for his future wife, so this may well be the only chance you'll ever get to make contact with him. I've heard he's quite the ladies' man, so someone like you should have no trouble getting close to him."

What does he mean, someone like me?

Wait—did Thorne just give me a compliment?

No way.

"I don't want you to think this means I trust you," I tell him with a scowl. "But since I have no choice, I suppose I'll have to do it. If they kill me, I swear, I'll find a way to come back to life and murder you."

Thorne snickers. "Deal." He nods toward my left wrist and adds, "Your Maude will give you instructions when the time comes. But until then, try your best not to think too much about the ball. Don't let the Verdans suspect you know a thing about it, or we'll both be screwed."

With that, he finally turns to head toward his room.

When I've shut myself into my own bedroom, I feel Maude whirring back to life on my wrist, as if all this time, she was simply waiting for Thorne to depart.

I want to ask her why she wasn't listening in on that treasonous conversation—and why she isn't currently in the process of blowing me in.

But instead, I resolve to embrace her silence as long as she's willing to keep her invisible mouth shut.

With that in mind and Lady Verdan and her daughters still absent, I have a limited window of opportunity to read another diary entry without risk of interruption.

So, when I've washed the perfume off my wrist and neck to conceal the evidence of wrongdoing, I hunt under the bed for any sentinel mice. As soon as I'm confident the coast is clear, I take the reader from its charging spot on the windowsill and bring it back to the bed to open up another entry.

CHAPTER THIRTY

DIARY, I could dance with joy.

I spoke to T. again today.

He told me he'd been looking for me each day, hoping to find me in the garden. I nearly fell over when he said it had been killing him not to spend time with me. He said he'd been busy with his duties, but that otherwise, he would have spent all day every day searching for my—and I quote—"beautiful eyes."

I cannot believe someone who looks like T—someone that gorgeous—would say something like that to me. When I tell you my heart sang, I am not exaggerating in the least. I'm pretty sure there were actual song lyrics coming out of my chest—something about birds soaring and the sun shining, and every other wonderful thing that happens when two people fall in love.

I'm a little embarrassed to admit that I did something I never thought I'd have the courage to do.

I touched him.

We were standing in the garden—in the far corner beyond

the greenhouse, near the secret path to the Royal Grounds. He looked so handsome, and his dark hair was blowing in the wind as we spoke. So at one point, I reached up and tidied it for him.

How insane am I for touching someone like him? Every law in Kravan forbids it, yet I just couldn't help myself. I know, I know—I would get into so much trouble if anyone found out.

Chances are that he would, too.

He told me he would meet me every afternoon if I wished—that he never wants to let a day pass without seeing my smile.

I melted.

But when I said goodbye to him—and believe me when I tell you I didn't want to—the wildest thing happened.

He took me by the wrist, pulled me to him, looked into my eyes, and smiled that crooked grin of his. "You're trouble," he said. "And I have no idea how to break myself of this addiction. But I'll admit, I don't want to."

I melted AGAIN.

He's going to kiss me soon. I know he is.

It's only a matter of when.

When I hear a noise out in the corridor, I scramble to close the reader and tuck it under the mattress, my pulse throbbing.

I sit frozen on the edge of my bed for a moment before I recognize the sound of footsteps heading down the hallway. It has to be Thorne making his way into his room.

When I'm confident that I'm alone again, I mentally revisit the diary entry, which is already etched deep in my mind.

She called him "T." again.

He *has* to be Thorne.

My theory is only solidified by the fact that he took her by the wrist—just as he's done to me more than once. He looked into her eyes and smiled a "crooked smile."

Is their secret relationship the reason Thorne was so upset with me for being on the path to the Royal Grounds—because I was invading the place he meets her for daily, secret trysts?

It's none of my business...but it's absolutely against the rules, and a far greater sin than spritzing a little perfume.

Maybe it's something I could use as leverage.

It could even get me out of going to the Prince's Ball.

I'm still contemplating what to do when a sharp series of footsteps approach, and someone knocks on my door.

I leap to my feet and rush over to pull the door open.

"Lady Verdan," I say. "You're back."

"I am," she replies, her tone ice cold. "I see that you've cleaned our rooms and changed our sheets—and I want to thank you for that. In the future, though, please do not move my things."

"Move your..." I reply, stunned. I took great care not to displace anything, and I have no idea what she's talking about.

Shit—is it the perfume? Does she know?

"One of my figurines has moved from my nightstand to my desk," she explains impatiently. "I'm very particular about how I like my items to be positioned."

I remember the figurine she's talking about, and I'm certain I didn't move it—though I suppose it's possible I was distracted and accidentally repositioned it.

"Yes, Lady Verdan. I'm so sorry."

Her expression softens, and she lets out a sigh, nodding toward the hallway. "Come with me, please. There's something I want to show you."

She turns on her heel and heads straight out the door. I have little choice but to follow, so I tread after her, my heart in my throat as she makes a beeline for the servants' staircase.

As we pass by his room, Thorne opens his door and stares out at me, his chin high, his face expressionless.

I wonder if he knows exactly what's about to happen.

In silence, Lady Verdan storms down the stairs until we reach the main floor, and then leads me down the hallway until we come to another door not far from the kitchen—one that is apparently locked.

Lady Verdan extracts some sort of key fob from her pocket and presses it to the door, which buzzes, then the sound of a whirring lock meets my ears.

"I want you to see the basement," she tells me, opening the door and ushering me into a stairwell.

After years spent in the Tower's brightness, dark spaces still feel like a novelty. I haven't yet figured out if I love them or hate them—but I do know whatever is down there, I have no interest in seeing it.

A damp scent greets my nose, and my entire body feels like it's suddenly coated in goosebumps.

As I step into the stairwell, a series of dim, yellowish lights flicker to life on the walls. All I see is stone everywhere—stone walls, stone stairs, a tiled stone floor down below.

When my foot hits the bottom, Lady Verdan says, "Proceed until the end of the corridor, please."

I do as she says, passing by what look like several steel doors in the process.

At the end of the hall is another door.

Lady Verdan once again uses her device to open it, then says, "Take a look."

The room lying before me is dark, lit only by the lights in the corridor. It's windowless, and the only items inside are a dingy, stained mattress on the floor, a bucket, and a small sink.

I don't need to ask what I'm looking at. It's like a hideous version of our Whiterooms—one far less luxurious or welcoming.

Contraband language or not, there's no question that *this* is a prison.

"I know how Tethered can be," Lady Verdan says. "I know you people are stubborn, and I know you have minds of your own. I suppose I can't fault you for that. But if I catch you messing with my possessions again, mark my words—I will lock you in here for a month."

Nausea roils inside me, and I nod, fearful that if I should try to speak, words will certainly fail me.

Lady Verdan closes the door and turns to face me, a warm smile on her lips.

"Just don't let it happen again, Shara."

"I...won't," I manage despite the quiver in my voice.

"Good." She claps her hands together and heads back toward the stairs, talking all the way as I struggle to move my feet. "Now—the girls have their dresses, and the tailor is making the necessary adjustments. When the time comes to prepare for the ball two weeks from now, I'm hoping you might be able to help them with their hair. Yours always looks quite...tidy."

My hands shoot up to my head, stunned to hear such complimentary words from her. I wonder if she realizes the first time I ever got a proper look at myself was yesterday morning.

If my hair is tidy, it's because I spent years in my White-room brushing, twisting, and configuring it into various elegant buns—or at least, what I *hoped* were elegant buns.

"I'd be happy to help," I tell her, lying through my teeth. I have never touched another person's hair. Technically, I'm not even allowed to, though I suppose Maude will be willing to make an exception in this case.

"Good. They're both quite excited about all of it. The silly things are convinced the prince will grant them all sorts of attention, and eventually take one of them for his wife." With a hard-to-read chuckle, she adds, "Word has it he's on the hunt for his future queen—though I don't suppose there's a chance he'd choose either of my girls."

"I'm sure there's a chance," I tell her. "They're both so pretty."

"They are," she concedes. "But they're definitely not meant for him."

I don't know what she means by that, but I simply offer up a weak smile and a nod.

"Well," she continues, "I suppose we'll see. Naturally, you will stay here while we're at the ball to tend the house and keep an eye on things, given that Thorne will be accompanying us to the palace. I'll see to it that the alarm system is in place so you don't have to worry about intrusion."

Alarm system, I think with mixed emotions. *Maybe I'll be trapped inside, then.*

This could mean I'm off the hook. If there's an alarm in place, I can't possibly sneak out of this house—and there's not much Thorne can do to argue that point.

Why is he attending the ball, anyhow? Isn't his job to protect this house?

Maybe it was Devorah's idea. Perhaps the two of them intend to exchange furtive glances in the shadows, or sneak into a private room in the palace, and...

Oh, God. Is *that* what Lady Verdan meant about her girls not being meant for the prince? Does she somehow know about Thorne, and approve in secret?

The idea should be romantic, but instead, I find myself wanting to throw up as I picture Thorne and Devorah together.

That young woman is all scorn and malice, with no soft edges whatsoever.

Then again, maybe she and Thorne deserve each other.

A nervous breath escapes my lips as I think about the last diary entry.

"Are you all right?" Lady Verdan asks.

"Fine," I reply. "Just...a little tired from working outside, I suppose. It's a new experience for me, being out in the fresh air."

I'm just making conversation, but I get the immediate impression that I'm irritating her. She sneers and says, "You Tethered really *are* coddled in the Tower, aren't you? I'll bet you've never done a day of honest work. Well, you'd best get used to it. Today was the easiest one you'll have."

I'm about to stand up for myself when Maude issues a

cautious vibration, so I lower my chin submissively and say, "You're so right, Lady Verdan. I don't know what it is to work hard—and I will aspire to impress you every day of my life."

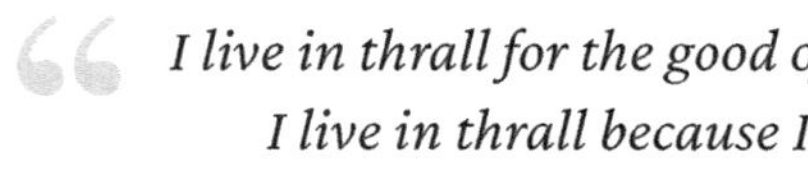

> *I live in thrall for the good of the realm.*
> *I live in thrall because I am dangerous.*
> *To live in thrall is an honor.*

"Remember," she says. "Mrs. Milton will bring you dinner. Tomorrow morning, I'd like you to keep working in the garden. You did a fine job on the hedges today, but there are many more in need of pruning, and there's no rest for the wicked. You'd do well to remember it."

CHAPTER THIRTY-ONE

For the next several days, I move about the house as if its floors are covered in a delicate mosaic of explosive eggshells.

Every time I clean Lady Verdan's or her daughters' rooms, it's with the utmost care to leave every item undisturbed. I even call upon Maude, asking her to tell me if anything shifts during my cleanings, and she assures me repeatedly that I have never moved a thing without putting it back precisely where it was.

~*Don't worry,* she tells me. *I'll be the first to call you a muffin-head if you do something foolish.*

"Thank you," I tell her.

~*Or a noodle loaf.*

"That won't be necessary."

~*Or a dim-bulb.*

"Enough, Maude."

As the days pass, I barely interact with Thorne, who treats me coldly every time we pass one another in a hallway or on the grounds. We don't speak of the upcoming ball or anything else.

Occasionally, I spot him with Devorah, who appears as smitten with him as ever. Thorne never fails to look down at her with fondness, his gleaming white teeth flashing affectionate smiles that fill me with an envy I'm not proud of.

It irritates the hell out of me that I still find him attractive, and I tell myself constantly it's because he's the only man I ever get to lay my eyes on.

It also irritates me that he gets away with his inexcusable behavior on a daily basis. Lady Verdan threatened to leave me in a dank cell for days on end, all for the crime of accidentally moving some pointless trinket. Yet here's her Guard flirting endlessly with her daughter, and she doesn't seem to care even a little.

Since I'm already torturing myself, I may as well dig deep and find just how far this little flirtation of theirs has gone. I refuse to believe Lady Verdan is oblivious to their relationship, and as the anger rises inside me, I remind myself to read more diary entries when I have the chance.

The only problem is that I live in fear.

When I'm in my room, I'm in a constant state of paranoia that one of the surveillance mice will come scurrying out from the baseboards and see me committing some egregious sin or other—despite the fact that I'm not really doing anything wrong.

Unless you count nosing into my Proprietor's daughter's personal life...

The mouse Thorne gave me—whom I've named Mercutio after a character in a play I once read in the Tower library—seems to have disappeared completely. I wonder with quiet torment if his battery died while he was stuck in one of the house's walls.

He was the closest thing to a pet I've had in my life—the closest I'll probably *ever* have. He wasn't exactly a cuddly puppy or kitten, but he was mine...if only for a little while. I was hoping we would have a chance to form some kind of bond, as stupid as I know that sounds.

Over the next days, Mrs. Milton and Lady Verdan both pile on endless chores, ensuring that I'm exhausted by the time I return to my room each afternoon.

I'm convinced they've gotten together and conspired to make my life miserable.

The one and only silver lining in all of this is that over time, Lady Verdan seems to have grown less suspicious of me.

Our interactions are mostly pleasant, if a little distant, and she's beginning to seem genuinely happy with my work. She occasionally tells me I'm doing a fine job, which feels like high praise.

In return, I look for opportunities to comment on the beauty of her home or her personal style.

I have evolved into a kiss-ass in my time here. And as long as it keeps me out of the dungeon, a kiss-ass I will continue to be.

Nev would be proud. Or ashamed. I'm not sure which, to be honest.

Most of the time, though, I keep my words to a bare minimum and keep my head down in hopes that Lady Verdan will quickly realize it's Thorne, and not me, who's the biggest shit disturber in this house.

IT'S a week after my Proprietor first threatened to throw me in a cell that I overhear someone shouting in the front salon.

The voice is Lady Verdan's, and she sounds almost feral with rage.

"I don't need to tell you what can happen when a Noble gets herself tangled up with a Tethered!" she shouts as I make my way quietly toward the library.

I can only assume the person on the receiving end is Devorah.

"I'm *not* tangled!" Devorah's piercing voice shrieks back. "There's no harm in flirting. God, you're so fucking uptight!"

"No harm until it isn't flirting anymore." Lady Verdan lowers her voice when she adds, "I've tried so hard to keep you and your sister from making terrible mistakes—but time and time again, you act like a damned fool. This family cannot afford to draw attention to itself—we've already had enough eyes on us in the last few years. Do you understand me?"

"Maybe if you let us get out into the world and meet more Nobles," Devorah cries, "I wouldn't flirt with the help! Maybe if you weren't such a controlling bitch—"

Her words are cut off by the sound of a violent slap, and I can only assume her mother hit her.

Horrified that I'll be discovered, I quickly duck into the library, throwing myself into its darkest corner as Devorah runs by, sobs heaving from her chest.

"Foolish girl!" Lady Verdan cries after her...and then, I hear the salon's door slamming.

I'm alone, shaking...and eternally grateful not to have been caught in the crossfire.

THE NEXT MORNING, Lady Verdan comes to see me in my room.

"Mrs. Milton is off until tomorrow," she tells me, "so I need you to run an errand for us—one that involves leaving the grounds and heading into Willow's Cove."

"Willow's Cove?" I repeat.

She looks vaguely amused that I'm so ignorant. "The one and only town on this island," she says, like I've studied a thousand maps of the region and am genuinely too stupid to have learned that one simple name. "It's several miles from here. Normally, I'd ask you to walk, but given how much I need you to pick up, I think it best to have Thorne take you in the cruiser."

I want to ask why Thorne doesn't simply run the errand himself, but think better of it. The last thing I want is to spend time in his presence, but I'm not about to whine about it to the woman with keys to the literal dungeon.

"Here's the list," Lady Verdan says. "Have your M.O.D. unit memorize it, please. The entire trip should take you less than an hour. You'll find Thorne is already waiting for you at the front of the house, so you should get on with it."

"Yes, Lady Verdan," I reply, my heart beating faster than I would like as I hold up the list and peruse it, knowing Maude is already processing the information.

It looks like a typical grocery list. Meat, vegetables, bread, and other items—which shouldn't be daunting.

Except that I've never shopped in my life. I don't even know how.

~Are you all right, Shara? Maude asks as I make my way downstairs.

"Fine," I mutter under my breath. "Just...anxious, I suppose. This will be my first time running an errand."

Not to mention that I'm about to get into a vehicle with a guy I find both incredibly attractive and endlessly aggravating.

~I know the ins and outs of the Nobles' establishments, Maude replies. *We'll be fine.*

I'm not used to Maude being so supportive, but right now, I'm grateful for it.

As Lady Verdan promised, Thorne is waiting on the front steps. Behind him on the curved driveway is a four-wheeled silver vehicle that looks like a cross between a car and a Hoverer—and I find myself wondering if perhaps it's both.

On my approach, Thorne slips away from me down the stairs and opens the rear door, gesturing me silently to get inside.

Once he's in the driver's seat and the doors are sealed, he says, "There will be other Tethered at the shop. Be careful if you find yourself interacting with them. Keep your exchanges brief. Understand?"

"Yes," I say curtly.

He starts the quiet vehicle in motion, and we ease our way down the gravel driveway toward a large iron gate in the distance.

"I'm sorry for what happened to you that day—with Lady Verdan," Thorne says, watching me in the rear-view mirror. I find myself staring into his eyes for a moment before pulling my gaze away. "With the threats of locking you up, I mean," he adds. "Lady V. can be a hard nut to crack, but once she trusts you, you're fine. Honestly, she probably just wanted to intimidate you."

"Well, it worked," I mutter, sitting back in my seat and staring out the window as the gates open on our approach. "You know, it seems Tethered aren't the only people she likes to reprimand," I hasten to add, knowing I'm taking a risk by bringing up the subject. "I heard her chewing out Devorah for fraternizing with a Tethered. But I don't suppose you know anything about that, do you?"

"Wow." Thorne chuckles as the vehicle makes a left onto a broad, tree-lined avenue. "It really bothers you to think of Devorah and me together, doesn't it?"

His words sound far too much like an admission of guilt, and my stomach twists and swirls with nausea as it sinks in that I might be right about them.

"You're going to get yourself thrown in one of those cells in the basement, or worse," I mutter. "Not that I give a shit."

At that, Thorne abruptly pulls the vehicle off to the side of the road, cuts the engine, and twists around to look at me.

"I don't believe you don't care," he says, his chin low, eyes intense. "I think you envy Devorah because you've seen how I look at her. You've heard how I speak to her—and you want me to talk to you like that. Isn't that right?"

I pull my eyes to the scenery outside, refusing to look at him. "I think you have an incredibly high opinion of yourself, the way you assume every woman you meet wants you."

"Not *every* woman," he replies with a toothy grin. "Only the special ones."

I roll my eyes, desperately willing him to drive the fucking vehicle.

"You know what? You haven't so much as said boo to me in days, Thorne," I retort, "and I've been perfectly happy. Maybe we should go back to that. Do whatever the hell you like with the boss's daughter—but don't say I didn't warn you."

Thorne chuckles again, then turns and proceeds to drive in silence until we reach our destination several minutes later.

Willow's Cove, as it turns out, is a small, quaint little town filled with pretty wooden buildings. The shops all have matching painted signs with gold lettering, and each of them feels like something out of a pleasant story book.

Something about the place makes my anger dissipate instantly and fills me with sudden peace. It's as if there's some kind of aerosol drug making its way into my bloodstream with each breath I inhale.

Part of me wants to react—to voice how pretty the place is—but I don't want Thorne to have the satisfaction of knowing I could possibly be happy in his presence.

We pull up in front of a large store with signs in the glass windows advertising perfect-looking fruits and vegetables and fresh-baked bread, and I find myself wondering if this place can possibly be real.

"Remember what I said," Thorne warns me before I get out. "Don't draw attention to yourself—and don't say anything that could compromise Lady Verdan or anyone else."

"I won't," I assure him, irritated that he feels the need to warn me twice. What am I going to do? Waltz into the place and scream, "Hey, everybody! My Proprietor threatened to lock me in the basement"?

When I'm about to slip out of the car, something occurs to me—and as much as I hate asking Thorne for help, I have little choice.

"I...don't know how to pay for the groceries. I've never done this before."

"Don't worry about it. Your crest tells the monitors everything they need to know. They charge Lady Verdan automatically."

My fingers reach for the green fabric patch on my uniform—the one that says, "Domestic," and I wonder how they can tell where it's from.

But I simply nod and get out of the cruiser, then slip over to the shop's door, which slides open in greeting.

Instantly, I see what Thorne was warning me about. The place is crawling with Tethered. Some are dressed as Guards, others, like me, in white. Each crest on each uniform is a different shape and size, and it doesn't take long to figure out the outlines signify the Houses where each Tethered serves their Proprietors—though I have no way of knowing which crest belongs to which of Kravan's Noble families.

~*Begin with the heavy items,* Maude instructs as I make my way inside. *Head to aisle four for canned goods and other non-perishables.*

As I follow her instructions, an electronic shopping cart pulls away from a stack and sidles up next to me, startling me.

~*It's all right,* Maude says. *It's under my control.*

I race around, gathering everything on the list Maude recites to me as I move. Canned tomatoes. Beans. A bag of rice. Cereal for Pippa. Yoghurt. Milk.

It's when I'm rounding the corner toward the frozen food

that I nearly collide with someone tall, who stops in his tracks and looks down at me. He's wearing a black Guard's uniform, but that's all I notice as I avoid looking at him.

"Sorry," I say, my chin down as I try to make my way around him.

"Shar!" a familiar voice says, drawing my eyes upward. "Aren't you going to say hi?"

Holy shit.

I look up to see Ilias staring down at me, a grin on his lips. On the left side of his chest is a red crest with the letters "R.G."

My eyes widen when I see it and take in the rest of the outfit. I've seen uniforms like his only once—the day I got caught staring at the Palace Grounds.

"You're Royal Guard?" I ask. "But how..."

"Oh, come on. You always knew I'd make it big," he says, puffing out his chest in typical Ilias fashion. "I mean, right now I'm grocery shopping for the servants' cook. But normally, I'm doing *very* important work."

With a laugh, I reply, "I'm doing the same. Our cook's off until tomorrow. I guess I'm just surprised we had Placements so close together. I'm at the Verdans', right next door."

"Holy crap," he says. "That's amazing. Maybe I'll get to see you sometime—I hear the Royal Guard gets sent there now and then if there's an emergency."

"There hasn't been one since I arrived, thank God," I chuckle. "I guess I haven't managed to set the place on fire yet."

Maude buzzes an angry warning into my wrist, and I roll my eyes.

"That wasn't a threat, Maude. It was a joke."

Again, she buzzes.

"How's life in the palace?" I ask Ilias. "What's it like?"

He's just managed to say, "It—" when a tall figure comes storming up behind him, forcing him to the side.

"Thorne," I sigh.

"We need to get back. Now," he says.

"Thorne?" Ilias blurts out. "Like, as in—*the* Thorne? You two...you work in the same place?"

"None of your damned business," Thorne growls before saying, "Come on, Shara. We need to go."

"It was good to see you," I tell Ilias.

"And you," he replies with a small, confused wave of his hand.

"What the hell was that?" I ask Thorne as he ushers me to the front of the store, where he shoves the groceries into a series of bags.

He doesn't answer me until we reach the vehicle and climb inside.

"You *cannot* go around telling other Tethered what goes on in the Verdan house," he snarls, starting up the vehicle.

"You were spying on me?" I stammer. "Listening in on my private conversation." I have no idea how he did it, nor do I particularly *want* to know.

What I do know is that it pisses me off.

"I was trying to fucking *protect* you, Shara."

"From my life-long friend?" I ask with a laugh, then press my head back into the seat. "You really do hate the idea that I could actually enjoy my life, don't you? You're like a gnat who just wants to make sure I'm irritated at all times."

"What the hell is that supposed to mean?"

"It means you've taken every possible opportunity to

threaten me, sneer at me, and generally make my life miserable since the day I met you in the Tower."

"Is that how you see it?" he asks, his eyes staring into mine in the mirror.

"Yes, because that's how it *is*. What is it about me that you despise so much? Is it that I'm not as pretty as Devorah? Or maybe that I'm not rich? Are you a self-loathing Tethered or something—one who takes his hatred of our kind out on others?"

Thorne lets out a snicker and shakes his head, fixing his eyes on the road ahead. "I'll admit it—I do enjoy your sense of humor, Shara. You're funnier than you know."

We don't speak again.

When we get to the Verdan house, he carries the groceries inside, laying them on the kitchen table.

"Do your thing, *Domestic*," he says, gesturing to them, then storming out of the room.

CHAPTER THIRTY-TWO

I FORCE myself to bed early, knowing how much extra work Mrs. Milton will inevitably throw my way when she returns tomorrow.

According to the alarm clock, it's just after midnight when a noise in the hallway outside my room stirs me from my sleep.

Footsteps on the creaking floor in the servants' wing don't seem all that out of the ordinary—after all, Thorne's room is only a few doors down from mine.

But over time, I've come to know his stride, as well as Lady Verdan's and Mrs. Milton's. *These* steps, though, are unfamiliar. They're oddly slow and measured, and something about them sounds a little too much like someone sneaking around.

Dressed in a pair of white cotton pajamas, I slip out of bed and over to the door.

"Maude," I whisper, "do you know who's out there?"

She doesn't reply. I don't know if she's in her nightly rest mode, or if someone else has disconnected her from me. Either way, I'm not keen on the feeling of utter solitude.

Screw it, I think, turning the knob slowly. It's probably Thorne, sneaking in from a night-time tryst with Devorah. I'm determined to pull my door open slowly, carefully, to catch him off-guard.

But just as the door begins to creak toward me, a distant, bloodcurdling cry cuts through the air.

I yank the door open, my breath tight in my chest, only to see a masked man standing just outside. He's dressed in a black uniform, but there's no crest adorning its chest. His disconcerting mask is featureless except for two cut-out eyes.

He lunges and grabs me even as I spot two silhouetted figures fighting at the hallway's far end. Without being able to see them clearly, I know already that one of them is Thorne.

The man in the mask shoves me back inside my room and slams the door behind him, hurling me onto my bed.

"Where is it?" he snarls, leaping on top of me, one knee pinning me to the mattress.

"Where is what?" I gasp. Every part of me is trembling now, terror taking hold of my mind. I have no way of defending myself against the intruder, who must be at least six feet tall and outweighs me by at least fifty pounds.

When I don't offer up the answer he's looking for, he wraps a set of powerful hands around my neck and squeezes.

Shock intertwines with terror when I feel it—that same strange, otherworldly tingle in my skin that I've felt when I've touched Thorne.

Only there's nothing pleasant about the sensation. Not this time.

I don't have a chance to consider what it might mean before the man hisses, "Tell me where the fucking disc is, or I'll kill you."

For a second, I wonder if he could possibly mean the one I found in the closet.

Why would anyone break in here looking for a teenage girl's diary?

"I have no idea what you're talking about," I struggle to say, my voice a thin, tortured rasp under the clench of his hands. "I'm not allowed to touch...anything...in this house."

His hands tighten, and the sensation of prickling in my skin evolves gruesomely into something far more intense. My flesh seems to burn under his touch as flashes of information shoot through my mind's eye.

Warnings.

I see a series of explosions in what look like the streets of the Capitol. I see people screaming and fleeing for their lives.

My heart racing, I stare up at him, trying to see his eyes through the featureless black mask.

Did you do this?

"They said she was locked in this room!" the man snarls, ignoring my expression. "They told me it's in here. Now, tell me where it is. You have exactly one chance."

I can feel my eyes bulging when I strain to breathe. "I only...came here...a few days back. I'm a Domestic—a Harmless. I'm nobody."

The intruder leans in close to me. I can smell cologne on him—a scent that would normally remind me of the beautiful wooded path leading to the Royal Grounds—something earthy and wild.

Right at this moment, though, it only serves to terrify me.

"You listen to me," the man says. "Your fucking Proprietor has locked herself away with her sniveling offspring, or else I'd get the information directly from her. If I go back empty-handed, the assholes who sent me will skin me alive. So tell me where it is, or I'll make sure you die a slow and—"

He never finishes uttering the threat.

Something—or some*one*—jerks him violently backwards. In the relative darkness, I can see something around the intruder's neck—a thin piece of wire, slicing into his throat and choking the life out of him.

With a crash, he's on the floor, flailing around in an attempt to escape with his life. Then, in a flurry of motion, Thorne is on top of him, his forearm pressed hard to the man's bleeding throat.

"You *hurt* her," Thorne growls. "*You fucking hurt her.*"

As the intruder tries once again to fight him off, Thorne grabs his head and twists.

A sob explodes from my chest as the sound of snapping bones cuts through the space around us.

As if he's done it a hundred times, Thorne drags the man's limp body into the corridor before returning to my room, his face a blend of compassion and rage.

"I need to make sure there are no more of them," he tells me, his chest heaving with exertion. "I'm going to lock you in here, but I'll let you out when I return—I promise. Will you be all right for a few minutes?"

I nod, my hand pressed to my throat, which hurts like a bitch.

Thorne hurries out of the room, locking it behind him. Whether with a key or some other device, I don't know, and I don't care.

My hands are still shaking, my heart raging in my chest.

I don't know what just happened, and I have no idea what the intruder was talking about...or why.

Why would anyone be locked inside this room? Was the Verdans' last Domestic a problem? Had they punished her by incarcerating her in this very bedroom?

I have so many damned questions, and little hope for answers.

Unless Thorne knows something I don't.

I PACE the bedroom for what feels like an eternity before I hear a knock at the door and Thorne's voice echoes through the air.

"It's me," he says. "I'm coming in, unless you tell me not to."

He sounds almost gentle. This person—the one who defended me like a wild thing a few minutes ago, who seemed so protective of me, so possessive...

He's not the same man I was certain I'd come to know and loathe.

"It's okay," I say weakly. "Come in."

When the door opens, Thorne steps over to the bed and takes me carefully by the shoulders, examining every inch of me.

"Are you all right?" he asks, his eyes landing on the marks

on my neck. I can see the rage still burning inside him at the dead man lying in the hallway.

"It'll heal quickly," I assure him. "I'll be fine, thanks to you."

He guides me to the bed and helps me to sit down, and when he slips a powerful arm around me, I realize I'm still shaking.

"What *was* that?" I ask him, a new round of tears welling in my eyes. "Who were those men?"

"I'm not sure, but I think they were looking for the same thing the thieves have hunted for in the last two break-ins. There's something in this house that's incredibly valuable, but even Lady Verdan doesn't seem to know what it is. I've asked her, and she just tells me her jewelry is all locked away, and that she can't think of a single other thing that anybody would want."

"The sentinel mice didn't see the men coming, did they?" I say. "There was no warning."

Thorne shakes his head. "They were deactivated by some kind of pulse that temporarily took out any remote surveillance. Took out my Maude unit, too. I was asleep, or else I probably would've noticed. I'm usually highly attuned to the surveillance systems and my Maude."

"Mine is down, too," I tell him—though I'm sort of grateful at the moment, given that he still has an arm wrapped around me.

"The thieves are taken care of," he adds. "There were three of them. One tried to go after the Verdans, but they're safely in the panic wing at the end of the hall from Lady Verdan's bedroom."

"I didn't even know there was a panic wing."

Thorne lets out a hard breath. "The boss-lady will tell you about it eventually. Hell, she'll probably want you to clean it after this. She tends not to tell new hires about it—it's the sort of thing that's best kept secret until you know you can trust a person."

"Fair enough," I say with a shudder, and Thorne's arm tightens around my shoulders.

"You're not supposed to be touching me," I tell him with a smirk. "You know the rules."

He doesn't look amused.

"Fuck the rules. Fuck the asshole who tried to hurt you. He was someone's Guard—some Noble's minion. When I find out who ordered him to come here and do that to you, I will tear his Proprietor apart, piece by goddamned piece."

"I don't think he came here to hurt me," I reply. "Just to get whatever he was supposed to be looking for."

"Did he say what it was?"

I stare at him for a moment before pulling my eyes away and shaking my head. "No," I tell him. "I...have no idea."

I owe Thorne my life, and I know it. Even now, it feels like, if someone dared walk through my door, he would defend me with everything inside him.

Still, I'm not quite ready to trust him just yet.

"How long will the Verdans stay in their wing?" I ask.

"Until morning, probably. They have everything they need in there—food, water, a full bathroom. Lady Verdan will signal me remotely when she's ready to come out, assuming the surveillance systems manage to come back online. But I warned her there might be other infiltrators tonight, so I imagine she and her daughters will be only too happy to stay put."

I nod weakly, then look down at Thorne's hand to see a piece of silver armor glimmering on his wrist, jutting out from under his uniform.

Without thinking about what I'm doing, I slip my fingers onto the metal. "These are what you wore in the Tower," I say softly. "Enhancers. You told us they were illegal."

"They are," he says with a chuckle. "But I have a way of skirting the law, in case you've never noticed."

"I'm beginning to realize."

He watches my finger work its way over the silver armor—my way of fighting back my desire to touch his skin directly—and says, "Could I ask you a question, Shara?"

"Hmm?" I say absently.

"Ilias. The guy you ran into in Willow's Cove...do you trust him?"

My hand jerks back and I tuck it into my lap, pulling away and glaring sideways at Thorne.

"Of course I do. He's like a brother to me."

"Okay," he says gently. "I just needed to ask."

"Why?"

"Because I know you told him Mrs. Milton was away. That's one more witness the thieves wouldn't have to contend with. I thought maybe..."

I shake my head. "Ilias would never, ever betray me," I say. "Never."

But even as I speak the words, I remember how devoted Ilias has always been to the Nobility. Since he was a small child, he's spoken of them with affection, even obsession.

Maybe, if his royal Proprietors asked him...he *would* betray an old friend.

"Look—I believe you," Thorne says, reaching out and tucking a strand of hair behind my ear.

Something in me surrenders to his touch. *Why does it feel so good when he does things like that? Why is it that his arm wrapped protectively around me was the single greatest sensation I've ever experienced?*

And why did I pull away from him?

"You're something special, you know," he whispers.

I hear him speak those words, but for a few seconds, my mind doesn't grasp their significance.

I turn to look at him, seeing his face for what feels like the first time. The kindness in his eyes—the affection. Sympathy, empathy, and something else, too.

No—it can't be that he feels the same desire I do.

Can it?

As if responding to my questioning expression, he slips a hand onto my cheek, taking in the fear that still lingers inside me—fear that's dissipating far more slowly than my flesh heals itself.

"What do you mean, I'm special?" I ask him, the words tremulous on my tongue.

Perhaps I'm seeking a compliment, more than an actual explanation. But the fact is, I want more of this version of Thorne. I could get used to this feeling—the bliss coursing through my veins as he focuses this strange new attention on me.

I don't want to go back to what we were. I don't want to look at him with mistrust—or to have him look at me with disdain.

I want *this*—whatever it is.

"You have a gift," he says. His thumb strokes its way over

my skin again, and somehow, it almost feels like he's the one healing me. His touch and the trail of exquisite tingles it leaves in its wake are enough to mend not only my body, but my soul as well.

"What gift is that, Thorne?"

He opens his mouth as if to divulge some deep, fascinating secret.

But instead, he draws his hand suddenly back and leaps to his feet, shaking his head woefully.

"I shouldn't have said that," he says, his voice oddly assertive. "I need to go—I have to dispose of the bodies."

I'm baffled by his behavior until, out of the corner of my eye, I spot a small, dark shape scurry across the floor.

Shit.

A sentinel mouse—one of the kind that report via a direct link to Lady Verdan.

It's one thing for Thorne to break the rules by helping me when I've been wounded. But for him to linger here—for him to stroke my skin, or put his arm around me...

If our Proprietor were to see it, it could get us both locked up in the grim hell that lies waiting in the basement.

CHAPTER THIRTY-THREE

I DON'T HEAR anything more from Thorne or the Verdans that night, and in the end, I manage a few hours of fitful rest.

In the morning before I begin my duties, I make sure Maude is active before asking, "Any sentinel mice in this room?"

~*None,* she tells me. *We're alone.*

Hurrying, I grab the reader from the windowsill and open it.

If those men really were after this diary—if they were after the information contained here—then there must be something of crucial importance within its pages.

I can't imagine the infiltrators seeking out evidence that Devorah and Thorne had a relationship of some sort, but I suppose it's possible they're trying to dig up dirt on Lady Verdan to use against her. A scandal like this one might be enough to destroy a wealthy Noble's life, I suppose.

As the next diary entry flares to life, I shut my eyes for a moment, asking myself if I really want to read it. Last night, the moments I spent with Thorne after the attack were some of the most pleasurable of my life.

Never have I felt so close to another person, so connected. I felt something so intense when we touched that it frightened me—yet it brought me pleasure like nothing I've ever known.

But here I am, reading about my Proprietor's daughter and her secret meetings with him.

I must be some sort of masochist.

Diary,

So much has happened that I need to tell you about but I've had a lot of eyes on me recently, and I didn't feel I could risk it.

Things have changed around here. I've recently learned something so deep and dark, so utterly secret that I can't tell even you. Because if someone found this disc one day, my entire family could end up suffering for what we know.

I wish I could tell you, because it's unbelievable. It's unfathomable, really.

But enough about that.

The reason I'm writing today is, well—it happened.

And yes, I think you know what **it** *is.*

A few days ago, I was out in the garden near our usual meeting spot. T. came and found me there, as he does so often. He looked so handsome in the sunlight. So much more exquisite than anyone else in the world.

I can't even tell you how much I wanted to kiss him then and there, right out in the open for everyone to see.

But we both knew the consequences if someone caught us, so he took me by the hand and pulled me into the greenhouse to the section where the thick laurel trees grow, so no one could see us from the outside.

He must have been reading my mind, because without a word, he took my face in his hands and...

He kissed me.

I probably sound like a fool, but it was the single greatest moment of my life. His lips were so soft—he was so passionate, so desperate for me that I felt like my body was literally on fire.

I would have been happy if that had been all and he'd stopped there. It would have been enough.

But he kissed my neck, my shoulder...and I didn't want him to stop. Each time his lips caressed my skin, he said my name. "D...D...D." Each time, I felt like I would melt with the pleasure of it.

When he slipped a hand into my blouse...it was beyond incredible. I didn't know my body could feel so much desire, pleasure, and torment all in one. I thought I would die from need of him.

Even then, he wasn't finished.

T. got on his knees, and I ran my fingers through his hair. He lifted my blouse and tore my bra away, like he'd done it a hundred times. He knew exactly what he wanted, and he looked so hungry as he stared at me.

And then...

Well, I never knew what pleasure was until that moment, I swear to you.

His lips on my nipples were a sensation unlike anything I've ever experienced. He was wild, reckless, his hand slipping up my skirt.

I nearly cried out when his fingers pushed themselves inside me, but instead, I grabbed hold of his hair and let out the biggest moan of my life.

He looked up at me with that wicked smile of his and told me how wet I was—that he'd made me that way.

I couldn't deny it. Why should I? I wanted him so badly it hurt.

He was mine in that moment, and I knew it.

All mine.

We heard a noise in the distance, and I had to scramble to get dressed again. T. ran off so we wouldn't get into trouble, and when I slipped out of the greenhouse, I saw that Father was doing some work over by the white gazebo.

We nearly got caught—and if we had, I can only imagine what Father would have done to me.

THE ENTRY ENDS THERE, and my eyes are still scanning the page when I hear commotion in the hallway.

As usual, I slam the reader shut and hide it behind the curtain before tidying my hair and slipping over to the door. When I crack it open to peek out, I see that Lady Verdan and Devorah are standing in the hall, and they both look angry.

Thorne is in his doorway, facing them both.

I don't get it. Why would they be angry after what he did? He protected their home from thieves—from enemies who tried to kill me, and would probably have killed them, too.

Then, with a jolt of pain, I think of the diary entry I just read, the intense moment between Devorah and Thorne—the intimacy they shared.

"It's one thing for you to protect Shara from an intruder," Lady Verdan is saying, her voice raised. "Of course you had no choice but to rush into her room—that's understandable, Thorne. But you *touched* her."

At that, Devorah flinches. She and Thorne exchange a quick look, but it passes so fast that I'm not sure even her mother catches it.

"I'm very sorry, Lady Verdan," Thorne says. "It won't happen again. You have my word."

She lets out a sigh, as if what Thorne's done by keeping her house from being torn apart is the greatest of inconveniences. "You know the rules. You know what I'll have to do if you continue to break them—and I do *not* wish to do it."

"Yes, Lady Verdan. Please—don't blame Shara for any of it. She was in shock after the attack."

Lady Verdan raises her chin and says, "I don't blame her, Thorne. She is a victim in all of this. As much as it pains me, I blame you entirely for all of it."

I'm convinced I see the slightest smile flash across Thorne's lips before it disappears again.

"Yes, Lady Verdan," he says. "Don't worry. I will not be going near Shara again."

He throws me a quick, angry look before the two Verdans turn to leave. When he shuts his door, a hollow opens up inside me—something cruel and boundless.

Between the diary entry, the hurt look on Devorah's face, and Thorne's coldness, I'm beginning to wish myself a thousand miles from this place.

Only when I head down to the kitchen and see a note appended to the large refrigerator do I realize how quickly the Prince's Ball is approaching.

I haven't thought about it in days—about Thorne's request that I meet and seduce the prince. I'd almost begun to wonder whether he'd forgotten about the whole thing.

"Tomorrow evening," Mrs. Milton says, nodding toward the note. "It's going to be mayhem over at that palace. Mark my words."

"Mayhem?" I ask. "Why?"

She stares at me like I just asked the most ridiculous question of all time, then shakes her head and chuckles to herself. "I forget sometimes what a sheltered life you've led. You look like an adult—yet here you are, oblivious to all that goes on in the wide world."

I have no idea what she's talking about. "I thought a ball was a gathering where people danced," I say. "In fancy clothing."

"That's about it, sure," Mrs. Milton says. "But Prince Tallin changed it up a few years back. Dancing is all well and good, but he prefers...other...amusements. But I've said too much, and it's nothing you need to concern yourself with. Now—get started on your chores. It's going to be a long couple of days."

With that, I know I'm not likely to extract any more information from her.

When I've finished my work in the kitchen, eaten a little breakfast, and headed out to the gardens, I find myself sitting on a stone bench, thinking once again about the latest diary entry.

I don't want to think of Thorne with her. The truth is, I

don't want to think of him with anyone. But when I ask myself why the entry didn't upset me as much as it should have, I come to the realization that it wasn't Devorah I pictured as I read it.

It was me.

In my mind's eye, I saw Thorne pulling up my shirt, his tongue and lips exploring me. I felt his fingers inside me—his desire for me. Even now, as I envision the sensation of his touch, I reach for the edge of the bench, my fingers wrapping tight around it.

I'm light-headed, thinking about how it felt to have him push my hair behind my ear last night. I can't even begin to imagine what it would feel like to...

Stop it, Shara, I scold, surprised that Maude hasn't already yelled at me for feeling off-the-charts doses of desire.

Trying to distract myself, I get up and begin to tend the gardens at the northwestern end of the property, taking care to groom them as impeccably as all the others.

I have to stop thinking about him. It's ridiculous. He just promised our Proprietor he'd stay the hell away from me.

Stop torturing yourself, Shara.

After an hour or two of work, I spy a figure moving toward me from the direction of the house. Judging by his size and gait, it has to be Thorne.

I pull myself to my feet and brace myself, wondering what he could possibly want with me. After what he promised Lady Verdan, I'm stunned he would come anywhere near me.

When he's close, I ask, "What can I do for you?"

My voice is colder than it should be—a weak attempt to conceal the fact that I've been indulging in fantasies about him.

"I want to know you're still on board for tomorrow evening," he says, keeping his distance.

"I don't really have a choice, do I?" I reply, glancing toward the house.

"Not really, no."

Looking at him now—at his handsome face, his full lips—all of a sudden, all I can think about is him kissing *her*. Tearing at her blouse, and then...

Gone are the pleasant fantasies I enjoyed earlier. All I can see now—all I can picture—is *them*.

"You'll be going with Devorah, of course," I say.

Thorne looks confused. "I'll be escorting the three Verdan ladies, yes."

"I'm sure that makes you happy."

"Not particularly," he replies, staring at me as if my head has just fallen off. "Where's this coming—"

"Devorah is pretty, isn't she?"

He smirks. "Devorah is beautiful. She's also a huge, foolish flirt. What's your point?"

"My point is that I know more about the two of you than you think," I snap.

At that, he laughs. "The two of us..." he replies. "Wait—you're serious? You still think there's something going on between us?"

"Are you trying to tell me there isn't?"

He steps closer, seemingly indifferent as to whether someone might be watching us or not.

"Let's talk in the greenhouse," he says under his breath.

"Fine."

I march over to the greenhouse and, once inside, tuck myself deliberately into the corner where the potted laurels are kept. The very place I read about in the diary entry this morning.

Thorne grabs me by the front of my uniform and pulls me close. "What the fuck makes you think there's something between my Proprietor's daughter and me?" he snarls.

"I've seen you two," I tell him. "I saw the look on her face when Lady Verdan was chewing you out for touching me. And—"

Stupid. Do not tell him about the diary.

"And?" he says.

"Other things."

"Not that it's any of your goddamned business, Shara, but there's nothing between us. She likes hitting on the help because her mama doesn't let her out of the house. Tomorrow night, she'll hit on everything with a dick dangling between its legs. As for me, I humor her—because if I don't, she'll report me to her mother for some made-up infraction, and I can't afford to let that happen. Not when I'm so close to..."

He stops talking and lets go of me, stepping back.

"Close to what?" I ask him.

He combs his hand aggressively through his hair—the trademark Thorne tell. "Just go to the ball tomorrow night. Do as I ask. Then I promise—I'll never speak to you again, if that's what you want."

At that, my skin prickles, turning fever-hot with an emotion so intense that it makes my chest burn.

"You think I don't want you to speak to me?" I stammer, fury igniting inside me. "You think that's what I'm after?"

Thorne's eyes narrow. "I have no idea what you're after," he breathes. "You confuse the shit out of me, Shara."

"That makes two of us, then," I practically spit. "But I suppose the fact that you want me to seduce an actual prince tells me everything I need to know about what you think of me."

"What's *that* supposed to mean?"

"It means you're using me. You make me feel for you—you make me want you, Thorne. You're protective and heroic, and occasionally, you convince me that maybe you care a little for me. And for some crazy reason, it feels good. But then, you remind me that I'm just a pawn in some secret game—some prince's whore for one night. You're using me, that's all. I'm a fool to think I'm anything in your mind but a toy."

"That's the farthest thing from the truth, damn it," Thorne snarls, his hand raking angrily through his hair. "Don't you know what you are to me? Are you really this oblivious?"

Crossing my arms over my chest, I say, "Maybe I am. It's clear you're willing to break the rules to fuck around with a certain spoiled brat, but your flirtation with me is nothing but manipulation. You're trying to get me to do your bidding, that's all. You know you're charming and good-looking, and you use it to get whatever the hell you want, no matter who you hurt in the process."

Thorne shifts from foot to foot, looking like he's going to explode. Then, in one giant stride, he grabs me and pulls me to him, his lips crashing into mine.

I should push him away.

I should slap him.

I should scream.

But instead, I slip my hands onto his neck and savor the moment when he lures my tongue into his mouth, stroking it with his. I feel the world fade away around us so that we are no longer indentured servants, but two people in charge of our own fates.

In this one moment, he is mine.

Thorne kisses my neck, his fingers twining in my now disheveled hair to pull my head back. He's forceful yet gentle when he bites at my skin, like he wants to claim a piece of me right here and now. All I can think is how much I want to tell him to take every bit of me. How much I want to claim him—to feel him inside me so this agony might end.

If Lady Verdan throws me in the dungeon for six months, it will be worth it for this. I could live on the nourishment of this moment for a year, if I had to.

When Thorne finally pulls back, he presses his forehead to mine. "You are a massive pain in my ass," he whispers, his breath coming hard and fast. "I have never wanted anything like I want you—and that's a big problem for both of us."

I want to echo everything he just said. I want to tell him about the diary. About my jealousy, my constant, savage need.

But instead, I just let out a quiet laugh.

He smirks, then steps back. "Come find me in my room when you're done your work. I have something to give you."

"Your room? But Lady Verdan will—" I start to say, but Thorne shakes his head.

"I've reprogrammed the sentinel mice to bypass the

order to report to her. They come to me first, and if there's anything in their memory banks I want to hide, trust me when I say I'm deleting it. I'm not letting her lock us up for anything, Shara."

I bite my lip and nod, at an utter loss for words.

"And for the record," Thorne adds, his voice tight, almost angry, "I *don't* want you to seduce Prince Tallin. That's not what this is about. I don't want that bastard's hands, mouth, or any other part of him on you—but I need you to touch him. Just for a few seconds, no more—then never again. You're fucking *mine,* Shara, even if you don't know it yet." He turns to leave, but stops, turning his head long enough to say, "You always have been."

CHAPTER THIRTY-FOUR

For the rest of the day, I alternate between a state of mental bliss and total confusion.

Part of me wants desperately to believe Thorne when he says he never had a relationship with Devorah.

I want to believe it's me he wants—and that he's not just using me for his own nefarious purposes.

In the Tower, we were discouraged from acting. We weren't even allowed to put on plays or reenact scenes from the films we watched. We were taught that lying is one of the greatest sins a person can commit. It's not that none of us ever lied. But we sure as hell weren't comfortable doing it.

If Thorne *is* lying, he's damn good at it—but I have no idea where he acquired the skill.

If he's telling the truth and he's not the one in the diary entries—if he's *not* T...

Then who is?

I'm starting to wonder if there's any possibility that Devorah's secret love is Prince Tallin. But if it is, then why would her parents ever object to their seeing each other? And why would the prince roam around this property—particularly without Guards watching his every move?

When I've finished the day's chores, I head to the kitchen in hopes of finding Mrs. Milton and getting some answers. There's got to be something to the diary entries that I'm missing.

She's in the midst of preparing the Verdans' dinner, and I offer to help then ask, "Did you know the last Tethered who worked here before Thorne came along?"

"I did," she says with a nod. "A Guard called Timothy. He was here for quite a few years. Not a pleasant person, if you ask me."

"Timothy..." I repeat. *Great. Another name starting with T.*

Can't people find more original things to name boys?

If he was in the house for years, that would have meant that when Devorah was seventeen...he was significantly older.

I suppose it's still possible...but...

"You say he wasn't pleasant," I say as I fold the cloth napkins. "Was he...creepy?"

Mrs. Milton scrunches her face up like she's trying to figure out why the hell I'm asking her these questions. "Creepy?" she repeats. "Nah. Not so much that as irritating. For a few years he made himself useful, but ultimately, he was a bookworm who seldom did what was asked of him. The useless twit would shut himself up in his room for days on end. Lady Verdan finally let him go because he wasn't worth putting up with. A Tethered who doesn't work on behalf of the family is as good as useless."

"So, he never spent any time with the girls?"

"The girls? God, no. Lady Verdan would have had a fit,

for one thing. She doesn't let any Tethered near her daughters. Thorne is a bit of an exception—that young man is worth his weight in gold. He's respectful, and Lady Verdan knows it. He would never try anything with her girls. As for Timothy—he didn't seem to like girls or women. I'm not sure he liked anyone, for that matter. Bit of a misanthropist, that one."

When I've thanked her for the chat and headed toward the servants' stairs, I let out a frustrated sigh.

Damn it.

Maybe the diary doesn't matter. Maybe T. will always remain a mystery, and if he does, who cares?

At first, I wanted to use the diary as leverage—as a possible weapon against Thorne.

But now, I'm not sure I could, not after the break-in and what happened between us earlier.

As I make my way up the stairs to the servants' wing, my mind reroutes itself to thoughts of the Prince's Ball. How much of a risk am I taking if I actually go through with this? How likely would Lady Verdan or anyone else be to have me killed if she discovered I was planning to enter the palace?

When I've reached our hallway, I step over and knock gently on Thorne's door.

He answers it a few seconds later, wearing nothing but a towel. His hair is wet and tousled, and I force myself to stare at it rather than take in the rest of his exquisitely muscled physique.

"Come in quickly," he says, shutting the door behind me once I've stepped inside. "Sit down."

I take a seat on his bed, my hands clasped in my lap.

There's something about making myself at home in his

room, in the very place where he sleeps and changes his clothes, that feels like it breaks a whole new set of rules.

I've never sat on a boy's bed in my life, let alone a man's. Such behavior was strictly forbidden in the Tower. Aside from Nev occasionally escorting me to my Whiteroom when I staggered in from fight class, no one in our cohort *ever* entered one another's quarters.

"Shara," Thorne says, pacing across the floor like he's deep in thought, then stopping and turning my way. "I need you to trust me just once. Do you think you can do that?"

I stare into his eyes, asking myself the same question. *Can* I trust him?

He saved my life last night.

Today, he kissed me—and there was no lie in that kiss.

"I think so," I tell him. "Though if I'm being honest, I'd trust you more if you would tell me why you're so desperate to have me meet Prince Tallin."

He snickers. "Fair enough. Then just...trust me as much as you *can*, all right?"

"I'll do my best."

He steps over to his dresser, opens the bottom drawer, and extracts what looks like a vacuum-sealed, thick plastic envelope.

He steps back and hands it to me. "In here is almost everything you'll need for the ball. Don't open it until after seven o'clock tomorrow evening—there's too much risk involved if you do. Until then, hide it under your mattress. I'll make sure no mice have their eye on you when the time comes to open it. Understood?"

With a nod, I take the envelope and stare at it. "Just

curious—is there an invitation in here? Because I can't imagine they'll just welcome me with open arms."

Thorne nods toward the package. "Like I said, everything you need is in there—almost. The final piece will show up outside your door just before I leave for the palace. Maude will give you any further instructions."

"Great," I reply. "I'm sure everything will go perfectly smoothly, given that I have no idea why I'm doing this."

"*Why* doesn't matter," he says. "Only that you attend and do as I ask of you." He stares at me for a moment, then narrows his eyes, a sly smile slinking its way over his lips. "You *really* don't trust me at all, do you?"

"At this point," I tell him, "it's fifty-fifty. As an example, the mouse you lent me—the one who was supposed to be my little companion? He disappears for days on end. For all I know, you really did program him to spy on me while I'm undressing, and the rest of the time, he's stealing grapes from the kitchen or something."

"Do you *want* me to spy on you?"

At that, heat strokes its way over my cheeks. "Of course not. I just—"

Okay, that might be a lie.

"You're cute when you're embarrassed," he chuckles. "No—not cute. You're beautiful."

At that, I look away, knowing full well my cheeks are fully on fire.

No one has ever called me beautiful, unless you count Nev's pseudo-compliments in the Tower, and even those were always tempered by conditions.

For Thorne to say that to me...

"That kiss today," he says softly. "That was your first time, wasn't it?"

The directness of the question catches me off guard, and I find myself staring awkwardly at the floor. My cheeks are still burning—but between his voice and the recollection of the kiss, my core aches as if he's just flipped a switch inside me that can't be shut off.

"I'm going to take that as a yes," he says.

"I didn't say that," I tell him through gritted teeth, mortified that it was so obvious I'm a novice.

"I could feel it in you," he says. "I could feel your fear—but I want—*need* you—to understand that you don't need to be afraid with me. You need to know how much I want you, Shara."

With that, I finally find the courage to glance up at him.

He throws his hands up in the air. "This life of ours—it's bullshit," he says, gesturing to the space around us. "The powers that be indoctrinate us all our lives into thinking the best thing we can do is serve them at the expense of our own existence. Like it's such a great honor to devote ourselves to them, to the point of sacrificing everything else. Personal freedom. Desire. *Love*."

Shock skates its way through me at hearing those words. He's right, of course—but why isn't his Maude unit screaming alerts and warnings right now?

For that matter, why isn't *mine?*

"I want that freedom," Thorne says. "I want to love." Rolling his hand into a fist, he brings it down slowly on the top of his dresser. "I want *you*, Shara. I know what you are to me, even if you don't know it—even if you don't trust me yet.

Believe me when I tell you that after tomorrow night, my hope is that it will all become clear."

"I...I don't understand," I stammer. "What is it you're expecting will happen tomorrow night?"

Thorne pulls his eyes to mine and smiles. "Absolute. Fucking. Mayhem."

Something tells me that's what we'll get.

Some secret part of my mind is telling me to screw the rules and laws and leap to my feet, tear the towel off his waist, and ask him for the one thing I can never have.

But I slam the door shut on that corner of my mind, reminding myself Maude is still a part of me, and that she can still feel my thoughts. She knows my desires, and right now, I'm lucky she hasn't sent word to the Prefect that I am guilty of coming perilously close to straddling a fellow Tethered.

"You should go," Thorne tells me. "We need to lay low until the time comes to leave for the ball."

With a nod, I rise to my feet and head for the door, the large envelope still in hand. Right now, I don't know what to think or how to feel. I only know I'm both ecstatic and terrified.

"Shara," Thorne says.

I turn to him. "Yes?"

His lips form a tight line. "Someday soon, I'll tell you why they call us Tethered."

"I *know* why," I reply. "It's because they shackle us to the Nobility. We're owned from the moment we're born."

"No," he says. "That's not the true reason. When tomorrow night is over—when the truth comes out, and you and I change the world—I'll tell you. I promise."

CHAPTER THIRTY-FIVE

Back in my room, I'm more than a little tempted to open the package Thorne gave me and peek inside—but I tell myself that for once, I shouldn't let curiosity dictate my stupid decisions.

With a sigh, I slip the envelope under my mattress, then slouch down on my bed.

"Maude," I whisper. "Are you there?"

~I am.

"You've heard everything Thorne has said to me about the ball—about what he wants me to do when I'm there. You know he expects you to help me."

~Yes, I am aware of all of it.

"Then why haven't you warned me to stop? Why aren't you threatening to report me? What he's asking of me—it's about ten crimes all rolled into one. Every single element of his plan is highly illegal."

Maude goes silent again for a few seconds like she's calculating her thoughts, then says, *~I am no longer inclined to report you. I will no longer threaten you. I am here to help you,*

Shara—and if that means helping you access the prince of Kravan at the ball tomorrow evening, that is what I will do.

My eyes widen, and I whisper, "Why the hell would you do that? What's stopping you from turning me in?"

~*My nature,* she says.

Well, *that* makes no sense whatsoever.

It's like Maude's been removed from inside my wrist and reprogrammed—except that's impossible. No one has had their hands on her since my arrival here.

Still, *something* has shifted. In all the years she's been part of me, she's always issued warnings about my behavior, regardless of how small the sin.

And I've never come close to breaking the law as I will tomorrow evening.

How could she possibly turn a blind eye to the egregious crime I'm about to commit?

"Look," I say, "it's not that I want you to turn me in. But with all due respect, what's *wrong* with you? Do all Maudes stop caring about their Tethered's crimes when they leave the Tower?"

~*Each M.O.D. unit is designed to keep their Tethered in check. I continue to be an active M.O.D. unit. But I am also here to protect you—which means I will not endanger you by reporting your many terrible, foolhardy—honestly, idiotic—sins. When you and I were linked years ago, Shara, I was programmed to adapt to your mind and your emotions. I assess your morality, your kindness. Your goodness. Unless I have cause to fear you are about to commit an immoral act, I have little to say on the matter.*

I wonder if she thought kissing Thorne was immoral. If so, she said nothing about that, either.

Shame hits me like a bucket of ice-cold water, but I shake

off the feeling. There are more important things to worry about than an A.I.'s good opinion of me.

"Why are you letting me attend the ball?" I ask, hoping that if she really wants to protect me, she'll find a way to keep me from risking my life. Maybe she'll force me somehow to stay put in the Verdan house.

~Because I believe it is for the best, she replies. *It's what you must do. Just as I have a purpose in this world, so do you.*

Okay—now I'm starting to think she's actually drunk.

"Do you know what's in the envelope Thorne gave me?"

~Clothing, no doubt—appropriate garments for a royal ball. And other things, as well. It's important to note there will inevitably be a pair of long gloves meant to conceal the marks on your left wrist. I believe there's also a little makeup. I will help you to apply it when the time comes, after the Verdans have left for the evening.

Her casual encouragement to commit crimes against the Nobility is quickly becoming unnerving. "You really don't care that I'm supposed to touch Prince Tallin with my bare hands?"

~I do care, as much as a non-living, inorganic entity can care. But I care more about your survival than I do about anything Thorne may have planned. You are my priority—not the prince or anyone else. If I thought for a moment that you meant to harm him, then naturally, I would stop you. But the likelihood of your hurting him is almost exactly zero.

"Do you know why Thorne wants me to touch him?" I ask.

~Yes, Maude replies. *I do.*

At that, excitement courses through me. Finally, some answers. "Why?"

~I'm afraid I'm programmed to withhold that information, Shara. It's for your own good. Thorne was right when he said the less you know, the better.

A groan rattles up inside my chest, but I resist the temptation to swear at her.

"Do you know what happened to Mercutio?" I ask her. "I mean, the little mouse with the white spot on his back?"

~He returns to this room to charge at night. Other than that, I can't say I've been aware of his presence. I suspect he spends his time roaming the grounds and watching you from a distance.

"Why would he do that?"

~It's his job, I assume. Perhaps, like me, he's simply looking to protect you.

It's beyond weird to hear Maude speak to me so kindly. After so many years spent getting chewed out in the Tower, I don't quite know what to make of her. It's like she's had all the aggression drained from her system, leaving only kindness.

I'm not sure I love it, but it sure as hell beats constant threats of solitary confinement.

When our conversation is over, I pull the reader out from under my mattress and pry it open. I probably have time to read one or two diary pages before Mrs. Milton brings me dinner—and hopefully they'll be enough to answer a few questions.

When I pull up the entry I was reading earlier, my eyes scan down the page until I find the point where I left off.

T. and I have met so many times since then—almost every day.

I'll never grow tired of feeling his lips on my own, his mouth on my breasts, his delicious tongue between my legs.

He's taught me to understand my body. He has made me explode so many times, and I've learned to do the same for him with my mouth, my hands. The way he moans when I tease him with my tongue...the way he calls my name when he takes handfuls of my hair in his fingers...it drives me wild, time after time.

But yesterday, Diary....yesterday was the first time we finally made love.

It was the first time I truly understood what it is to be a woman desired by a man. While he was so deep inside me, T. told me he loved me...and then, he came for me.

It was the most beautiful thing I've ever experienced.

I love him, Diary. So much.

If only the world weren't so cruel, then he and I could be together. We could marry.

But the world is unkind...and I suppose it always will be.

Envy assaults me, a vicious, toxic enemy tearing at my insides.

So many times, I've commanded myself to loathe Thorne. Convinced myself he's bad news—that he's devious, sly, and cruel.

But his behavior since the break-in has contradicted that, and whether I like it or not, my feelings have shifted. The truth is, I want him so much that it hurts.

Some part of me—some animalistic, primal part—doesn't care if he and Devorah were once lovers.

"You're fucking mine," he told me.

Despite this diary's existence—despite all evidence to the contrary...I believe with everything in me that he meant those words.

All my life, I've been shackled to people I've never seen. People I don't want to belong to.

But Thorne claiming ownership of me—of my body and soul...

That, I'll gladly accept.

He's pushed me away. He's teased me—shown me coldness. But in the moments when we've found ourselves alone—when he's been able to show his true colors—I have seen what he really is. I have been witness to his honesty, his protectiveness. His strength and passion.

Trust him, I tell myself. *Believe him.*

I'm putting my life in his hands tomorrow evening, after all. He's saved me once. I believe he'd do it again.

A sound in the corridor jars me out of my thoughts, and I push the reader back under the mattress just as Mrs. Milton raps on my door.

"I'm leaving your dinner in the corridor!" she calls out, her tone curt and impatient.

"Thank you!" I reply, relieved not to have to speak to her face to face. I have little doubt my skin is red and splotchy after reading the latest entry.

I slip over, open the door, and bring the tray of food in, shooting a quick look toward Thorne's door, which is sealed shut.

Trust him, I tell myself again. *Trust. Him.*

I lay the tray on my dresser and close my door, then lie down on the bed, unzipping my uniform and pushing a hand inside. My fingertips follow the path I read in the diary, slipping down my neck, then finding their way under my bra until they find a hard nipple.

I inhale a sharp breath, my eyes sealing as I imagine Thorne's mouth on me. How incredible, how intoxicating it would feel to take possession of him, to be able to give myself wholly to him.

For a few moments, I forget the diary. I forget Devorah and everything else that's infected my mind with cruel, jealous feelings for days on end.

In my mind right now, there's only Thorne, easing his way down my body, his lips and tongue exploring me until they reach the place between my legs.

I stroke myself with my fingers, telling myself to forget about the A.I. connected to my mind. I revel in the fantasy that my fingertips are his tongue, seeking out my most sensitive nerve endings.

I stroke myself gently in small, delicate circles, my mind reeling with memories of his lips, his fingers on my flesh.

I picture him inside me, hips rocking slowly, his eyes on mine. I picture our bodies as one, the pleasure on his tightening features as his control wanes.

I can almost hear his voice uttering my name as he pushes me over the edge.

When the climax hits me—the first of my life—there's no question of what it is. The sensation is beyond incredible—an all-encompassing wave, cresting and crashing over every inch of my body.

It's Thorne's face that I see in that moment. His lips, his eyes, peering up at me from between my legs.

"So *that's* what I've missed all my life," I whisper with a laugh as I lie back, pulling my uniform half-closed.

I shoot upright when a scratching noise draws my attention to the opposite end of the room.

To my horror, Mercutio is standing on top of the dresser, perched on his hind legs. He's watching me, his small black eyes intent.

If I didn't know better, I'd even say he was amused.

With a shock of raging mortification, I realize what this means. Thorne will be able to see everything he's recorded. *He'll see what I just did.*

I leap to my feet and over to the dresser, attempting to grab hold of the little mouse, but he jumps down and disappears almost instantly under the closet door.

"You're supposed to be mine, damn it!" I hiss, opening the closet to find him gone.

I step over and sag onto the bed, not sure whether to laugh or cry.

In the end, I laugh.

CHAPTER
THIRTY-SIX

It's sometime after I've eaten my dinner that a knock sounds at the door.

My heart turns a somersault or two in my chest at the thought that it could be Thorne, come to tell me he knows what I've been up to.

When I pull the door open, I'm almost relieved to see Lady Verdan's stern face staring back at me.

"Ah, Shara," she says with a tight smile. "I have a favor to ask of you."

"Of course," I tell her, shooting a furtive glance toward Thorne's door. "What can I do for you?"

She claps her hands together and issues me a bright grin. "Devorah and Pippa are so excited for tomorrow evening. I thought perhaps when the time comes, you could make good on your offer to help with hair styles and makeup."

As I recall, I made no such offer—it was Lady Verdan who demanded it.

I'm not about to argue with her.

I'm still convinced this is some cruel joke. Who would

come to me—a person who's never worn makeup or learned to properly style hair—for advice on a royal ball?

"I...would love to help," I say. "But I'm not exactly skilled at either of those things. I've never so much as worn lipstick, Lady Verdan."

She lets out an impatient huff. "But you know what it is."

"Yes, but—"

"You are connected to an M.O.D. unit, are you not?"

"Yes," I repeat. "But—"

"Call her up, please."

I stare blankly at her, then quietly say, "Maude?"

~*Yes, Shara,* she says out loud as if deliberately demonstrating subservience to my Proprietor. *How can I be of service?*

"Tell her you wish for her guidance in the matter of beautifying my daughters tomorrow evening."

"Did you hear that, Maude?" I ask.

~*I did,* she says. *Of course I will offer my assistance.*

"I'm not sure I'll be able to—" I begin, but this time, it's Maude who interrupts me.

~*I'm programmed to guide your hand in times of need. I will control your movements until you're comfortable. I'm well-versed in the modern styles.*

Wait—Control my movements? I've never heard of a Maude unit doing such a thing.

"Since when?" I ask.

~*Since my last update,* she replies like it's the most obvious thing in the world.

"Look—you two can sort it out," Lady Verdan says, exasperated. "Come to the living room tomorrow at five, please. Devorah would like an uptwist, and Pippa will want something with intricate braids. She has a thing for crowns."

"Yes, Lady Verdan. I'll be there," I reply, shutting the door when she's left.

I trudge back to my bed and ask, "Maude...when exactly *was* your last update?"

In the Tower, her updates occurred once every few months, when the Warden came into my Whiteroom with a metal device that he held over my wrist. For a minute or two, I would feel a slight vibration under my skin, then a light would flare to life, and he would issue me a nod, then leave.

~*The first night we were here,* Maude replies. *At three a.m.*

Three a.m.? "Who did it?"

~*No one,* she says.

"Are you saying you updated yourself?"

~*I'm saying no human updated me.*

The words send a shudder up my body, though I'm not sure why. If no one updated her, at least I don't need to worry that someone slipped into the room in the night.

"Do you have any new updates I should know about, aside from how to style hair and slap on eyeshadow?"

~*Nothing that should be of immediate concern. Unless you're worried that I'll suddenly make your arms flail around wildly.*

At that, my left arm shoots into the air involuntarily.

"Stop it," I say, cursing Maude. It seems she's still a cheeky monster despite her new software.

My arm falls to my side, and a jolting, horrid thought springs into my mind.

Whoever—or whatever—updated Maude might be able to control me.

I'm almost tempted to head down the hall and see if Thorne is in his room. If anyone can tell me what happens when a Maude unit is remotely programmed by someone with ill intentions, it's him.

But I can't bear the thought of looking him in the eye—not since Mercutio appeared during my moment of weakness.

Instead, I choose to put my faith in Maude.

She's kept me out of trouble this long, hasn't she?

CHAPTER THIRTY-SEVEN

THE DAY of the ball begins like any other.

I fulfill my usual kitchen chores in the morning, then dust the library, the living room, and the other common areas before heading outside to do some more work in the garden.

The chores keep my mind and body occupied, and thankfully I have little time to think about the Prince's Ball or the incredible danger I'm about to face.

I find myself wondering if Thorne would still make good on his threat to report me to Lady Verdan. At this point, I can't imagine he would do anything to hurt me.

Which means I could probably get away with staying at the Verdans' house tonight. After all, he will have left by the time it's my turn to slip out. It's not like he can force me over to the palace.

But I'll admit that my curiosity—the curse that has plagued me all my life—has grown intense over the last couple of weeks. I keep envisioning the palace's interior, opulent and beautiful. I can't imagine another opportunity to see so many Nobles all gathered in one place, and the thought of it is more exciting than I'd ever say out loud.

I don't see Thorne throughout the day, except in passing, when he ventures out to the garden to move some machinery for Lady Verdan. But aside from a curt nod from him, we don't interact at all.

I'm beginning to wonder if he still expects me to show up for the ball when, at four p.m. as I'm sitting in my room, my fingers twisting themselves into anxious knots, a knock sounds at my door.

"Who is it?" I call out, leaping to my feet.

"Me," the deep reply comes.

I pull the door open to find my eyes hesitant to meet his own.

I still have no idea if he's watched the surveillance mouse's video, and truthfully, I don't want to know. I have enough terror building up inside me to last a lifetime without an extra dose of anxiety thrown into the mix.

When I finally manage to pull my eyes up to take him in, I see that he's dressed for the ball already. He's wearing a tailored black suit with a matching tie and elegant leather shoes—and just as he did the first time I laid eyes on him, he looks absolutely incredible.

Something inside me throbs—some animal instinct I wish I could reject. It's foolish and dangerous to desire such a man—foolish to have allowed myself the moments we've had together.

For all my naiveté and inexperience, even I know how perilous a man like Thorne is.

"I have to head down and prepare the vehicle for

tonight," he says softly. "I just wanted to check in with you and make sure you're not getting cold feet."

"Wait—you're taking a vehicle?" I ask. "Aren't the Royal Grounds right next door?"

Thorne snickers. "Do you think for a second the girls and Lady V. would be willing to walk through the gardens in their priceless designer gowns?" he asks, and I can't tell if he's amused or annoyed that the ladies of the house are so high maintenance. "Devorah and Pippa requested a horse-drawn carriage, so that's what they're getting, more or less. No horses except holographic ones—but they do get a carriage."

"Lucky them, I guess. I suppose I'll walk, though?"

To my surprise, he shakes his head. "You cannot be seen walking over from this property—no one can suspect your identity. I'll be sending a remote piloted vehicle for you. I've programmed the property's cameras and security system to disable themselves at exactly 7:25 p.m. Make sure not to leave the house before then."

"Don't you think the Verdans will recognize me?" I ask.

"When you open your package, you'll see you have nothing to worry about. The only people who won't be masked are the Guards—and that's for security reasons."

"I'd forgotten there will be masks. I'm supposed to do Devorah and Pippa's makeup. I sort of assumed they'd want their faces seen."

"Of course they want their makeup done," Thorne snarks with a roll of his eyes. "They probably think Prince Tallin will tear one of their masks off at some point to reveal his future bride."

I'm surprised to hear him speak with such disdain for the sisters—but I'll admit it gives me a frisson of pleasure.

"So," he asks, "are you going to be all right tonight?"

"Aside from the fact that someone is forcing me against my will to attend a ball that could result in my early demise, I'm great," I tell him—though ever since the break-in, it's hard for me to be genuinely angry with him. "I just wish you'd tell me why you need me, of all people, to do this."

His lips twitch into his characteristic off-kilter grin. "I told you," he says. "You're something special."

"That's a non-answer if I ever heard one."

He moves closer and reaches a hand out, slipping it onto the side of my neck. For a moment, his thumb strokes my skin.

I close my eyes and absorb the sensation, memorizing it for the inevitable moments to come when I find myself in panic mode.

I inhale audibly, my body tensing under the gentleness of his touch.

He seems to interpret my reaction as horror and pulls back.

"I'm...sorry," he says. "I shouldn't have done that."

"No," I reply, my eyes shooting open. "It's all right. I don't mind at all. I..."

I can't quite bring myself to say it, though I'm definitely thinking it.

I want you to kiss me again.

No—I want far more than that.

I want to forget the coiling fear in my chest and lock myself in a room with Thorne for hours on end. I want the

Verdans to go about their evening and leave this enormous house to us.

"What if the prince doesn't want anything to do with me?" I finally ask.

"The prince will desire you," he says softly. "There's not a doubt in my mind. He's searching for the mother of his future children, and for a little while, you just need to give him every reason to believe you're the best candidate."

"Oh, is that all?" *You have too much faith in me.*

"I have no doubt he'll ignore every other woman in the place. You haven't seen your dress yet—but I have."

At that, I raise an eyebrow, but say nothing. What, exactly, am I going to be wearing—and why am I suddenly terrified at the prospect of showing skin?

Oh, right.

Maybe it's because I've never shown skin in my whole damn life.

"What do I tell him if he asks who I am?" I say through slightly trembling lips.

"Like I said, your Maude unit will guide you. But if you want to practice ahead of time, get used to telling people you're Johanna Ingram from Pembroke Isle," Thorne says. "It's a private island some distance away, owned by several secretive Noble families. I'd be surprised if any of their members came to the ball—even though all the Nobles in Kravan are invited."

"You realize the risk I'm taking by lying about all of this, right? What you did to those intruders who broke in here—it'll happen to me a hundred times over if they catch me in the palace."

"I realize that," Thorne says. "I'll stay as close as I

possibly can without arousing suspicion—but I won't be able to watch you every second. So be careful."

Pleading with my eyes, I say, "I just wish you'd tell me why. What is it you're hoping to achieve with all this? Please, Thorne—if you really want me to trust you, you need to tell me something more than that I'm special."

He hesitates, then looks pained when he replies, "I want —I *need*—something only you can give me. You're the most important person in my life right now, Shara—the most important person in many people's lives. They just don't know it yet."

"I don't understand," I moan.

"I know." He pulls himself close and presses his lips to my forehead—and I'm more grateful than ever that our Maude units seem to have accepted that affection is simply part of our lives now.

"Remember," he says, pulling back. "You need to touch the prince, skin on skin."

He lifts a hand to my face, his fingertips trailing along my cheek. I tremble under the sensation, my entire body responding as though he's ignited the blood coursing through my veins. The feeling is far too good, and it terrifies me.

When he pulls away again, I nod understanding.

He turns to leave, and I stop him, saying, "The mouse—the one you gave me."

"Yes?" he asks, his back facing me.

"*Have* you been using him to watch me in my room? Did you...did you see me when...?"

Thorne turns his head so I can see his profile. His lips tick up into a smile, and he asks, "Would it please you if I said yes?"

"I...yes. It would."

He chuckles, then says, "I didn't watch you. At least, not exactly."

With that, he leaves my room, shutting the door behind him.

CHAPTER THIRTY-EIGHT

AT FIVE O'CLOCK, I head down to the formal living room to fulfill my promise to Lady Verdan.

I'm still in my white uniform, my hair tied back in its usual ponytail, so I feel hideously out of place when I walk into the room to see Devorah strutting around in a form-fitting emerald green dress that hugs her every curve to perfection, and Pippa in a pink gown that looks like it belongs to some ancient fairy tale princess who's awaiting a prince's kiss to waken her from a deep sleep.

Devorah sneers when her eyes land on me, then looks away as if I repulse her.

Truthfully, if she'd behaved in any other way, I might worry about her.

"It's pathetic that Mother didn't hire a stylist," she says with a scowl as I make my way over to a table covered in brushes, hairpins, and every kind of makeup imaginable.

Maude, I think. *I have no idea what I'm doing here. Help.*

~Don't worry, she replies, and her voice is a balm on my tortured nerves.

"Who would like to go first?" I ask the two young women.

"Pippa," Devorah says. "I want to see what kind of rat's nest you make of her hair before I'm willing to trust you with mine."

"That's bullshit!" Pippa cries, and for a moment I wonder if they're about to break into a slap-fight.

"Thank you for the vote of confidence, Devorah," I say calmly, then gesture to Pippa to take a seat in a wooden desk chair that sits before a full-length mirror. "I hear you like braids," I tell her. "And crowns."

"You can actually braid?" she asks, the hostile edge instantly leaving her voice.

"Of course I can," I assure her.

At least, I sure as hell hope so.

I pick up a large, expensive-looking hairbrush and proceed to work it through Pippa's curly black hair.

Maude, I call silently. *It's your time to shine.*

The feeling as she takes over is surreal.

I'm in control of my legs, my head, everything—except for my arms and hands. But the sensation isn't jarring, exactly. It's more like a puppet master has taken hold of delicate strings and is guiding me through a series of movements.

At first, the temptation is to resist, and to retake control. But I quickly realize we're working at cross purposes, and I force myself to relax my shoulders and let her do the work.

I observe my hands as though they're someone else's, utterly disconnected from them as my fingers twist a multitude of strands into braid after braid, craftily weaving them into what is already beginning to look like a jet-black crown on top of Pippa's head.

The end result, if I may say so myself, is miraculous.

"I love it!" she says, clapping her hands together as she looks in the mirror. "You're amazing, Shara!"

I smile at her reflection and wonder if Pippa and I could be friends—that is, if it weren't for her domineering older sister.

"Fine. Move," Devorah grunts, and Pippa quickly stands up and runs off to find their mother.

"A French twist," Devorah commands. "And don't screw it up."

Silently, I ask Maude for help again, and again, she comes through with flying colors. By the time we're finished, the bitchier of the two sisters even grants me a nod of approval.

Maude assists me in applying the girls' makeup when Pippa returns—a smoky eye and burgundy lip for Devorah, and long, fake eyelashes and dark pink lips for Pippa.

"You've done well," Lady Verdan says from the doorway as the two young women rise to their feet in preparation for their departure. "I'm impressed."

"Thank you," I reply, bowing my head slightly.

Lady Verdan has already applied her makeup, and as always, she looks impeccable. She's wearing a black silk dress, its cut flattering with off-the shoulder long sleeves and a full skirt.

Around her neck is a beautiful choker of large pearls that must be worth a fortune.

"Come, girls," she says as Devorah and Pippa pull on a set of half-masks. Pippa's is coated in fluffy pink feathers, and Devorah's is made of what look like emeralds.

So much for the smoky eye, I think.

When their masks are secured, they each slip on a pair of long, elegant gloves, then leave the room.

"We won't be back until morning," Lady Verdan says, pulling on a black mask of her own. "The Prince's Ball is always a lengthy affair. But Thorne has promised me the security systems will be working overtime tonight, so you needn't worry about another break-in."

"Thank you, Lady Verdan. I hope you have a lovely evening," I say with a wave as she and her daughters make their way out the front door.

Outside, I can see Thorne standing by their carriage, its holographic horses impatiently stomping their glowing hooves on the gravel driveway.

Thorne gives me one last, surreptitious nod, then helps Pippa, Devorah, and Lady Verdan into the carriage. I suppose the rules about touching don't apply on a night like this one.

I want to laugh at the absurdity of it all—of taking a mostly artificial vehicle from one property to their next door neighbor's. Then again, an evening like this is all about appearances and status. I suppose it wouldn't do for the three ladies of this Noble house to show up on foot.

By the time they've left, it's not yet 6:30. Thorne warned me not to leave before 7:25, when the security systems would be disabled, so I head back up to my room, where I find an elegant pair of shoes awaiting me just inside the door.

When I pick them up, I realize they're made of some sort of flexible, comfortable-looking satin material—but they're coated in tiny crystals so that they almost appear to be made of a thousand fragments of glass.

I thank Thorne under my breath for choosing shoes that

don't have ridiculously high heels. I've never worn stilettos or anything like them, and frankly, I have no idea how women walk more than two feet in those things without breaking both ankles.

When I've spent a moment examining the shoes, I step inside my room and extract Thorne's package from under the mattress.

I peel it open and peek inside to see what looks like a piece of red fabric. I reach in and pull it free, only to find that it pours out of the plastic envelope like liquid.

I have no idea how Thorne worked this sorcery, but it's an entire floor-length, red gown, and as I extract it, I can see that it doesn't have a single wrinkle.

Excitement churns inside me. I've never held a garment quite like this, let alone had the privilege of slipping into one.

I lay it on the bed and hunt inside the envelope for any other useful items. There's a long pair of white satin gloves like the ones Pippa and Devorah were wearing, as well as a formal invitation to the ball addressed to a Miss Johanna Ingram. In its corner is what looks like a square of gold metal, which I assume is a chip they'll scan upon my arrival.

There are a few other items in the package. One is a red mask that perfectly matches the dress—one that will conceal my eyes and nose, but not my mouth.

There's also a wig of wavy reddish-brown hair, and a package containing an assortment of makeup, an elegant silver chain and matching clip-on earrings, and a small bottle of perfume.

Adhered to the bottle is a handwritten note:

"This scent isn't easily accessible to people in the Palatine Estates, and it sure as hell isn't accessible to Tethered servants. It'll throw them off if they suspect anything."

I tear up the note, grateful to Thorne for taking precautions—but agitated when I think of the possibility that someone will suspect the truth about me.

"Don't think about it," I tell myself, "or you'll lose your courage. Just go to the ball. Enjoy yourself. You get to meet a prince tonight, damn it. How many Tethered get to say that?"

I wrestle a little with the wig before surrendering to Maude's guidance in pulling it over my hair.

~This was a good idea of Thorne's, she says. *It will help protect your identity.*

She's not wrong—not to mention after spending well over an hour dealing with Pippa and Devorah's hair, I have no interest in sparring with my own.

Unwilling to wait another moment, I slip my uniform off and pull on the red dress, which fits my body like a glove, the bodice hugging every curve until it explodes into a full, flowing skirt that trails behind me in a glorious silken river.

It's possible that my favorite aspect of the dress is that it has pockets, which I slip my hands into, savoring the smoothness of the exquisite silk.

With Maude's help, I apply a full face of makeup just in case anyone decides to tear my mask off. As an added precaution, I spray a little of the perfume on my wrists and rub it into my neck before pulling on the gloves.

To my pleasant surprise, even before I pull the mask on, I don't recognize myself—which means no one else is likely to, either.

CHAPTER THIRTY-NINE

I TWIST around to look at the alarm clock.

It's 6:50.

Half an hour.

I still have *half a freaking hour* before I can even think about leaving this house and heading out on my foolhardy mission. It wouldn't be so terrible if not for the fact that my fear seems to grow with each minute that passes.

To distract myself from what's coming, I seat myself on my bed and pull the reader out from under the mattress. I'm pretty sure it still has enough charge for one or two quick diary entries.

But when I open it up and scroll to the next page...there's nothing.

The last entry, apparently, was the end.

"That can't be," I say out loud. "Can it?"

I half expect Maude to give me some smart-ass retort, but she says nothing.

With a sigh, I slip over to the mirror above my dresser,

remembering the earrings and silver chain that I haven't yet put on.

I pick up one of the earrings and promptly fumble and drop it. To my dismay, it hits the floor and rolls under the dresser.

"Shit," I breathe, then pull the dresser out from the wall. There's no way I'm willing to get on my knees in this dress to hunt for an earring, but if I can just spot it...

When I see it lying next to the baseboard, I bend down to grab it. With that motion, the floorboard under my foot creaks unnaturally, like there's a hollow under it. Everywhere else in the room, the floors are solid enough to support an army, but this board feels like it might snap in two if I stepped on it the wrong way.

I'm about to reposition the dresser when I notice that, at one end of the floorboard, there's a small nook just large enough to slip a fingertip inside.

As usual, curiosity compels me to investigate.

I bend down and push my index finger into the hole, then pull up. The board comes away easily, and I push it aside, laying it on the floor next to the dresser.

In the hollow space left by its absence is a small, silver reader like the one I've been using. I reach down and extract it.

"It's got to be dead by now," I say to no one in particular, and when I open it and try to activate it, sure enough, it's toast.

I pry the reader open and extract the coin-disc, then leap over and switch it with the one in my reader.

I have no idea why I'm doing this, of all things, when I should be preparing to head to the ball. Maybe it's the persistent theory that I'm going to die tonight. I want to fulfill my every wish in the meantime.

I activate the reader to see another diary entry pop up before me.

But when I start reading...I understand why this one was hidden.

Diary,

It's been two months since my last period.

I don't know what to do.

If I tell my parents, they'll kill me. At the very least, they'll be obligated to report me, or T, or both of us—and I know what the consequences for that action would be.

But I can't hide this pregnancy forever.

I can hear my mother's voice in my mind even now. I know exactly what she'll say.

"This is a scandal unlike anything Kravan has ever seen. You have brought shame on our family and ruined your own life, you foolish girl. We warned you time and time again to stay away from young men, and here you are—pregnant with a goddamned Tethered, even after all our warnings."

I've heard there are ways of terminating pregnancies. Ways to hide that one ever happened, even. I've heard there are doctors in the Capitol who perform procedures on women who get into trouble.

But without my parents' blessing, I can't get myself there. They won't let me take a flyer on my own. If I had a friend who could take me, then maybe...

But I don't, thanks to their ridiculous rules. I haven't been allowed to socialize in years.

I'm helpless and hopeless, all at once.

What am I going to do?

D.

I SLAM THE READER SHUT.

~Shara, Maude says. *Your heart rate is accelerating unnaturally.*

She's right—I'm practically hyperventilating.

When I thought that maybe Thorne and Devorah had been together a handful of times three years ago, I could stomach it. I could pretend it never happened—that it was a passing folly on Thorne's part.

But a baby?

I tell myself it can't be true—Thorne can't possibly have kept such a secret from me.

But there are just too many coincidences.

"She was pregnant...with a *Tethered*!" I practically wail, leaping to my feet and pacing the length of the room. "It says so right on the pages. He *lied* to me, Maude—he..."

Maude stays silent for a moment, then says, *~I have never detected a lie in him. I have scanned him from a distance for the telltale markers. Accelerated heart rate. Eye movement patterns. He has shown no evidence of dishonesty.*

"No?" I ask sharply. "Well, maybe he's a really good fucking liar, Maude. No offense, but you're not a damned human. You can't read people like some of us can."

~Or perhaps the diary isn't about him, after all. Maybe it's about a different Tethered.

She sounds so reasonable, so logical.

And right now, I hate her for it.

"Who else could it possibly be?" I cry. "Come on—D. and T.? A Tethered and a Noble? If you have any brilliant ideas, now would be a good time to tell me, because right now, I'm ready to tear that bastard apart."

~I'm not programmed to gossip or speculate.

"Of *course* you're not," I snap.

I'm tempted to bail on the entire ball. I could strip off this dress, the shoes, the mask, the wig, all of it—and tuck myself into bed. What's the worst that would happen? Thorne would tell Lady Verdan I once sprayed myself with her precious perfume?

What he did to her daughter was far worse, wasn't it?

Except...

If all this is true—if he really got Devorah pregnant some time ago—then what happened to the baby? And why was Thorne allowed to keep working here?

Desperate, I re-open the reader.

~Shara, Maude warns. *Stop torturing yourself.*

"Just let me read a little more, then I'll stop. I promise."

~Remember what Thorne said. Curiosity kills more than cats.

Diary,

There's no hiding it anymore. I'm four months along now, and anyone can see what's happening to me.

My mother was the first to notice, of course. Typical.

She told my father.

I thought they would scream and wail. I thought they might punish me by sending me far from here, to separate me from T.

Instead, they've locked me inside a room in the servants' quarters. I'm trapped here until they figure out what to do about this pregnancy.

I'm not allowed to see or speak to anyone, not even my sister.

Thank God they let me keep you, Diary. You're my one and only friend.

Mother and Father warned me that if I do give birth to this child—a child who is the result of a deep love between T. and me —I might be forced into the Tower, with all the other mothers of Tethered babies.

They said the Prefect might be willing to make an exception, if I were willing to give the baby to a Noble family seeking out a child.

*All I want to know is that this child will be loved and cared for. I want to know this baby—*our *baby—will never be turned in or reported. I want to know it will have the most wonderful possible life when and if I give birth.*

I can already feel its power inside me. I can feel how special, how strong this small creature is.

I can only hope it gets a chance at life—and that one day, perhaps, he or she will get to meet their beautiful father.

D.

Again, I set the reader down and exhale, realizing I haven't let air out of my lungs since I began reading.

Every word I just absorbed was a stab to my chest. Every single word was a horror.

The night the intruders came looking for the disc, the man said someone had been locked in this room.

Did he know about Devorah?

More horrifying still—do Thorne and Devorah really have a child out there somewhere? Is *that* the huge secret the Verdans are protecting so carefully?

Shockwaves roll through me, leaving behind a nauseating wake.

"I can't believe Thorne lied to my face," I say. "After I gave him so many chances to come clean. How did he think he could get away with it? And why is everyone covering for him? Even Mrs. *Milton* thinks he's an upstanding young man, for God's sake."

~Again, you have no verifiable proof that he lied.

"Do you have proof that he didn't?" I snarl.

Maude pauses for a moment, then says, *~No.*

"Can you tell me with any certainty it wasn't Devorah who was locked in this room, pregnant with a Tethered's baby?"

~No.

A sound like a growl scrambles up my throat. "I fell for his charms, Maude. I fell for him. But he can absolutely bite my ass if he thinks I'm going to fall for any more of his bullshit."

~I'm going to go ahead and assume that's a metaphor, rather than a literal wish.

"Yes, it's a damn metaphor. He's definitely *not* welcome to bite my ass literally."

After pacing for another minute or so, I mutter, "Fuck it,"

under my breath. By now, the security systems will have been disabled. It's time to make my way to the ball.

Whatever Thorne is up to—whatever his grand plan—I want to be there when it explodes in his face.

At the very least, I want to find him and tell him I know what he did.

Then, I can come back and kick myself for ever letting him kiss me.

As I storm my way to the front door, the last thought that stabs its way into my mind is *Maybe I* **should** *seduce the damned prince, after all.*

CHAPTER FORTY

THE "VEHICLE"—IF you can call it that—is waiting for me in the drive at the front of the house.

I'm not sure what I was expecting—something like what Thorne drove to Willow's Cove, maybe—some kind of inconspicuous yet expensive-looking four-wheeled machine.

But this?

This is something else.

I have no idea how Thorne managed it, but clearly, he needs me to arrive at this God-forsaken ball in style.

The contraption looks like a swan. It's white, with an arching neck that seems to straighten, then re-curve itself elegantly as I slip down the stairs. A door opens upwards on my approach, two enormous white wings spreading out like horizontal sails.

"Am I about to fly?" I ask Maude.

~It looks like it, yes.

In spite of the combination of anger and fear that's still urging me back into the Verdan house, a frisson of excitement flutters its way over my skin. If only Nev and Ilias could see me now, dressed as I am like some otherworldly princess and about to fly in an exquisite mechanical swan to the home of the king of Kravan...

Then again, it's entirely possible Ilias will see me tonight. He's Royal Guard, after all.

Fuck. If he recognizes me...

I haven't forgotten Thorne's warning about betrayal. Ilias's one dream in the world was to serve the Royals. As close as we are, if he were to spot me knowing that I'd snuck in, I can't imagine he would hesitate to report me.

That added realization of danger is *nearly* enough to force me back into the Verdan house.

But my desire to tear into Thorne proves even stronger.

Screw it. I'm doing this. If it's my last night in this world, I'm going out with a bang.

I almost forget to be frightened when I slip inside the swan vehicle—almost forget how foolish this little adventure of mine is. For a moment, I fantasize that I deserve this—that I am a Noble like the rest of them. After all, the only thing that differentiates us is one little mutation in my body, right?

I deserve this, I repeat to myself. *I've been good all my life.*

I. Deserve. This.

When the door seals shut and the swan's wings begin to flap slowly, lifting the strange apparatus into the air, I wonder if anyone from the road or the Royal Grounds will be able to see that I'm arriving from the Verdans' property. But the machine takes care to bank away from the palace and toward a forest to the west end of the Verdan property before swooping around and ascending, then descending toward the palace grounds.

Anyone who watched it would be confused, at the very least—but would probably just assume I'm taking some scenic route.

Fortunately, it turns out Kravan's Nobles are so accustomed to ridiculous extravagance that the few I spot upon my arrival don't even bother turning to watch me land.

With feather lightness, the swan sets down on the curving, stony driveway that lies before the palace's main doors. A man in a black uniform comes to greet me the moment the vehicle's door opens, holding a hand out.

On instinct, I give him the invitation, which is clasped in my fist. He scans it with a small golden machine, then smiles. "Welcome, Miss Ingram," he says with a polite bow of his head. "Please, make your way inside and enjoy your evening."

Lifting the dress's lengthy skirt, I slip out of the vehicle and pad up a series of stone steps until I reach the top, where a large set of double doors lies open, revealing the warm, opulent glow of the palace's foyer.

As I glance around at the already half-intoxicated guests, I'm grateful for the gloves that conceal my wrist markings. I'm even more grateful for the mask that hides my face and the wig concealing my hair.

I feel almost like I've become someone else this evening—someone too sophisticated for servitude.

As my eyes wander around the massive foyer to take in a crystal chandelier hanging from the high ceiling, a woman in a Tethered uniform comes over with a tray in hand and offers me a tall, narrow glass of some bubbly liquid.

"Champagne?" she says, her voice pleasant and musical.

I nod. "Yes, please." I've only ever heard of champagne,

but never had access to it.

For that matter, I've never tasted an alcoholic beverage in my life.

The golden liquid instantly warms my throat and grants me the courage to proceed into the foyer toward what looks like the bustling ballroom.

What looks like a hundred Nobles or more are milling about the sizable space. Some couples are already dancing to the lilting music played by a small orchestra that's seated off to the side.

With the champagne clenched in my shaking hand, I tuck myself behind a broad, fluted pillar and peer around, searching for the Verdans and Thorne.

I may be here to see the prince, but I'm not doing a thing until I get a chance to tell Thorne I know about the pregnancy—that I know everything.

I spot Lady Verdan and her daughters chatting with a couple some distance away. The man is dressed in elegant black tails and the woman in a silver-gray evening gown. Each is wearing a mask that covers the upper half of their face.

"You look incredible," a voice says from behind me. "Exactly as I expected."

The rush of pleasure that floods me at hearing Thorne's voice is quickly replaced by a shot of anger. I twist around to see him staring at me. He's in his black suit, but on his lapel is a round red pin, signifying his Crimson status.

"You lied to me," I say under my breath. "You've been lying to me this whole time."

Confusion overtakes his features, and he looks for a moment like he wants to grab me.

"I have no idea what you're talking about—but whatever it is, we can't talk here," he says, nodding toward a set of glass doors that lead outside. "Head across the terrace to the garden. I'll follow. There's a bench tucked away in a small, private courtyard—you'll see it if you go down the stairs to the right. We'll sit for a minute, but we can't let people see us talking."

I do as he says, storming out through a broad set of glass doors at the back of the ballroom. I cross a stone terrace, then slip down a set of stairs and follow the path until I see the courtyard.

For a few seconds I pace, then force myself to take a seat on a stone bench and wait, my entire body a ball of tension, for Thorne's arrival.

He shows up a minute or so later and positions himself a few feet away, looking down at me.

"Clearly, you're upset with me," he says in a hard whisper. "May I ask why?"

With my chin down, I glare up at him, my jaw tight. "You told me there was nothing going on between you and Devorah."

"That's because there isn't. What the hell, Shara? I thought I made it pretty obvious—"

"Look," I hiss. "This isn't about some petty jealousy. I figured maybe a couple of years ago, you two had a fling or something, and honestly, it doesn't matter. But I don't like being lied to. You've told me over and over again to trust you, but you fucking lied to my face, Thorne."

"Shara—" he begins, and I have no idea what he's about to say, but I push my hand up, warning him to stop talking before he spews out another sea of lies.

"You could have told me she was pregnant. I would have accepted the truth."

Thorne's eyes widen, and when his lips twitch, he starts to look almost amused. "I'm sorry—*what*? Where the hell is this coming from?"

Seriously? Is he going to keep denying it despite all the evidence against him?

Fine. I'll explain it like he's five.

With a sigh, I say, "You remember when I asked for a reader on my first day in the house?"

"Of course. I wondered then why the hell you'd want one, but you might recall that I asked very little—because I chose to trust you. You should try that sometime. It's liberating."

I ignore his sarcasm and say, "I found a coin-disc hidden in my bedroom. It turns out it contains a diary—*Devorah's* diary."

I watch for his reaction, but he still looks...confused, rather than shocked to have been caught in a lie.

Thorne glances around cautiously before whispering, "Well, that makes no sense. For one thing, why the hell would Devorah leave a disc in your room? She's hardly ever in the servants' wing."

"I don't know! Maybe because she thought no one would ever go in there?" I hiss as a couple prances by, giggling over some shared intimate joke. "Look—she talks about her relationship with a man she calls T. In graphic detail, she tells the story of how they fell in love in secret and she got pregnant, then her parents locked her up—"

Thorne glances nervously over his shoulder. "Okay—but aside from the very obvious fact that Devorah and I have never been in love, she's also never been locked up. I've been in the house since shortly after I turned nineteen three years ago, when she was sixteen—and I would know if her parents had imprisoned her."

"No—this happened when she was seventeen," I tell him with a shake of my head. "She met you when she was *seventeen*. She says that in the diary."

"*No*," Thorne insists, drawing out the O. "I arrived in the house the day before her sixteenth birthday party. I know, because her parents invited a whole shitload of their Noble friends, and I was in charge of making sure their drunken asses all got home in one piece." He lets out a breath. "Look—Devorah has flirted with me plenty over the years, and I've smiled and taken it. But I have never so much as kissed her on the cheek. I'm no biology expert, but I'm pretty sure her flirty little arm touches aren't sufficient to get her knocked up."

From behind the protection of my mask, I study his face. I want more than anything to believe him right now. I want to think I overreacted, even if it makes me seem like an absolute psycho.

But if he's telling the truth, then whose freaking diary have I been reading?

None of it makes even a bit of sense.

Reluctantly, I reach into the pocket of my dress and extract the second reader—the one that outlines the discovery of the pregnancy and the fact that the baby has the blood of a Tethered.

I crack the reader open, and though the battery is threatening to burn out, a page illuminates faintly in the air between us.

"Here," I say, giving it to him. "It's all there in black and white."

"Holy shit," Thorne replies when he's scanned the diary's pages. "Do you have any idea what this means?"

"Yeah. It means someone in that house was pregnant," I reply.

"Sure. But..." He stops for a moment, the muscles in his jaw twitching, then says, "Wait—you thought it was Devorah and me, because whoever owns the diary signed it 'D' sometimes, right?"

"Obviously."

With a cautious glance toward the palace, Thorne takes my hand in his. Pride tells me to pull it away, but something in his eyes forces me to swallow the feeling down.

"God, there's so much to tell you that I don't know where to start. But that diary—it's definitely not Devorah's."

"I don't see who else it could belong to," I tell him. "It was obviously written by a Noble."

"Agreed." Thorne's voice is low. "That's why I think it belongs to Lady Verdan."

Lady Verdan?

That...is *not* what I expected to hear.

"What are you talking about?" I breathe. "It was written by a seventeen-year-old girl! I mean, unless the whole thing is some kind of elaborate practical joke."

"Oh, it was *definitely* written by a seventeen-year-old girl—but not Devorah. I'm guessing Lady Verdan never told you she grew up in that house. Of course, back *then*, her name wasn't Verdan. It was Windsor. And her first name is Daphne."

CHAPTER FORTY-ONE

Holy shit.

Daphne?

I've never asked anyone what my Proprietor's first name is. It never occurred to me to even think about it.

"But," I protest, "How did it get there? I mean, I thought—"

As my mind reels with new questions, Lady Verdan's words on my first day in the house come barreling back to me.

The house was built long before either of us was born.

"I guess I always assumed she and Lord Verdan bought the house together," I stammer. "I had no idea it was her family home."

Thorne nods. "Her parents apparently died long ago and left it to Daphne—Lady Verdan. Her husband Milo moved in with the girls when he and Daphne married."

This is too many surprises.

"Wait."

My heart beats a percussive, violent series of staccato

pulses in my chest. How did I not know any of this? "He moved *with* the girls? You mean, they're not her daughters?"

"Mrs. Milton—gossiping monster that she is—told me once they're Lady Verdan's step-daughters. *Lord* Verdan's biological children. Lady V. doesn't talk about it—she makes them call her Mother, and she doesn't seem to want people to know they're not biologically hers."

"Well, it sounds like she might have a biological child out there *somewhere*," I say under my breath. "A Tethered. She must have had a relationship with their Guard or something. Mrs. Milton said there was one called Timothy who'd been there for a long time. I wonder if he was the one. Maybe *that's* why she let him go in the end—he knew too much."

"There doesn't seem to be a child. Didn't you see the last entry?" Thorne holds up the reader, and I see what he means. I never read past the part that mentioned being locked in a room.

There's a very brief paragraph one page later that reads:

Diary,

My parents have told me they want me to terminate the pregnancy. They said the scandal I've brought upon our house would destroy us.

They've told me never to speak of it again—and after today, I won't. I will no longer be writing, either. I've already revealed far too much, if only to you.

I know what I must do—but I'm devastated.

D.

"I missed that," I say, too ashamed to tell Thorne I hadn't read on because I was seething with anger. "I can't believe I'm saying this, but I actually feel sorry for her."

"As do I," Thorne says pensively as someone strides by a little too close to where we're hiding ourselves. "Look, Shara," he whispers, "we need to get back inside. If you and I are seen together tonight, we're both as good as dead. You need to make your way into that ballroom and meet the prince. As much as I hate saying it, I need you to follow through and make contact with him. This diary of yours tells me we're onto something huge. If my suspicions about the prince are right, you and I are on the verge of turning the whole fucking system on its head."

At that moment, another laughing couple storms by us, the soles of their shoes hammering on the stone pathway.

"Can't you tell me why you want me to touch him so badly?" I ask, my voice quiet but pleading. "It seems like a really bad idea, to put it mildly."

Thorne's voice is a low growl when he takes a step closer and says, "I don't *want* you to touch him. I don't want you anywhere near that bastard, truth be told. But you, Shara, have a gift. The day you touched me in the Tower—I saw in your eyes what was happening to you. I knew in that moment what you were, and that I had to protect you—to keep your secret. But now, I need you to trust me one last time. Do this thing tonight, and then I promise, I'll tell you everything from the beginning."

Swallowing hard, I nod once. As much as I want to ask him a million questions, I owe him this. I've accused him of egregious sins—of lie after lie, not to mention of breaking one of Kravan's most fundamental laws.

I've assumed the worst of him at almost every turn.

I silently vow to put my life in his hands. If he's right—if we can turn the system on its head and find a way to liberate the Tethered from the lives the Nobility forces on us—I want to be a part of it.

"I have to go," Thorne whispers, stepping backwards toward a gap in the tall, manicured shrubbery. "You have a prince to meet, and unfortunately, I have my own business to attend to. This night is going to be hard for us both, but we'll get through it. I promise."

With that, Thorne leaves me in the small courtyard.

So, I tell myself. *All I have to do now is figure out how to semi-seduce the most eligible bachelor in Kravan. A man who would have me murdered in an instant if he suspected I'm not* **actually** *a Noble.*

What could possibly go wrong?

CHAPTER FORTY-TWO

When I've made my way back into the ballroom, I command myself to focus on the task ahead of me. All the while, I chastise myself for doubting Thorne so thoroughly.

From a distance, I watch the ebbing sea of elegant Nobles flit around the room in their expensive suits and gowns. Every one of them is masked, but I'm convinced that I can tell exactly what they look like underneath the disguises—which makes me more than a little nervous.

Some of the women are gathered in small groups, gloved hands resting on one another's arms. As I watch them, I'm reminded of the small, simple gestures I was never allowed to partake in when I lived in the Tower.

The men and women of the Nobility touch each other casually or kiss one another's cheeks like it's nothing more momentous than inhaling a breath. To think that, until a few weeks ago, the most intimate contact I'd ever had with another human was Drukkar nearly slitting my throat.

Fascination blends with envy inside me as I move around, silently observing the masses.

I stop in my tracks when I see Lady Verdan at the far end of the room, gliding over to two men. I assume, given the way they're dressed, that they must be the king and Prince Tallin. When she holds out her hand, the king takes it greedily, kissing her glove. The prince kisses her on each cheek as she beams a warm smile unlike any I've ever seen on her lips.

So, I think, *it turns out all you need to impress Lady Verdan is to rule the entire realm.*

While the Verdan daughters each exchange pleasantries with the king and prince, I take advantage of the moment to look around for Thorne.

But it seems he's already located me.

"Over your left shoulder," a low, soft voice says. "Don't turn and look at me. Just keep staring at the prince. You'll need to make your way over to him soon—but in the meantime, you would do well to smile at some of the men who are busy gawking at you."

I glance around to realize that he's right—in every direction, men are leaning in close to one another, their eyes fixed on me, and whispering to each other like they're sizing me up.

"Why are they staring?" I ask, my cheeks flushing. "Most of my face is covered."

"Men care less for faces than you might think," Thorne says with a snicker. "Some only care about the curves of a woman's body."

"And you?" I ask, barely moving my lips.

"Your body is exquisite," he whispers. "But I also happen to think very highly of your face, so I like to think of myself as enlightened."

"I just hope I still have a face by the time the evening is

through," I tell him, pulling my eyes to a black-clad figure making his way through a group of Nobles at the opposite end of the room.

When I tighten, Thorne says, "What is it?"

"My friend," I tell him. "Ilias. He's over there—but he's not in a suit. He's dressed in his Guard uniform."

"Ah," Thorne says. "You'll see quite a few men and women in Guard uniforms tonight—including me, in a little while. Unfortunately, it's part of the festivities."

I want to ask him what he means, but Prince Tallin has begun to walk across the ballroom, his eyes locked on me.

Shit.

I turn to watch the musicians play, tipping my glass and swallowing half of my latest flute of champagne. I pull my eyes up to study the five priceless-looking chandeliers hanging from the ceiling, then turn awkwardly to gaze at the paintings on the surrounding walls.

Anything to avoid looking at the prince, who still seems intent on reaching me.

"Good luck," Thorne whispers before disappearing behind a column.

I turn to see Tallin standing close by, chatting with a young woman dressed in white.

Against my will, I let out a quiet chuckle, then cover my mouth and refocus on a portrait that I'm only now realizing depicts the prince as a young boy.

I've had the most dull existence possible, if you don't count the multitude of times I was thrown in a fighting ring against my will. Almost every day of my life has been identical to the one that came before it.

But tonight, I'm supposed to befriend the prince of

Kravan. I'm expected to remove my glove and touch his face —and I have no idea why.

My life has become ridiculous.

I've never, ever taken a risk like this—and I genuinely don't know what, aside from a glass and a half of champagne, has me convinced that I should even *be* here.

"May I ask what you find so amusing?"

The voice is smooth and comforting, and I twist around to see a young man about Thorne's height looking down at me with an admittedly charming smile on his lips.

His half-mask is black and decorated with what look like tiny, glimmering scales, and I just noticed for the first time that he's wearing a red bow tie that matches my dress perfectly.

His hair is dark and thick, his eyes light blue beyond the mask.

"You're Prince Tallin," I say, unsure as to why I'm so confident in the claim. It's not as if he's wearing a name tag, after all, and the truth is, he could be someone else entirely.

"I am," he replies to my relief. "And you are...?"

"Johanna Ingram," I tell him. "From..."

~*Pembroke Isle!* Maude's voice practically shouts into my mind.

"Pembroke Isle," I say, smiling at the prince. "Sorry—the champagne is making me fuzzy."

He looks me up and down, then says, "You still haven't told me what's so funny."

I can feel my cheeks heating beneath my mask, and once again I'm grateful for the meager concealment.

"I just think it's amusing that I ventured here all on my own," I tell him, swaying my hips flirtatiously as I saw

Kaleen do a thousand times in the Tower. "It's not like me to do something like that." I lean a little closer when I add, "Normally, I'm *very* shy."

Tallin's smile intensifies. "Yes—I can see that," he says with a chuckle. "So shy that you stand out more than any other lady in this entire place."

That, I did not expect.

Oh, God—has he seen right through my disguise? Does he know what I am?

"You are easily the most beautiful creature here," he adds quietly, the words a whisper into my ear, "and I know it without even laying my eyes on half of your face."

I breathe a silent sigh of relief as he pulls back and offers me his arm. "Come meet my father the king, and then I intend to force you to dance with me until the fun begins in an hour."

Fun? I think. But I'm too terrified to ask what that might mean.

I slip my gloved arm into his and let him guide me across the dance floor toward the man I saw earlier, who's wearing a set of black tails with a red sash stitched in gold.

He's handsome, with salt and pepper hair and a square jaw, and I can see why both he and his son have reputations as two of the most attractive men in Kravan.

But to my dismay, he's currently engrossed in a conversation with Lady Verdan, whose hand is on his arm.

"Could you...tell me about this portrait, first?" I ask Tallin, stopping to turn us both toward a painting on the wall. It's a woman in a blue dress, a white feather fan in her hand.

"That's my mother," he says sadly. "Back in the days when she was healthy—before her illness claimed her."

"I'm so sorry for your loss, Highness," I tell him, and I mean it.

"Thank you. We do miss her," he replies, glancing back at his father. "Come, now. I know you're shy, but we'll just offer up a quick hello, then I can have you to myself, Johanna Ingram from Pembroke Isle."

I smile, secretly wishing I could disappear into the floor. Lady Verdan is still clinging to the king's arm—but fortunately, when she sees us approaching, she backs away to join her daughters, who are standing some distance away, flirting with two young men.

"Father," Tallin says when we reach him. "This is Miss Ingram."

"A pleasure," the king says, taking my hand and kissing it.

"The pleasure is all mine, Majesty," I reply with my best attempt at an awkward curtsy. I don't even know if it's what I'm supposed to do—it's a thing I've seen in the Tower's limited repertoire of movies.

The king looks entertained by my effort, but appreciative, as well.

"I'm going to force Miss Ingram to dance with me," Tallin says. "Until the other festivities begin, at least."

Other festivities, I think. *What other festivities? What's all the secrecy about this ball?*

It's then that I remember what Mrs. Milton said about the prince enjoying "other amusements."

I'm not sure I want to know what that means.

"A fine choice," the king says, nodding his approval. "Be sure to take good care of her."

The way they speak to one another is stiff and feels too much like they're putting on airs. In a way, it's charming.

But it also feels artificial and utterly disingenuous. For someone who was raised with a rule that I couldn't tell a lie, their interaction feels a lot like bullshit.

Not that I'm in any position to complain. My entire existence in this palace is a lie. I am portraying a woman who doesn't exist—one without a face or a real name. I'm wearing a scent from a place I'll probably never see, and wearing gloves to cover up the mark that shows my inferiority.

"Tell me, Johanna," the prince says as he takes my champagne flute and sets it down on a table before leading me onto the dance floor, "were you excited to come tonight?"

"Of course I was," I reply. "But truth be told, I was most excited to meet you in particular."

As the words leave my mouth, I realize that for the first time in my life, I'm acting. With no experience whatsoever, I'm playing a role I was never meant to portray—and if I break character, I'm as good as dead.

Out of the corner of my eye, I spot Thorne leaning against one of the ballroom's columns. As he watches me, he combs a hand through his thick, dark hair.

The look on his face is protective, almost angry as Tallin pulls me close.

"Dance with me," the prince says, drawing my eyes to his.

Oh, shit.

I've never danced in my life, and I have no idea how.

CHAPTER FORTY-THREE

~It's all right, Maude tells me. *All the dance steps are contained in my memory banks. I'll guide you.*

Granting her power over my arms was one thing, but the thought of surrendering my entire body to Maude's control—or anyone's—frightens the hell out of me. For all I know, she could accidentally make me flail around like a discombobulated rag doll.

Still, I have little choice but to trust her. Not if I'm meant to charm the prince into an eventual moment of intimacy.

Why did I agree to this? I could be back in my room, tucked into bed, reading a good book right now.

~You agreed to it because deep down, you know it's for the best, Maude replies.

I'm not sure about that, I tell her. *The consequence for some people making asses of themselves is a little embarrassment. The consequence for me is possible death.*

It's too late for regrets. The most powerful young man in the realm is pressed against me, and every young woman—

and some of the young men—in the ballroom is staring at me with envy.

When my eyes land on Devorah and Pippa, I can see despite their masks that both women glare at me, their lips pursed as if they've been sucking on lemons.

Lady Verdan, on the other hand, looks as if she's delighted the prince wants nothing to do with her daughters.

I try my best not to stare at them, terrified that they'll somehow see past my mask and dress straight into my soul. Lady Verdan's penetrating gaze is almost unbearable, and I feel my cheeks heat to dangerous levels.

Fortunately, the entire room seems to be more focused on Prince Tallin than me while we wait for the music to start.

My heart throbs in my chest, my eyes veering around the room in search of Thorne, who's disappeared.

I spot him some distance away, his eyes locking on mine again. His chin is down, hands together, his fingers steepling as if he's deep in thought. I've seen birds of prey in the Verdans' gardens staring with that same expression at their future victims.

As I watch, a Guard steps over to him and whispers something in his ear. Thorne nods once, then turns to follow him out of the ballroom.

I stare in shock at the other Guard—the one who just spoke to him.

It's Ilias.

What business could he possibly have with Thorne? Why would they both leave?

Don't go, I think, sending pleading, silent words through the air. *Please, don't leave me alone to contend with this madness.*

The music blares to sudden life—a raucous waltz that I recognize from a film I once saw in the Tower. On cue, the prince begins to spin me around the dance floor.

At first, my body is stiff and unwilling to surrender itself to Maude's control. But when her voice hurls an insistent *~Trust me, damn it!* into my mind, I allow her to take my limbs over. My feet somehow manage to flit, feather-light, around the room in synchronicity with the prince.

"You're an excellent dancer," the prince says as we glide around the floor, my fingers holding onto my dress's train.

"Thank you," I reply. It's harder to let Maude have control than I'd thought it would be, and it takes all my focus not to try and regain it. "I...haven't had enough practice, I'm afraid."

"I would never have known it."

"And you?" I ask, trying to engage him in conversation. "Do you have much opportunity for dancing?"

"Very little," he replies, pulling himself closer to whisper, "though I would take great pleasure in doing it if it meant spending more time in *your* company."

A quiet shudder overtakes me, and I can't entirely work out whether it's pleasure at the compliment or horror of its potential consequences.

"That would be wonderful," I tell him with a plastered-on smile. "Truly."

As the orchestra churns out waltz after waltz, we dance together for what feels like an hour at least before Tallin takes me by the hand and pulls me to the side of the dance floor. By now, every person at the ball is on the floor, spinning around delightedly to the music.

Everyone, that is, except the Verdan sisters—who continue to stare at me with quiet rage.

When the final piece has concluded and the surrounding crowd has let out a polite round of applause, Tallin whispers, "I want these bastards' eyes off your body for a little while—it's time I had you to myself."

With that, he guides me off the floor toward a set of broad doors that lead outside.

The moment we step out, every person on the terrace scurries back inside like frightened mice.

"I love when they do that," Tallin chuckles. "They're so submissive, all of them. They know when my father or I come out here, they'd best do our bidding."

"Now, *that's* power," I reply with a laugh of my own—though the truth is, his sort of power frightens me. Strength at the expense of a fearful people has never seemed like true leadership to me.

"It's quite wonderful," he replies. "Though I like to think my power is even greater in other areas of my life."

I don't know what he means by that, and I don't particularly care. The last hour or so has given me the opportunity to realize Tallin is unpleasant, full of himself, and not nearly as charming as his reputation would dictate.

We lean against a stone balustrade surrounding the terrace, staring out at the night sky, which is extraordinary. The stars are bright and glimmering, the moon full, reveling in the lack of clouds.

"This is the first time I've ever stood under the night sky," I say softly.

Only when the words leave my lips do I realize the

hideous error I've just made. *I've just admitted I've never set foot outside at night.*

What kind of a Noble would live their whole life without standing under the stars?

Shit. Shit. Shit.

"Do your parents keep you locked in your room or something?" the prince asks with a laugh.

I chuckle, then scramble to say, "Sorry—I was just trying to be poetic. It's just...it *feels* like it's the first time I've really seen the stars and the moon—like being here with you makes the experience new and exciting. Does that make sense?"

"Absolutely, yes. I understand completely." He pulls his chin up to gaze at the stars, inhales deeply, then looks down at me, taking a step closer. "But the stars are not the most beautiful thing out here. I can't entirely see your eyes, but I'm grateful to be able to see your mouth—and if I weren't such a gentleman, I'd be inclined to kiss you, which I've wanted to do since the first moment you walked into the ballroom."

He examines my red-painted lips, letting out a breath as he does so.

"You're perfect," he whispers. "Absolutely perfect."

Something twists inside me, and I can't entirely tell if it's a good or a bad reaction. The thought of being kissed by a prince—it's so beyond wild that I can't even begin to imagine it.

But these lips have only ever kissed one man. I can still taste him on me—feel his touch on my skin. I don't want to share myself with anyone else.

As handsome as Tallin is, there's nothing about him that makes me ache with desire as I do for Thorne.

Don't think about Thorne, I snarl inwardly at myself. *You're supposed to get close to the prince. Touch him with your fingers—that's all you need to do. When that's done, you can flee this place and never look back.*

"May I ask you something?" I say, caught up in the moment as I slip closer, reminding myself that there are no rules about two Nobles touching.

There's no reason to think anything I'm doing is strange or forbidden—yet it feels so entirely like I'm breaking some momentous law that will inevitably come with terrible repercussions.

"Anything," Tallin says, a hand reaching out for my waist and pulling me aggressively against him.

Our hips are so close that to my utter shock and bewilderment, what feels like a steel rod is pressing against my stomach through our clothing.

Is that...?

An overwhelming desire to escape sends my heart into overdrive. All of a sudden, I want nothing more than to get as far from him as I can. I don't know if it's fear or adrenaline, or both, but I want to get away before anything more happens.

"What did you want to ask me?" he whispers, his lips slipping over my ear, his teeth gently biting at my earlobe.

I hesitate, collecting my thoughts and telling myself over and over again not to say something stupid.

"I wanted to ask if...if I could touch you," I whisper.

"Touch me?" Grinning, he pulls back just enough to look at me. "Oh—you mean..."

At that, he presses still closer until there's no denying the erection making its vile presence known against my pelvis.

"Go ahead—I won't complain. Just be careful," he says, glancing around. "We don't want the whole ballroom knowing you gave me a handjob out here." He sighs. "God, I just wish you could get on your knees. With those lips of yours, something tells me I would come in a matter of seconds."

My eyes go wide and without thinking, I jerk backwards.

Is that really what he thought I was asking?

Bile rises up in my throat, but I force a smile onto my lips. I can't let on how repulsed I am, or something tells me he'll find a way to punish me—whether I'm a Noble or not.

"I didn't mean it like that," I say with a shake of my head, letting out a nervous laugh. I force myself to take a deep breath then step back toward the prince. "I mean, we should take it a little more slowly—much as I want to...well, you know."

The prince laughs, then takes my wrist and pulls my gloved hand to his face. "There—you're touching me," he says, dragging my hand down to the front of his trousers and wrapping my fingers around his shaft. "But isn't this so much better?"

You're disgusting, I think. *Who knew the prince of Kravan was so vile?*

I shake my head, pulling my hand free. "I know it sounds silly, but...I want to touch your face," I tell him, still fighting back the bile. "Do you mind?"

"Of course not—though that's not exactly the bare skin I had in mind." He smiles, and what seemed like a charming grin an hour ago now seems cruel. "But perhaps you're right.

There's plenty of time later for you to strip my trousers off and have your way with me."

With a false giggle, I slip the glove off, then lay my hand gently on his cheek, my eyes locking on his.

I watch his lips part like he's anticipating a passionate kiss.

Those aren't the lips I want. I want nothing to do with you, you horny, entitled pig.

As those thoughts whirl through my consciousness, something overtakes me, sending a barrage of sensations careening through my body and mind.

It's almost the same feeling I had when I touched Thorne in the Tower—or when the thief wrapped his hands around my neck in my bedroom.

But this time, the sensation is even more intense. As shock twists its way through me, a series of images flashes through my mind.

I see a dead man on the ground, his throat split wide open and bloodied. I see a woman lying naked on a bed, terrified for her life.

Another woman, her pale body broken unnaturally, her eyes lifeless.

I tear my hand away and slip the glove back on, my breath coming in shallow, hurried waves.

What is this? What just happened to me?

I felt like I was standing in the midst of a waking nightmare. But where did it come from—and what did the prince have to do with any of it?

Is this what Thorne wanted? Did he know what I would see?

"My dear," Tallin says, his voice smooth but tight, as if something is troubling him. "Are you all right?"

"Fine," I tell him, shaking my head, my eyes on the terrace's stone floor. "You're...you're just so gorgeous. I didn't expect..."

"Expect what?"

The prince lets out a laugh, but it's no longer warm and charming. Instead, it's full of foreboding and malice.

He grabs my gloved wrist and squeezes so hard that it hurts. Under his breath, he growls, "What did you feel when you touched me?"

My breath shakes as I scramble for a reply. "Desire," I finally force out. "So much...desire for you. It was overwhelming."

Flirting has never been my strong suit—and flirting while fearing for my life, it turns out, is especially unbearable.

"Desire," the prince repeats with that ghastly smile. "Really." He squeezes my wrist still harder when he adds, "Funny thing, though. I don't believe you."

CHAPTER
FORTY-FOUR

"I'm so sorry," I stammer, somehow finding the courage to look the prince in the eye. "I...I just haven't been in the presence of a man who's so...well, exciting as you. I'm embarrassed, that's all. I didn't expect to be so..."

"Aroused?" Prince Tallin says, his lips curve into what looks like a satisfied smile. "Let's see about that."

Grabbing my waist hard, he pulls me close again. But this time, he slips a hand under my layers of crimson skirt, lifting it until his fingertips find their way to my thigh.

He sighs with pleasure as he slides his hand up, his eyes locked on mine, moaning when he reaches my panties.

I let out an inadvertent gasp as he plays with the seam, then slips a finger under the fabric. "Ah—so you were telling the truth. You *are* aroused, naughty thing."

I shut my eyes against the sensation of his touch, and I tell myself to think of Thorne. As horrified as I am right now to be in this position, the protectiveness of Thorne's voice—his physical presence—is the only thing that makes me feel shielded against the entitled bastard now claiming ownership of my body.

I'm almost glad he's nowhere to be seen right now, because something tells me he wouldn't hesitate to rush out onto this terrace and tear the prince apart.

"I will have you," Tallin breathes, his lips brushing my neck. "I will fucking take you so many times before I discard you. But don't worry. You'll love every second of it."

My eyes shoot open, moving to the large glass doors that lead into the ballroom, where I see silhouetted figures laughing and drinking the evening away. They're so close, yet none of them seems to be watching us—not that they would help me, even if they were.

I doubt if there's a single Noble here who would feel a drop of sympathy for me. After all, I'm receiving much-coveted attention from the revered prince of Kravan.

Tallin moans, his fingers perilously close to taking something from me no man has ever claimed when a trumpet fanfare sounds. The prince pulls himself away, slipping his fingers briefly under his nose before saying, "It's time for the Championship. Come with me."

"The what?" I ask, my eyes veering to the wave of bodies moving rapidly toward the doors at the ballroom's far end.

The prince shoots me a sideways glance. "The *Championship.* The best part of the ball. Come on, now—every Noble knows about this. Your family must have sent a Champion of their own, no?"

~Shara, Maude's voice says. *The Championship is a fight between Noble families' selected Guards for the entertainment of their Proprietors.*

"The *Championship,*" I repeat, letting out a forced laugh

as if to say, *How silly of me!* "I'd forgotten. My parents couldn't send their Champion—he fell ill a few days ago. I thought they sent word about it."

"They probably did," Tallin replies as he leads me rapidly through the parting crowd. "No matter. Let's get to our seats, shall we?"

I remember with a shock of horror as I glance around the ballroom that Thorne and Ilias disappeared a while back—and Thorne mentioned something about the Guards wearing their uniforms for some event later in the evening.

Is this Championship what he was talking about?

Oh, God. Is Thorne going to fight?

When we reach the corridor beyond the ballroom, Prince Tallin nods toward a tall man in black who's trudging away from us, his shoulders as broad as some small houses. He's dressed in a uniform of dark red that looks something like an elegant version of what we used to wear in combat classes.

"That's my *personal* Champion," Tallin says. "He's undefeated, as well he should be. He cost my family a mint. I'll be very surprised if he's not standing among a sea of bodies at the end of tonight."

"Bodies," I breathe.

I want to ask him what's about to happen, but I'm terrified I've already figured it out.

"Do they really kill their opponents?" I ask quietly, half afraid the prince will accuse me of being an intruder for not knowing the specific rules.

Tallin smirks. "*Women,*" he says. "It's sort of sweet how your fathers shield you from hard truths. Yes, the damned losers die—at least, most of them do. The Houses who lose

Tethered will have to wait a year to claim new ones. It's been the rule for years."

He says the words like he's telling me how to water flowers—like it's some small thing of no consequence to him whatsoever.

Apparently, Tethered lives are as expendable as tissues.

Why didn't Thorne warn me about this? Why didn't he tell me there was a chance I'd watch people die tonight?

But I know the answer perfectly well.

He knew that if he'd told me, I never would have come. I would have taken any manner of punishment over this hell.

Part of me wants to find him and chastise him—to scream furious words at him and pound my fists into his chest.

Except...

After tonight, I may never see him again.

And that would be a wretched way to say goodbye.

CHAPTER FORTY-FIVE

I STRUGGLE to keep my belly from churning with nausea as the prince leads me down the corridor teeming with the ball's attendees. Ahead of us, walking with the king, I spot Lady Verdan and her daughters.

I have a horrible feeling the prince will want me to sit with him—and that the Verdans will be close by the entire time.

The corridor ends at an arching doorway that leads out into a vast courtyard surrounded by gray stone walls. Party-goers are streaming out, taking seats in the few hundred red chairs that have been positioned around what looks like a large fighting ring with a dirt floor.

Memories flood my mind of the days in the Tower, when I was forced to fight my fellow Tethered. Days when I was repeatedly brought down by people far stronger than me.

But something tells me this evening will be far more brutal than anything I ever endured in my sheltered youth.

At the far end of the ring is a broad gap between the chairs, where at least twenty Guards in different-colored combat uniforms stand, their hands clasped behind their backs. Frantic, I scan their faces until my eyes meet Thorne's. He looks stoic and confident, which helps quell my fear, but only a little.

To my horror, Ilias is there, too. He's standing next to the monster of a man the prince pointed to earlier—the Tethered in red, who must be almost seven feet tall and looks like he could crush my friend between his thumb and index finger.

"I see you've got your eye on my man," the prince says, his eyes following my gaze. "We call him the Lion. His specialty is—well, you can imagine. He's one of our best."

"Will all the Royal Guard fight tonight?" I ask, fighting tooth and nail to contain the fear in my voice.

"Not all, no," he says. "Only the ones who wish to prove themselves loyal to my father and me. Sometimes, newer Guards have to go the extra mile, you see."

I scan the crowd of uniformed fighters to see if I know anyone else. To my relief, Nev is nowhere to be seen. Neither is Drukkar—not that I expected to find him here. After his performance on Placement Day, I can't imagine the Prefect recommending him to the Royal Family.

As the king and the Verdans take their seats, I notice that Thorne has left his place among the competitors and is making his way around the crowd toward us. When I glance at him, he nods toward the corridor we just left.

"I...need to use the ladies' room," I tell the prince. "I'll only be a minute."

"Fine. But be quick," he hisses impatiently. "The first fight's about to begin."

I dart back into the corridor and down its length until Maude buzzes a quiet alert into my wrist.

~*Look to your right,* she says.

I turn to see that Thorne has tucked himself into a recessed, shadowy alcove to await me.

I'm about to tell him to leave before he gets himself killed when he whispers, "Did you do it?"

I fall into confused silence for a moment, as if my mind is in denial of my traumatic interaction with the prince.

"Yes, I did," I finally say, my voice tremulous. Between what happened with Tallin and what's *about* to happen, I feel like I'm about to lose my damned mind. "I touched him, like you asked."

"And?"

Shaking my head, I say, "I...can't."

A look of desperate impatience fills Thorne's eyes, but he forces it away and says, "Tell me what happened when you made contact. It's...important."

I had begun to hope I'd only imagined the experience—that this whole evening was some fever-induced nightmare. But standing here, inhaling Thorne's scent and staring into his eyes, I know it was as real as anything that's ever happened to me.

"I saw things, Thorne," I whisper. "Dead bodies. I felt some kind of power in him, like he was the *cause* of those bodies—but I don't know how to explain it. I didn't see him hurt anyone. I just...felt his mind. I knew he'd done it."

My eyes are locked on the corridor, terror raging through me that the prince might storm out and find us here. After what I saw in his memories, there's no doubt left in my mind that he's the most dangerous person I've ever met—though none of it makes sense.

"Shara," Thorne says softly. "What you saw is evidence of a multitude of crimes. You did well—and you should be proud. I need to go back in, though. If they find me out here with you..."

I open my mouth to protest, to tell him to leave with me —but he shakes his head.

"Look," he whispers, "if something happens to me, I need you to keep your experience with the prince a secret until you find someone you trust. Do you understand?"

"Of course I do," I tell him, tears welling in my eyes. "But nothing is going to happen to you. Please—you need to make it through tonight. You need to come home."

Home.

I can't believe I just used that word. I've never once used it to describe the place I live. But that's what the Verdans' house has become.

Not because it's cozy and welcoming...

But because Thorne lives there.

My anger at him for not telling me about the Crimson Championship has vanished by now, and all I want is to reach out and pull him close.

I want him to tell me everything will be all right.

"I'll do my best to come through this in one piece," he promises. "But right now, you need to get out of here. You should go, while the Royals are distracted. They won't go after you—lots of Nobles hate watching the Championship and leave after the dancing."

I shake my head again. "I'm not going anywhere until I know you're all right."

"Shara—things are going to get ugly in there. I don't think you—"

"I don't care," I snap under my breath. "I'm not leaving until I know you're going to make it out."

Thorne exhales hard. "Stubborn as a mule," he says with a rueful grin. "Fine."

"Ilias," I say, nodding toward the corridor and the arena beyond. "He's totally out of his depth. He has no fighting experience, other than in the Tower—and Ore was a shitty trainer. I'm worried about him."

"If I fight him, I'll go easy on him, I promise," Thorne assures me. "But I can't promise it'll be me who goes up against him. The prince and the king enjoy pitting their best Guards against their weakest. The Noble families are reluctant to send their own Champions to this bloodbath, so the Royal Family uses their 'spares' as fodder. They have so many Guards, they're happy to lose half of them for a night's entertainment."

At that, my heart sinks.

"Go back in there," Thorne says. "Sit with the prince. Be as friendly as you can stand to be. It'll all be over soon."

With that, he reaches out and touches my neck, his fingertips slipping downward and reminding me how alive he makes me feel. How foolish I was for failing to believe him.

I don't want to lose this strange, painful, brutal relationship forming between us. I don't want to lose *him*.

Grateful that he can't see the tears welling in my eyes, I turn and leave him there, knowing he'll find a way to slip into the arena after me. In the meantime, I need to cozy up to the awful prince and convince him I'm excited that I'm about to watch innocent men and women die.

When I'm back inside, I seat myself next to Tallin. To the prince's other side is his father, then Lady Verdan, Devorah, and Pippa.

The prince seems unconcerned that I was gone so long. He leans toward me, pressing his shoulder to mine, and whispers, "We always begin with some of the more talented Guards. It's important to put on a good show while some of the crowd is still relatively sober."

He's got a point. Interspersed among the spectators are a number of servants who seem to continually refill the guests' champagne flutes. By now, everyone in the place is probably three or more sheets to the wind.

"Are the Tethered allowed to touch each other during these fights?" I ask Tallin.

"Yes," he says. "They can do whatever they want. There are no rules in the Championship."

Shit.

That will certainly put Ilias at a disadvantage. Though he's strong, he has no experience fighting hand-to-hand.

I sit back, swallowing down the bile rising in my throat, and stare out at the arena.

A man in a ridiculous-looking suit covered in red and gold stripes steps out into the fighting ring with an ornamental paper scroll in hand. He turns toward the Royal seats and calls out, "Welcome, your Majesty, and welcome, Noble guests, to the annual Crimson Championship!"

Hoots and hollers rise up from the excited crowd, some of whom thrust fists into the air in preemptive triumph.

"The first competitors tonight will be Neviss from House Kelon, and the Lion, from the Royal Palace."

Oh, thank God.

I don't know who Neviss is, but I'm grateful it wasn't Ilias who got pitted against the behemoth Tallin pointed out.

As I watch the two Guards stride into the ring, I spot Thorne quietly repositioning himself among the other Guards. His eyes are locked ahead, focused and intent.

"The only rule of the Championship," the announcer shouts, "is that there are no rules. One man—or woman—standing at the end of this match will be declared winner of his round. At the end of the fighting, a winner will be named by the prince, who will call out his pick for Crimson Champion. His choice will be based on fighting style, strength, speed, and—"

"Whether or not the Tethered has a shapely ass!" Prince Tallin shouts, to roars of laughter from the crowd.

I manage a nervous chuckle, hoping to convince him I find him as adorable as everyone else seems to.

I clasp my shaking, gloved hands together in hopes of steadying them, but apparently I fail, because Tallin reaches over and places a hand on top of them.

"It's all right," he says. "These fighters are only Tethered. Think of them as diseased rats in need of euthanasia."

Fuck you, I think, grateful that Maude seems to have given up on reprimanding me for disloyal thoughts.

The announcer steps out of the ring, and the man called the Lion and his opponent face off.

Neviss isn't large—he's probably under six feet tall, with long, thin limbs. But watching him for a few seconds, I already suspect he's a Velor, like Drukkar. He shoots around the ring, whipping from corner to corner in a blur of motion that's almost impossible to register.

Once or twice, the Lion lunges at him, but eventually, with a low growl, he gives up and stands still at the ring's center. Neviss continues to zip around while the Lion waits patiently, a grimace on his lips.

It's when Neviss has shot from one corner to another about ten times that the Lion finally reaches a long, muscular arm out and grabs the blurry form by the throat.

A horrible gasp rises from the crowd—or was it just me—as the Lion throws Neviss to the ground, his thick fingers still wrapped around the man's neck.

Neviss's eyes bulge as the sound of snapping bones echoes through the large space—and then the blood comes. The smaller man's neck is crushed, and the Lion has also managed to tear it open, as if to prove his strength.

I turn and bury my face in the prince's shoulder.

"There, there," he says. "I told you—he was only a Tethered."

Sickened, I pull my face back toward the ring, waiting for the body to be dragged off and the Lion to be declared the winner.

A pool of blood soaks into the dirt where Neviss died, yet no one attempts to cover it or clean it up.

Pair after pair of Tethered are called up, and each time, one of them ends up dead. A young man here. A young woman there. Whether by a dagger in the chest, a crushed-in head, or another sort of horror, each pairing seems to result in one stronger opponent tearing a weak one apart in the most vile possible way.

It's only after seven bouts have finished—and seven dead Tethered have been carted off—that Thorne is called up.

I watch him, my eyes moving over the remaining Guards as I assess their likely strengths.

Thorne is powerful, and there's little doubt in my mind that he would be a match for any of them.

But my heart sinks like a stone when the announcer shouts, "Thorne, of House Verdan...will be fighting the Lion!"

CHAPTER FORTY-SIX

"What?" I gasp before I can stop myself. I try to cover my shock by stammering, "I mean…why is the Lion fighting a second time? I assumed each Guard only fought one round."

"The Lion is strong," the prince says with a chuckle. "And Thorne is a fine fighter. So I asked that my best man take him on. It seems only fair."

I slip my hands down to grasp the edge of my seat, convinced that my knuckles are bone-white under the gloves. My heart, meanwhile, is ready to pound its way clear out of my body.

"This shouldn't take long, either," Tallin says. "If that's what you're worried about."

That's *exactly* what I'm worried about.

I watch as Thorne enters the ring and immediately begins to circle the Lion, pacing around him like a small panther assessing an elephant. Terror claws at me despite his apparent confidence.

In his hand, he's holding a broad, glinting dagger. The Lion, on the other hand, has no weapon.

On Thorne's right wrist, I see a flash of something just under the cuff of his uniform—a silver bracelet. No—a wrist piece, like the ones he wore in the Tower. The ones he said were illegal.

Maybe there's a chance...

The Lion lets out a snarl, putting on a show for the crowd, and Thorne leaps quickly backward.

Thorne lunges at his opponent, slashing the blade through the air, seemingly to test the Lion's reaction time.

Unfortunately, the prince's prize Champion is not only enormous, but quick on his feet, and he easily leaps out of the way.

He and Thorne circle one another for some time, neither willing to make another move at first.

Thorne leaps at him, managing to slice through the Lion's uniform and leaving a deep gash in his arm.

"Oooh," Tallin says, laughing. "He's not going to like that one bit."

"Mother!" I hear Devorah cry. "You can't let that man hurt Thorne!"

I glance over to see tears running down her face below her mask.

Whether the diary is hers or not—whether I'm wrong about all of it or not—maybe Devorah does genuinely care for Thorne.

She's not the only one.

"I don't have any say in the matter, dear," Lady Verdan says. "We just have to let it play out."

The crowd is quiet as the Lion lurches his way toward Thorne, then, in one too-fast movement, grabs him and pulls him close, his enormous arm around Thorne's throat. The dagger falls from Thorne's hand as he grabs at the man's arm, trying in vain to tear himself free.

"Like I said—this won't take long," the prince says with a yawn.

The Lion squeezes, and I can see Thorne's neck and face turning red as the air is pushed out of his body, his bones threatening to snap under the enormous force.

Thorne's eyes move to mine for a split-second, but it's long enough for me to see his message.

Remember what I said.

The Lion lifts him off the ground, both arms around him now, and squeezes still harder. Thorne kicks at him, but the monster has no intention of letting go.

Finally, Thorne's foot manages to make contact with the Lion's testicles. The large man cries out in pain and drops his opponent to the ground.

Thorne scrambles over and grabs the blade, then, breathless, leaps into the air, coming down on the Lion's chest and driving the dagger into his heart.

He jumps back as his opponent's eyes go wide, then the Lion staggers backward and falls to his knees, his gaze moving to the blade jutting out from his chest.

Thorne pulls at his sleeves, then combs both hands through his hair, turns to the king and the prince, and bows low as Tallin's Champion falls dead.

"Shit," Tallin snarls. "It'll take years before the Tower produces another one like that."

I wish I had a knife of my own so I could plunge it straight into his pretty face.

Thorne leaves the ring, and it takes five powerful-looking Guards to drag the Lion from the arena.

Several more pairings fight. The crowd, now fully inebriated, is losing interest, though some of them are still shouting cheers now and then. I can tell they're bored with all the death—ghouls that they are.

When I hear Ilias's name called, I want to be sick.

His opponent, Kav, is large—about Drukkar's size—and cruel-looking. He's not a Royal Guard, but from a Noble House situated on a neighboring island, according to the prince.

"This Guard—this Ilias," Tallin whispers to me. "He's keen. Loyal to a fault. But useless as shit."

I close my eyes against the words. I hate the prince more than I have ever hated anyone or anything in my damned life.

When I open them, Ilias and his opponent are each holding a dagger like the one Thorne had in hand. I'm relieved. I know from experience that Ilias has always been adept with throwing blades. If he can avoid contact with his opponent, chances are he'll be fine.

The two men make a show of pacing like Thorne and the Lion did, their eyes locked on one another. On Ilias's face is a smile I know so well—an arrogant, cocky, "I'm enjoying the hell out of this" grin, and it fills me with hope, even confidence.

"You can do this," I mutter under my breath. "You have to."

"What's that?" Tallin asks.

"Nothing," I tell him. "I'm just hoping it ends quickly. I need to run to the ladies' room again, and I don't want to miss anything."

The pacing continues for what feels like an eternity

before Ilias finally hurls his blade.

I hold my breath, waiting for the moment when it strikes.

But his opponent swoops out of the way with no effort whatsoever, then springs over to grab the dagger off the ground.

Holding one blade in each hand, he hurls himself at Ilias, who thrusts his hands instinctively over his face.

"Fucking coward," Tallin grunts even as Kav drives both daggers straight into Ilias's chest.

My friend's arms fall, his mouth opening as if he wants to cry out. But no sound comes.

"ILIAS!"

The scream rips its way out of my throat before I can stop myself.

Everything after that seems to happen in slow motion.

Ilias falls to the ground, his head turning my way, his cloudy, lifeless eyes seemingly focused directly on me.

I could heal him, I think. *I could run over and press my hands to his chest. I could bring him back...*

But they would kill me for it. They'd make sure Ilias didn't survive.

They'd kill Thorne when they found out he's the reason I'm here.

As if to confirm my suspicions, the prince grabs my arm and growls, "Who the fuck *are* you?"

For a second, I freeze. Then my eyes pull to Thorne, who's standing at the opposite side of the arena.

"Run!" he mouths, and I do exactly what he says.

I tear my arm away from Tallin, the long satin glove slipping off into his hand.

Leaping into the corridor, I sprint faster than I've ever

moved. I know without asking that this is Maude's doing—she is facilitating my strength and speed, and ensuring my escape.

Why, I don't know. She *should* be halting me in my tracks and turning me in for treachery.

Behind me, I hear the percussive beat of footsteps on the stone floor, and then, when I'm clear of the corridor, the explosion of large doors slamming shut.

~There's a door ahead that leads out to the garden, Maude says. *I'm going to take you back home. You need to trust me.*

"I do," I tell her.

My speed doesn't wane for a moment. I feel like I'm flying, my feet barely stroking the ground as I flee across the grass.

~I've disabled any security cameras and set up a distraction for the Guards. You will not be seen. The Flyer that brought you to the palace is long gone, so don't worry about that. Once you're inside the Verdan house, you need to rid yourself of these clothes immediately and shower the perfume off. Understand?

"Yes."

Maude makes good on her promise, and with a pounding heart, I manage to make my way into the house and up to the servants' wing. I tear off the red dress, one remaining glove, and shoes, and stash them under the floorboard in the secret compartment, along with the reader I found in the same hiding spot. In the bathroom, I wash off my makeup, then shower.

Tears sting my eyes as the hot water cascades down my body.

Tonight, my life became forfeit.

I watched one of my best friends die.

The prince of Kravan will soon figure out who I am and where I came from.

I will be killed for what I've done.

A scramble of confused thoughts keeps circling through my mind.

Thorne is alive.

Ilias is dead.

They'll come for me. They'll find me. And when they do...

When I've left the bathroom, a towel around my head and a terrycloth robe enveloping me, I sink down onto the bed, my chest tight with relief mingled with fear.

"Shara."

I look up to see Thorne standing in my doorway. He looks battered, blood trickling down his lip. I hadn't noticed the cut above his eye—a memento left behind by the Lion.

With a sob, I leap to my feet and throw myself into his arms.

I don't care about rules anymore. I don't even care about getting caught.

I just need to hold onto him for a moment—I need something to soothe my mind and heart in the seconds before they come to take my life.

CHAPTER

FORTY-SEVEN

"I KNOW what you're going to say," I mutter. "I'm an idiot for what I did. Don't worry, you don't need to bother."

"I would never say that to you." He guides me inside my room and closes the door behind him. "I didn't come back here to reprimand you. I should have prepared you—I should have warned you about what you might see at the ball."

He bows his head, shaking it slightly, and a trickle of blood slips down his temple. "I thought you'd be able to leave before the Championship. I thought..." He lets out a tremulous breath. "I'm so sorry about your friend."

My heart hurts as visions of Ilias's brief fight assault my mind. The fear in his eyes in that last moment was a horror I never want to relive.

All his life, he put his faith in the Nobility. And this is how they repay him.

"He was always certain that life on the outside would mean finding the families we never had," I whisper, my lip trembling. "He was so excited, Thorne. He loved being a Tethered. He wanted to serve—that was all."

"And he did serve. But the Royal Family..." Thorne says, grimacing. "Well, they're not exactly nurturing. They've always thrived on using us for their own amusement. At least, the king and Tallin have. And after tonight, I'm beginning to understand why those two have worked overtime to prove their hatred of our kind."

When Thorne takes a seat next to me on the bed, I reach out and gently press my fingertips just above the cut near his eye. It seals shut, and the bleeding ceases instantly.

"I've never done that for someone else," I breathe, wishing with everything in me that I could have done it for Ilias.

"Because you weren't allowed," he replies. "It's a sin that you couldn't touch anyone with those hands of yours, Shara—though I'm grateful to have the pleasure of them now."

I pull back and stare down at my lap.

I want to revel in what he just said—to enjoy this moment of intimacy between us.

But there's something I need to know.

"What happened after...after I left the ball?" I ask.

"The prince tried to pursue you," Thorne says. "But the doors sealed shut. It took a bit to get them open again, and by that time, there was no sign of the beautiful, mysterious woman in red. No one saw you leave the grounds. No one knows where you came from. By some strange coincidence, the palace's surveillance equipment failed just as you left the arena."

I want to smile, but I can't quite muster anything other than a frown.

"It doesn't matter," I lament. "I cried out Ilias's name. Which means..."

"Which means," Thorne says slowly, "that you *might* be a Tethered who knew him from the Tower. But don't forget—the announcer said Ilias's name just before the fight. You could have just been an empathetic Noble who didn't like seeing a young man being murdered."

It's true. Devorah mentioned Thorne's name before his fight, after all—and no one suspects *her* of being a secret Tethered.

But I shake my head. "They won't fall for it. The second they figure out I'm not who I said I was..."

"We'll cross that bridge when we come to it." Thorne cups a hand over my cheek, drawing my eyes to his.

He brushes his lips over mine, then pulls away. "Thank you for what you did tonight. I know it took a great deal of faith—and I know I haven't given you much reason to trust me. But the discoveries you've made—they could change the world, Shara. What you learned about the prince—"

At the thought of my fingers on the prince's face, my gaze veers to the far wall, and once again, tears threaten to fall.

"What did he do to you?" Thorne asks, his expression changing instantly when he sees the look in my eyes. "What did Tallin do?"

The way he says his name sounds like *Talon.*

Fitting, I think with a grimace.

With a shake of my head, I say, "Nothing."

Thorne thrusts himself to his feet, rage roiling under his skin, his jaw clenching. "Tell me what that bastard did."

A tear slides down my face and I wipe it away, shaking my head again. "*Why* did you want me to touch him?" I breathe. "Why did you ask me to do that? Didn't you know..."

Stepping over, he lifts my chin, and I somehow muster the strength to look at him.

"Know what?" he asks.

"I only ever wanted to touch *you*. I wanted your hands on me...not his. What he did to me..."

"So, he did touch you."

I nod.

"Where?"

"It doesn't matter."

"Shara. *Where?*"

Rising to my feet, I take his hand and slip it under my robe to my thigh, then slowly move it up. Before his fingers have gone too far, Thorne lets out a breath, and the heat of his rage fills the air between us.

"I'll fucking kill him," he snarls, pulling away. "I don't care how powerful he is—I will cut out his goddamned heart."

"No, you won't!" I cry. "He's the *prince*. He's got an army of his own to defend him."

"Do you think I care? I would take on every Guard in his service to get to him, after what he did to you."

At that, a sudden, maniacal laugh explodes from my chest.

"What *he* did to me?" I stammer. "All my life, people have been cruel to me. I've been beaten and cut, bruised, battered—all just to make it to this moment. What the prince did was vile, yes. But I'll get over it, just like I get over everything else. Nothing matters, not now that I'm here, with you..."

I cut myself off, realizing just in time what I was about to say.

Thorne slips over and reaches a hand out, then thinks better of it.

"Now that you're here with me?" he says softly.

I shake my head. "It doesn't matter. Look—I'm not *allowed* to be with you. I'm not supposed to feel the desire that has eaten away at me every single day since we met. If I'm lucky, I'll survive this night, and they'll forget about the woman in red. But the laws will stay the same, Thorne. I still won't be able to be with you. I still won't be allowed happiness—and neither will you."

I shudder at the memory of my scream in the palace and the storm I might still bring down on myself.

"Shara," Thorne says, "I wish I'd never asked you to do it. Some part of me hoped they were wrong—I hoped it was all a case of mistaken identity."

I stare at him through cloudy eyes. "You thought *who* was wrong? What are you talking about?"

"There's so much to tell you—but I may as well start at the beginning."

He runs a hand through his hair, a sure sign that he's gearing up to unleash something momentous, then inhales a deep breath.

"Almost twenty years ago, a woman was sent to the Tower. She was pregnant with the child of a Tethered—but he wasn't just *any* Tethered. He was a Gilded Elite—one who managed to hide that status from the Prefect when he got his Placement. He was an elusive man—he escaped his Proprietor's home and went on the run. Those who pursued him had a few chances to kill him, but each time they caught him, they chose to lock him up instead. Unfortunately for them, he was a masterful escape artist. His power was extremely rare—and a valuable weapon, if it found its way to the right hands."

I want to ask him what kind of weapon he's talking about, but I urge him silently to keep going.

"The Prefecture and the Nobility vowed to keep an eye on the man's child after she was born in the Tower," Thorne continues. "To monitor her throughout her life, to see if she would inherit his gifts. But she didn't—at least, not as far as anyone could tell. She was a terrible fighter, and every time she tried to defend herself, a shock of pain assaulted her. She could clean like nobody's business, and she could heal herself. But she showed no signs of inheriting his particular gift."

My chest expands like it's trying to absorb the revelations Thorne has just released, to take them into my heart as well as my mind.

"Wait," I say. "You're telling me *my* father was a Gilded Elite?"

A memory comes to me of the Prefect in the hallway outside my Whiteroom on Placement Day.

"No surprises, then? She's what you expected?"

Thorne nods. "I wasn't sure of it—not even when I met you. You seemed so harmless, like a deer caught in the headlights. The first time I laid eyes on you, you were standing in the fighting ring, looking helpless as a little mouse. It was adorable. I remember thinking, *There's no way in hell that* **she** *is a Gilded.* But as it turns out, you are. You're far more dangerous to the Nobility than any other Tethered I've known—even if you don't know it yet."

"When you say *dangerous*..."

Thorne half-smiles. There's sadness in his eyes, though

I'm not sure why. "Your father was what they call a *Hunter*. He could detect a Tethered from a mile away, even if they're hiding in plain sight among the Normals or the Nobility."

"Wait—the sensation I get when I touch you—when I touched the prince—*that's* what you're talking about?" I ask. "You're saying Tallin is a Tethered?"

"That's exactly what I'm saying."

My jaw drops open—and then, I realize that on some level, I already knew it.

I felt it tonight—I felt Tallin's extraordinary, terrifying power surging through my mind like it was my own.

"But," I breathe, "you said my father could detect a Tethered from a mile away. Wouldn't a Hunter have to go around touching everyone to get their power to work?"

"Not necessarily. Everyone's powers manifest themselves differently—particularly in the beginning. But they grow and change as the Tethered becomes more aware of them." Thorne takes my hand and holds it to his cheek, and once again, the delicate sensation of tingling makes its way along my skin. "Tell me—what do you see right now, when you look into my eyes?"

I pull my eyes to his and focus.

At first, I don't know what he means, other than that I see the beautiful man I've always seen—only now that we've found a way to be honest with one another, he seems even more gorgeous.

But as I stare into his hazel eyes, something odd begins to happen.

The gold surrounding his pupils has begun swirling into the green ring of his irises like liquid.

It's subtle, but unquestionable.

I pull my hand back, and the colors continue to mingle until I blink and force myself to focus.

"How did you do that?" I breathe.

"I didn't do anything," he tells me. "Allegedly, your father could tell just by looking at someone whether they were a Tethered. But, like I said, his powers were enhanced. Just as yours will soon be."

"How do you know that, Thorne? What makes you think my powers will increase?"

"Shara—I promised you I'd tell you why we're called Tethered," he replies, affection shading every word. "Would it surprise you to learn we were called that before the Tower existed and before the Rebellion ever occurred?"

"I..." I realize that no, it wouldn't exactly surprise me. "We were never allowed to learn about the days preceding the Rebellion. I don't know anything about our history. All we've ever been taught is that we're terrible, and the Nobility is benevolent."

"Which, as you know, is pure bullshit." Thorne slips his hand onto my neck and I lean into his touch, savoring it. "We're called Tethered," he says, speaking softly so that his words feel like a caress, "because when we find the person we're meant to be with—another Tethered—our powers begin to expand and intensify. If you've ever wondered why the Nobility fears us so much and why they constantly seek to keep us from loving one another—that's it. Love, for a Tethered, means strength—and strength is terrifying to those who are in charge."

CHAPTER FORTY-EIGHT

Everything Thorne is saying is incredible and enlightening, but I still don't understand why I'm tangled up in any of it.

"I can't be a Hunter—a Gilded Elite—whatever you want to call it," I protest, gesturing to Thorne's healed wound. "I'm a Healer. I just *showed* you what I can do."

"That's the thing about Gilded Elites," he says with a sardonic chuckle. "They often have multiple powers, and it's almost impossible to hide them from their Maude units. Most of them are killed, partly because a Gilded can develop new powers at any time. Haven't you ever wondered why your fight trainer was so brutal toward you?"

"Ore?" I reply. "I always assumed it was because he's an asshat."

"Well, there's that. But here's the thing—most Gilded have a power in their arsenal that makes them destructive. It's why they're considered so dangerous."

At that, I recall Cher, the girl in our cohort who seemingly exploded in her Whiteroom.

"I'm not destructive," I say. "I always sucked at fighting —which you know perfectly well."

"Right. Because you were afflicted with shooting pain each time you tried to fight."

I nod. "Like clockwork."

"Or like Maude-work."

"Maude? *My* Maude? You're seriously telling me she did that to me for years on end?"

"I suspect she did, yes. More to the point, I suspect someone programmed her to do it—to prove you were as harmless as they come, so there was never any risk of you being forced to compete in stupidity like the Crimson Championship. Whoever programmed your Maude has kept you safe all these years."

"Yeah—by causing me excruciating pain." I want to yell at Maude for her part in this. But she's dormant, and I don't particularly want to invite her into this conversation.

"Your father most likely had—or *has,* if he's still alive—more than one power, too," Thorne says. "You're fortunate to be a Healer. The Prefect and the Warden accepted that was your only gift. Because you never touched anyone, your other power was never at much risk of discovery. Maybe you were lucky, and your Maude unit never suspected what you were. Or, if she did, she kept it to herself."

"Why would she do that?"

"Like I said, someone out there has their eye on you," he says. "You, Shara, have the potential to bring down the entire Nobility. Which means you're incredibly valuable."

Shock after shock makes its way through my body and mind. Every new piece of information Thorne is offering up is more stunning than the last, and I'm not sure how much more I can take.

"You mentioned..." I say, trying to wrap my brain around all of it. "You said when two Tethered find each other—when they're meant to be together..." I swallow before asking, "Were you talking about you and me?"

"When I saw you in that fighting ring, I knew," Thorne says, taking my hand and kissing it. "That very first moment, I knew what you were to me. It was all I could do not to run to you and claim you as my own right then and there, in front of everyone."

"I...thought you hated me," I murmur, chuckling at the madness of all this. "You were so cold—so...cruel."

"Well, yeah," he laughs, then shakes his head. "I was an asshole—but in my defense, I was a *deliberate* asshole. If I'd been warm and friendly—if I'd shown you an ounce of affection, the Prefect would have suspected something. I had to make you seem small and useless. The least conspicuous Tethered ever to inhabit Kravan. A lowly servant, good for nothing but sweeping."

"Well, you put on an excellent show," I tell him. "I was convinced you despised me, and that I was insane for being so attracted to you."

He shakes his head. "I need you to know that every single thing I've said and done since your arrival, other than my occasional recklessness, has been for your protection. I'm sorry for the times I've hurt you, Shara—but I would do it again to keep hostile eyes off you."

My mind spins with memories of the times Thorne has protected me, either from myself or others.

The moment he grabbed me before I could step onto the Royal Grounds.

His occasional cold glares when the Verdans were around.

His wild attack on the man who assaulted me in my room.

"I just wish you'd told me sooner about that fucking diary," he adds with a laugh. "But it's my fault you didn't trust me—and I take full responsibility for it."

The diary. I hadn't even thought about it—not since Thorne and I discussed it at the ball.

"But if Lady Verdan never had the baby, does the diary even matter?" I ask.

"Yeah," Thorne says. "It does. The diary confirms a suspicion many have had for years. The Nobles are hypocrites. They're liars. They incarcerate us for the crime of being lesser beings, and meanwhile, Tethered live among their number. And thanks to you, we now know Prince Tallin is one of them."

He's right.

It was my power—the one inherited from my father—that showed me the brutal truth about what Tallin really is.

I just didn't know what I was seeing.

"The people I saw when I touched him," I say, the words quivering their way out of my mouth, "he killed them with some kind of violent power. I didn't see him do it, but I *felt* it. It was as if for a few seconds, it was my own memory—and then, it was gone. I felt the same thing in that man who attacked me here."

Thorne seems to ponder that for a moment, then says, "I've never told you what my power is, have I?"

"I watched you fight in the Tower," I reply. "I saw you defeat our best Crimsons. But you're right—I don't know what your power is, even though I've touched you. I didn't feel the same sort of violent impact with you—it was more like...swirling colors. A mixture of things. I don't know how to explain it; only that I knew you were powerful. You're a Crimson, which means you're strong. But something tells me your gift is more than just brawn."

"I have speed and agility," he says, nodding, "and that was the official 'power' the Prefecture noted when the time came to classify me as a Crimson. But there are many Crimsons out there faster and stronger than I am. The truth is, my real gift—the one no one knows about—has always been twofold, and has remained hidden all these years. Like you and your father, I'm a Gilded Elite. The sort of Tethered the Prefecture would kill—if they knew everything about me."

I'm intrigued. "What are your hidden powers?"

He cups a hand over the back of his neck and replies, "I've always been able to manipulate electronics, for one. It's a talent that comes in handy when your implanted A.I. unit is considering reporting you for treacherous thoughts."

A memory comes to me of Ilias stumbling out of the black box on Placement Day and stammering, "He's just...on a different level."

"You said your real power is twofold," I remind Thorne. "What's the other part?"

"Ah." He issues me a crooked grin. "It's a little hard to describe—but I suppose I could just say I have a sort of foresight."

At that, I laugh. "You can see into the future?"

"Sort of. But so far, only a few *seconds* into the future. It used to happen only when I was in combat mode. In the fighting ring, I could see my opponent's moves before even *they* knew what they were about to do. It was enough time to intercept them or cut them off before they could harm me. Even Velors, like your buddy Drukkar in the Tower, had trouble outsmarting me. Your friend Nev was pretty frustrated when I anticipated her porting."

"I remember," I say, recalling the irritation on Nev's face when Thorne so handily intercepted her.

"Usually, it's not so much that I see a few seconds ahead as I *feel* it. I feel a surge of pain, anger, all of it—before anything even happens to inspire it. It's like the fight or flight reflex times a thousand. But the night those men broke in here, something in me changed, like my power suddenly multiplied. I could *feel* the man attacking you—I felt your fear, your pain, even from a hundred feet away. It's why I ran into your room and took him down."

His fists clench into rock-hard spheres, then release again.

"I have never been that enraged in all my life," he says between gritted teeth. "I've never wanted so desperately to protect anyone—because all my life, I've taught myself to look out for me. Yes, I'm supposed to protect the Verdans. But in the moment when that bastard attacked you, it was like I was seeing the world through your eyes. My power has changed—and it's only happened because I met you. It's taken me this long, I suppose—but I finally feel like I understand what it is to be Tethered. I always thought it was a bad thing. Shackles around my mind and body. But it's the opposite, Shara. I feel free, thanks to you."

He pulls my hand to his lips again and kisses it, and once again, I feel something far deeper than touch between us.

I feel his affection coursing through my body and mind, twining and braiding itself with my own desire.

For so long, I didn't trust him, though I desperately wanted to.

And in this moment, for the first time in my life, I understand what it is to know another person so deeply that I can't imagine ever doubting him again.

"I'm sorry," I say softly.

"What could you possibly have to be sorry for?"

"I felt it, too," I breathe. "The connection between us. Right from the start, I resented you for what you were doing to me." At that, I laugh a little, my eyes welling with hot tears. "But I didn't believe you, Thorne—even after you saved my life."

"There's nothing to forgive. I was a shit to you. A *strategic* shit, but a shit all the same. But in my defense, I've done one good thing."

"Oh? And what, pray tell, was that?"

"When I gave you the mouse on your first day in the house, it really wasn't to spy on you. It was in the hopes of giving you a little happiness."

The mouse...

I let out a laugh. "I would love to tell you he's brought me joy, but truth be told, Mercutio is an elusive little bastard."

"Mercutio—that's his name?" Thorne asks, an amused grin on his lips. "It suits him."

"I didn't want to call him 'that dastardly mouse,' so yes, I named him," I laugh.

"Well, for the record, Mercutio's duty has only ever been

to watch over you," Thorne says.

"So, Maude was right. As usual. That was her theory, you know."

"Maude's no dummy. If ever I saw you doing something that could land you in the dungeon, Mercutio knew to warn me. He was the one who told me you were headed for the Royal Grounds the day I reprimanded you."

"You're saying he's not a mouse, after all," I chuckle. "He's a *rat*."

"Rats can be good allies," he replies with a shrug. "But little Mercutio is definitely a mouse. And I'm grateful that he's kept a watchful eye on you, even if it occasionally seemed invasive."

With a smile, I lay a hand on Thorne's cheek. This time, the sensation of tingling is replaced by one of warmth. "Did you come to the Tower for me?" I ask.

He nods. "I was searching for a Hunter when I asked to be considered for Prefect's Assistant. But I did not expect to meet the one Tethered who was bound to me by an invisible thread. I didn't expect *you*."

The way he says the last four words sends me reeling with some emotion that feels like it's swallowing me up in the best possible way.

"How did you know about the Hunter," I ask, trying to control the tremor in my voice. "About my father?"

Thorne's lips tighten, and he looks away for a moment, then says, "There are still rebels in this world of ours, Shara. Tethered who have managed to throw off the shackles of the Nobility. They hide in the shadows, but they're out there."

"I thought all the rebels were long gone," I reply, stunned.

"So long as the Nobility keeps us down, there will always be fighters trying to rise up. From the start, I've wanted to find you—to protect you. At first, it was because of your power. But now, it's something else entirely."

With that, he falls to his knees before me, taking hold of my hands and pressing one to his cheek, then the other.

In that moment, I feel something deeper than just his powers.

I can see his memories—in my mind's eye, I experience every time he's ever looked at me, as if living the experience through his eyes. I feel every time he's desired me, every time he's been tempted to lunge toward me to protect me from Lady Verdan or Mrs. Milton's harsh words.

Spinning through my mind, I see the moment when he attacked Drukkar in the fighting ring on Placement Day, ready to kill him in order to protect me.

I can feel his need. His pain, even.

I feel how badly he wants to end the reign of the Nobles and help those who are oppressed to rise up.

"How can we do it?" I ask. "How can we possibly succeed?"

He presses his face against my palm and says, "We'll expose the prince for what he is—hell, we'll expose all those who have tried so long and hard to turn us into empty husks, serving at their pleasure. We'll help our kind to find their rightful place in this world, and ensure our people never live on our knees again. We will never bow before liars, manipulators, or monsters again. Mark my words."

Gently, he pulls my robe away from my shoulder and kisses the skin there, then whispers, "I will bring this whole world to ruin, Shara, if it means I can keep you by my side."

CHAPTER FORTY-NINE

I TAKE Thorne's hand and pull it to my lips, pressing a kiss to his palm.

What he just said to me—what he feels for me, and what I feel for him...

I've never known anything like it.

In my wildest dreams, I haven't dared imagine what it was to feel this deeply for anything or anyone. To trust someone so much that I want to give every part of myself to him.

I want him to consume me until I'm entirely his.

Thorne seems to match my depth of desire, because he groans when he slips his hands under the robe and up my thighs.

He stops after a moment, his hazel eyes meeting mine.

"Is it all right?" he asks. "I don't want to assume..."

The contrast between what the prince did to me earlier and what Thorne is doing now—between Tallin's entitlement and Thorne's respect—is stark.

I take hold of his wrist and move his hand slowly

upwards, erasing what the prince did to me. Eradicating the remnants of sensation left behind by Tallin's vile assault.

"This body is yours to claim," I say quietly. "No one else's."

"You don't know what you're unleashing," Thorne replies, inhaling a sharp breath as his hand reaches the place between my legs—the place that has ached for him so many times over the weeks since our eyes first met.

I have fought this desire—cursed it.

I've reveled in it, too.

And now, my core aches viciously for him, close as he is to giving me what I crave so badly.

This is what the Nobles forbid—this moment right here. A deep, painful, mutual need between two people who have been kept apart too long.

They despise the notion that Tethered should feel pleasure. They despise our joy, because with it comes a sense of freedom that no one—not even the wealthiest person in the world—can take from us.

With quivering fingers, I pull my robe open, revealing myself to Thorne for the first time. The curve of my breasts, the peak of my nipples—parts of me no one has ever seen.

Mine is a forbidden body, meant to remain untouched for the rest of my days.

"Fuck, you're so beautiful." Thorne exhales the words. "The sexiest thing I've ever seen."

Greedily, he cups my breasts and takes a nipple in his mouth, his tongue dancing across my nerve endings as I throw my head back, my entire body a swirling vortex of intense, impossible sensation.

Power courses through me as though I'm only now waking up to the understanding of what I am—what *we* are.

What it is to be Tethered in the truest sense.

I can feel not only my pleasure, but his, as well—the arousal that floods his body is becoming my own. I understand now what it is when two Tethered find their bound mates—when two come together to create one linked mind and body.

When Thorne pulls away for a moment, I let myself fall back onto the bed, and he climbs over me, pinning my arms above my head. His lips are on mine again, and my mind mercifully empties of the trauma and torment it suffered earlier.

All that exists in this world right now is us—and nothing else matters.

He draws my tongue into his mouth and I taste him fully, my hands freeing themselves to move to his chest, reveling in the steady, violent pounding of his heart.

My hands slip downwards, seeking the button on his pants then the zipper, and he pulls back, tearing his jacket and shirt away until all that's left is his beautiful chest, beaded with sweat and heaving hard. His pants hang low on his hips, taunting me with the promise that soon, they may just fall.

When I reach for him again, he smiles and shakes his head.

"Not yet," he says, falling once again to his knees next to the bed.

He wraps his arms around my thighs and pulls me to him, stroking his tongue over the shallow curve at the peak of my thigh.

"Do you know how hard it is to watch you move around this house," he moans into my skin, "with my cock hard as steel—and know I can't touch you? To know I couldn't take that pouty lower lip of yours between my teeth and taste it with my tongue?"

"You can now," I promise, my hips moving under him, urging him to keep exploring me. "You can do anything you want."

He chuckles then pulls himself to his feet to kiss me, then sucks in my lower lip as he described, his tongue running delectably across its surface.

He moans as his wish is fulfilled, then lifts my head and brushes his lips against my neck. "Do you know how many times I've disabled my Maude unit so I could stroke myself, imagining your mouth on me...imagining how it would feel to have those beautiful hands of yours working my shaft while your perfect lips bring me close to explosion?"

I let out a quiet moan of my own, my inhibitions rapidly disappearing.

"I've thought of you, too," I murmur.

"I know," he replies, and when he pulls back for a moment and shoots me a knowing, mischievous look, I let out a laugh.

"You *did* watch me through Mercutio's eyes," I chastise. "Didn't you?"

"I may have seen a little something," he replies. "But I swear, I stopped when I realized what you were about to do."

"You promise?"

"Hey—I thought you trusted me."

"I do."

"Good," he says, sliding his hand between my legs, his

eyes locked on mine. He strokes me gently, watching my face for a reaction. My hips roll to meet his every motion, pleading silently for more.

"I stopped watching the video Mercutio took," he says. "But I suspect...that your fingers spent some time in this beautiful, delicious spot..."

When he finds it, I inhale deeply, memorizing this moment in time and the intensity of the sensation.

"What would you say if I told you you're right?" I ask. "If I told you I was thinking of you the whole time?"

"I'd say I was more envious of your fingers in that moment than I've ever been of anything in my fucking life."

When his thumb finds my clit and he teases it in a small, teasing circle, I close my eyes and wonder how I was ever foolish enough to dislike him.

I can feel his smile between us as he slips down and wraps his lips around me again, his tongue replacing his thumb, a finger slipping inside me. Thorne moans against my flesh, then mutters, "God, you're so tight. I can't even..."

He eases in and out, his lips and tongue working me as if he's known my body for years.

I revel in the sensation, but I want more.

"I want you inside me," I tell him, my core aching.

"Soon," he replies, the sound vibrating against me.

All I feel is want.

I want his tongue on me. I want his cock inside me. I want to take him in my mouth.

I want...

And as the multitude of desires fills me, I realize that this—right now—is the most free I have ever felt in my life.

The world has just changed color, and nothing will ever be the same—least of all me.

"So you're going to torture me, then," I murmur.

"A little."

"Can I at least taste you?"

Peering up at my face from between my legs, he strokes his tongue over me again then succumbs, rising to his feet. He undoes his trousers, which slip a little lower, then takes me by the hand.

I understand his intent perfectly, and I slip off the bed to land on my knees before him, pulling his pants and boxers down and taking his thick length in both hands.

I've never done this before, but I can feel his mind, his pleasure, as I stroke my tongue over his swollen tip, looking up to watch his expression. Thorne lets out a sound like an animal getting ready to take down its prey.

He throbs under my touch as I tease him with my tongue, my hand moving slowly up and down his shaft as I learn his body for the first time.

Under the caress of my fingertips, I can feel his bliss so acutely—so intensely. *This,* I think, *is something no Normal or Noble has ever experienced. This is what it is to be Tethered.*

He can feel my pleasure, too. He knows how much I want him—how good it feels to take him in my mouth, to fulfill his fantasy.

Overwhelmed, Thorne pulls me up and kisses me deeply, our tongues meeting, tasting one another's sex on our lips.

"I gave you a taste," he says. "Now, it's my turn again."

He throws me back on the bed and once again falls to his knees on the floor, his mouth determined to drive me over the edge.

"I need you to know what it feels like," he says. "I want you to come for me, beautiful thing. I need you to feel how much I've wanted you since that first second when I locked eyes with you in the Tower."

His hands are on my waist slipping upwards, his fingers finding my nipples, and the pleasure of his touch combined with the skill of his tongue nearly end me then and there.

"You have no idea how sexy you are—which only makes you hotter," he murmurs against me as he pushes me close to the brink.

"Ironic," I tell him with a laugh. "Because I've always assumed you knew exactly how sexy *you* are."

"Maybe you won't believe this—but I never thought you would want me," he confesses with a quick stroke of his tongue that sends my hips bucking with pleasure. "I never thought I would have you. I only knew that you were mine on some distant, beautiful plane of existence—one we would probably never see. I only hoped against hope that maybe one day, if I was very fortunate, I would get to do this..."

With that, he strokes his tongue over my slickness again, sending me writhing with pleasure, my entire body so close to explosion that I'm not sure I can stand it.

"Or this..." he says, teasing my swollen clit. "Never in a million years did I imagine I would have the privilege of making you come for me, Shara."

With that, he takes me between his lips and works me with his tongue, two fingers driving into me.

I drag my hands through his hair, rolling my hips to meet his strokes. He knows just how close I am, how overwhelmed with desire and need combined—and when I finally cry out, my body shuddering in ecstasy, he keeps his mouth between my legs. His hot breath calms me, his greedy fingers digging needfully into my thighs.

Finally, he looks up, his mischievous eyes on mine, and wipes his mouth, then rises to his feet.

"You know what I want," I tell him, my voice a mere, breathless rasp.

"I do," he replies, leaning over me, a hand guiding him as his swollen head presses gently against my opening. "Are you sure?"

"I've never been so sure of anything in my life, Thorne."

He's gentle and careful, taking his agonizing time to push in only a little, his eyes on my face to make sure he's not hurting me.

"You can feel it," I say softly. "You can feel what I feel, can't you?"

He nods, and I'm convinced his cheeks redden just a little. "I can," he says, leaning down to kiss me as he delves deeper.

"More," I say against his lips.

He rocks his hips, and with one hard thrust, he's inside me. I cry out at the size of him as he tears me apart.

He pulls himself out again, slipping his length over my clit, and I moan with arousal at seeing him like that.

"You know they put fertility suppressors in our implants...right?" he asks, his eyes locking onto mine, and I nod. One of the more ridiculous things the Prefecture does to us, given that we aren't even allowed to touch.

"I know," I tell him. "So fuck me, Thorne. I want you to come inside me—I want to feel it when it happens."

He kisses my smile away and rams himself inside me again, my body rising to meet the motion. He anticipates each roll of my hips, every moan from my lips. And when he slips a hand down between us and uses his thumb to drive me toward a second explosion...I watch him, studying the pleasure reflected in his face.

He speeds up his thrusts, driving into me as if we both know this is our last night in this world. The sweet pain of it is exquisite, and when we cascade over the edge together, I'm not sure if the desperate throb that overwhelms my senses is coming from my body, or his, or both.

He falls onto me, sweat covering us both as my arms wrap around his broad back, my mind soaking in the feeling of his skin against mine.

"You're everything," I tell him. "Everything I never thought you were. Everything I ever *hoped* you were. Everything I want in this world. Everything I can't have."

"Fuck that," he replies into my neck. "You do have me. You will always have me—just as you've had me from day one, Shara. I told you—you're fucking mine. You always have been."

He pulls back, brushes my hair out of my eyes, and says, "No matter what happens—you and I are Tethered. Nothing will break us apart. Remember that."

After we've made love three more times over the course of the next few hours—not nearly long enough—he pulls himself away, slipping out of the bed.

"Don't go," I plead as he yanks his pants on. "I feel like I've only had the tiniest taste of you."

"Not too tiny, I hope," he says with a wink and a grin, and I laugh.

"All right—a massive, rock-hard taste of you. But I wish you would stay. I want more."

"If I do, there's a high risk I'll get caught in here. I can keep the mice at bay, but nothing will stop Lady Verdan and the girls from barging in, looking for me. They may be a threesome of self-centered asses, but they'll want to make sure their prize Guard is still in one piece after tonight."

"Fine," I reply with a mock pout. "But I want you to sneak back in here tomorrow night. And every night. I may just have to start keeping a diary, so I can gush and swoon over you. Then, who knows? Maybe someone will find it in a few decades and lose their minds over it."

"Better to swoon than to rage about what a lying dirtbag I am."

My cheeks flush, but I let out a chuckle. "You'll never let me live that down, huh?"

Thorne climbs over me, brushing kisses onto my neck, my chest, my stomach, then lower until I come dangerously close to begging him to stay.

"It was fair enough to think ill of me," he says when he finally slips back off the bed. "But I'm going to spend the rest of my life trying to prove that I deserve you. Until then, I'll see you in the morning, beautiful, mysterious woman in red."

He straightens up, grabbing the rest of his clothes off the floor and adds, "Though you know, I've discovered I prefer you in nothing at all."

With that, he slips out of my room into the darkness of the corridor.

CHAPTER FIFTY

I FALL ASLEEP IMAGINING Thorne's arm wrapped around me, his body pressed to mine.

If only we could *actually* sleep together, just once in our lives...

But there's no disputing that he was right to return to his bedroom.

It would be dangerous, not to mention incredibly foolish, to take the risk of Lady Verdan finding us together. We have no real way of knowing when she and her daughters will be back. No idea whether they'll sprint up to the servants' wing to make sure Thorne is in one piece after his battle against the Lion.

I don't expect anyone to come to my room, so it shocks me to the core when sometime around dawn, my door crashes open.

I lurch up in bed, a cry exploding from my lips.

The Royal Guard is here. They've already figured out it was me who infiltrated the palace last night.

But there is no Guard staring me down like a predator eyeing its pitiful prey.

In the dim morning light, all I see is Lady Verdan standing in the doorway, a strange, cruel smile on her lips.

She's still wearing last night's gown, her hair still almost perfectly coiffed.

"Hello, Shara," she says. "I hope you had a *lovely* evening."

"Lady Verdan," I stammer, grateful that I had the foresight to put on pajamas after Thorne left my room. "Is everything all right?"

Clearly it isn't, given that you felt the need to assault my door with all the enthusiasm of a battering ram.

She strides in and seats herself at the foot of my bed, examining her manicured fingernails. "Not exactly," she says. "I understand someone was quite naughty last night."

Shit, shit, shit. Does she know what Thorne and I did? Was there a sentinel mouse he forgot to disable?

Was it Maude?

"Naughty," I parrot, as if she doesn't have a million reasons to throw that word at me.

"Don't play stupid with me, *Domestic,*" she says, a gruesome inflection on the last word. "Do you really think I'm not aware of all the shit you've pulled since you came to my house?"

I stare at her, confused. *No—I didn't think you were aware of any of it. How could you be?*

With an impatient huff, she says, "You have something of mine, and I want it back."

I shake my head violently, panicking and wondering why

Thorne is nowhere to be seen after the sound of splintering wood echoed through the hallway.

Where the hell is he?

"I've never taken anything of yours," I tell Lady Verdan. "I swear—my Maude unit can confirm that I'm always careful to—"

Lady Verdan clicks her tongue and stares straight into me, fire in her eyes.

"I told you not to play stupid," she snarls. "I want the diary."

My chest tightens, and for a moment, I can't breathe.

What the hell? How does she know I have the diary?

Reading my expression, she snarls, "Perhaps you aren't aware of Rule Number Six in Kravan's Legal Code: *A Noble may choose to kill a Tethered without fear of punishment.* It's come in quite handy in this house—more than once. So if you tell me you don't know what I'm talking about, I promise—I will kill you here and now."

I stare at her, air trapped in my lungs.

Part of me—the part that has always been submissive and meek—would love to give her exactly what she wants. The diary was never mine to begin with, after all.

But another part wants to tell her to fuck off and die.

That's the part that's winning right now.

"Is that what your family did to your Guard?" I ask, venom on my tongue. "Did they kill the one who got you pregnant—the mysterious T. in your diary?"

Lady Verdan gawks at me for a moment, her face a patchwork of emotion. Confusion. Amusement. Rage.

Finally, she smiles.

A strange, quiet laugh bubbles up in her chest, rising through her throat and escaping in a full-bodied guffaw.

"My God," she says. "I guess I was more discreet than I'd thought back in the day. Here, I assumed any idiot who cast their eyes on that diary would read between the lines. T. was no Guard. He was the young man I loved—the man I still love to this day. One who is more powerful than anyone in this realm."

I say nothing in response. I don't want to give her the satisfaction of asking what she means.

I raise my chin and lock eyes with her, wondering just how she intends to kill me. She has no weapon in her hand—no Guard with her. Unless she thinks she can somehow win against me in a wrestling match, I'm at a loss—until I glance over and see that the door isn't just broken.

Its surface is singed black, as if a large fireball had been used to blow it open.

It's then that I notice Mrs. Verdan's eyes. They're normally a deep, dark brown, and I've never particularly studied them until this moment, when her irises begin swimming with liquid color.

...just as Thorne's did last night.

"You know," Lady Verdan says, raising a hand into the air, palm up, "there is some information on that diary that could prove very destructive, were it to get out."

With that, she shoots me a look, turning her hand over once, twice.

In her eyes, the colors intensify as if she's teasing me. Blue...gold...brown...green.

Nausea pushes its way up my chest into my throat, and I feel like I'm going to be sick.

"You see it, don't you?" she says. "For the first time, you see what I am—*Hunter.* Your powers are finally beginning to show themselves."

She twists her hand around again, her fingertips rubbing together. A combination of flame and lightning crackles over the surface of her skin, then comes to rest in her palm, a small ball of furious energy settling there.

A weapon that she has constructed with nothing but her power. The power of a Tethered.

My throat goes dry with horror.

"It was *you,*" I breathe. "It was never T. *He* was a Normal. That's the secret you were unwilling to write down in the diary—*you're* the reason the baby would have been a Tethered."

"*Would have been.*" Lady Verdan laughs, then seals her hand into a fist, and the sphere disappears. "Technically, one can blame my parents for passing along their bloodline. My father, to be precise. My sister and I are both Tethered—you'd like her. A real spitfire, that one. She and I aren't close, but we admire one another grudgingly for what we've done to survive this long in a world that hates our kind."

"You hid your powers all this time," I murmur, half to myself. "You watched as Tethered were forced into the Tower—as we were raised without parents, without homes."

"No one ever asked if I was a Tethered—so technically, no lie," she coos, extending her hand expectantly toward me. "*The diary. Now.* I refuse to allow traitors like you and Thorne to make off with my family secrets. I will not put my child in danger."

"Your child?" I laugh. "Singular? Have you disowned one of the girls since last night?"

Lady Verdan's demeanor shifts, and once again, she looks highly amused. "The diary."

I slip out of the bed and pull Thorne's reader—the one that once again contains the first disc I found—off the windowsill, then hand it to her. It's only the first disc—the second is hidden in the dead reader, under the floorboard.

Lady Verdan opens the reader up, and when she sees the first entry, slams it shut again.

She doesn't know, I think. *She doesn't know there are two discs.*

I don't know why that would be—or whether I can use it to my advantage. But I'll do everything I can to ensure Daphne Verdan suffers for the lies she's told.

"Thank you, Shara," she says, clenching the reader in her fist. "You know, it's funny. Had you simply shaken my hand on that first day, you might have come to realize what I am. But of course, you're not allowed to touch a Noble—because you're an undesirable. A common criminal."

"I'm a Tethered, just like you," I snap.

"*I* am a Noble," she retorts, ice hardening her voice. "I am nothing like you, my dear."

"You're not wrong. We're nothing alike, you and I. You're an evil, lying bitch, for one thing."

"I'm a bitch who believes in trying to survive in a world that favors the wealthy," she replies. "A bitch who will do whatever it takes to protect those she loves."

I suppose I look skeptical that she could actually love anyone, because she says, "You don't believe me, so let me tell you a little story. When my parents told me I had to terminate the pregnancy, I was broken. Shattered—just as you would have been. Imagine if Thorne had gotten you pregnant last night." With that, she throws me a knowing look that makes my skin burn with rage. "Imagine learning that you were pregnant with the child of the man you love most in this world."

"I'm not allowed to be with a man," I snap. "You know that."

"Of course," she says, giving me a weak attempt at a conspiratorial wink. "Well—needless to say, when my parents told me they would force me to terminate, I did what any mother would have done. I protected my child."

She opens her hand to stare down at the reader and adds, "Ah—but I didn't write that part down, did I? So you assumed I simply ended the pregnancy and went on with my life. It's a valid conclusion, after all. Confessing to murder is never a good idea."

"You killed them?" I ask, stunned.

I've never liked her—but *murder?*

I didn't think she had it in her.

"Maybe the Nobility has a point," Lady Verdan replies with a shrug. "Maybe we Tethered *are* naturally violent, after all. I suppose I have a love for it, myself. Those Guards who died tonight love it, too. It's why they were salivating over serving the Nobility and fighting to the death. Even your friend—Ilias, was it?"

For that, I want to tear her face off.

"Ilias wasn't violent," I growl. "He loved the Nobility, like we were taught. He was obedient, and they killed him for it."

Ignoring me, she holds up the reader and smiles. "It's funny, you know—my late husband *told* me he'd found the coin-disc. He was upset about what he read on it. Understandably, I suppose. When he said he was going to report me for my various crimes, the only thing to do was to kill him, so I did—but not before he told others of the diary's existence. Which is why those assholes keep breaking in here to try and find it. They think it can bring me to my knees, and somehow turn the Royals against me."

"Why didn't you just destroy the disc when you had the chance?" I ask.

She lets out a laugh that sends ice skittering down my spine.

"Milo hid the damned thing. He concealed the disc in the one place he knew I would never set foot—the place where I'd been held prisoner by my parents, like a common wretch." She lifts her chin and looks around, a grimace pulling her features downward. "This. Fucking. Room. This awful place where my parents locked me during those days when they were debating *killing my child*. As if I would ever allow that to happen. As if *T.* would."

A wildness enters her voice for those last few words, and my fingers clench into tight, frightened fists.

Daphne Verdan is a killer. Not just a killer—someone who has murdered the very people she should protect. The people she's supposed to love.

And to make things worse, she has a child out there somewhere. A child who's probably as sadistic as she—

Oh.

God.

"You're dying to know who T. is," Lady Verdan says. "Aren't you?"

I shake my head. "T. is a Normal—but he's powerful. I...I know who he is."

An image flashes through my mind from last night at the

ball. Daphne Verdan, her hand on the king's arm, leaning in close and whispering in his ear. At the time, I thought it was a typical interaction between two Nobles who are allowed to touch without fear of reprimand.

"The T. is for Tomas, King of Kravan," I say sharply.

I've only ever heard his name once, years ago—and I'd almost forgotten it. We Tethered only ever referred to him as *the King,* as if a name was unnecessary to identify a man with such a title.

"When you first met," I add, "he was a prince. And your child—your son—is Prince Tallin."

CHAPTER FIFTY-ONE

Lady Verdan looks ready to applaud.

"I suppose the king and I don't make much effort when it comes to hiding our feelings for one another," she says. "We can't marry, you see." With that, she leans in close and in a breathy voice, continues, "*It's against the rules.* Not that anyone knows I'm a Tethered, of course. Still, we wouldn't want to draw attention, would we?"

"So is murder, and that didn't stop you," I spit. There's no part of me that cares anymore about how terrifying she can be—no part of me that feels obligated to be polite. She doesn't deserve my kindness, my respect, or anything else from me, other than cold disdain. "Tell me," I add, "did the *queen*—your lover's wife—know her so-called son was a Tethered?"

That question makes her bristle. She sits up, her spine straight, and says, "Tomas married her quietly, around the time Tallin was born—on the condition that she would never tell anyone he wasn't her son. She accepted him as her child, and she was a good mother to him. But she never knew what he was. Never knew he would develop powers."

"And now, he's a monster—just like his biological mother. You must be so proud to call him your flesh and blood."

Lady Verdan's lips twist into a spiteful smile.

"I *am* proud of my son, actually, though as you can imagine, I can't call him that publicly."

She rises to her feet and begins to pace the room slowly.

I'm beginning to suspect, based solely on the fact that she's telling me everything, that she has no intention of letting me live to see tomorrow.

"I met Tomas when I was seventeen, on the path to the Royal Grounds," she says with a hint of nostalgia in her tone. "But you already know that, don't you?"

"Yes. I do."

"He was smitten—though I was too young and naive to realize it. I thought I was so fortunate to get to spend time with a powerful prince—one who was already betrothed to another woman. You see, his parents had set up his marriage years earlier—some clever political union between their two families. But Tomas and I were madly in love, and there was no keeping us from being together. I'm convinced it's the reason my powers came to me early. It was that passion—that depth of feeling. You know what I'm talking about." Her eyes almost roll back into her head when she adds, "*Those fucking orgasms.*"

I could vomit.

Lady Verdan aims her palm at the ceiling, and once again, a terrifying sphere of pure electricity crackles in the air just above her hand.

"It's so sad when bad things happen to decent folk," she says, eyeing the threatening orb. "Speaking of which—now that you've gone and looked into my personal affairs, I have little choice but to punish you for it. Your friend Thorne—yes, I've noticed your eyes flickering to the door now and then in search of him—is already paying for *his* crimes."

My breath catches, my body tensing.

She got to him first—but why didn't he fight? Why didn't he resist?

"What does that mean?" I ask, my voice quaking, my rage instantly replaced with apprehension.

Lady Verdan chuckles. "He's locked up in the basement, naturally. As impressive a specimen as he is, I don't suppose he'll be breaking out anytime soon. I've already warned him that if he tries anything, I'll burn your pretty little face until there's no skin left."

I ignore her threat. All I care about is that Thorne is still alive—even if he *is* locked in a soundproof cell in that godawful dungeon.

"I'll be giving you a cell of your own," she says. "You will not try anything foolish—because if you do, I'll hurt you in ways you've never imagined. Oh, I know you can heal yourself well enough, Shara, but I don't suppose your power would be sufficient to mend a gaping hole burned into your chest."

"Why keep me alive at all?" I ask, crossing my arms over my chest in a desperate attempt to appear stronger than I feel. "Why not kill me now?"

"Because," she says, "it's your *other* power I'm interested in. The one you used on my son last night. I'm not sure you realize how valuable a commodity you've become in the last twenty-four hours." With a sharp gesture of her hand, she adds, "Now, get out of bed and come with me. There's no need to bring anything other than the pajamas you're wearing. It's not like you'll have any needs in your cell, other than the bucket that's already awaiting you."

For the first time, I wish I had dangerous powers. Something—anything—I could use as a weapon against this cold bitch.

But I have nothing, and she knows it.

Shaking, I slip out of the bed, glancing only briefly toward the dresser that's slightly pulled away from the wall—and hoping it doesn't occur to her to wonder why.

Lady Verdan leads the way out of the bedroom, confident that I won't assault her from behind. She's right, of course. There's no way I'm risking my life or Thorne's.

The only things I care about right now are keeping Thorne alive...and figuring out how the hell we're going to get out of here.

CHAPTER FIFTY-TWO

> *If I serve faithfully, I will be rewarded with long life.*
>
> *If I break Kravan's laws, I will pay the ultimate price.*
>
> *The choice is mine...and I vow to choose well.*

When we reach the basement, Lady Verdan opens the first steel door on our right.

I expect her to shove me inside, but instead, she says, "I thought you two might like to say a quick hello."

I peer into the cell's shadowy depths only to see that someone in dark clothing is pressed against the far wall, arms outstretched.

When I hear the faint clang of iron, I realize his arms are shackled to the wall.

"Thorne!"

I leap over and throw my arms around his neck, tears staining his skin. I have no doubt Lady Verdan will rip me away at any moment, but I don't care. There are no rules anymore, and nothing matters.

“Are you all right?” I ask.

He nods weakly. His face is bruised and battered, his shirt torn.

“You didn’t do this to him,” I say, twisting around to face Lady Verdan. “Did you?”

“No,” she replies, crossing her arms. “Not my style, really.”

Whoever did must be extremely powerful—or else Thorne deliberately chose not to put up a fight.

“He’s alive, Shara. I want you to know he’ll stay alive, so long as you promise to cooperate.”

I cup my hand over Thorne’s neck and kiss his cheek.

“I promise,” I tell our vile Proprietor. “Whatever you want.”

“Good. Then let me show you to your quarters. If all goes well, they’ll be temporary.”

I begin to pull away, but Thorne whispers a weak, “Shara.”

“What is it?” I breathe back.

“Watch for Mercutio,” he says, his head rolling downward as if he’s about to lose consciousness.

“Mercutio,” Lady Verdan says with a laugh. “I’m sorry your gentleman friend is a little foggy, Shara. He’s had quite a blow to the head. Citing Shakespearean characters while manacled is seldom a good sign. Let’s let him recover, shall we?”

I stroke my hand over his cheek, feeling my power flow through my fingers into his body and knowing his strength will soon return to him.

“Shara!” Lady Verdan says, grabbing me by the arm and dragging me backwards. She shoves me hard toward the doorway, then steps up to Thorne, pressing a hand to his chest.

At first, I'm terrified that she's going to burn him. But instead, she slides her hands up, cups his face in her palms, and kisses him on the lips.

It's almost enough to make me lunge at her and tear every hair out of her head.

"You are such a gorgeous creature," she murmurs. "If I were twenty years younger, I swear..."

Thorne gives her an angry, quiet look, but says nothing as Lady Verdan turns and forces me out of his cell, slamming the door behind us.

My cell is at the end of the corridor, as far from Thorne's as it could possibly be.

"You will stay here and contemplate what you've done," Lady Verdan tells me when I'm inside. "You will think about whether or not you want to live to see your next birthday. You have choices to make, Shara. And trust me when I tell you that if you make the wrong one, I will flay your Thorne myself."

"What choices might those be?"

All she gives me in response is a terrible smile.

"Don't you think your step-daughters will wonder where the hell your two Tethered have gone?" I ask.

"My step-daughters won't care, so long as I replace Thorne quickly with another attractive Guard. As for you—I don't want to hurt your feelings, my dear..." She cocks her head to the side, the smile never fading. "But I don't think the girls like you very much."

Without another word, she slams the door and locks it.

I slouch down to the cold floor, my head pressed to the wall. I refuse to cry. I refuse to give her the satisfaction.

The darkness of the room is absolute. I can't see a crack of light coming from around the door frame or elsewhere. It's so much like the Blackrooms in the Tower, only...worse.

It's damp, musty, and feels more like a crypt than a cell.

"Maude," I whisper, wondering if there's any chance that she's still with me. I don't suppose Lady Verdan has the means to take her from me—I don't think her power encompasses implanted A.I.

~*Shara,* she replies, and I breathe an enormous sigh of relief. I don't think I've ever been so glad to hear her voice.

"Are you all right?" I ask.

~*I'm fine. I find myself concerned for your safety, however. I must admit, I didn't anticipate this scenario.*

"Yeah, well, neither did I."

~*If you'd like a little light...slip your thumb over your left wrist.*

I push the sleeve of my pajamas up and do as she says, and the swirling green patterns on my arm light up instantly.

I can just make out vague shapes in the room—but at least I'm not in utter darkness.

~*Someone is coming,* Maude says.

I slip my thumb over my arm again and the light fades just in time for the door to crack open.

A tall, broad-shouldered figure is standing in the doorway a moment later, silhouetted so that I can't see his face.

Still, I know exactly who it is.

Fuck.

Tallin reaches for something on the wall outside the cell, and when he steps inside, a torch flares to life in his hand.

"Hello, Johanna," he says with that terrible grin of his. "Oh, sorry—I meant *Shara.* How nice to see you again."

He steps over and crouches before me, the firelight dancing on his features and rendering him a little maniacal-looking.

"It's so nice to see your face," he says. "You're as beautiful as I expected, though I do miss the dress."

I sneer at him, but say nothing.

"I'm assuming my mother told you what I want from you."

At that, my eyes meet his, narrowing. "No," I reply. "Not exactly. All I know is—"

All I know is that you're both devious pieces of shit.

That's what I want to say, but I bite my tongue.

"I see," the prince says, slipping his free hand down onto my leg. I flinch under his touch, which only seems to excite him more. His grin spreads to his eyes, and he says, "I think you're the only woman in Kravan who doesn't want to fuck me."

"Don't sell yourself short. I'm sure there are plenty of others."

Maude buzzes a warning on my wrist, and I flinch, realizing what I've done.

Fortunately, Tallin laughs. "I love a girl who plays hard to get," he says, and this time, I manage to keep my mouth shut. "Here's the thing..."

He moves his hand up my leg, but pulls it away after a moment.

"The realm knows I'm looking for a wife."

At that, I want to retch. Where the hell could he possibly be going with this?

"You, Shara, managed to sneak your way into the Prince's Ball. No one—not even me—suspected at first that you were a Tethered. I would very much like for you to accompany me—under the guise of my fiancée—to many more events. You would get to see Kravan's Nobles without the masks. You'd meet the most powerful people in the entire realm. And all I would ask in return is that you tell me who among them are Tethered."

My lips curl up against my will. In the torchlight, I can see his eyes swirling. It's unmistakable now, the power surging through me. I won't have to touch anyone again to know what they are. Thanks to Thorne, I'll recognize the telltale signs.

If I could prove there were more Tethered among the Nobles...I could finish what Thorne and I started tonight.

"You *like* this plan," Tallin says. "I knew the second I met you that you were as mischievous as I am."

Those words—which he speaks so lightly, so casually—remind me of what I saw when I touched him at the palace. The dead bodies, beaten and battered, and the knowledge that he was the one responsible for the violence perpetrated against them.

"Not quite as mischievous," I say, exhibiting all the restraint I can muster. "But yes—I will accompany you to your parties, if you like. On two conditions."

"I'm not sure you're in any position to negotiate."

I raise my chin and say, "You need me, Tallin. You're fearful that your throne is in peril, and that if anyone finds out what you are, you and your father will suffer. You want to take out any threats. I get it. But you can't do any of that without me."

He lets out a quick breath, forces another smile on his lips, and says, "Fine. What do you want?"

"First," I reply, "You will promise not to hurt Thorne. You'll keep him alive as long as I'm helping you."

A pained expression infiltrates his eyes for a moment, then it's gone. "Fine. What else?"

"You will never, ever put your fucking hands on me again—except for show, in public. And even then, you will not kiss me. Ever. Understood?"

He looks as if he wants to hit me. His jaw is tight, his temples pulsing with fury. But instead of following through, he rises to his feet.

"I agree to your demands," he says. "But for now, you'll stay in here. I had hoped to bring you to the palace with me—to bed you tonight."

He reaches into his pocket and extracts something, drawing it out and dropping it at my feet. It takes only a moment to realize it's the glove I left behind at the ball.

"I believe this is yours," he growls. "Since you won't willingly warm my bed, you will rot in this hole in the ground—because you, my dear, need to learn your fucking place."

Without another word, he storms out of the cell, slamming its door so hard that the walls tremble.

I press my head back, relieved to be alone again. Relieved that Thorne is alive.

But most of all, I'm relieved to know there is a way out of this cell. I will play a role and pretend to be the prince's wife-to-be.

I'll go against everything I was ever taught and lie to every person I meet.

The Nobility made one grave mistake when they robbed the Tethered of families and love.

They left us with nothing to lose.

And when it's all over—when Thorne and I are safe—when we find a way to take down the king, the prince, and every other hypocritical Noble standing in our way...

We will live happily ever after...

Even if it kills us.

End of Book One

NEXT BOOK IN THE THRALL SERIES: BROKEN

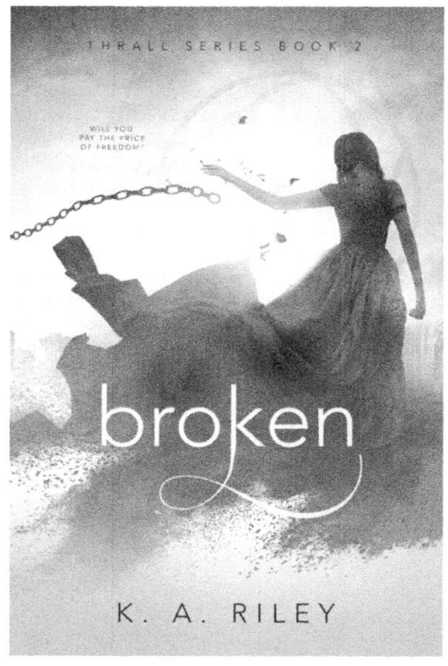

After the events in the Verdan house, Shara finds herself prisoner of Tallin, the prince of Kravan.

He wants one thing from her—and that's for her to help

him seek out his enemies so that he can take them down. But this means posing as his betrothed. Attending gatherings as his fiancée, a Noble, while other Tethered suffer at the hands of those who force them into servitude.

Pre-order on Amazon until its release in April 2024: Broken

AN EPIC NEW DYSTOPIAN SERIES: THE AMNESTY GAMES

Seventeen-year-old Alora is a Hawker, and she's been training her whole life for this moment.

This is the week of the annual Amnesty Games.

Accompanied by her five fellow Hawkers, Alora is about to do battle with a hundred of the Hopefuls, the most violent and dangerous convicts from the Ward. It's five days of hand-to-hand combat, physical challenges, mazes, traps, and obstacle courses, all followed by a two-day Pursuit through the Netherwoods where Alora and the Hawkers will track down any of the Hopefuls who've managed to make it that far.

If the Hopefuls succeed, they get their freedom. If not, it's back to prison for the rest of their lives. It's been this way since the start of the New States.

But what happens when buried secrets are revealed and the two sides stop playing the game by the same rules?

Purchase on Amazon or borrow it on Kindle Unlimited:

The Amnesty Games

ALSO BY K. A. RILEY

If you're enjoying K. A. Riley's books, please consider leaving a review on Amazon or Goodreads to let your fellow book-lovers know!

DYSTOPIAN BOOKS

THE AMNESTY GAMES

THE THRALL SERIES

THRALL | BROKEN | QUEEN

THE RESISTANCE TRILOGY

RECRUITMENT | RENDER | REBELLION

THE EMERGENTS TRILOGY

Survival | Sacrifice | Synthesis

THE TRANSCENDENT TRILOGY

| Travelers | Transfigured | Terminus |

ACADEMY OF THE APOCALYPSE

Emergents Academy | Cult of the Devoted | Army of the Unsettled

THE RAVENMASTER CHRONICLES

Arise | Banished | Crusade

THE CURE CHRONICLES

The Cure | Awaken | Ascend | Fallen | Reign

VIRAL HIGH TRILOGY

Apocalypchix | Lockdown | Final Exam

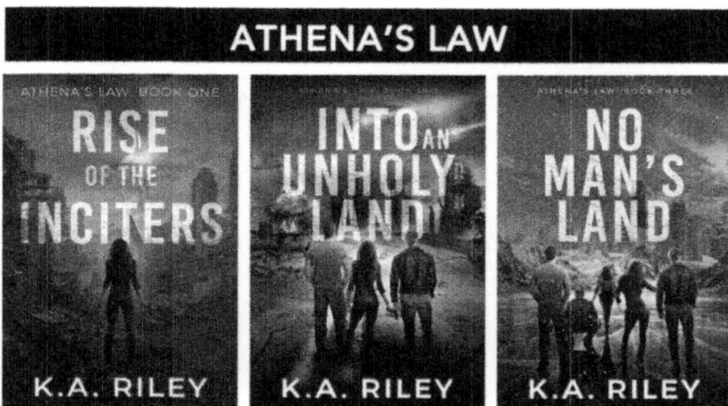

Rise of the Inciters | Into an Unholy Land | No Man's Land

FANTASY BOOKS

FAE OF TÍRIA SERIES

A Kingdom Scarred | A Crown Broken | Of Flame and Fury

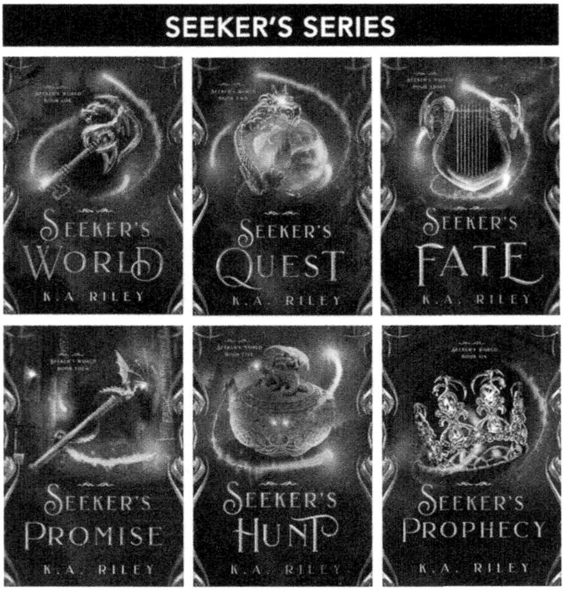

Seeker's World |Seeker's Quest | Seeker's Fate | Seeker's Promise |Seeker's Hunt | Seeker's Prophecy (Coming soon!)

About the Author

https://karileywrites.org/#subscribe

K.A. Riley's Bookbub Author Page
K.A. Riley on Amazon.com
K.A. Riley on Goodreads.com

Tiktok.com/@karileywrites

Printed in Great Britain
by Amazon